Pisgah Press was established in 2011 to publish and promote works of quality offering original ideas and insight into the human condition, the realm of knowledge, and the world around us.

Copyright © 2025 Pisgah Press

Printed in the United States of America

Published by Pisgah Press, LLC
PO Box 9663, Asheville, NC 28815
www.pisgahpress.com

Book & cover design: A. D. Reed, MyOwnEditor.com

Library of Congress Cataloging-in-Publication Data
Sefrin, Eliot
Port City/Sefrin

Library of Congress Control Number: 2025902159

ISBN: 978-1-942016-95-3
Fiction/Historical Fiction

First Edition
First Printing
May 2025

AUTHOR'S NOTE

Port City is a work of fiction. While portions of the novel are based on real-life events, the characters, companies, place settings, emotions and actions depicted are either products of the author's imagination or are used in a fictitious manner. Any similarities to actual persons, living or dead, are purely coincidental.

For my granddaughters Ava and Stevie.

PORT CITY

A NOVEL

ELIOT SEFRIN

Pisgah Press, LLC
PO Box 6993
Asheville, NC 28815
www.pisgahpress.com

New York is everybody's port ... the Grand Exchange not just of America, but of the world. It is the universal seaport.

—*James Morris*

Chapter 1

January 31, 1946

Henry McFarland was running late to his meeting, but he wasn't inclined to rush. He seldom was.

To Henry, adhering to schedules that he himself hadn't fashioned was far beneath someone at his lofty station in life. Henry made his own schedules—his own rules, too—rarely acceding to the whims of others, least of all the tugboat union negotiators he was obligated to meet with that morning. He'd get to his 10 a.m. collective-bargaining session when he was good and ready, not a minute sooner. If those noxious union reps took exception to that . . .

Well, the entire bunch of them could go straight to hell!

Besides, Henry was otherwise occupied on this blustery winter morning, immersed in a mountain of paperwork at the summit of his company-owned office tower in the heart of Lower Manhattan's Financial District. The business matters requiring his attention, Henry had deemed, were every bit as important as the contract negotiations he was scheduled to attend. He wasn't budging from his desk until those self-proclaimed priorities were attended to. *Not a goddamned inch!*

"Pardon me, Mr. McFarland."

Henry's longtime secretary Elena Karas, smartly attired in a charcoal suit, pillbox hat, and snow-white gloves, peeked timorously through the doorway to his office.

"Your messages, sir," she said.

Henry, riveted to his paperwork, no more than waggled his fingertips. Cued by the wordless command, Miss Karas tiptoed in, steno pad in hand.

"What do you have for me?" asked Henry, seeming vexed by the intrusion.

"A reporter from *The Times* phoned," Miss Karas informed him.

"And what did he want?"

"An update on the status of the tugboat workers' contract negotiations."

Henry waved a hand flippantly, as if shooing a gnat.

"The *Times* will get its update after this morning's bargaining session," he snorted. "Just like every other newspaper in town."

Henry spoke in the terse, clipped cadence of a man clothed head to toe in self-confidence, a business mogul accustomed to wielding power and seeing it neither questioned nor defied. Miss Karas, long inured to her boss's sulky demeanor, seemed unruffled. Henry could be overbearing at times, snapping at skittish underlings and forcing them to walk on eggshells. Miss Karas was expert at parrying those exchanges, however. In the rare instances when prudence was impossible, she also knew how to put her boss in his place: firmly, but with the utmost respect. She was among the handful of Henry's legion of employees who could manage such dissonance—and only because she was also steadfastly loyal, an attribute Henry valued above all others.

"Anything else?" he asked, a half-smoked Lucky Strike cradled between his knuckles.

"Morris Dubinsky phoned to say your suits are ready," Miss Karas chirped.

"Already?" Henry perked up. "Damn . . . that old Jew works fast!"

Miss Karas nodded. "He's certainly an excellent tailor, isn't he?"

"Only the best on Seventh Avenue!" Henry said. "Maybe all of New York!"

He swelled with self-approbation, as if his personal tailor was a private treasure stashed in Manhattan's teeming Garment Center, available only to a tiny circle of privileged elitists—of which, Henry felt, none were more privileged or elite than himself.

"It's such a pity, though." Miss Karas sighed.

"What is?"

"You know, sir . . . what happened to Morris's people."

"His people?"

"I mean, all those poor souls . . . millions, if you believe the reports coming out of Europe. Innocent Jews stripped of their possessions and separated from their families. Herded into boxcars and shipped to Nazi death camps. Incinerated. Gassed. Stacked in bunkbeds like human skeletons."

Miss Karas shook her head glumly. "It's impossible for me to fathom, sir . . . how all of that could have happened."

"Well," Henry said blithely, "perhaps Morris's 'people' should have been stronger."

"Stronger, sir?"

Henry drew on his Lucky, his sunken eyes shrouded by a billow of smoke.

"What I mean," he said, "is that perhaps the 'poor souls' you're referring to should have mustered the gumption to stand up to the Nazis, even if it cost them their lives. Perhaps they should have found the backbone to resist . . . instead of going to their graves like sheep."

"Some of them did resist," Miss Karas demurred.

"Well," said Henry, "apparently not enough."

Miss Karas cleared her throat, treading more guardedly now.

"Pardon me for saying this, sir . . . but don't you think that sounds a bit, um—"

"Callous?"

"Perhaps."

"Simplistic?"

"I suppose."

"As if I'm blaming the victims for the misdeeds of the perpetrators?"

"Uh-huh."

"Well, I'm sure most people might view it that way," Henry conceded. "But I have my own perspective."

He stubbed the remains of his cigarette into a crystal ashtray on his desktop.

"To me," he said, "there's an invaluable lesson to be learned from what happened to the Jews in Hitler's Europe."

"A lesson, sir?"

"Yup." Henry nodded. "I've seen it time and again—in business, politics, warfare . . . even the contract negotiations I'm up to my eyeballs in now." He unleashed a croupy smoker's cough into the hollow of his fist.

"Weakness," he croaked derisively. "All it ever leads to is certain demise."

Miss Karas studied her boss as he fired up another in an endless chain of Luckies and drew a twisting plume of smoke through his nostrils. So resolute. So cocksure. So high and mighty behind his massive mahogany desk.

"Reveal even the slightest hint of weakness," he said, "and your adversaries will pounce . . . abandon all civility and seize what they believe is theirs—

rightly or not. It's human nature, Miss Karas. Has been that way since the dawn of time."

Henry drew on his cigarette, relishing the way his smoking calmed his nerves, lent clarity to his thoughts, and buttressed his imperious boardroom countenance, an almost lordly haughtiness. Miss Karas bit her tongue. It was always judicious, she knew, to grant Henry his stage. He didn't take kindly to being contradicted. Not by employees. Not by anyone.

"Adversaries can never be contained by passivity or appeasement," Henry said. "Hitler demonstrated that . . . and, thankfully, so did the Allies."

He grew pensive, dragging again on his cigarette.

"Who can truly explain why the Jews have lived through centuries of persecution, oppression—and now this mass murder they're calling 'genocide'?"

He exhaled a velvety stream of smoke.

"Perhaps Jews view passivity, for some reason or another, as a virtue . . . or see their endless persecution as a betrayal by God, or a punishment for some terrible sin. Perhaps in building their credo of 'helping their fellow man,' they've never truly learned to help themselves."

He took another pull on his Lucky. "My point," he said, "is that passivity never prevails. Never! Weakness, I suspect, is like a feral scent that triggers the savage beast . . . rendering the compliant vulnerable to the basest whims of humanity."

Miss Karas, slack-jawed, remained mum.

"And how," asked Henry rhetorically, "does one repel a savage beast?"

"How, sir?"

"With fortitude! Resistance! Strength!" Henry grinned assuredly. "The only way to contain your adversaries is by bucking them head-on: mustering whatever backbone you possess and demonstrating, beyond a shadow of a doubt, that you won't be intimidated! Won't be trampled upon! Won't be defeated!"

Miss Karas, once again, said nothing. Discourse, she knew, was futile in the face of Henry's soliloquies. You'd never prevail in any kind of an exchange—and the damage could be irreparable. Henry clung fervently to his beliefs; rarely was he dissuaded.

Besides, he signed the paychecks. That alone, it was generally assumed, gave him a leg up when it came to polemics—certainly among the thousand or more people on his payroll.

"Well," Miss Karas relented, "thankfully, Morris managed to escape harm's way, and get his family out of that dreadful ghetto in Warsaw."

"And thankfully, he brought his talents with him to New York." Henry grinned. "Because hands down, he's the finest couturier I've ever had. Professional. Courteous. Reasonable in price—especially for a Jew. And grateful for every penny of business I provide."

He glanced at his desktop, anxious to resume work, musing to himself, Everyone on my payroll should be that accommodating. Especially those goddamned union malcontents!

"Oh . . . one more thing," Miss Karas said. "Otto Blackburn also phoned."

Henry looked up again, his interest clearly piqued.

"And what did Mr. Blackburn say?"

"That he needed to postpone your one o'clock phone call."

"For how long?"

"An hour."

"Did he say why?"

"Only that he was working on a report for you, but wasn't quite finished," Miss Karas said. "He said you'd know what report he was referring to . . . and that it was important enough that you'd be willing to await its completion."

Yes, Henry knew the report being referenced. Yes, it was important. And yes, he'd await its completion—for however long it might take.

"Is that all for now?" he asked, his patience wearing thin.

"Well, sir," Miss Karas replied sheepishly, "I assume you're aware of the time."

Henry nodded, fully aware that the morning was rapidly slipping away. Thirty floors below his office, a Packard limousine idled at the foot of the building, its driver waiting to transport Henry to the Waldorf-Astoria for his collective bargaining session. Already, it was a quarter to ten. Henry knew full well that by the time his driver delivered him to Forty-Ninth and Park, assuming the usual traffic, he'd be half an hour late—at the very least.

No matter.

"The contract negotiations," he said flippantly, "can wait till I arrive."

"Certainly, sir," Miss Karas said, closing the door as she departed.

*   *   *

Alone again, and mollified, Henry returned to his paperwork, routine matters for an executive at the helm of a company like his: a purchase agreement on diesel-electric engines for a trio of tugboats; a contract with a European shipping firm; a series of bids for the construction of a North River dry dock. Working in shirtsleeves, he navigated deftly through the documents, scribbling notes with a gold-nibbed fountain pen, wholly at ease in an office befitting the master of a far-flung corporate empire. Shafts of sunlight poured through curtain walls on two sides of the spacious corner suite, outfitted with a cushy leather couch, guest chairs, and matching accoutrements.

Henry's outsized desk fronted a wall plastered with citations from trade associations, civic groups, and charitable organizations. An adjoining wall was adorned with photos of Henry posed alongside prominent public officials: New York Governor Thomas E. Dewey at a black-tie GOP fundraiser; Cardinal Francis Spellman at a charity dinner for the Archdiocese of New York; Fiorello LaGuardia at ribbon-cutting ceremonies for the opening of the George Washington Bridge.

Even more impressive than the office, however, was the stunning vista: a sweeping panorama of New York's majestic Inner Harbor, the gateway to America's preeminent city, its sparkly gunmetal waters lapping the Battery Park promenade and bleeding into the woolly horizon. Cargo ships, oil tankers, and other vessels sat anchored near the Statue of Liberty, its gold-leaf torch barely visible through wisps of factory smoke. Double-decker ferries crossed to and from the Castle Garden and Staten Island commuter terminals. A pair of tugboats, their smokestacks belching exhaust, nudged an ocean liner toward its North River berth. Miles of cargo piers, shipyards, warehouses, and refineries hugged the shorelines of Manhattan, Brooklyn, and Queens.

Henry paused to soak it all in. It was something he did often: stealing quiet moments in his harried workdays to revel in the harbor spectacle and bask in the expansive waterfront domain over which he held iron-fisted sway.

He was entitled to such affirmation. Indeed, Henry McFarland was a towering figure on the New York City waterfront in 1946, a business magnate of nearly unrivaled import. As owner and CEO of McFarland Marine Towing Inc., he presided over a multi-million-dollar corporate empire that spanned hundreds of miles of waterways and operated the city's largest tugboat fleet. He was also chairman of the Gotham Harbor Alliance, a coalition of tugboat firms that controlled nearly all commercial traffic in New York Harbor and its environs.

As such, Henry's realm transcended that of even the most prominent public officials. Shipping firms of all sizes and specialties used his company's services. Thousands of operatives did his bidding. Politicians of every ilk heeded his call. No one in either the private or public sphere dictated his actions. New York Harbor was, in many ways, Henry's personal fiefdom—and Henry, accountable solely to himself, was every bit its lord and master.

But today wasn't a fitting time for basking in professional vainglory. Henry's thoughts were elsewhere—and with good reason. The Gotham Harbor Alliance was neck-deep in negotiations with New York's tugboat workers on a new labor contract, and Henry was squarely in the middle of those talks, his viewpoint critical to their outcome. And that was an ominous prospect.

It was ominous, in large measure, because Henry was in an especially foul mood these days, seething over his dealings with Local 88 of the United Stevedores Association, the labor union representing the city's tugboat workers. And largely because of Henry's deep-seated rancor toward the union, New York—and in many ways America itself—was facing a crisis of dire proportions.

Here it was, the final day in January, and the existing labor contract between Local 88 and the Gotham Harbor Alliance had expired the previous June. The months since then had yielded little more than gridlock, acrimony, and angst. For all that time, New York's tugboat workers had been laboring, grudgingly, under the terms of their former contract—with negotiators on both sides of the squabble solidly dug in, and a frigid, contentious cloud shrouding the talks. Tugboat owners were refusing to budge off their single wage-and-benefit offer. Strike threats were being voiced by an increasingly hostile union. Collective bargaining had descended into a bellicose ritual of pettiness, bickering, and personal attacks. And all the while, city officials—like much of the public—had greeted the standoff with a collective yawn.

All of which was understandable. For decades, there had been a predictable pattern to labor disputes in America's largest city. Despite the verbal jousting, saber-rattling, and brinksmanship typical of collective bargaining, negotiated settlements had invariably been hammered out, often at the eleventh hour. It was de rigueur for labor relations in New York. And a similar outcome had been expected in the current dispute.

But things were different this time. For one thing, the warring parties were uncommonly at odds—light years apart on potential contract terms—with anger and vitriol ruling the bargaining sessions, bitter rivals tearing at each other's throats, and acerbic new voices muddying the waters. A volatile chemistry was also in play: now that World War II had ended, organized labor was flexing its muscles as never before, and a seismic wave of strikes was washing across America's heartland. To exacerbate matters, the window on a negotiated agreement was closing rapidly, the stalemate approaching a critical mass on this frosty winter morning, during which the final bargaining session was scheduled. A strike, threatened for midnight, was more than merely a possibility. By now, it seemed all but inevitable.

And that was the reason for the impending crisis. Unlike other work stoppages, a New York tugboat strike in 1946 would hardly be a trifling occurrence. To the contrary, its impact could well be calamitous. New York's ascent to prominence—in some ways, its very existence—had always been tied inextricably to its superb natural harbor. While manufacturing and finance fueled the city's economy, shipping and trade comprised its commercial backbone. Nearly half of America's maritime imports and exports—hundreds of ships, along with most of the nation's railway and truck lines—entered and exited the Port of New York each year. The port, the largest and most important in America, represented a vital link to a burgeoning global economy, the beating heart of a metropolis primed to soar to unparalleled heights as the postwar capital of the world.

For all its modernity, however, New York was tethered in many ways to its centuries-old past. Major thoroughfares remained antiquated, linked by rickety bridges, crumbling infrastructure, and gaslit, cobblestoned streets. Firewood, produce, block ice, and milk were still delivered to many neighborhoods by horse-drawn wagon. And coal was still the city's primary source of energy—powering its factories, running its transit system, and heating and electrifying its homes, businesses, hospitals, and schools.

That's where tugboats entered the picture.

With much of the city separated from mainland America, most commerce was reliant, in one form or another, upon water. The bulk of New York's coal supply, along with oil and other fuel, was still being transported to local power plants by barge from nearby refineries and storage facilities. Agricultural produce, livestock, dairy products, construction material, and other key commodities arrived in similar fashion, as did most U.S.-bound cargo. The city's fleet of tugboats enabled the movement of those critical resources; maneuvered the endless stream of cargo ships, tankers, passenger liners, and other vessels through the city's narrow, congested harbor; and helped haul tons of trash and other refuse to ocean dumpsites. In short, it was tugboats that allowed America's most important city to function, to subsist, to matter.

A tugboat strike of even fleeting duration would bring commercial traffic in New York Harbor to a virtual standstill, crippling the city's economy and resulting in untold hardship to millions of people. Incoming shipments of coal and fuel oil, along with tons of food, medical supplies, and other necessities would be disrupted. Factories, hospitals, businesses, and schools would be forced to curtail operations. The Consolidated Edison Company and the New York Steam Corporation, which supplied electricity, heat, and power to the city's eight million residents, would see service interrupted. The rapid-transit system would grind to a halt. Tens of thousands of jobs would be disrupted.

None of this, however, seemingly weighed even the slightest on Henry. Outwardly unmoved by the gravity of the impending work stoppage, he sat cavalierly at his desk, attending to paperwork, indulging his three-pack-a-day smoking habit—and seething with anger and resentment.

"Goddamned, fucking piss-ants!"

Henry's sentiments, guttural and raw, spewed almost inaudibly from his lips—couched not in the genteel vernacular that usually marked his speech, but in the coarse and vulgar parlance of the city's rough-and-tumble waterfront.

"They're pygmies—every damned one of them!" Henry spit the words, as if expunging a bitter taste from his mouth. "A monkey could do their job . . . a trained, fucking seal! And for a lot less money, too!"

He exhaled, cigarette smoke venting his nostrils like steam from a locomotive.

"If it weren't for the jobs I provide, most of those union miscreants would be out digging ditches!" he wheezed. "They're commodities . . . nothing more! Ingrates! Malingerers! Leeches! I can fire all of them, and thousands more would happily line up for the wages I pay!"

Henry vented a lot like that in recent days, exploding in choleric, unfiltered diatribes laced with profanity. Never publicly, of course. Vulgarity, after all, was hardly befitting a man of his genteel lineage. But to himself? That was different. If you made your living, as he did, on New York's seedy waterfront, Henry reasoned, why not speak the language? If you were forced to deal with the kind of workplace scum he employed, he thought, why not communicate in a voice they'd comprehend?

"Half those union bastards never made it past grade school!" Henry ranted. "Never had the brains or the balls to amount to anything more than a crock of shit! Never aspired to anything beyond a paycheck and their weekends off!"

Henry dwelled on the objects of his venom: the thirty-five hundred members of Local 88, roughly a third of whom he employed on his hundred-vessel tugboat fleet. He thought about how contract negotiations, contentious from the very start, had languished for months, and how he'd grown irritated over the futility of the talks, increasingly at odds with union reps who grated on him like fingernails on a chalkboard, angering him with demands he deemed outlandish, grievances he deemed petty, minutiae he deemed inane.

As for their leaders, Henry grumbled, "They can go fuck themselves! Greedy, lowlife thugs! Stirring up trouble! Working less, but always demanding more!"

God, how Henry hated labor unions. Hated them for all they purported to be but, in his mind, weren't. Hated how their leaders claimed to champion workers' rights, but instead promoted laxity, cheating, and incompetence. Hated how their rank and file had become so coddled, so entitled, so sullied by power, that they'd lost all incentive to work—cutting corners, constantly complaining, simply covering their asses on the job. Hated, most of all, how organized labor served as a counterweight to everything businessmen like him endeavored to do—chipping away at corporate profits, threatening free enterprise, and degrading the tugboat trade with their corruption and crime.

"Fucking unions!" Henry muttered. "They're destroying my company!

Destroying the city! Destroying America!"

In time, Henry was convinced, organized labor would do nothing less than bring New York to its knees. Drive costs sky-high. Cripple businesses. Force companies to flee the city. Kill the very jobs the unions were trying to protect.

"Enough of their baseless demands!" he groaned. "Enough of them pleading poverty, holding my feet to the fire, bleeding my business dry! Enough!"

Henry could barely contain himself anymore. His heart hammered wildly in his chest. His cheeks were purple as plums. Unable to focus, he shoved his paperwork aside, capped his fountain pen, and glanced at the gold Rolex on his wrist.

It was 10 a.m. already—time to get going. No longer any leeway for flimsy pretenses about conflicting priorities or pressing demands. No more postponing the inevitable. It was time for Henry to stop dawdling and get himself to the Waldorf. Time to face those carking, uncouth union lowlifes. Time for another round of demands and threats—another fruitless, maddening tug-of-war at the bargaining table.

As he crammed a sheath of papers into a monogrammed leather briefcase, he thought, *Those union pricks are going to get an earful from me! They've got no idea, the heartache they're bringing on themselves by pushing me to this point!*

They'd find out soon enough, though, Henry vowed—find out as surely as if they'd been whacked across their collective skulls with a wooden two-by-four. He stuffed a pack of Luckies into the breast pocket of his suit and rose from his chair. Then, just as abruptly, he took his seat again.

Let those sons of bitches wait! Let them take their meeting time and shove it up their asses! Let them just try to start their negotiations without me!

He flicked his cigarette lighter open, lit another smoke, and gazed out his office window. The harbor, at midmorning, had grown somber and forbidding. A tempest was brewing, bound up in the charcoal sky, the banks of bulbous clouds, the wind gusts quartering across the choppy, whitecapped water.

And Henry's thoughts meandered once again—not to the scope of his tugboat empire this time, or to the transcendent power he wielded, but to Morris Dubinsky and the plight of the Jews in Hitler's Europe:

In business—as in politics, warfare, even life itself—he had long known that weakness and appeasement would result only in certain demise, and that adversaries would inevitably pounce at the slightest hint of timidity, abandon all civility, and seize whatever bounty they could. He also knew that in contract negotiations there was but a single way to conduct oneself: by remaining hardnosed and steadfast. Never budging. Never giving in. Never succumbing to loyalty, sympathy—or, worst of all, charity.

I'm Henry McFarland! Ruler of New York's tugboat trade! Lord and Master of the city's waterfront! And nothing—not an obligatory meeting or a negotiating mandate or an impending public crisis—will dictate my schedule, or set my priorities, or determine how I go about my business.

No one, Henry vowed, was going to tell him where to be, or when. No one was going to bully him, intimidate him, or impose their will.

He alone would call the shots in the tugboat workers' contract negotiations, Henry pledged. He alone would put the uppity labor unions in their rightful place. He alone would chart the fate of his harbor. His city. His port.

CHAPTER 2

January 31, 1946

The union reps had never set foot inside anyplace like this. Sure, the two of them had been to ritzy Manhattan hotels before, plenty of times. The Commodore, even years past its Roaring Twenties heyday, was still first-rate. So were the Algonquin, the Roosevelt, and the St. Moritz, all of which had served as meeting venues across eight months of collective bargaining with New York's tugboat owners.

But the Waldorf-Astoria? That was in another league entirely.

Benny Logan and Tommy Duggan, born and raised in working-class enclaves in New York's outer boroughs, had never ventured into a hotel even remotely resembling the Waldorf, with its high-class ambience and stately Old-World opulence. But the glitzy landmark hotel was precisely where the men found themselves on this sullen winter morning, the pair seeming wholly out of place with their raffish demeanor and off-the-rack business suits, bowled over by an aristocratic ambience that clashed with the dingy union halls and waterfront haunts where the two of them usually plied their trade.

"Willya get a load of these highfalutin digs!" gasped Benny, trying to stifle a laugh.

"Ain't nothin' like it in the Bronx, that's for sure," Duggan said.

"Brooklyn, either." Benny cackled. "I can vouch for that!"

The two reps, struggling to feign nonchalance, wound their way through the Waldorf's ornate lobby, sneaking glances at the lavish, Georgian-style furnishings, marble fountains, Art Deco fixtures, and nine-foot-high Exposition clock, adorned with the bronze relief figures of six American presidents and England's Queen Victoria.

"Guess we finally made it to the big leagues." Duggan snickered. "Go figure . . . coupla workin' stiffs like you an' me!"

"Fuckin' unreal . . . how the upper crust lives." Benny shook his head.

"Guys like us will never know from it," Duggan said. "That's for fuckin' sure."

"Ahhh," Benny pooh-poohed. "Who needs this shit anyway?"

And the two of them burst out laughing.

But while the Waldorf's palatial grandeur offered a lighthearted diversion, the men had arrived at the hotel on serious business. Benny Logan was the shop steward for Local 88 of the United Stevedores Association, the labor union representing New York's tugboat workers; Tommy Duggan was the local's recording secretary. The pair was present to attend a pivotal collective-bargaining session with officials of the Gotham Harbor Alliance, the coalition representing the city's tugboat owners. Business didn't get more serious than that for Local 88's thirty-five-hundred-member rank and file—or for its Committee on Wages & Negotiations, on which the two men served.

"Christ Almighty!" Duggan chuckled. "The fuckin' Waldorf!"

The two men, mouths agape, sashayed through the hotel's sprawling reception hall. Uniformed bellmen rolled luggage trolleys bulging with steamer trunks, garment bags, and custom-leather suitcases. Soigné women in mink stoles and diamond-studded jewelry walked arm in arm with tuxedoed, top-hatted men.

"I've been livin' in New York for forty years," Duggan quipped, "an' the only time I ever laid eyes on this place was at the RKO Regal on the Grand Concourse . . . in a movie!"

"Ya mean *Weekend at the Waldorf*?" Benny snickered. "The flick with that 'sweater girl' they discovered in a Hollywood malt shop?"

"Lana Turner," cooed Duggan, blowing a kiss.

The two men, cackling, conversed in the earthy patois of New York's immigrant-rooted working class, their wisecracking, profanity-laced discourse high-pitched and clangorous.

"Whaddaya suppose a night in this joint would set a guy back?" Duggan asked.

"Probably more than our two bankrolls combined," Benny replied.

"Just imagine, though," Duggan said, dreamily. "Silk sheets. Fresh towels. Bellmen an' chambermaids waitin' on ya hand over fist!"

"I think I could live with that," Benny said.

"You an' me both!"

They made their way through the Waldorf's stately main corridor, past fashionable salons and smoking rooms, Peacock Alley banquet halls and tony cafés, terracotta walls and an alabaster bust of Marie Antoinette.

"Who the fuck is that?" Duggan asked.

"Damned if I know." Benny shrugged. "Some French broad, I think."

The two reps, sniggering, ascended a winding travertine staircase leading to the gilded conference room where their negotiating session was scheduled to begin in minutes. Constrained now, they tiptoed in, settling into leather armchairs alongside a pair of union colleagues seated at a conference table strewn with notepads, ashtrays, drinking glasses, and pitchers of ice water. A pair of tugboat owners, courtly in their custom-tailored three-piece suits, nodded dourly from across the table.

"They sure seem chipper," Duggan said facetiously. "Got a feelin' they ain't exactly thrilled to see the two of us."

"Tough shit!" Benny snapped. "I ain't thrilled to see them, either."

The reps unzipped their faux-leather portfolios, plopping legal pads and ballpoint pens on the conference table. Cigarette smoke clung like a fogbank along the white-tiled ceiling. Steam heat hissed as it coursed through cast-iron radiators set under a row of windows opaque with frost.

"Looks like the gang's all here," said Duggan, scoping out the room.

"All except for one," Benny grumbled.

His inference was obvious. Nearly everyone required for the collective-bargaining session—five union reps and a quartet of tugboat owners—was present and accounted for. The sole absentee was Henry McFarland, arguably the man most critical to the negotiations. With bargaining unable to start without the Gotham Harbor Alliance chairman, the negotiators had no choice but to bide their time. Duggan and the other negotiators sat rigid as statues, staring dully into space. Benny, deep in thought, drummed his fingertips idly on the tabletop. The only sound—garbled chatter and raucous bursts of laughter—emanated from the far end of the room. There Paddy O'Boyle was holding court.

At age sixty-two, Pádraig Aloysius O'Boyle had served roughly half his life as president of the United Stevedores Association, or USA, the union that represented thirty-two thousand longshoremen on America's East and Gulf

Coasts, while also serving as parent for New York's tugboat workers' local.

As the USA's top dog, O'Boyle was ostensibly the chief strategist and negotiator for Local 88. His chatty demeanor suggested otherwise, however. Unlike the other union negotiators, sullen and standoffish, the USA president seemed not even remotely at odds with the tugboat owners he'd come to bargain with. To the contrary, the stout, silver-haired union boss was engaged in lighthearted banter with two of the owners, his voice raspy and booming, his laughter coarse and braying, his craggy face flushed with the remnants of a sunburn.

"Lookit that sonofabitch," Benny groused disdainfully. "Here we are, at the ass-end of January, no new contract in sight, an' good ol' Paddy sits yakkin' with his 'buddies' . . . lookin' like he just strolled in off a goddamned beach!"

"Where did he sun his ass this time?" Duggan asked. "Vegas? The Caribbean?"

"Who knows?" Benny seethed. "Does it even matter? Negotiations are in the shitter, our union brothers are freezin' their nuts off in the harbor . . . an' that crusty old bastard takes off in the middle of everything for a little R&R? You believe that bullshit?"

"Guess Paddy figures he's earned himself some time off," Duggan said.

"Well, he ain't earned shit!" Benny snapped. "Not till our union gets a new contract!"

The prospects for any such contract, however, seemed remote at best. The union was bucking for a four-percent across-the-board wage hike, retroactive to the expiration of its former contract. The tugboat owners had countered with a proposed increase of two percent. Anything beyond that, they had argued, would necessitate a reduction in tugboat crews, a notion the union deemed a nonstarter. Other management proposals—changing the length of the workweek and forfeiting previously earned benefits—were similarly rejected, as were alternative union demands.

In reality, though, the contract negotiations were about more than simply wages, working conditions, and benefits. Nor was the squabble confined exclusively to New York's tugboat trade. Indeed, eight months of collective bargaining had underlined a key question tied to labor relations throughout post-World War II America: what would be the relationship between workers' wages and corporate profits now that the war was over?

The answer was very much up in the air.

Throughout America's involvement in the war, the federal government had scrupulously controlled both workers' wages and the price of goods and services, holding key price controls in place once the war ended as a means of curbing inflation. Tugboat owners were seeking White House assurances that the remaining price controls would soon be lifted, enabling the businessmen to recoup higher labor costs by raising their towing rates. But because the government had balked thus far at lifting the controls, the owners argued that their hands were tied when it came to pay hikes. The union had countered with claims that tugboat firms, having profited handsomely throughout the war, could hike wages without raising towing rates, and still turn a healthy profit.

Time hadn't softened either side's stance. To the contrary, the current proposals had been on the bargaining table for months, with each side offering little more than head feints, scare tactics, and trial balloons. The owners had proposed replacing hourly wages with a flat daily rate—an offer the union rejected, claiming it would reduce weekly pay. Another proposal floated by management would have hiked wages more than the desired two percent, but reduced contributions to the union's pension fund. That, too, was voted down.

And that's when the negotiations had turned testy.

Henry McFarland, speaking on behalf of the Gotham Harbor Alliance, had made it clear that the owners were in no mood to offer additional wage concessions. Union leaders had made it equally clear that they were unwilling to soften their demands—and fully intended, if push came to shove, to stage a harbor-crippling strike. Indeed, as if to reinforce their stance, Local 88's five-man Committee on Wages & Negotiations had recently been renamed as its "Strike Committee." A deadline had been set for midnight that night. Either a deal would be struck by then, or enough progress made in the contract talks to temporarily avert the threatened work stoppage. Neither prospect seemed likely.

"I'm tellin' ya, Tommy," Benny groused. "I'm sick an' tired of seein' our men take it up the ass from those money-grubbin' tugboat owners."

Duggan nodded. "I hear ya."

"Think the owners give a hoot about us an' our families?" Benny asked. "Think they're willin' to pay us fairly for the work we do?"

"No way!"

"Goddamn right!" Benny scowled. "To men like Henry McFarland, guys like us are nothin' but a means to an end. For us, money is about payin' our rent an' feedin' our families. To penny-pinchers like McFarland, though, it's a religion. Guys like him have no regard for anything but the Almighty Buck. Never have enough of it! Never stop pickin' people's pockets in their pursuit of more!"

"Give 'em an inch," Duggan said, "an' they'll steamroll us, pay us coolie wages, fire us on a whim. They think they own us, control our lives."

"Well, I've had it up to here with bein' controlled!" Benny seethed. "Fed up with earnin' peanuts. Fed up kowtowin' to those corporate tightwads!"

Jacket slung over the back of his chair, Benny rolled his shirtsleeves up, his tattooed forearms knotted like rope, his craggy face resembling a clenched fist.

"Maybe those greedy fat cats will just have to shave some of their ungodly profits," he muttered. "Or cut some of the executive pay they dole out."

"Don't matter how they find the money," said Duggan. "Long as they do."

The men cut short their private discourse, their attention shifting to Paddy O'Boyle, busy amusing his negotiating counterparts with a litany of raunchy bar jokes.

"That crooked Mick has been sellin' out our union for years." Benny scowled. "The backstabbin' sonofabitch shouldn't even be sittin' at the bargainin' table with us!"

"Should be on the owners' side," said Duggan. "Where he belongs."

The men's contempt for the veteran union boss was resoundingly clear—reflective, too, of a growing number of Local 88's rank and file: angry, disgruntled militants like Benny Logan and Tommy Duggan, longtime confidantes and best of friends.

"Paddy's nothin' but a stooge for the owners," Duggan said. "A sellout."

"Might as well be on Henry McFarland's payroll," Benny scoffed. "The only thing that crooked bastard cares about is gettin' his palm greased."

"Guess he figures a last-minute contract settlement is a sure thing," Duggan said. "Ya know, business as usual: good ol' Paddy ridin' in on his big white horse to pull a new deal out of his ass, an' declare himself a conquerin' hero."

"Well, Paddy's got another think comin." Benny glowered. "See, he don't call the shots for Local 88 anymore. Those days are over. If Paddy don't know that by now, he'll get the message soon enough!"

"An' I suppose you'll be the guy who delivers it?"

"Goddamned right, I will!"

Duggan laughed. "An' I suppose you got a message for McFarland, too?"

"For that greedy prick, I got a belated Christmas present," Benny said. "Thirty-five hundred pissed-off tugboat workers, ready to shut the harbor down unless we get the contract we deserve!"

Duggan shifted nervously in his seat. "Think our local has got the muscle for that?"

"You doubt it?"

"Dunno," Duggan shrugged. "We're battlin' a bunch of heavyweights here . . . men who've never been taken to the mat before. An' a union our size? Let's face it, Benny: we ain't exactly an army."

Duggan had a cogent point. Local 88 was barely a speck on organized labor's map, too trifling to even be granted its own charter, its jurisdiction overlapped by a powerful parent union whose corrupt old-guard leadership worked in cahoots with New York's tugboat owners.

"I'll admit the cards are stacked in the owners' favor," Benny said. "But it ain't the size of our union that matters, Tommy. What matters is who we are . . . an' what we do."

"It ain't that complicated," he said, speaking quietly to his friend. "New York Harbor is the chokepoint of the economy—not just for the city, but for all of America. If the harbor shuts down, commerce halts. If commerce halts, money dries up. An' if money dries up—"

"The city," said Duggan, "stops breathin'."

"Bingo!" Benny grinned. "An' what controls commerce in New York Harbor?"

"Tugboats."

"An' who mans those tugboats?"

"We do."

The gist of Benny's argument was abundantly clear. Indeed, just as the actions of corporate tycoons like Henry McFarland impacted tens of thousands of people, New York's tugboat workers, despite their paltry numbers, occupied an outsized place in the daily life of America's greatest city. Such was the critical role played by the vessels they manned.

"All of that makes our 'puny' little union pretty damned powerful, wouldn't ya say?" Benny argued. "In fact, there ain't many unions our size, anywhere, that have the leverage we do."

"Sounds like we've got a lot more muscle than we give ourselves credit for."

"Enough," said Benny, "to grab power brokers like Henry McFarland by the short hairs . . . an' pull."

"McFarland thinks he calls all the shots in the tugboat trade, thinks he can treat workers like field hands just 'cause he's rich an' powerful?" Benny said. "Well, that arrogant prick's got another think comin'!"

"An' all this so-called muscle we've got?" Duggan asked. "How come we never flexed it before?"

"We never had the stones," said Benny. "Or the leadership."

The two men glanced again at Paddy O'Boyle, doubled over with laughter from a bawdy one-liner.

"Speakin' of leadership," Duggan asked, "what about Paddy?"

"Don't worry 'bout him," Benny vowed. "I'll take care of that problem."

"An' McFarland?"

"I got no problem pokin' that bear, either."

"Dunno, Benny," Duggan sighed uneasily. "This is a huge step our union may be about to take. A tugboat strike could wreak havoc on the city."

"Ain't that the point?"

"Maybe so. But a lotta people could get badly hurt . . . most of all our men."

"Then I guess our men," said Benny, "will be put to the test, see what they're made of."

"Think they can handle the shitstorm they're about to face?"

"I guess we'll find that out."

"An' the owners? Think they'll push us to that point?"

"Well, unless Henry McFarland does an abrupt one-eighty in his bargainin' position," Benny said, "I don't see how a strike can be avoided."

Duggan shook his head. "McFarland's sure a pigheaded sonofabitch, ain't he? Pissed off. Anxious to show us he's wieldin' the hammer. Ready to go to war."

"So am I," Benny vowed. "I'm every bit as pissed-off as that connivin' prick. Wieldin' just as powerful of a hammer. An' just as ready to go to war."

CHAPTER 3

August 4, 1945

Summer that year was daunting, breaking into the tugboat trade in the throes of a record heat wave: dense humidity, savage thunderheads, and storm-tossed ocean swells that swept in over the shoals of the harbor mouth and tossed tugboats around like bathtub toys.

Crewmen could perish in those fierce, unbridled squalls—tangled up in spaghetti-skeins of hawsers and towlines, then tossed overboard and crushed between rampaging vessels, or swallowed up by the swirling, turgid waters. The scorching heat could sap you, too. Cramp your muscles. Bleach your bones. Wilt you like a flower starved of sunlight and rain.

But the stifling heat and ferocious storms were only part of what made that summer so grueling. The workdays were interminable, the conditions perilous, the learning curve steep. Then there was the punishing daily grind, the relentless drumbeat of scutwork at the world's busiest port: hauling barge flotillas of fuel oil, coal, scrap metal, and trash to refineries, storage silos, junkyards, and ocean dumpsites; ferrying scows of lowing, bleating livestock from the Jersey stockyards to slaughterhouses and wholesale meat markets; docking an endless spate of cargo ships, tramp steamers, and oil tankers at their North River berths; ushering a steady stream of ocean liners through the Narrows, then out past Sandy Hook for their transatlantic crossings.

All that summer there was scarcely a letup, no dodging the moil and the sweat, the danger and the grime. Not for fledgling deckhands like Jack Logan. Not for anyone working tugboats in New York Harbor's post-World War II heyday, when the city's waterways thrummed with traffic and the workdays ran dawn through dusk, and legions of workmen toiled at the shipyards, docks, and quays.

But then there were the mornings.

Jack loved being aboard *Jupiter* in the glimmer of first light: the sky brush-stroked in shades of scarlet, coral and pink; the salt air bracing and cool to the skin; the harbor at slack tide smooth as glass, tranquil and crystal clear at the crack of dawn.

Perhaps it was the steadfast rumble of *Jupiter*'s engine that made Jack feel so grounded, so sanguine and full of hope. Perhaps it was the gentle sway of the tugboat as it plowed through gauzy curtains of fog, or the sense that Jack was so close to the city's beating heart that he could feel its doughty pulse, or the way the briny sea scent could cleanse a man from the inside out, and open his eyes to even life's simplest blessings.

Perhaps it was all those things. It didn't really matter.

What mattered most to Jack was that it was possible in the golden glow of morning to feel upbeat and alive again, easy to believe—even after all he'd lived through, and all he'd seen—that life could still be good and the world could seem idyllic, scrubbed of chaos and conflict, free from the detritus of the long and terrible war. It had been years since Jack felt so heartened, long enough ago that he had wondered at times if he'd ever feel that way again, or even if he could. But he felt that way on his mornings aboard *Jupiter*, felt it that summer.

And why wouldn't he?

World War II was all but over by then, receding like a tempest blowing out to sea. Hitler and Mussolini were dead, the Axis enemy vanquished in Europe, the Pacific campaign winding to a close. Troopships packed with homebound G.I.s were arriving like clockwork in port, greeted by pealing church bells and water-spewing fireboats and cheering dockside throngs. Ceremonies and speeches hailed the Allied triumph. Victory parades wound their way through Broadway's Canyon of Heroes.

Best of all, Jack was home again, discharged three months earlier after four years of army service in England and France. Nestled again in the comforting bosom of family and friends. Newly married and soon to be a father. Angling, like all the other war-weary ex-G.I.s, for a fresh new start.

The war had, inevitably, changed Jack. No one who ever left to fight a war ever returned home quite the same. Jack was barely twenty years old when he'd shipped overseas to Europe. He was all of twenty-four now—older than his years in many ways, yet still in the flower of youth—audacious enough to harbor faith, bold enough to chase his dreams, and bullish enough to believe that the tumult of the past four years may truly have quieted and the arc of his life might finally ascend and that, bathed in the lambent radiance of postwar America, he could live the soldier's most fervent wish: to forget the horrors of all that he'd seen; to pick up the pieces of his former life and somehow start anew; and to discover, in the city he called home, a concrete, lasting peace.

Jack clothed himself in those emotions now, reveling in how his mornings aboard *Jupiter* could feel so buoyant, so peaceful and bulging with hope. Not simply the cusp of a brand-new day, but the dawning of a whole new life.

Some mornings, in the dusky half-light, he'd stand on *Jupiter*'s foredeck as the tugboat, running light and fast, would ride a freshet along Manhattan's eastern flank, gliding past the settlement houses, rookeries, and pushcart peddlers of the Lower East Side, and the oil-skinned fishmongers at the South Street docks, and the souvenir stores and bubble tea shops of Chinatown. Past the crenulated shorelines of Brooklyn and Queens, and the newspaper-printing plants on Park Row, and the Turtle Bay construction site where workmen would soon be laying the foundation for the headquarters of the United Nations. Past rocky promontories and rutted stone embankments and small islands housing hospitals and prisons, mental asylums and squatters' shacks, umber housing projects, and the ghostly ruins of old, abandoned forts.

Sometimes, gliding through the cynosure of the city, williwaws blowing off the jagged midtown spires, Jack would try to envision what all of it must have looked like centuries earlier, when the riverbeds were virgin, the oil-slicked water pristine, and the shorelines lush with soaring primeval forests. He'd try to imagine what the early European explorers must have seen, fanning out in a quest for power and riches, and stumbling instead upon a slender, rugged island and a natural harbor unlike any on earth: an intricate network of navigable waterways washed by ocean tides and rivers, and anchorages sheltered from ice and storm. Inlets and bays. Creeks and coves. Estuaries and lagoons. Barrier islands and salt marshes. A veritable paradise of timber and fur, tobacco and cotton, shellfish beds, and ecosystems ideal for human settlement. A whole new world!

Standing aboard *Jupiter* on those idyllic summer mornings, Jack would try, too, to envision what all of it must have looked like decades after its discovery: trees along the riverbanks felled; teams of laborers clearing land, planting crops, and building earthwork cabins; the Wall Street Slave Market teeming with traders and auctioneers, African fieldhands and domestic servants, white householders and wealthy homesteaders.

Then, a century later, through the Ages of Sail and Steam, a city in adolescence, buzzing with commerce and exchange: its waterfronts lined with boarding houses, mercantile buildings, and chandleries; its harbor a forest of steamers and frigates, coastal schooners and clipper ships, canal boats and river sloops; its wharves swarming with sailmakers and riggers, shipwrights and seamen, carpenters and blacksmiths; its docks piled with imports of coffee and tea, whiskey and sugar cane, ivory and spice, molasses and silk, and exports of timber and fruit, tobacco and wool, rice and salt, cotton and wheat.

It looked nothing like that anymore, of course. Not by the summer of '45.

New York, by then, was a sprawling, brawny port city, brimming with energy and self-confidence, fresh off America's triumph in the war. Its miles of river frontage had long since been transformed into a welter of factories, warehouses, and industrial lofts; refineries, grain elevators, and ferry terminals; chemical plants, lumber mills, and railyards. Acres of shipyards, dry docks, and deepwater piers glutted shorelines abutted by a seemingly endless landscape of bridges, elevated subway lines, and traffic-clogged thoroughfares. Beyond its waterfronts lay a patchwork of disparate neighborhoods, a teeming alloy of races, ethnicities, religions, cultures, and social classes. At its core, lay a vast expanse of office towers and apartment buildings, restaurants and taverns, hotels and retail shops, railroad and bus terminals, police stations and firehouses, hospitals and schools, nightclubs and movie houses, government buildings and houses of worship, and block upon block of discrete commercial districts: garments, meatpacking, theater, advertising, insurance, finance, jewelry, flowers, cosmetics, toys, printing, and wholesale foods.

This was the city Jack had returned to after four years at war: the city that had nurtured and shaped him, that housed his fondest memories and grandest hopes and highest aspirations. The city in which he'd try now to raise a family and reboot his education and ply a trade, and start all over again.

God—it felt so good to finally be home, cloaked in the grandeur and the grit of New York, the sights and sounds of the old neighborhood, the embrace of family and friends, the adulation of strangers coming up to clap him on the back and shake his hand and thank him for all he'd done to help America win the war.

He felt so lucky, too. Lucky to have made it back, sound in body, mind, and spirit—unlike the legions of men and women who'd been lost, and the countless others damaged and broken by the war. Lucky that his brother Benny, a rising star in union circles, had helped him land a stopgap job aboard *Jupiter*, queen of New York's tugboat fleet, so that he could re-enroll in college at night, and pursue the teacher's degree he'd put on hold.

And lucky, most of all, to have crossed paths with Kate, the British bride who'd followed him to New York from the rubble of melancholy, war-torn London.

Kate.

Jack thought a lot about his new wife, too, on his mornings aboard *Jupiter*. He imagined her fully astir by then: padding about the apartment in Williamsburg that the couple shared for now with his parents. Brushing her hair. Slipping into nylons and flats. Applying lipstick and rouge. Donning a skirt and blouse instead of the starched white apron of a British nurse. No more wounded Tommies for her to tend to in the blood-spattered wards of St. Bart's. No more firebombs raining down on her dank, beleaguered city. No more victims to pull from the rubble, or missing children to be found, or grieving parents to console.

None of that anymore. Not in postwar New York.

Sometimes, in the blush of morning, Jack would wonder if Kate was thinking about him at that very moment, too. Embracing each new day, just like he was. Trying to purge the nightmares and the flashbacks, the horrors of the Blitzkrieg and the harrowing nights at the hospital. Envisioning a life together in the pith of good fortune, the quietude of a world at peace.

Jack wanted to believe all of that, wanted to believe Kate felt that way now that the war was over and the two of them were finally together in the opening act of their conjoined life; wanted to believe that his wife of eight months, pregnant with their first child, felt as hopeful as he did, grateful for even the meager holdings they possessed, heartened by her audacious leap of faith—marrying a young G.I., a stranger in many ways, and following him to a new home in America.

The past two decades—first the Great Depression and then the war—had been fraught with heartache and struggle, privation and uncertainty, separation and sacrifice, the wretched lot their generation had been forced to endure. But maybe, Jack thought, the turmoil, the struggle, the waiting—all of it—would somehow be worth it in the end. Maybe there'd be a pot of gold awaiting them all, a payoff, a reward.

Misery and sacrifice? Conflict and travail? That couldn't be all there was to life—could it? No. There had to be something better. Something more. Maybe, Jack reassured himself, he and Kate could put the past behind them, reboot their lives, and chase the dreams they'd harbored for so long. Maybe, at long last, he thought, their time had finally come.

Things felt different now that the war was over. Spirits were lifting. There was promise in the air, an era of peace and prosperity about to begin. You could hear it in people's voices, see it in their eyes.

Jack was tired of the fighting, the hardship, the struggle. All he longed for now was a second act, a peaceful, ordinary life. Nothing grandiose. Just a chance to turn the page, a chance to work and study and raise a family and build a life in a city where anything seemed possible now: optimism, healing, faith, love.

Anything at all.

The last thing Jack wanted was for New York Harbor to become the backdrop for something ruinous and frightful. The last thing he wanted now was yet another war.

CHAPTER 4

January 31, 1946

He waited another full half hour, simply out of spite. Purposefully disregarding the scheduled start time for his collective-bargaining session, Henry remained sequestered in his office, busying himself with mundane paperwork and vengeful musings about all the ways he saw organized labor leaving an indelible stench upon corporate America. He could have spent the entire day on the latter topic alone, such was the depth of his contempt for labor unions.

By 10:30, however, he decided that he'd delayed the start of contract negotiations long enough. Further delays, he reasoned, would only prove needlessly damaging. Already, his tardiness was ruffling feathers in the Waldorf-Astoria conference room where union and tugboat-owner negotiators anxiously awaited his arrival.

Grudgingly, Henry gathered his belongings, donned a camel's hair topcoat, and rode the elevator down to the lobby, exiting his building and slipping surreptitiously into the sleek, black Packard awaiting him. Invisible behind tinted windows, he reclined on the plush rear seat as his driver, Billy Murdock, pulled from the curb.

A retired NYPD captain who augmented his police-union pension by driving for Henry, Murdock handled the limousine like someone long accustomed to navigating Manhattan's streets, skirting thoroughfares jammed with delivery trucks, buses, and fleets of yellow Checker cabs, before heading uptown on the FDR Drive, where he could exit at Forty-Second Street, shoot across town to Park Avenue, and make his way seven blocks north to the Waldorf.

"Looks like traffic is movin' . . . for a change," Murdock said through the limo's partition window.

"We'll see how long that lasts," Henry groused.

"Probably not for long." Murdock agreed.

Driving adroitly, the ex-cop whisked Henry uptown on the winding shoreline parkway, newly named for the three-term president who had died that April. Across the East River, the industrial landscapes of Brooklyn and Queens loomed like grainy tintypes. Volcanic plumes leaked from the smokestacks of factories, refineries, and chemical plants. Derricks, steam shovels, and cranes rose like sculptural abstracts from the water's edge. The entire city seemed cast in gray: the river, the smog, even the battle-scarred flanks of the mothballed warships anchored bow to stern at the Brooklyn Navy Yard.

"Looks like snow," said Murdock, nodding at the darkling sky. "Sure is cold enough."

"I suspect things will heat up rather quickly, though," Henry said, a reference to the impending contract talks.

"Pivotal bargaining session today, huh?" Murdock inquired.

"Likely the final one too," Henry said ominously.

Murdock pointed at a coal-barge flotilla being towed by a trio of Henry's tugboats.

"Well, at least your tugboats are still out there, earnin' their keep," Murdock said. "Gotta keep them boats on the water, huh?"

"That's exactly what I intend to do," Henry vowed. "By hook or by crook."

And he meant every word of it. Even in the face of a potentially calamitous strike, Henry's bargaining stance hadn't softened one iota across eight months of collective bargaining. To the contrary, the Gotham Harbor Alliance chairman had become even more belligerent, more unyielding and resolute.

"Fucking labor unions!" he griped. "Think they run the goddamned city!"

Murdock, treading lightly, peeked through the rearview mirror. Despite conflicting loyalties—living jointly off both his union pension and Henry's good will—he was savvy enough to know where his bread was buttered these days. When push came to shove, he'd play the loyal sycophant, siding with Henry on labor-related issues. Anything short of that, he guessed correctly, would likely cost him his job.

Then falling silent, Henry shifted his focus, thinking not about the tugboat workers' union, or the impending contract talks, but staring uncomfortably at the scowling visage mirrored in the limousine's valance window.

Fuck—is that really me? he wondered.

Indeed, it was difficult for Henry to believe—the way he looked now. Harder even to accept. He'd once been so strikingly handsome, after all: elegant and lean, with tightly whorled chestnut hair, chiseled jawline, and piercing cobalt eyes. But that was thirty years ago, and Henry had long since let himself go: too many cocktails, cigarettes, and meals at political fundraisers and charity events; too many sumptuous client dinners and late-night snacks; too many broken promises to curb his eating, quit his smoking, and get himself to a gym.

And now it was far too late. The once-dashing tycoon, past the cusp of middle age now, had morphed at age fifty-two into a corpulent, doughy presence, the epitome of a paunchy, over-the-hill pencil-pusher: his jaw wrinkled and droopy; his hair grayish and thinning; his hands fleshy and pink—nothing like the sinewy, calloused hands of the tugboat workers who drew his wrath.

Fuck!

Henry ran his fingertips, clubbed from decades of smoking, along the flaccid skinfolds of his neck, staring at his dour, bloated countenance. It hurt to see how the passage of time had been so unpropitious—hurt even more to dwell on it. So he cast his gaze inward, thinking instead about how his tugboat empire was tied so intrinsically to the city he thought of as his own, and how he'd made his livelihood and his life on New York Harbor, rooted firmly in both its present and its past.

*   *   *

Indeed, for Henry it had been a long and eventful ride: three-plus decades clawing his way to the summit of New York's corporate stratosphere; shepherding McFarland Marine Towing through triumph and setback, and perpetuating an eighty-five-year legacy spawned when his immigrant grandfather, Aidan, founded the eponymous tugboat firm that Henry now headed.

By the time Aidan McPharlin, sixteen years old and penniless, arrived from County Cork shortly before the Civil War, New York was already the world's largest Irish city. Irish refugees were flocking to the city in an endless flood tide, pouring through the Castle Garden immigration center, before streaming onto Manhattan's alleyways and backstreets. The ocean crossing, for most, had been an excruciating test of perseverance and fortitude. Hundreds of émigrés were packed like chattel into the steerage compartments of iron-hulled steamships. So many people died on the arduous, dayslong transatlantic voyage that the vessels were known as "coffin ships."

For many immigrants, conditions weren't much better ashore. Legions of new arrivals found New York to be overwhelming, menacing even, in its clamor and scope. Crowded into filthy vermin-infested tenements, thousands fell victim to typhus, smallpox, cholera, and other infectious diseases. Others became tethered to a lifetime of indentured servitude, their passage to America financed by overlords who owned them now, body and soul. Anti-Irish bigotry also ran rampant, with pitched battles raging between nativists and refugees over religion, ethnicity, and class.

Aidan, however, found New York to be neither pernicious nor intimidating. To the contrary, the ambitious young Irishman saw his adopted city as invigorating and rich with promise, the antithesis of a homeland blighted by famine, pestilence, and persecution. In Ireland, Aidan had seen his family's potato crops ravaged by drought or seized by British overseers. In New York, he discovered a bustling, vibrant city that could untether him from the shackles of the Old Country, a land of plenty where refugees could reimagine their lives and become the people they always wanted to be.

Dogged, resourceful—and, unlike many Irish refugees, literate—Aidan managed to dodge the notorious waterfront "runners" who preyed on new arrivals, shepherding the refugees to disease-riddled hovels after swindling them out of their savings. Instead, he found shelter at an almshouse run by Jesuit priests at the Five Points, a teeming Irish slum where he went about shedding his thick native brogue, adopting an American surname, and finding work.

Bottom-feeders on the lowest rungs of the socio-economic ladder, Irishmen were landing mostly pick-and-shovel jobs in New York then: laying railroad ties and streetcar tracks; laboring as hod carriers and sandhogs; digging aqueducts, tunnels, and sewers. Aidan set his sights elsewhere, however: on the city's bustling harbor. He was hardly alone. New York Harbor was a magnet for hordes of Irishmen drawn to jobs as ballast handlers, stevedores, chandlers, and livery boatmen. So many Irish-owned vessels operated in New York Harbor at the time that the fleet was dubbed the "Irish Navy."

Aidan began his career modestly, rebuilding a rickety old schooner that he used to transport building materials, grain, and other cargo between ships and piers. Partnering with his two brothers, he augmented the business with the purchase of a sidewheel steamer that made seasonal runs to nearby tourist attractions. The brothers then solidified their growing foothold by acquiring a trio of tugboats. Thus McFarland Marine Towing, Inc. was born.

Business was booming in the company's first few decades, as New York Harbor fueled the city's robust economic engine through its sheltered deep-water anchorages and navigable links to the Atlantic Ocean, nearby rivers, and the network of canals that extended the harbor's reach into America's fertile heartland. Time and again, the harbor was modified to accommodate the city's growth: its waterways widened, its shorelines buttressed, its channels dredged to allow for the passage of larger, deep-draft ships. By the turn of the century, tugboats had become all but ubiquitous in New York, as much a symbol of the booming metropolis as any of its world-renowned icons.

Over the decades, McFarland Marine Towing attracted entire generations of family members: brothers and sons, uncles and nephews, cousins and in-laws. Henry joined the firm upon completing his formal education at Yale and, later, The Wharton School, assuming corporate stewardship at age twenty-two upon the sudden death of his father Liam, a heart-attack victim at fifty.

The tugboat business then was a dog-eat-dog enterprise whose formula for success was both simplistic and cutthroat. Incoming ships would arrive at the mouth of New York Harbor and tugboats would literally race one another for the right to tow the ships into port. McFarland tugboats, often as not, claimed the bounty.

But McFarland Marine Towing wasn't merely swift. It was also smart. Shortly after becoming CEO, Henry reasoned that rather than racing competitors for the business, it made more sense to negotiate docking rights with shipping firms in advance of their vessels' arrival. For weeks at a time, Henry journeyed to Europe, South America, and the Orient—pitching his company's services, building relationships, and closing deals. Before long, McFarland tugboats no longer had to race competitors for the business; the company held most major ship-docking contracts before U.S.-bound vessels even set sail. Of equal importance, it possessed a valuable form of collateral: access to the financial institutions needed to borrow and invest.

Like his forebears, Henry found New York Harbor a sumptuous buffet at which to feed. Tireless, driven, and remarkably prescient at times, he proved masterful at running his burgeoning empire, seizing new opportunities, broadening his revenue base, and generating the capital needed to modernize and expand his fleet. Corporate debt was retired, assets managed skillfully, profits reinvested in the business. Family members were systematically bought out, potential investors spurned, offers to take the company public repeatedly rebuffed. Fiercely independent, Henry invariably chose to fly solo, determined to keep his company closely held, free to make decisions outside the purview of partners, shareholders, and others who could stand in his way.

McFarland Marine Towing operated the finest tugboats, retained the most seasoned crews, and employed skilled shipwrights and mechanics to keep its vessels in tiptop working shape. The company also pioneered key advances in technology—converting from sidewheel to propeller-driven vessels, and from steam to diesel engines—and was the first tugboat firm in New York to install ship-to-shore radios, reducing unprofitable running time by eliminating the need for vessels to return to shore to receive new assignments.

For Henry, each of these moves paid major dividends. Revenue soared, profit margins rose, and weaker companies languished. With investment beyond the financial means of most, competing companies were forced to operate antiquated vessels, or were limited to salvage work and similar low-profit jobs. Others saw their assets gobbled up by corporate predators, or were forced to bite the dust.

In time, it became obvious that Henry was a business savant, ideally suited for the job he'd inherited. Every nuance of personality generally considered flawed—egotism, autocracy, obsessiveness, cunning—proved an asset in running his tugboat firm. Whatever character trait was required, Henry adopted it, cultivated it, leveraged it. If that meant being ruthless or callous, so be it. If it meant putting in hundred-hour workweeks, that was okay, too. If it meant currying favor, or donating to political campaigns, or financing lobbying efforts—those too were part of the game—as was bending, even rewriting, the rules, a business practice Henry regarded as a simple matter of expedience, a prime requisite for success.

And, Henry, by most standards, was wildly successful. The darling of New

York's business press, "Mr. Big" of the waterfront to the city's spicy tabloids, he was lauded for his ascension to fortune and fame, hailed as a modern-day Midas who occupied a plateau reserved for men of soaring ambition and unremitting drive, visionaries bold enough to reach for the stars and brilliant enough to soar to those heights.

Inwardly, Henry saw through those canards, knowing full well that there was more to success than good fortune or some mythical Golden Touch. Success, he knew, was neither preordained nor dispensed willy-nilly. Instead, men ascended to the heights by outhustling their rivals and setting themselves apart with bold, outside-the-box thinking. They persevered by learning from setbacks and mistakes. And they flourished by standing their ground and letting no one wrest from them what was rightfully theirs. Not competitors. Not bureaucrats. Not politicians. And certainly not the labor unions.

Was the ascent to the corporate summit always easy?

Hardly. Dogged competition forced Henry at times to engage in vicious price wars, dole out costly favors, and cut backroom deals with city officials and others. Graft and corruption were deeply rooted facts of life on New York's waterfront, a spiderweb of extortion, bribery, and deceit. Unscrupulous harbor masters, charged with supervising the berthing of ships, ran their jurisdictions like personal fiefdoms, often demanding payoffs in exchange for prime wharf space. Customs inspectors, city officials, and underworld associates posed challenges of their own.

Nor was business always so robust. The tugboat trade, like others, rose and fell with the fortunes of New York. Business cycles fluctuated; revenue streams ebbed and flowed. Just as the tugboat industry mirrored the rising tide of its first half-century, it plummeted to earth when the financial bubble burst. World War I saw overseas shipping come to a screeching halt, rendering working capital scarce. The Wall Street crash hit harder yet, forcing the closure of many waterfront enterprises, decimating the city's tugboat fleet, and reducing Henry's company to a handful of aging vessels and a payroll a fraction of its usual size.

But through all the challenges, McFarland Marine Towing managed to persevere. Henry, almost singlehandedly, saw to that. When bureaucratic palms needed greasing, he proffered the necessary indemnity. When special interests came calling, he procured loyalty with the requisite tributes. When revenue evaporated, he hired his tugboats out for charter-fishing and tourist excursions. When the equities markets collapsed, he consolidated his assets, eschewed paychecks, cut overhead to the bone, and trolled the harbor's backwaters for any job he could scrounge.

The tugboat trade was boosted mightily by lend-lease shipments of war materiel to European allies during the military buildup preceding World War II. The war itself proved an even greater boon, especially once Henry procured a lucrative Defense Department contract to transport naval munitions through New York Harbor. By war's end, competition had weakened, passenger and cargo ships were once again sailing the Atlantic, and McFarland Marine Towing was busier than ever.

New York was different in 1946 than at any time in its history. Freed from the economic grip of the Great Depression—and, unlike other major cities, unscathed by World War II—New York had risen to prominence as the financial, cultural, and communications capital of the world. America's largest manufacturing and wholesale center. It was also home to the greatest concentration of wealth and power in history and stood as the world's pre-eminent port, the hub of all global trade. And McFarland Marine Towing Inc. stood at the center of it.

More than a hundred of Henry's tugboats operated in New York Harbor now, his company's annual earnings upwards of twenty million dollars, its prospects as rosy as ever. Months earlier, Henry had signed a lucrative multiyear contract with New York's Sanitation Department to haul the city's trash to offshore dumpsites. That deal alone would assure the company's success for at least another decade, at which point Henry could pass the torch to his sons Patrick and Paul, already being groomed to eventually assume control.

But there was more to McFarland Marine Towing's success than simply its financial posture. Far more.

Henry was proud—damned proud—of everything he saw his tugboat enterprise embodying: a classic American success story, grounded in an immigrant's dream and built through decades of intellect and sacrifice, resiliency and faith. He was proud that his company had survived the tugboat trade's wild-and-woolly years, outlasting competitors that had long since gone belly up; proud that it was free of the petty lawsuits and personal squabbles that marred many family businesses; proud of the indelible imprint it had left on New York. No company, after all, had deeper ties to the city's all-important port. Few were so ingrained in the fabric of America's greatest city. Fewer yet had established such a legacy, forged such a tradition, made such a mark.

Henry was equally proud of the mantle he occupied in the city's social strata. He was the waterfront's most powerful business magnate, an exalted twentieth-century oligarch wholly immersed in New York's ruling class, scion of a company that had survived two world wars, a Depression, and the passing of two generations of leaders, and one of a tiny handful of wealthy power brokers who ruled the roost in New York's business circles.

Henry reveled in all that—and reveled, too, in its fruits: vacation getaways to Europe, Hawaii, and the Caribbean; lifetime memberships at Winged Foot and Shinnecock Hills; prime seats at Yankee Stadium, Madison Square Garden, and Broadway theaters; standing reservations at The Copacabana, The Stork Club, and The Rainbow Room.

Then there was his home. Henry owned a penthouse apartment on Manhattan's East Side, a Tuscany chateau, and a Waldorf-Astoria suite that he used mainly for business. His primary residence, though—his pride and joy— was in Sands Point, on Long Island's North Shore.

The most fashionable retreat in Greater New York, the North Shore had earned the nickname "The Gold Coast" for its landscape of opulent, Gilded Age mansions and private preserves, many of them built by wealthy industrialists, financiers, and corporate titans. Sands Point, and Henry's home, sat at the very heart of it.

A replica of a medieval Irish castle, the lavish estate sat atop a hillside that offered a commanding view of Long Island Sound. Entire rooms had been constructed in Europe, dismantled, and rebuilt alongside formal gardens, tennis courts, a skeet-shooting range, and an Olympic-sized pool. A string of yacht clubs and horseback-riding stables was within walking distance. Families with names like Guggenheim, Vanderbilt, and Rockefeller occupied nearby chateaus and villas.

Henry loved being nestled in the comfortable bosom of the North Shore's Old Money. He loved residing in a palatial estate that stood as a testament to his status and success; loved rubbing shoulders with affluent burghers whose fortunes had been made in railroads, shipping, textiles, and steel; loved moving among the prominent patricians who dominated New York's business, cultural, philanthropic, and political circles.

He, too, had earned his place in that rarified atmosphere. Busted his ass for decades. Overcame every challenge he ever faced. Proved time and again he was worth every penny of his six-figure salary and perks, his multi-million investment portfolio. He'd also earned the right, Henry reasoned, to carry himself with the same aristocratic cachet as other Gold Coast bluebloods, with a vocal inflection and patrician bearing that implied he was a cut or two above the common workmen he employed, and head and shoulders above the social climbers moving in droves from New York now, ruining Long Island with their shopping malls, suburban sprawl, and cookie-cutter homes. Bad enough he had to negotiate with the riffraff who ran the labor unions, Henry reasoned. Now he had to live near them, too?

And if his mindset mirrored a holier-than-thou countenance, Henry thought, then so be it. If it branded him as an elitist—tough shit. Arrogance, he understood, was an acquired trait, accruing through the years like layers of skin, and erasing all traces of humility. Henry wasn't changing. Not now. Not ever. Nor would he make apologies for his lavish lifestyle, or the cold and calculating way he ran his business, or the petulant, arrogant snob he'd become.

Why should he? Henry McFarland was the epitome of success, the living, breathing embodiment of the American Dream. Everything about his life had fallen into place precisely as he'd scripted, precisely as he'd planned. Except, of course, for what happened to Carolyn.

That, Henry had never bargained for. Never could he have foreseen how the circumstances that befell his wife of thirty years would cast such a somber shadow over the tugboat empire he had built and the city that housed it. Never could he have envisioned how all that he had accomplished, and all that he had become, might have planted the very seeds whose toxic fruit would foster his personal dissolution and destroy him from within. But in fact, it would take a scant two weeks to witness all of that, twelve days of heartache and chaos wrought by the crusade Henry was prepared to embark upon now.

CHAPTER 5

January 31, 1946

By 11 a.m., Benny Logan had had about as much as he could take. Local 88's collective-bargaining session with the Gotham Harbor Alliance, delayed an hour already, seemed permanently on hold, much to the angry dismay of both union and tugboat-coalition negotiators. Paddy O'Boyle continued his friendly back-and-forth with a pair of tugboat-owner cronies. Henry McFarland was nowhere in sight. And Benny, wound tight as a drum, seemed about at the end of his rope.

"So tell me, Tommy," he muttered. "Where the fuck is 'Mr. Big'?"

"Damned if I know." Tommy Duggan shrugged.

"An' what's with the holdup?" Benny squirmed in his chair. "Some kind of power play? McFarland's way of showin' the world what a big shot he is?"

Duggan, closemouthed, shook his head.

"Well, I got an idea." Benny grinned impishly. "How 'bout we start our negotiations without that pompous prick?"

Duggan winced. "I ain't sure what that'd accomplish, Benny."

"You ain't?"

"Uh-uh. McFarland is the tugboat owners' puppet master, their mouthpiece. You know that better than anyone, Benny. Hell . . . the other owners don't so much as fart without his say-so."

"That right?" Benny stiffened. "Well, maybe if we start our contract talks without him, we can knock McFarland off his high horse, put him in his place."

Duggan laid a palm on Benny's wrist, trying to assuage his high-strung friend.

"No, Tommy!" Benny pulled away. "This is bullshit!"

The pithy exchange caught the attention of several other negotiators. Benny toned it down, but not by much. He didn't care who heard him anymore, or what they thought.

"People like Henry McFarland make me wanna puke!" he railed. "That arrogant bastard thinks he can come an' go as he pleases? Thinks his bankbook gives him license to set all the rules?"

"I suppose," Duggan conceded.

"Really? An' why does 'Mr. Big' get to set all the rules? 'Cause he's somehow better than the rest of us? 'Cause peons like you an' me are beneath him?"

Duggan shrunk in his seat. It was difficult to reason with Benny when he got riled up like this. Better, Duggan knew, to simply let him off steam.

"An' tell me somethin' else," Benny growled. "What makes McFarland such hot shit in the first place? 'Cause he lives in some fancy 'Gold Coast' mansion, an' talks in that highfalutin' 'Locust Valley Lockjaw,' an' pals around with other rich pricks?"

"Well, money's been known to affect people that way," Duggan said.

"That's exactly my point!" Benny argued. "Muckety-mucks like McFarland? Their money goes to their head . . . convinces 'em they're above us 'little guys,' an' can push us around however they see fit."

"Maybe so."

"No maybe about it, Tommy. I'm tellin' you for certain: Men like Henry McFarland don't think the way 'normal' people do, don't relate to the challenges men like you an' me face."

"They live in a whole other world," Duggan conceded. "Never had to get their hands dirty to earn a buck, like we do."

"Wouldn't know a callus," said Benny, "unless it grew on their ass!"

The two men stifled a laugh.

"I ain't kiddin'," Benny said. "Most of the city's tugboat owners were born with a silver spoon in their mouth, or made their fortune off the backs of workin' stiffs like us. We break our balls to eke out a living, an' those rich pricks ride our coattails an' rake in the dough."

"Nothin' new there." Duggan shrugged. "Been that way from day one in the tugboat trade. The rich get richer . . . the workingman takes it up the ass."

"Well, it's time for that shit to end!" Benny seethed. "Time we stopped gettin' pushed around by these 'captains of industry.' Time for them to share the bounty with the men doin' the heavy liftin'!"

"Well, that's why we got a union, ain't it? So we can push back on the shit the corporate bigwigs dole out, an' fight for our piece of the pie."

Benny grinned. "Hey . . . maybe that's what I oughtta do."

"What's that?"

"Ya know . . . me an' Henry McFarland, dukin' it out in a boxing ring, the way men settle their differences in Brooklyn."

"A lot of us'd love that, Benny." Duggan said with a laugh. "Our union gets the contract we deserve, an' you show McFarland how working-class New York feels about him."

"It'd be worth shavin' a point or two off our wage demand." Benny grinned. "Payback for all the grief McFarland doles out."

The two reps, snickering, fidgeted in their chairs.

"You know," said Duggan, "there is a small consolation to all the bullshit we're forced to swallow." He nodded at the conference room's ornate trappings: the hand-carved woodwork, frescoed ceiling, mahogany furnishings, and mirrored walls. "These are sure some high-class accommodations we get to plop our ass in."

But Benny was unmoved, his face wooden and cold. "The joint is fancy," he said. "I'll grant ya that. But promise me one thing, Tommy."

"What's that?"

"Promise me that whatever happens in this conference room today—whatever is said or done—you'll never, even for a split-second, act like you don't belong."

*   *   *

Benny Logan may have seemed grossly out of place in a Waldorf-Astoria conference room, his earthy persona clashing with the hotel's genteel surroundings. But that dissonance didn't matter one bit. Not when it came to negotiating labor contracts on behalf of New York's tugboat workers. Not when it came to voicing Local 88's viewpoint on issues of import to its rank and file. Not when it came to trading punches with people in high places.

It didn't matter to New York's tugboat workers that Benny was a high-school dropout whose crowning scholastic achievement was a D-plus average.

Nor did it matter than he lacked the worldly patina of bluebloods like Henry McFarland, or that his gruff demeanor rankled most management-types, or that he carried himself as if he had a perpetual chip on his shoulder, pissed off and spoiling for a fight. None of that mattered, not in the least.

Benny Logan was precisely who Local 88's rank and file wanted at the contract-bargaining table: a cagey, iron-willed negotiator who walked the walk and talked the talk of New York's roisterous waterfront, a tough-as-nails foot soldier who'd started out as a nobody and climbed the ranks to emerge as the union's conscience, its driving force, its voice.

The eldest son of Scottish-Italian immigrants, Benny made no pretense about his rough-hewn façade. Nor did he try to distance himself from his indigent roots, or make excuses for the way he comported himself. To the contrary, Benny wore his feisty workingman's cloak like a badge of honor—and, just as often, as a disguise.

Indeed, Benny loved nothing more than locking horns with the highbred negotiators, prep-school elitists, and Ivy League hotshots who mistook him for some bumbling, uncouth schnook, or thought that their pedigree and bank account made them better than him. He took equal delight in tweaking his polished, well-off adversaries, foiling their machinations and watching their demeanor change from haughtiness to timidity when he ambushed them with his guts and his guile, and they realized they were in a dogfight with someone they hadn't seen coming—someone lionhearted, agile, and sharp as a tack.

Proving his worth to people who snubbed their nose at him? Benny lived for moments like that. And winning the battles he waged was even sweeter yet.

To Benny, contract negotiations were a chess game of sorts, a test of wits that mirrored fortitude and character, tactical skills and steely nerves. There was a blueprint in play as well, a roadmap for leveraging authority, creating expectations, applying pressure, setting traps, avoiding pitfalls, winning concessions, and breaking deadlocks.

But prevailing in negotiations meant more to Benny than merely a transactional triumph. At its heart it was a means of affirmation, a way of demonstrating that a nobody from the streets of Brooklyn could wage war with the Big Boys—a case of the scrappy underdog spitting in the face of the Almighty Establishment, David bringing Goliath to his knees.

And the ironies made the exercise even sweeter yet. Indeed, to Benny, his humble pedigree and lack of schooling were hardly drawbacks at the bargaining table. To the contrary, they were precisely the attributes that fueled him, toughened him, and made him hungrier than the men he bargained with. Most of those men, after all, had never had to scratch and claw simply to earn a buck, or prove that they belonged. Most had no clue what it felt like to get hired and fired at the whim of some pompous corporate lackey, or to have a guillotine hanging over their head each day at work. Most had never been forced to grin and bear it while some clueless empty suit called the shots, made the rules, and dictated everyone's fate.

But Benny knew about those things, knew about them firsthand.

Benny knew what it felt like to have earned his keep from the age of ten, knew what it took to survive the streets of Depression-era Brooklyn and earn whatever cachet he could by outhustling and outmuscling men in neighborhoods where guts and fury settled most disputes. He knew what it felt like to breathe the fetid air of New York's blue-collar workplace; to be low man on the totem pole; to feel vulnerable and helpless while heartless fat cats held all the cards; to give every ounce of his body and soul to a corporate entity driven solely by greed, at companies where loyalty was a fairytale and reciprocity illusory, and good men got eaten alive and kicked to the curb when they were all used up.

He knew those things because he'd experienced that, and more, across twelve-plus years in New York's tugboat trade, half a dozen of them as a union official—when he'd also learned what it felt like to discover a voice, exert his own strength, and sway the balance of workplace power.

And all of that fueled him, too.

Benny Logan was driven by everything he'd experienced across his blue-collar work-life: dedication, sacrifice, and pride; humiliation, outrage, and deceit; injustice, heartache, and insults; triumphs, stalemates, and setbacks. And all of that carried enormous weight with the union members whose challenges he'd lived, and whose interests he now championed.

Benny's time as a tugboat worker afforded him credibility and insight. His role as shop steward afforded him license to speak, with no holds barred, on the union's behalf. His personality afforded him the means for communicating in fiery, combative language that the rank and file could connect to, draw inspiration from, and rally around.

"The tugboat owners don't like me?" he'd bellow from a makeshift stage at union headquarters. "They think I'm too uncouth, too angry, too unyielding?"

Then he'd bust out laughing. "Well, I say tough shit!"

And the men would laugh along with him. And raise their fists. And cheer.

"The owners say that I demand too much . . . that I'm too defiant an' not willin' to settle for easy compromise!"

More raised fists. Another round of cheers.

"Well, I say you men are worth more than they pay you for the work you do!"

And the men would cheer even more lustily. Believe it, too. With every fiber of their being.

"Without you men," Benny would say, "the owners have no companies! Their tugboats sit idle at their docks! Their revenue dries up! Their profits disappear!"

Then a cadence of silence. And wholesale concurrence.

"Truth is—I don't give a shit what the tugboat owners think about me," Benny would say. "The only thing I care about is what you men think about how I represent the interests of Local 88. If the way I conduct business is acceptable, I ask for your support. If it's not—well, you can throw my ass in the goddamned harbor!"

That was Benny: as feisty and belligerent as he was cunning and tough; desperate to prove his mettle; the proverbial outsider vying for recognition and respect. And shaped by deprivation and penury the same way Henry McFarland had been shaped by privilege and wealth—not in moneyed preserves like New York's Gold Coast, where a landed gentry presided, but in darker, poorer quarters of the city, where a lower, less-privileged stratum walked the streets.

* * *

Born in Chelsea, a working-class enclave on Manhattan's West Side, Benny Logan had lived his early childhood in a tiny, cold-water flat sandwiched between a brothel and a church—or, as his father Gus liked to say, somewhere between heaven and hell. Mostly hell.

The epicenter of New York's working waterfront, Chelsea was unimaginably squalid, lined with block after block of Old Law tenements, dilapidated firetraps, and shotgun hovels. Armies of roaches resided in mold-riddled ceilings and walls. Ragpickers and rats combed through piles of rubbish. Homeless drifters lived on stairwells and fire escapes. In many apartments, tenants unable to pay their rent took in indigent boarders who slept on mattresses set in hallways, alcoves, and kitchens.

The Logans had it better than that, though not by much. Gus Logan, his name anglicized from the Scottish Gustav O'Loughlin, earned eleven dollars a week at an East Village sweatshop that supplied bedding to hospitals and nursing homes, his sixteen-hour workdays spent sifting through bedsheets soaked in urine, feces, and blood. The family's windowless, two-room flat had no heat, hot water, electricity, or toilet facilities. Blankets nailed to leaky, paint-chipped ceilings separated one kerosene-lamp-lit room from another. Wall crevices stuffed with steel wool kept rodents at bay. Benny and his brother Gabriel, six years younger, bathed in their parents' bathwater, slept head to toe in a single bed, and went barefoot in summer so that their cardboard-soled shoes could last a full year. Their mother, Agnes, cooked their meals on a cast-iron coal stove—that is, when the family wasn't subsisting on cucumber sandwiches, baked beans, and potato soup.

When the boys were still young—Benny aged nine and Gabriel three—the Logans joined the flood tide of working-class New Yorkers pouring across the East River with the expansion of the city's subway system, settling in the Williamsburg section of Brooklyn so they could live near a new job Gus had procured. By then, a third boy, Jack, had been born, and the family's twenty-dollar-a-month railroad apartment was spacious enough for a bedroom that the three brothers shared.

With electricity, gas, and steam heat available, kerosene lamps were a thing of the past; so were cold-water baths and sleeping together in a single bed. Gus's new job paid decent-enough money, especially with overtime. Agnes, an expert seamstress, did her part by taking in piecework sewing jobs. Benny pitched in as well, hawking newspapers, working as a bowling alley pin boy, and scrounging the neighborhood for glass bottles redeemable for cash. And the family scraped enough money together to make ends meet, wholly ingrained in the threadbare fabric of their neighborhood.

Ramshackle, bustling Williamsburg was the most densely populated enclave in New York then, with tens of thousands of Eastern European immigrants, first-generation Italians, and Hasidic Jews crammed into tenement apartments, boarding houses, and brownstones. Factories, shipyards, and industrial lofts dotted the local landscape, along with a handful of churches, synagogues, and schools. Trolleys and buses rumbled along wooden and cobblestone streets lined with grocery stores, butcher shops, pharmacies, produce stands, and round-the-clock taverns. The air, especially on smoggy days, was thick with the scent of coalsmoke, chemicals, and paint.

The Logans lived a stone's throw from the East River, on Roebling Street, named for the engineers who designed the Brooklyn Bridge. The family's six-story brick tenement, bordered by a shoemaker and a rubble-strewn lot, stood directly across from a fortress-like National Guard Armory, and around the corner from Brewer's Row, heart of New York's beermaking trade. The family's dingy third-floor walkup contained a galley kitchen, living room, closet-sized bathroom, and twin bedrooms overlooking a railway yard. Dozens of freight trains rumbled past the building each day, leaving locomotive soot to seep through windowsills and wall cracks and blacken clothing, furnishings, and food.

All that was commonplace, however. Countless working-class New Yorkers lived in similar fashion, in humble enclaves often defined by ethnicity, religion, and culture. Williamsburg, like similar neighborhoods, was populated by legions of blue-collar workers, most of whom lived paycheck to paycheck, barely making ends meet.

In the same way that the Logans mirrored that working-class template, Benny fit another common construct. Like many Brooklyn youths, he grew up largely in schoolyards, playgrounds, alleyways, and rooftops—a gifted athlete who excelled in punchball, stickball, stoopball, and other popular street games. As a youngster, he'd dazzle onlookers by doing dozens of handstand pushups. In the sixth grade at P.S. 84, he set school records for rope-climbing and chin-ups. Later, at Eastern District High School, he won the scholastic handball championship in both his freshman and sophomore years.

Most of all, though, Benny could fight.

He wasn't very big—five-foot-eight, maybe, on the tips of his toes—but Benny was rock-solid, lightning-quick, and thick in his shoulders, arms, and chest. By his teens he was spending most of his free time honing his fighting skills at a local Police Athletic League gym. By age sixteen, he'd slugged his way to a welterweight title in the Golden Gloves, a prestigious amateur tournament. A year later he was vying for nickel-and-dime purses at fight clubs throughout Brooklyn and Queens.

And he was good. Benny's fighting style mirrored his personality. Feisty, combative—and blessed with boundless stamina—he was a fearless, indomitable warrior, willing to push himself to the very limit of his endurance. When it came to fighting, Benny knew only one way: plow ahead, hit hard, and absorb whatever punishment his opponents dished out.

Benny didn't win all his fights, but his scrappy, hardnosed persona earned him something even more valuable: respect, an accolade that carried considerable weight in neighborhoods like Williamsburg, where toughness was a form of currency, affording a status that most men aspired to, the only acclaim they'd ever truly achieve. It meant a lot to people in Williamsburg that there were gutsy scrappers like Benny Logan around: guys with moxie; guys with heart; guys who wouldn't be beaten unless they were carried half-dead from a fight.

Benny's fighting skills made him a celebrity of sorts in Williamsburg, whose streets were as much a laboratory and a classroom as a playground and stage. Everything of genuine value that Benny ever learned—the art of social interaction, the ethics and duplicity of commerce, how to cope with the spontaneous and the unpredictable—was learned outside the purview of parents, teachers, and the parish priest: on rooftops, alleyways, and streets; in schoolyards, city parks, and gyms.

And he'd learned those lessons well.

Rugged, resourceful, and streetwise, Benny was expert at navigating gritty enclaves like Williamsburg. He learned how to mimic the body language of tough guys he saw on street corners and movie screens, mastered the artful parlance of the street, and spoke enough Italian, Yiddish, Russian, and Polish to get by amidst Williamsburg's stewpot of ethnicities, languages, and cultures. He also learned how to instantly distinguish friend from foe, sense danger and fortuity, bargain and trade, affect a cocky bravado, and exercise common sense enough to simply walk away. Though Benny could always fight his way out of trouble, more importantly, he knew how to talk to people—and, equally paramount, how to listen: how to read faces, discern emotion, and relate to setbacks and triumphs, aspiration and fear. Call it charisma, simpatico, whatever—Benny possessed it in spades. Effortlessly, instinctively, he knew how to build trust and inspire confidence, courage, and strength.

All those attributes came in handy in the workplace. Arduous and unforgiving, tugboat work fit Benny's personality like a glove. From day one he flourished in the trade, starting out as a deckhand and rising to first mate before being elected to a full-time post as a Local 88 trustee. More recently, he'd led a slate of youthful insurgents in winning election as shop steward, the primary conduit between union members and management—and a job ideally suited to his temperament and skills.

Serving effectively as shop steward required a robust advocacy on behalf of the union's rank and file, even if that meant getting down and dirty with management. Down and dirty wasn't a problem: not only did it come naturally, but the job afforded critical legal protections, including the right to advocate on the union's behalf without fear of penalty or reprisal. Becoming shop steward also put Benny squarely on the front lines when it came to contract negotiations.

And that's where he'd really made his mark.

Like most working-class New Yorkers, Benny had lived an entire lifetime believing that the world consisted of essentially two kinds of people: big guys and little guys, haves and have-nots. Each cohort, to Benny's way of thinking, was inherently at odds with the other, vying for power and control, and harboring an innate animus that inevitably led to conflict.

To Benny, the people who owned and managed companies instinctively took advantage of the workers they considered subordinate: repressing them, exploiting them, and ultimately discarding them, often ruthlessly, once they'd outlived their usefulness. But that was only part of it. To Benny, the true enemy wasn't so much corporate management as it was privilege itself: the universe of wealthy, well-connected elitists who thumbed their nose at "little guys" like him. Benny had long ago grown tired of battling that mindset, of seeing birthright outweigh other virtues, of being victimized by age-old dictums regarding status and social class. Labor unions stood as instruments of liberation, the only vehicle that men like him could leverage in their struggle to buck the system. For Benny, the fight wasn't simply a battle over paychecks. It was about respect, the belief that men like him had value, that their existence mattered.

Shrewd and unflinching, Benny was far more aggressive than the union's old-guard leadership in his contract demands. To him, Paddy O'Boyle and his sidekicks in the United Stevedores Association were too comfortable, too beholden to men like Henry McFarland, too willing to settle for swift, expedient compromise. Benny, in contrast, was anything but comfortable or beholden or passive. Even now, his boxing days over, he retained a steely edge: defiant, tenacious, spoiling for a fight.

And that had captured tugboat workers' attention.

Local 88 had never had a president of its own *per se*; Paddy O'Boyle filled that role, ex officio, as head of the parent union. But tugboat workers were demanding change. Months earlier, an insurgent faction led by Benny and Tommy Duggan had formed a "Committee for Activism," a reform group vying with incumbent leadership for control of the local. Benny, at thirty-three, had emerged as Paddy O'Boyle's most ardent rival. While O'Boyle still controlled the lion's share of union members, Benny was leading a growing cohort of dissidents, many of whom viewed him as Local 88's future president.

But that was down the road. For now, Benny had been named chairman of Local 88's Strike Committee. In effect, he'd been asked to take the reins in collective bargaining despite O'Boyle's presence—serving, in effect, as de facto union president. Benny possessed enough clout to recommend that the rank and file ratify or reject a contract proposal, remain on the job, or strike. The odds were favorable that the men would follow his lead.

And why wouldn't they? Benny Logan was the ideal spearhead for a union on the brink of taking an unprecedented leap of faith—not some bloated beer-hall figurehead, but fervid, irrepressible, forthright, and committed; a rebellious, no-holds-barred streetfighter who'd stand up for a restless, disaffected rank and file, and serve as a steward for workers who felt unappreciated and abused. Indeed, if Henry McFarland owned the hearts and minds of New York's tugboat owners, Benny Logan stood in perfect counterpoint: Just as headstrong. Just as combative. Just as willing to make a stand.

CHAPTER 6

June 4, 1945

The job was entirely Benny's idea. Jack had never given tugboat work so much as a passing thought, not even as a financial stopgap after returning from the war. Tugboats, after all, were Benny's stock in trade. Jack aspired to a very different line of work, a whole other life.

Necessities were unappeasable, however. Always are. Jack needed a steady paycheck, and Benny pitched the tugboat job hard. He'd caught wind of the deckhand opening through a union connection, quietly pulled some strings at Local 88's hiring hall, and before long was chasing after Jack like a birddog tracking a scent.

"You just stepped in shit, kid!" Benny crowed, three months after Jack's Army discharge. "A job opened up at the harbor . . . an' it's got your name written all over it."

Kid.

Ever since they were young kids, Benny had applied that doting sobriquet to his younger sibling. Still did—even though the two of them were hardly kids anymore. But Benny was nine years Jack's senior, and in his mind, he'd always be the Big Brother: mindful, benevolent, protective. And Jack? He'd always be simply "kid."

"What kind of job are you talking about?" Jack asked.

"Deckhand." Benny winked. "On a tugboat."

"A tugboat?"

Jack was caught off guard. It wasn't simply that the job had materialized wholly out of left field, it was more the nature of the work. While Benny was a natural for the tugboat trade—ideally suited for the work in body, mind, and spirit—a deckhand job hardly seemed a perfect fit for Jack. Indeed, the brothers were, in many ways, polar opposites, different as siblings could possibly be.

Jack, a lanky six-footer, seemed far younger than his years, with a beguiling smile, cleft chin, and shock of tousled black hair. Benny, half a foot shorter, looked more like an uncle than a brother: his craggy face stubbled, his body thickset and sinewy, his salmon-hued scalp peeking through a ring of thinning brown hair. Even more inconsonant than their outward miens, however, were the brothers' demeanors: Jack as circumspect as Benny was impetuous, as placid as Benny was combative, as comfortable in a classroom or a library as Benny was in a boxing ring or a waterfront saloon.

But personal dissonance meant little to Benny now. He was offering his brother a much-needed, highly coveted job. In truth, he was offering far more than that, as Jack would come to learn.

"Who's the job with?" Jack asked.

Benny puffed out his barrel chest. "McFarland Marine Towing."

"McFarland?"

"That's right, kid!" Benny declared. "Only the biggest tugboat outfit in New York, a job a lotta guys would kill for . . . an' one that I know you need."

Benny was right on all three counts. His Army stint over, Jack had re-enrolled in Manhattan's Pace University, attending classes three nights a week on the G.I. Bill. Earning a bachelor's degree would take two full years, however, and a steady paycheck couldn't wait till then. Not if Jack and Kate wanted to move from his parents' apartment to a place of their own; not if they wanted to live the life they aspired to. Besides, with Kate pregnant, who knew how much longer she'd be able to work, or if the couple would have enough money to make ends meet?

But that was only part of Jack's dilemma. Jobs were hard to come by in New York. With World War II all but over, and America's postwar economy yet to reboot, ex-servicemen like Jack were caught in a bind, with military contracts being cancelled left and right, and defense facilities laying workers off in droves, even as legions of mustered-out G.I.s were returning stateside. Jack had been fruitlessly searching for a job since his discharge that spring.

"Tugboat deckhand, huh?" he asked. "Tell me about it."

Benny lit up. Hardboiled and callous most of the time, he wasn't prone to revealing a softer, gentler side. He was different when it came to Jack, however. Benny had a soft spot in his heart for Jack: he would move heaven and earth if called upon for his earnest younger brother. It had always been that way.

"McFarland operates about a hundred tugboats in New York," Benny said. "That's a lotta work, kid. An' it just so happens they're lookin' for a deckhand on their flagship tugboat. Strictly grunt work, I ain't gonna bullshit ya. But we're talkin' about a union job here: full-time, solid benefits . . . an' the paycheck ain't too shabby either."

"What does it pay?"

"Fifty-four bucks a week." Benny grinned. "With time an' a half for overtime."

Jack nearly keeled over. He'd earned only a fraction of that during his four years of Army service. Fifty-four dollars a week seemed like a windfall. In many ways, it was.

"An' there's even more than that in the pipeline!" Benny boasted. "The union's about to open negotiations on a new contract, an' we're buckin' for a hefty raise."

"Think you'll get it?"

"I'd say there's more than a decent shot." Benny winked knowingly. "None other than 'yours truly' is heading Local 88's Negotiating Committee."

Jack was impressed—and with good reason. Benny was climbing the ranks swiftly in the tugboat workers' union, becoming a pivotal figure in labor circles throughout New York.

"You're pretty high up on the union's food chain, aren't you?" Jack asked.

"High enough," said Benny, "to throw my kid brother a lifeline."

Jack's interest, by now, was fully piqued. And Benny went for the close.

"Look," he reasoned, "you gotta make ends meet till you finish college, right?"

"Uh-huh."

"So . . . got any irons in the fire?"

"Nothing solid."

"An' how're you fixed for cash, if ya don't mind me askin'?"

"Kate's paycheck is all we've got coming in at the moment."

"Enough to pay the freight?"

"Just barely."

"Well, the deckhand gig is a real job, paycheck plus benefits," Benny said.

"An' it's yours for the takin', kid. Fuck . . . I'm handin' you the gig on a silver platter!"

Jack was appreciative. Interested, too. Still, he remained reticent. Not only did the notion of nepotism run counter to his beliefs, but he'd never been comfortable accepting favors—especially from family. Abetments meant obligations, and that could be tricky. Troubling to Jack was the fear that by accepting the job he'd be beholden to his brother. Jack didn't want to chance being on the hook for a potential payback. He wasn't sure, if called upon, that he'd be able to deliver.

"Don't get me wrong," he hedged. "I appreciate what you're doing for me, but—"

"Whoa!" Benny recoiled. "What's there to think about?"

"Well, for one thing, aren't there men ahead of me on the waiting list?"

"Your name," said Benny, "got bumped to the top of the list."

"But I didn't even apply."

"I applied for you."

"Okay . . . but am I qualified?"

Benny snickered. "You got arms an' legs that function?"

"Of course."

"Half a brain?"

"Sure."

"An' can you take orders from people higher up?"

Jack nodded. He'd had plenty of experience doing that in the Army.

"Then you'll be fine," Benny said. "Besides, kid—there ain't no better qualifications than having a 'rabbi' like me lookin' out for your interests."

That was Jack's opening. "Well, now that you've mentioned it, I suppose that's my problem," he said. "It doesn't seem fair for me to jump the applicants' waiting line just 'cause my brother is a muckety-muck in the union."

Benny smirked. "Listen, kid. Most things ain't fair. You know that by now, don't ya?"

Jack nodded. He knew it all too well.

"Okay," Benny said. "So, long as that's the case, it might as well be you who games the system, right? 'Sides, what's the big deal if your brother goes to bat for ya?"

"It's not that big of a deal, I suppose," Jack conceded.

"Course it ain't!" Benny cackled. "Look at it this way: It's only a temporary gig, somethin' to get you an' Kate on your feet. Put in a coupla years, then graduate college, an' you're on to bigger an' better things. What's the problem with that?"

"Nothing I can think of," Jack said.

"So . . . whaddaya got to lose?"

"Nothing, I suppose."

"Besides," said Benny, "isn't this what brothers are supposed to do?"

"I guess."

"Damn right!" Benny said. "Brothers are supposed to be there for each other in a pinch . . . supposed to have each other's back."

Jack nodded as if he'd heard that sentiment before. And he had. For as long as he and Benny had been bonded by blood, far more times than he could count.

*　*　*

Indeed, when it came to his brothers, Benny had always been squarely in their corner. Watching over them. Safeguarding their interests. Shielding them from harm.

Serving as a stalwart guardian for his two younger siblings was at the very pith of Benny's existence, tied inexorably to his sense of self. To Benny's way of thinking, brothers were tethered by more than simply the ligature of common lineage. There was a moral contract in play as well, an immutable code of conduct to abide by. Brothers took care of one another. Regardless of circumstance, they were there to turn to, to lean on—and, when necessary, to defend.

Benny had lived and breathed that mantra ever since he, Jack, and their middle brother, Gabriel, were young boys. Even at an early age, Benny had been a steadfast champion to his siblings, a steward and savior, hero and guiding light. And for most of their boyhoods, he'd fulfilled that role without hesitation.

With his reputation as a gutsy, hardnosed fighter cemented by his teens, Benny was afforded a wide berth throughout Williamsburg, a product of the adulation he'd earned in the boxing ring. Not even the local wise guys or the knife-wielding street gangs ever busted his horns. Nor did anyone trifle with

Gabriel or Jack, both of whom basked in their older sibling's aura, enjoying an exalted status simply because they were Benny Logan's brothers.

But there was more to the sibling bond than that. Far more.

Gus Logan, the boys' father, worked nearly round the clock, leaving the family's apartment in the wee hours each morning and returning home past nightfall. Meals together were an anomaly, family outings and vacations rarer yet. For days at a time, Benny and his brothers hardly saw their father—and on the rare occasions when they did, he was usually in and out of their apartment in a rush, or far too tired to talk.

Not that talking was Gus's strong suit anyway. Awkward in most social circles, Gus Logan wasn't prone to idle conversation. Chitchat, to his way of thinking, was a pastime engaged in exclusively by women. Men, in contrast, were supposed to be silent and strong—staunch, dependable providers who shouldered their burdens stoically, and fulfilled their familial obligations with neither colloquy nor complaint.

In no way, by fatherly standards, could Gus be called malevolent. He wasn't a malingerer or a philanderer, didn't gamble or drink, never raised a hand to Agnes or his sons. His paternal delinquency manifested itself in an all-too-common form of benign neglect. Like many men of his generation and Old Country pedigree, Gus resided in a perpetual pool of silence: taciturn, brooding, rarely conveying emotion or engaging his sons in any meaningful way. To Gus, the paycheck he brought home validated his role as man of the house. Gus put a roof over his family's head, food on their table, and clothing on their backs. Emotional sustenance was an asset he was unable to provide.

So Benny did.

With Gus perpetually absent, distant as a ship at sea, Benny became a de facto father to his two young siblings, a cagey, streetwise surrogate who took the boys under his wing and taught them the ins and outs of the urban landscape they inhabited—and, in many ways, about life itself.

Benny took Gabriel and Jack on buses, trolleys, and subway lines that roared through serpentine tunnels and soared overhead on elevated cast-iron trestles. He taught the boys how to purchase nickel tokens, read transit maps, and use paper transfers to travel to distant corners of the city; taught them to identify local landmarks and boundaries, and how to traverse Williamsburg's fickle terrain, steering clear of deserted alleyways and dead-end streets where potential danger lurked. In winter, he took the boys sledding in Prospect Park; in summer, to ballgames at Ebbets Field and the Polo Grounds, the penny arcades at Coney Island, and to local movie houses where the three of them escaped into Buck Jones westerns, Tarzan jungle sagas, and action thrillers about gangsters and soldiers, daredevils and pirates.

But that was only part of it. Each year, as the boys matured, Benny introduced his brothers to new life-lessons—trying, in his own way, to teach them how to cope with their surroundings, address the challenges of growing up, and become men.

In the schoolyard at P.S. 84, he taught his brothers how to field ground balls, line drives, and pop-ups, and how to hit a Spaulding rubber ball with a sawed-off broomstick. On Williamsburg's occluded streets, he taught them how to play punchball, stickball, ringolevio, Johnny on the Pony, and skelly—and later, how to flip baseball cards, toss dice, and play blackjack and poker. In the alleyway alongside their building, he taught them how to do pushups, sit-ups, and leg squats, and how to use dumbbells and handsprings to increase their mobility, balance, and strength. At night, huddled around their Philco console, he introduced the boys to *The Lone Ranger, The Shadow, Captain Midnight,* and other popular radio serials. In the privacy of their room, he told them off-color jokes, let them steal peeks at his secret stash of girlie magazines, dab Brylcreem in their hair, and sip from a bottle of Trommer's malt beer he hid in their closet.

Benny also introduced Gabriel and Jack to the rudiments of boxing and the techniques of the fighters he revered—Benny Leonard, Henry Armstrong, and Barney Ross—each man known for his combination of toughness, intelligence, and grit. Being handy with their fists, Benny taught his brothers, was a useful faculty to master in tough, forbidding neighborhoods like Williamsburg, and relied upon far more than simply stamina and technique. They needed to be able to think on their feet, he told the boys, stay a step or two ahead of the other guy, and always keep their wits about them.

In a similar fashion, Benny told his brothers that winning a fight was about more than simply leveraging their strengths and exploiting their opponent's weaknesses. It was about channeling their emotions and conquering their fear.

Make adrenaline your servant, never your master, Benny advised Gabriel and Jack. Understand the value of discipline, preparation, and sacrifice. And more than anything, learn to take a punch.

Making their way in neighborhoods like Williamsburg, Benny explained, was a lot like living in a jungle, the streets populated by predators as well as prey. At all times, he said, they needed to keep their eyes open and antenna tuned; understand when to speak or shut up, to stand their ground or step aside. They also needed, he told them, to become calloused, resilient, and tough.

Toughness, Benny told his brothers, was essential for making their way in the world, and a trait they'd best acquire early in life. Never, he said, should they display anxiety or panic, weakness or pain—all of which could be exploited. Never should they cede control, or succumb to intimidation, or fail to grasp the basic tenets of self-preservation.

Indeed, toughness was a tenet that Benny both practiced and preached— and that's what Gabriel and Jack grew up believing. Both were far better students than their older brother, possessed of exceptional aptitude in reading, science, and math. Benny, however, was blessed with an attribute that neither boy possessed—and one that they craved. Being tough was a currency of far greater worth in Williamsburg than being genteel or studious. Toughness garnered attention; it engendered respect. It was a big part, the boys believed, of what made you a man.

And whatever Benny told his brothers then, the two of them believed. Gabriel was eleven at the time; Jack was eight. And Benny, at seventeen, was lord and master of their world—their shepherd, their role model, their idol. It was downright comical at times, the way Gabriel and Jack trailed their older brother around like puppies, craved his approval, sought his counsel, and affected his gestures and expressions: the insolent, cocksure way he swaggered about; the way he hitched his trousers, combed his ducktail hair, and spit through a gap between his two front teeth. They even spoke like him, mimicking his vocal inflection, his favorite expressions, his penchant for crude profanities.

And Benny ate it up.

He never said a word about it, but inwardly he loved the fact that his two younger siblings worshipped the ground he walked on. He loved being at the center of their universe, perpetuating the Big Brother role he scrupulously nurtured, showering the boys with tokens of his affection: Hershey bars, Tootsie Rolls, and Life Savers; bubble gum, egg creams, and comic books.

And all of it was easy enough to understand. Indeed, for all the adulation he drew throughout Williamsburg, Benny had always been a problem in the eyes of his father. Hyperactive and easily distractible as an infant and toddler, Benny was a late talker and had difficulties sounding out words, learning nursery rhymes, and identifying numbers and letters. Reading was a monumental challenge, spelling and memorization virtually impossible, failure a common occurrence.

Sympathetic to her eldest son's plight, Agnes was a staunch, kindhearted ally, tutoring Benny patiently for hours on end, offering support as he alternately raged and cried in frustration over the futility of his efforts. But nothing Agnes did made a palpable difference. Nor did the efforts of teachers, tutors, and others.

Beneath it all, Benny was frightened, lonely, baffled by his shortcomings. But he squirreled those emotions away, masking them beneath a façade of apathy, humor, and bravado. Acting out, focusing on his physicality, playing for laughs—those were Benny's ways of diverting attention from his limitations, and staving off mockery, isolation, and fear. Dyslexia—Benny's bane—was an enigma in those days, usually ridiculed and dismissed as an incapacity, rarely diagnosed, and usually untreated. And so Benny's condition persisted, even worsened with time—as did his behavior.

As did his behavior. By his teen years, Benny was more than either his parents or his teachers could handle—rowdy, abrasive, downright incorrigible at times: sneaking into movie theaters and ballparks; copping free rides on buses and subways; hanging out in pool halls, betting parlors, and strip joints; running numbers for policy-slip sellers and whiskey for local bootleggers.

Benny thumbed his nose at traditional teenage constraints. In junior high, he was suspended repeatedly for truancy and other infractions, and placed in a special class for so-called slow learners. In high school, he was kept back a grade. Most nights he stayed out till all hours, brawling, carousing, hustling handball games, and running with a crowd that seemed destined for reform school, the welfare rolls, or prison.

Boxing helped enormously, winning Benny notoriety, teaching him discipline, and helping him channel his pent-up energy and rage. Through boxing, Benny discovered that he could focus his attention for lengthy periods of time, and overcome his innate deficiencies with endurance, power, and speed. He also discovered that he had been blessed not simply with stamina, reflexes, and power, but with other redeeming qualities: an ability to instantly discern patterns in people's behavior; make fast, instinctual decisions; and not only outslug opponents but outthink them as well. Perhaps he couldn't excel by traditional standards, but Benny discovered that talent, intellect—even brilliance—weren't confined solely to the classroom. He could be special in his own way, he learned; become worthwhile not only to others, but to himself.

None of that mattered, however, to his father. Indeed, if Gus Logan had always seemed incapable of providing his sons with emotional sustenance, in Benny's case he also seemed unwilling. Repetitively, and without fail, Gus chastised Benny for the way he conducted his life, invariably drawing on unfavorable comparisons with Gabriel and Jack, studious, obedient, model sons in every way. To Gus, his eldest son's lifestyle was nothing short of contemptible. The fact that Benny drew more adulation from the boys than their father—and for seemingly all the wrong reasons—only exacerbated Gus's angst. He could never understand what Gabriel and Jack saw in their wayward brother, or fathom why they idolized Benny more than they did him. And he resented it.

As Benny grew increasingly incorrigible, Gus took to constantly berating his eldest son, scolding Gabriel and Jack for emulating him, and predicting that Benny would never amount to anything more than a no-good, two-bit bum. Benny, in turn, grew to despise his father—offering his brothers the adoration and approval that he had never received; shielding them from the heartache he'd endured; harvesting from them the paternal gifts he'd never received;.

Gabriel and Jack couldn't fight like Benny, but that didn't matter. Benny could fight for them. He could guide them, teach them, safeguard their wellbeing. And he did.

Gabriel and Jack always felt watched over, protected, and safe when Benny was around. They knew that, come hell or high water, he'd be there in a pinch. Never leave them in the lurch. Never let them down. Never let anything bad happen to them.

But something bad did happen.

These were the 1930s, a time before New Deal money began pouring into

Depression-era New York and WPA workers set about building playgrounds, parks, and swimming pools in neighborhoods like Williamsburg. Instead, kids found respite from the summer heat at local beaches and public bathhouses, in jets of cold water from open fire hydrants, or by swimming in nearby rivers. Gabriel and Jack did a lot of that, under Benny's watchful eye.

River swimming could be treacherous, however. Swimmers had to be unwaveringly vigilant, keep an eye on each other, and cling to shorelines where the water was tranquil and shallow. And even that could be perilous. New York's riverbanks were pockmarked with auto carcasses, industrial waste, and other debris. Rotted wood pilings lay hidden in the mudflats and seagrass. The oil-slicked water was clogged with the flotsam of a populous, working city.

And one day, trouble arrived.

Benny, Gabriel, and Jack were swimming with a group of friends off an abandoned pier on the Brooklyn side of the East River, several blocks from home. Everything was going fine until Gabriel dove headfirst off the pier, where the shoreline was littered with hidden slabs of concrete and stone. When he didn't surface immediately, Benny began shouting his name.

"Gabriel!"

No response.

"Gabriel!"

Still nothing.

"Gabriel!"

In the blink of an eye, before any of the boys knew what was occurring, Benny launched himself from the pier. Deep beneath the river's surface he dove, groping in the murky water for shadowy forms, pulling up clumps of cardboard and weeds. Arms flailing, gasping for air, Benny shouted his brother's name again and again, more desperately each time.

"Gabriel! Gabriel! Gabriel!"

But still no sign of anything.

Desperate now, Benny drew a deep breath and dove again, clear to the muddy riverbed this time, cleaving his way through the brackish water, clawing through layers of sediment, coal tar, and silt. Above, swarms of mosquitos and midges swirled about. Below the surface, gribbles and water rats nipped at his arms and legs.

And still, he couldn't find a trace of Gabriel.

Until, soon enough, the other boys did. Panicked, shouting, they pointed to a spot some twenty yards off the pier, where Gabriel, arms and legs splayed, floated downstream with the current. Several of the boys ran for help; others simply ran away. Jack stood helplessly at the pierhead, shivering in his wet bathing suit, crying and shouting his brother's name, then watching as Benny swam to the middle of the river.

Benny was a strong, intrepid swimmer, as fearless in the water as he was on land. But the rain-swollen East River, running high and swift that day, was a daunting challenge. Benny was in the open water now, being pummeled by crosscurrents and tidal surges, swept past seawalls and wharves, struck time and again by chunks of wood and floating debris. There was nothing to cling to. Nowhere to rest and catch his breath.

Lungs afire, arms and legs leaden, Benny swam for all he was worth. Even in the height of summer, the East River was icy cold, and clogged with rivulets of oil, silt, and gobs of human waste. Time and again, he slipped beneath the surface, swallowing water, gasping for air, struggling to stay afloat. Still, he wouldn't quit. Benny would never quit. He'd die if he had to, trying to save his brother.

And he very nearly did. A gaggle of dockworkers, witnessing the unfolding drama, joined in the rescue effort. So did a group of recreational boaters who happened on the scene. Their efforts were fruitless, however. Gabriel's lifeless body, tangled in the pilings of a derelict pier, was fished from the river half an hour later, efforts at resuscitation fruitless. Benny was pulled from the water too, utterly spent, wailing in anguish and grief.

When a police car brought the boys home—Gabriel stretched like a cord of wood across his brothers' laps—it was all anyone could do to assuage a grief-stricken Agnes, who hurled herself to the sidewalk, pummeling the concrete until her palms were bloody and raw. There was no consoling the boys' mother, her heartbreak seemingly boundless. It took an army of neighbors to lift her from the sidewalk and carry her upstairs to the family's apartment. Other neighbors stood idly by, statue-like, silent. Jack clung to the cast-iron stanchion of a nearby lamppost, crying and quaking like a leaf. And Benny—still in his bathing suit, a threadbare woolen blanket wrapped around him—stood in abject silence, watching a pair of morgue attendants slide Gabriel's body into the rear of a solemn black hearse, before pulling from the curb and disappearing into the ether of the city.

Then it was as if Roebling Street simply stopped moving.

The entire block seemed motionless as a still-life. Traffic halted. Children ceased playing. Neighbors stood gawking, eyes riveted on Benny as, slowly, he sank to his knees, his entire body wracked with sobs.

It was a spectacle no one had ever imagined witnessing: Williamsburg's dauntless warrior—its heroic, fearless fighter—overwhelmed, vanquished, shattered by grief. No one knew what to do or say, how to offer comfort or assuage Benny's anguish. Seconds passed like hours. Finally, Jack loosened his grip on the lamppost and rushed to Benny's side, clinging to his brother as if he'd never let go, the pair hugging and crying. Several neighbors approached too, encircling the brothers, trying to stanch their grief.

But not their father.

Shackled by his prisonlike silence, unable to verbalize a fitting response to the tragedy, Gus Logan stood silent, stoic, clutching a concrete balustrade on his building's stoop. Then, as if untethered from an unseen restraint, he approached his two sons.

"P-p-p-pop," Benny stammered. "I couldn't save him. I'm s-s-sorry. There's nothin' more I could've—"

But he never managed another word. Never had a chance to explain what had happened: how Gabriel had dived into shallow water, striking his head on a concrete block; how he, Benny, had tried with every fiber of his being to save his brother's life: battling tidal currents and swirling water; swimming through garbage and clinging to debris and swallowing human excrement, and nearly drowning himself.

Benny never had the chance to tell his father how his steadfast, gallant heart was breaking, or how riddled he was with torment and guilt, or how he wished it was him instead of Gabriel who had drowned. Gus never gave him that chance. Never offered a gesture of consolation or solace. Never uttered a word of absolution or remorse. Instead, letting loose with a feral grunt, Gus reared back and slapped Benny across his face.

Right there, in front of everyone.

Once, twice, three times, Gus slapped his eldest son, each slap more forceful and impassioned than the last. Who could have anticipated such a baseless, wanton attack? How could it possibly be explained? Defended? Or forgiven?

Stunned by his father's baseless outburst, Benny backpedaled, resisting his instincts to hit back, covering up with both hands before tripping awkwardly over his own feet, tumbling backward, and striking his head on the sidewalk.

"Pop! Please!" he sputtered, his palms abraded, the back of his head bleeding. "I'm s-s-s-orry, Pop! It wasn't my fault! I did everything I could!"

Sobbing, wallowing on the sidewalk, Benny pleaded with Gus to halt his mindless assault.

"Please stop!" he spluttered. "Pop! Not here! Not in front of everyone like this!"

But his anguished pleas went unheeded. Unrelenting, pulling from the grasp of stunned neighbors, Gus leapt atop Benny, straddling him and pummeling him repeatedly as Benny lay helplessly on the sidewalk. Bewildered. Humiliated. Shattered.

Then Gus—the father who rarely engaged his sons, rarely conveyed emotion, rarely spoke at all—uttered words that stung far more than his senseless, impassioned blows, that cut Benny to his very core.

"You were supposed to take care of him!" Gus bellowed. "You were supposed to watch your brother! Take care of him! Protect him!" Then, still more harshly: "What kind of brother are you anyway? I'll tell you: you're nothin' but a lowlife piece of shit . . . a two-bit bum who belongs in another family!"

Then, without another sound, Gus rose to his feet, turned his back, and made his way up the stoop, leaving Benny curled prenatally on the sidewalk, Jack wailing like an infant at his side. One brother dead. A proud and dauntless brother shattered. An entire household soiled and broken and ruined.

Chapter 7

January 31, 1946

By the time Billy Murdock got him to the Waldorf, an hour late for his collective-bargaining session, Henry's rancor toward the tugboat workers' union had reached fever pitch—an emotion, to his way of thinking, that was wholly justified.

Indeed, Henry's contempt for organized labor had been festering like an open wound for decades, its seeds sown by corporate forebears who had raised the Gotham Harbor Alliance chairman on vengeful sagas about how America's labor movement had been founded largely in lawlessness and violence—and how unions had endeavored to undermine McFarland Marine Towing Inc. literally from the company's inception.

The stories weren't simply hyperbole. Organized labor, even in its nineteenth-century infancy, had recognized that to gain control of New York's lucrative tugboat trade it was necessary to build a powerful chain of union shops while eradicating independent, non-union firms. McFarland Marine Towing, the city's most prominent tugboat operator, drew the lion's share of labor's attention—and the heaviest flak. Union organizers, financed by Tammany Hall politicians and a cartel of special interests, invested countless manhours and sums of money to establish a foothold in Aidan McFarland's fledgling firm, knowing that even if a simple majority of its workers joined the nascent tugboat workers' union, management had no choice but to bow to the union's right to serve as bargaining agent for all workers.

Union recruitment campaigns were relentless, malicious, and often illegal. Cleverly disguised union sympathizers, known as "salts," were paid to infiltrate the company, organize from within, and disrupt operations. Rather than conducting secret-ballot elections, as required by law, organizers badgered, bribed, and strongarmed workers to win their support. Corporate assets were stolen or destroyed, shipping firms pressured to boycott the company, McFarland family members—including young children—were demonized and harassed. The company was also barraged by a litany of false propaganda aimed at damaging its reputation, undermining management, and threatening its very existence.

Naturally, Henry's predecessors fought back.

Founder Aidan McFarland, a rock-ribbed anti-unionist, used every trick at his disposal to thwart the growing labor movement, countering the union offensive with injunctions, restraining orders, and other legal maneuvers aimed at halting coercive conduct, restraint of trade, and other common-law violations. Union elections were rigged, organizing drives undercut, lockouts imposed, recruiters fired and blackballed from working other firms. Undercover operatives known as "missionaries" employed rumor, innuendo, and whisper campaigns to defame union leaders, sow discord, and wreak havoc at workers' meetings. Aidan's son, Henry's father Liam, unleashed a similar litany of anti-labor tactics, using industrial detectives to monitor union activities while forcing prospective tugboat workers to sign "yellow dog" contracts, ironclad oaths pledging that the men, if hired, would refrain from joining a union. Both Aidan and Liam also summoned National Guardsmen, state militias, Pinkertons—even indigent migrants whom they quartered in livestock pens—to forcibly quash union-led work stoppages.

In the end, though, none of those tactics made a palpable difference. Even in the face of steadfast resistance, McFarland Marine Towing was forced to accede to organized labor's demands. And even then, union pressure ratcheted up. By the time Henry assumed control of the company, America's legislative pendulum had swung in favor of organized labor. Right-to-work options were eradicated at most tugboat firms, workers forced to accept union representation whether they wanted it or not. Union officials also found guileful ways to leverage their power: skirting regulatory oversight, gaining control over hiring and firing, and systematically raiding the corporate till.

"Goddamned sons of bitches!"

Henry barked the expletive loudly enough to startle Billy Murdock as the ex-cop inched the limo through the final stretch of midtown traffic, mere blocks from the Waldorf now.

"Those union pricks are going to get a hot poker shoved up their asses for trying to extort me with their unconscionable demands!" Henry fumed. "They're like rabid dogs. The only way to deal with them is to put 'em down . . . once and for all!"

Then, as earlier on the drive uptown, Henry grew silent, his thoughts fixed not on the roots of his corporate empire or the labor unions that bedeviled his tugboat firm or the pivotal bargaining session that was mere minutes away. Instead, his eyes pooling, his heart tumbled into a gaping chasm somewhere beneath his chest.

"Carolyn," he whimpered, his voice cracking and his body aching from head to toe.

* * *

They were college sophomores when the two of them met: Henry at Yale, debonair, whip-smart, destined to head a lucrative family business; Carolyn at sister school Vassar: talented, popular, a spirited Irish-Catholic girl with a smile that could brighten a room and just enough foibles to make her even more fetching, more human.

Theirs was a perfect match, a storybook romance right from the start. Carolyn Elizabeth Byrne, daughter of a prominent Boston couple, was an accomplished pianist and equestrian, with interests and aspirations that overlapped those of Henry. She, too, came from a monied pedigree. She, too, shared Henry's passion for classical music and jazz; for Joyce and Yeats and all the other great Irish writers; for sailing and swimming, theater and gourmet dining, ballroom dancing and travel abroad. She also harbored Henry's deepest yearnings: an expansive waterfront home far from the bustle of the city; a passel of children; festive gatherings with family and friends; the financial wherewithal to support favored cultural and philanthropic endeavors.

Beguiling in her flapper-style dress and cloche hat, Carolyn was introduced to Henry at a Roaring Twenties-styled fraternity mixer between their schools. Within weeks, their lives were intimately entwined.

They were inseparable throughout their final two years in college, then through grad school, with a teaching stint for Carolyn, and Henry's entry into the corporate realm. Their marriage seemed scripted in Hollywood: picture-book wedding at a century-old Sands Point church; monthlong honeymoon in Maui; sprawling Gold Coast mansion; a trio of bright and healthy children. They enjoyed all the blessings of a joyous, decades-long union, and together found in each other the fortitude and wisdom to weather life's setbacks.

The Wall Street Crash . . . two world wars . . . the collapse of New York's tugboat trade . . . Carolyn was there through all of it. Never wavering. Never faltering. There at Henry's side, every step of the way.

She was there when Henry plunged to the depths and clawed his way to the corporate mountaintop again; there to raise their sons Patrick and Paul, and their daughter Sallie Ann, while Henry was working hundred-hour weeks; there to revel in Henry's triumphs, mitigate his setbacks, share good times and bad.

"Carolyn."

Henry breathed her name, his mind flooding with remembrances of all the ways she had abetted and buttressed him, nurtured and comforted him—and liberated him from a life awash in loneliness, uncertainty, and tumult.

The youngest of six siblings, the only boy, Henry had been painfully insecure throughout much of childhood: sheepish, lethargic, browbeaten by his hard-hearted father—and gripped by a crippling fear of the tugboats at the center of his family's life.

Just as Aidan McFarland had bequeathed his tugboat empire to Henry's father, so had Liam McFarland harbored the belief that his only son would follow in those footsteps as heir to the corporate throne. But Henry, bumbling and meek in prepubescence, seemed patently ill-suited for any such role. Indeed, the first time his father brought him aboard a tugboat, at eight years old, Henry was so traumatized by the massive ships sailing through New York Harbor that the only place he felt safe was in the tugboat's engine room far below deck. It wasn't until years later that he fully outgrew that fear. In some ways—known only to him—he never truly had.

Liam McFarland was hellbent, however, on molding his diffident young son in the imperious image of a corporate tycoon. When Henry turned twelve, his father banished him from the family's Central Park townhome and enrolled him in an all-male, military-style boarding school hundreds of miles from home, with explicit instructions that administrators "make a man" out of Henry—toughening him up and teaching him discipline, self-sufficiency, and leadership skills.

Precisely the opposite occurred, however. At least at first.

Tormented by feelings of abandonment, Henry plunged headlong into an emotional morass that only exacerbated the festering pain of his childhood. The school's regimen of military drills, physical training, and advanced coursework proved debilitating. Its tie-and-jacket dress requirements, disciplinary codes, and autocratic instructors made matters even more insufferable.

Worst of all, though, was the bullying. Deeply ingrained in the academic culture, bullying at Henry's boarding school was normalized—accepted, even by parents, as a form of character-building. Protests over the practice were sloughed off, ridiculed, or dismissed as expressions of weakness, rebellion, or betrayal. There was nothing to stop it. Nowhere to hide.

Henry, like other plebes, was victimized by the school's "fagging" system, a merciless ritual of hazing, browbeating, and humiliation during which vulnerable young students were roughed up, terrorized, made the butt of jokes, and forced to perform servile tasks on behalf of dormitory prefects and despotic older students. Passive and sloth-like, Henry was forced to scrub floors, shine shoes, fetch snacks, and run a gamut of fool's errands. Clothing, toiletries, textbooks, and other personal belongings were pilfered or defaced. Communal showers became excruciating forms of sexual innuendo and body shaming. Corporal punishment—including sleep deprivation and paddling with wooden yardsticks—was administered for even imagined breaches of conduct.

With no means to blunt the toxicity, and no one to turn to for help, Henry adapted to his tortured existence the only way he knew how: by retreating even further into himself and developing an inviolate suit of armor, a defensive veneer that shielded him from his vulnerabilities. Feelings of weakness and trepidation were subjugated. Expressions of vulnerability were patently off-limits. Substantive relationships were avoided at all costs. A hard-shelled, duplicitous persona supplanted that of the mousy, anxiety-riddled young boy.

As he rose through the ranks at the school, Henry shielded himself from further torment by turning to aggression, treachery, and subtle forms of manipulation that soon became more overt. Having grown half a foot by his junior year, he whipped himself into physical shape, focused almost obsessively on personal grooming, and immersed himself in manly sports like wrestling, rugby, and lacrosse. He also vowed that he would never again appear vulnerable or meek in the eyes of others, never again allow himself to be bullied, never again be a victim. As naïve, younger students entered his orbit, he adopted a posture of arrogance, pugnacity, and dominance. By his senior year at the school, he was King of the Hill: calculating, hard-edged, every bit the "man" Liam McFarland hoped he would become . . . at least in his outer appearance.

In truth, Henry was a poseur, far from the cocky, condescending tyrant he pretended to be. Feelings of inadequacy plagued him; attractive, self-assured women sent him scurrying. Terrified by the notion of intimacy, Henry was convinced he'd never be able to sustain a meaningful relationship, or ever truly be loved. Even as he sailed through his first two years at Yale, he was tormented by a closely guarded fear that he could never confess to his weaknesses, never surrender to emotions like frailty or dependence, never escape a troubled existence increasingly marred by insomnia, irritability, and bouts of drinking, debauchery, and depression.

But Carolyn turned those troubling emotions squarely on their head. A year younger than Henry, though infinitely more insightful, Carolyn helped her new beau recognize that freedom from the shackles of his tortured inner self was more than merely a misguided hope. By encouraging him to open a window to his emotions, and earning his unbridled trust, the upbeat young co-ed became ballast for her fickle, high-strung suitor, a savior from the psychic storms that roiled him, wakening him to parts of himself that he never knew existed, emotions he never knew he could feel, possibilities he'd never dared envision.

Carolyn allowed Henry to forgive his innate failings, encouraged him to admit to his most troubled emotions, and granted him permission to shed his veneer of autocracy, braggadocio, and posturing. Assertive, independent— and light years ahead of her time—Carolyn had little patience too for the way women were treated in America. She mandated that Henry discard gender-based archetypes; taught him that women were worthy of both social standing and respect; decreed that he listen as well as speak, give as well as receive. More than anything, Carolyn afforded Henry the freedom to be loved, and to grant another person unconditional love in return.

The years that followed reinforced that relationship.

As a wife, and a later as a mother, Carolyn blossomed into a woman of not only intelligence and sensitivity but compassion and warmth; an aesthete who furnished their home with artwork and ceramics, sculpture and antiques; an altruist whose charitable donations aided a multitude of philanthropic endeavors; a beneficent hostess who regaled houseguests with piano concertos by Mozart, Beethoven, and Brahms; a companion and partner who brought laughter and joy into Henry's pressure-cooker life.

Of all the people whose paths he had ever crossed, only Carolyn had truly touched Henry, inside and out. Only Carolyn knew what made him tick, what fueled him, wounded him, frightened him, and warmed his heart. Only Carolyn eased his burdens, smoothed his briary edges, forgave his darkest instincts, made him feel worthwhile and whole.

Only Carolyn.

What happened to her, Henry thought now, was never in the cards. Never did he think his wife of nearly three decades would ever get sick. Not with the way she looked. The way she cared for herself. In the prime years of her life.

But Carolyn did get sick. Very sick. And there was nothing Henry could do about it but flail helplessly at her illness and watch her succumb. Even with all his import. All his connections. All his money.

The doctors tried everything imaginable: radiation; chemotherapy; surgery; experimental new protocols that bordered, in some cases, on voodoo. But none of it made a difference.

Carolyn withered like an orchid deprived of sunlight and moisture. Stripped of her persona. Robbed of all dignity. Wasting away to a point where Henry could barely recognize her, couldn't bear to look or to talk to her or to touch.

She didn't deserve that, he now thought angrily. *Not that!*

And he didn't deserve to lose her. Not at forty-eight. Not so soon. Not after everything they'd been through, all the years they thought they had left. They had such plans now that their children were on their own and there wasn't the slightest concern over money. The places they were going to go! The things they were going to do! The times they were going to have!

But all of it meant nothing. Carolyn was gone, that's all that mattered. She was gone—and along with her, everything that Henry held dear, everything they'd accumulated across half a lifetime as sweethearts, soulmates, husband, and wife. Only Henry was left behind: wounded and empty; cheated and lost; longing and disillusioned. Padding around his lifeless mansion with no one to be with, or talk to, or love. Pouring himself nightcap after nightcap to blunt his emptiness and heartache. Awake all hours of the night, tossing and turning in bed, waiting for first light so he could shower and dress and get to the office and bury himself in work, and not have the time to think or to feel.

"Carolyn." He murmured her name again, tears dribbling down his cheeks.

"Almost there!" Billy Murdock chirped as he angled the limo to the curb, the trio of flags over the Waldorf's entrance flapping in a stiff, cold breeze.

And Henry's heart drummed with the imminence of his mission: collective bargaining that made him feel as if he'd sunk into a slimy morass; union negotiators whose presence made him want to puke; another round of contract talks destined to crash and burn.

Henry reclined in his seat, mulling a new revelation now: Maybe Carolyn's death eleven months earlier was the reason he felt the way he did. Maybe her death was why he was so frustrated and bitter, so empty and disaffected, so isolated and besieged. Maybe what had happened to her was the reason why he harbored such an unremitting, white-hot rage. Angry at the tugboat worker's union. Angry at everyone and everything. Angry at nothing at all. Angry all the time. So fucking angry!

"Goddamned parasites—feeding off my enterprise, my energy, my ideas!" Henry muttered, his thoughts fixed on the tugboat workers' union, and all of organized labor.

"Those bastards are out to bludgeon my business and ruin the city with their endless power plays! They'll never understand what it's like to run a company like mine: the challenges I face, the decisions I'm forced to make!"

Billy Murdock pulled up to the Waldorf's entrance and a doorman helped Henry exit the limo, escorting him beneath the hotel's wrought-iron marquee to its revolving glass doors.

I'm the one supplying the money and the brains! I'm the one putting my ass on the line! I'm the one working endless weeks, while the only thing those money-grubbing malcontents do is show up, cover their asses, and punch out at quitting time!

Those were Henry's thoughts as he strode purposefully into the Waldorf's lobby Resolute. Itching for a fight. And again thinking: *That fucking union is going to strongarm me? After all I've done for them, for their families? After everything my company has meant to this city?*

His insides raging now, his heartache and anger were ready to find a voice and make the union a punching bag for his bitterness, his loss, his unrelenting grief. He was more intransient than ever. Wasn't budging on his contract offer, wasn't giving an inch—not even in the face of a strike that could cripple his business, impact millions of lives, and ravage America's preeminent city.

It wasn't a prudent strategy, walking into a contract negotiation while carrying this kind of prickly, unabashed rage. The rational part of Henry, the businessman, understood that full well. It didn't matter, though. Henry welcomed his anger now, embraced it, used it as tinder for the bonfire that burned inside him, the rancor he was about to unleash.

I'll show those union cocksuckers! he thought. *They're going to dictate terms to me ... tell me how to run my business? Over my dead fucking body!*

Up the twisting, travertine staircase Henry walked. Detemined. Flush with righteous indignation. Making his way to the conference room where negotiators from Local 88 and the Gotham Harbor Alliance anxiously awaited his arrival.

The union wants a tugboat strike? he thought. *Fine! I'll oblige them! I'll give them a strike to end all strikes! I'll give them a strike the likes of which this country has never seen!*

CHAPTER 8

June 4, 1945

Sometimes, in summer's high heat, the brothers would flee their family's stifling railroad flat to bed down for the night on their building's rooftop and catch the cooling breezes blowing in off New York Harbor.

Gabriel was still alive back then, the Logan household intact. And some nights Benny and his two young siblings would clamber up the three flights of stairs to their tarpaper roof, to sleep on beds of old newspapers and gaze across the sprawling urban landscape—a city that, even in the grip of the Great Depression, seemed awash with possibilities, boundless as the boys' imaginations. "Tar Beach," the brothers called their rooftop oasis, a refuge in which the three of them could loosen the tethers of their hardscrabble existence and give their dreams free reign.

From their sixth-story perch, high above the streetside tumult, Benny and his brothers could gaze across a sweeping expanse of northern Brooklyn, a craggy terrain of storefronts and elevated subway lines, rowhouses and Beaux Arts apartment buildings, church steeples and red-brick schools. They could see the brawny frontage of factories and warehouses, machine shops and foundries, grain elevators and breweries; see rooftops cluttered with chimneys and water towers, clotheslines and pigeon coops; streets canopied by ailanthus and London plane trees, and backyards lush with tomato vines and cabbage plants, rose bushes and hedgerow ivy.

Hugging the East River shoreline were the shipyards, coaling towers, graving docks, and chemical plants of New York's industrial waterfront; the hovels and shantytowns where sallow, hollow-eyed squatters lived in cardboard huts, tin shacks, and holes in the ground; and, just across the river, resplendent in the night, the shimmering butte of stone façades and masonry-clad spires that people in Williamsburg called The City.

Then there was the harbor. The boys could see that, too.

Peering out from their rooftop vantage point, the Logan boys could trace the labyrinth of rivers, tidal fingers, and canals that coursed like chiffon blood vessels through the serried urban tissue, winding through riverine neighborhoods and threading beneath roadways and railroad trestles, then converging in a giant basin at The Battery, before flowing through the Narrows bottleneck where the Lower Bay opened to the ocean and the ocean opened to the world.

They could see bridges glittering like diamond necklets, the umber domes and minarets of Ellis Island, and the pale-green Statue of Liberty, its gold-leaf torch aglow against the sooty, starless sky. They could see the string of filigreed North River pier sheds where the Cunard and White Star Lines docked their famous ocean liners, the Old Slip Piers where workmen offloaded boatloads of bananas, and the corrugated-tin buildings at the Fulton Fish Market, where fishmongers hawked their daily catch beneath the blazing glow of floodlights.

But there was more to New York Harbor than simply a visual feast for a trio of boys lost in reverie. To Benny, Gabriel, and Jack, the harbor was unique to their citified existence, an almost-mythical centerpiece to their otherwise-mundane lives. It wasn't simply that the harbor possessed prodigious symbolic weight, the entrepôt through which generations of immigrants—including their parents—had passed on their flight to a better life. Nor was it simply that the harbor served as a portal for global trade or possessed strands binding it to the very fabric of America.

The Wall Street crash of 1929 had hit America's greatest city especially hard. Half of New York's factories had been shuttered, its financial heart decimated, a third of its workforce thrust from their jobs. Williamsburg, like other neighborhoods, was littered with symbols of misery and loss: breadlines queued with human casualties; vacant lots converted to Hoovervilles; women and children scavenging for food; broken men, rheumy with defeat, selling apples on the street.

But the harbor stood in stark contrast to all of that.

To Benny and his brothers, New York Harbor was nothing short of magical: a wellspring of mystery and adventure, wonderment and romance, inspiration and hope; an awe-inspiring spectacle that lifted the boys high above the city's prevailing heartache and squalor.

In a city that was cacophonous, unforgiving, and often menacing, there was something comforting about living in the company of the harbor's sights and sounds: the baying of foghorns, cawing of seagulls, and clanking of signal bells from channel markers and buoys; the nighttime glow of welders' sparks at the Brooklyn Navy Yard; the metallic grind of cargo-hoisting gear at the docks; the lapping of water against wooden pilings and pierheads.

Benny and his brothers were enthralled by the harbor's intoxicating aura, captive to its magnetic pull, its aura of worldliness and intrigue unlike anywhere else in the city. Sailors from faraway lands frequented its flophouses, tattoo parlors, and brothels. Merchant ships sailed in and out under the flags of foreign countries, their hull markings and hieroglyphs whispering tales of intrigue and adventure. Majestic ocean liners, funnels ablaze like torches, rode the evening tide as they sailed across the ink-black water on their way to sea.

Living at the harbor's doorstep reminded the boys, too, that New York was part of a world that stretched far beyond the stunted geography of home. Williamsburg was their neighborhood, its topography familiar, its landmarks distinct. But Williamsburg was finite; you could only see and do so much. Brooklyn was much the same.

Even The City had an impenetrable ceiling. Manhattan could be enticing and intoxicating; a repository of mysteries and wonders, triumphs and hopes; a polestar of prestige and power, fortune and fame. But it could just as easily be solemn and unwieldy, chaotic and menacing, far too massive and unwieldy to ever be tamed, seemingly close enough to touch, yet forever beyond the boys' reach. Manhattan could inspire dreams—but it could just as easily smother them, reduce them to hopeless, puerile fantasies. Even the grandest of dreams could wither in Manhattan's steel-and-concrete canyons. Its buildings alone were colossal enough to blot out the sky.

But not the harbor.

To the Logans, New York Harbor had no such ceilings, no such constraints. The harbor didn't kill dreams; it birthed them, nourished them, allowed them to take flight. If for millions of immigrants the harbor was a way in—a portal to a land of opportunity and hope—for Benny and his brothers it was a way out, a conduit to a life of adventure and romance, liberation and dreams. Gazing across its waters on those vernal summer nights, the boys could unleash their fettered spirits, loose their imaginations, and map the course of their lives.

The prepubescent Gabriel and Jack fantasized about stowing away on a tramp steamer and sailing to far-flung lands in search of fortune and fame, like the heroes they worshipped from radio serials, comic books, and newspaper funny pages. Benny, more grounded and mature, dreamed of making the harbor his workplace, and applying his energy, moxie, and street smarts to the muscly scale of commerce at the Port of New York. All of them believed in their reveries, too, just as they believed they could move through boyhood unscathed. The same way they believed that their lives, like their city itself, would stretch to the distant horizon, winding through the years like the ribbons of water that gave New York its identity and its vitality, its energy and its hope.

Then Gabriel drowned. And the Logan family crumbled to pieces, and all the boyhood fantasies came crashing abruptly to earth.

The same harbor that had stoked the brothers' dreams and tendered them hope had taken one life and ravaged four others. Gabriel's death would prove a scourge to last a lifetime, an affliction that not even New York Harbor on a summer night could ever possibly mollify.

* * *

Benny left home the day after Gabriel drowned—quit high school in the middle of his junior year. Fudging his age, he enlisted in the Merchant Marine, and fled as far from Williamsburg as possible. No one had the slightest clue where his odyssey led him, save for an occasional postcard from some far-off exotic port. It wasn't until his discharge, five years later, that he returned to New York, settled in the Bronx, married, fathered two daughters, and fulfilled his boyhood dream of working at the harbor, landing a succession of tugboat jobs before assuming a full-time post with the union.

And eleven more years passed.

None of the Logans would ever be the same after Gabriel's death, each of them damaged in some elemental, intractable way. Jack—his childhood aborted, his bearings unsteady, absent not just one but both his brothers now—drifted aimlessly through high school and two years of college before enlisting to fight in World War II. Gus retreated to the only place he'd ever felt safe, reporting like clockwork to his job, and logging in as many hours as his company would allow.

Agnes changed, too.

Inconsolable for months in the wake of Gabriel's death, Agnes, like Benny, went missing: lost somewhere deep inside herself, inaccessible to family and friends, finding solace only in hours of mundane housework and weekly sojourns to the parish church. Terrified by the prospect of losing another son, and vying desperately for God's good graces, she lit row upon row of votive candles, praying for Jack's safe return from Europe, and threw herself into wartime volunteer work: sewing tattered American flags, baking communion bread, and assembling relief packages for shipment to POW camps.

There were subtler changes, as well. Throughout a thirty-five-year marriage that began for her at age fifteen, Agnes had fulfilled the role of the dutiful homemaker: cooking, cleaning, shopping, washing and ironing clothes, and subjugating nearly all her needs to those of her husband and children. But Gabriel's death had opened a fissure in that marital bond. An unspoken frigidity had crept into Agnes' relationship with Gus, a subtle form of rebellion born of bitterness and resentment. Increasingly, Agnes had begun punishing her husband, at times indelicately, for his lack of emotional accessibility, his unremitting silence, and the heartless way he'd treated Benny in the wake of Gabriel's death. Exercising a growing sense of autonomy, she'd purposefully expanded her home-based sewing enterprise to include embroidery, crochet, and macramé, selling her work at church bazaars, flea markets, and similar venues—and increasingly leaving Gus to fend for himself. Most nights, feigning fatigue, she retired to their bedroom early and fell instantly to sleep. Leftovers supplanted fresh-cooked meals. Wifely affections were invariably withheld.

Another significant offshoot of Gabriel's death continued to mar the Logan family. Since the day of the drowning, Gus and Benny had never been in one another's presence. Nor had they spoken. Not a word in sixteen years.

Nothing.

More distant and taciturn than ever, Gus refused to even acknowledge the existence of his eldest son, his silence a prison from which words nor emotions could seemingly escape. And Benny, haunted by the ghost of his brother, riddled by condemnation and guilt, simply hardened as the years passed, severing the cord binding father and son, punishing Gus unremittingly for his paternal sins. Never forgiving. Never forgetting. Never letting go of what happened that fateful day, turning his torment and remorse to resentment and rage. Neither time nor distance could assuage his emotions. Even becoming a father in his own right didn't palliate him—not when it came to Gus. To Benny, it was as if his father was dead. For all intents and purposes, he was.

In 1942, the Logans, like many American families, subscribed to telephone service, and no longer had to receive their calls from a booth at the local drug store. Benny phoned like clockwork. Every Sunday at 6 p.m. he called to check on Agnes and to keep tabs on Jack, overseas in the European theater by then. Not once did Gus come to the phone . . . nor was he summoned. Agnes and Gus were permitted to visit their granddaughters, but only in the presence of their daughter-in-law Ginny—never Benny. All father and son had between them now were distance, rancor, and the burden of that ghastly day.

In time, speaking to Gus no longer mattered that much to Benny. He'd found a more receptive set of ears by then, a whole other path to acceptance and vindication. As a rising star in the union, Benny had attracted a dedicated group of minions he could command—a legion of men, unlike his father, who lauded his talents and tendered him admiration and respect.

Benny was thoroughly at home on New York's waterfront, a hardboiled world of swagger, vulgarity, and sweat. Just as boxing had once been a means for proving his mettle, union leadership provided that bounty now, offering direction, fulfillment, and a sense of purpose. Benny was the same dauntless warrior he'd been in the boxing ring: feisty, indomitable, contemptuous of the status quo, a passionate, incorruptible champion for the city's tugboat workers—a beleaguered, disillusioned constituency that, until Benny's emergence, had been bereft of power and hungry for a voice.

And all of it formed a perfect circle.

To Benny, the union filled the gaping chasm his brothers once filled, the part of him that yearned for absolution from a father who had condemned him and a brother he was certain he had failed. In many ways, the union was everything he needed now: a fellowship akin to the brotherhood he had always craved; a defensive bastion that shielded men like him from the corporate bigwigs who treated "little guys" as if they counted for nothing.

There was an abiding ache inside Benny, an unrequited longing that would torment him his entire life. In the union, however, he could leverage those emotions and meld them with his street-smarts and iron will into something of substance and import. He could make a genuine difference too, succeed at something tangible, just like the other self-made social climbers shaped by New York's jumbled psychological landscape: outsiders denied credence due to their humble pedigree; poor boys who craved a chance to poke a finger in the eye of the smug elitists who belittled them and sold them short.

And there was no reason Benny couldn't make a mark. Anyone who could handle himself on the streets of Williamsburg surely could do so in a union hall or a corporate boardroom, on a tugboat or at a contract-bargaining table. In many ways, it required the same attributes. The same moxie. The same fuel.

Benny had leveraged his innate faculties to become a champion for the disgruntled, undervalued, and maligned—a courageous, rebellious truth-teller who stared defiantly in the face of power. And, in the process, he had discovered a sense of worth he was certain he would never attain in the eyes of his father: a calling, a powerful, intoxicating identity that transcended anything he could discover elsewhere. In the union, Benny had also inherited an entirely new family. His fellow tugboat workers were his brethren now. Redefined by his setbacks, more resolute than ever, he could tend to Local 88's rank and file the same way he'd tended once to Gabriel and Jack—the vigilant, mindful brother he'd always aspired to be.

And by the time Jack returned from the war, Benny could pick up where he'd left off, reclaim a semblance of what he'd lost, be the brother he couldn't be for Gabriel, the brother he still needed to be—even if all he had to offer now was a shadow of what he had once tendered, a totem as minor, as basic, as a tugboat job.

"So, this job I'm tellin' ya about, kid," Benny said, after Jack had finished his Army stint, home again and in dire need of a paycheck. "Whaddaya think?"

Benny was brimming, Jack sensed, with an odd sort of hope.

"We're talkin' about an honest day's work," Benny said. "Pretty damned important, too. You know about New York Harbor, an' all that it means to the city . . . right?"

Jack nodded. After all, he'd never forgotten the childhood nights on the rooftop in Williamsburg: the sights, the imaginings, the dreams.

"The men workin' tugboats are nothin' more than foot soldiers in the city's workin'-class army," Benny said. "But they count for somethin'. They count a lot. Those same guys are the blood an' guts of the workforce that built New York from the ground up, an' make it run—"

"'Sides kid, let's face it . . . you need a job."

Jack, keenly aware of that, needed no further coaxing. Any reticence he'd initially felt—concerns about nepotism, about owing Benny a favor—had evaporated by now.

"What do I have to do?" he asked.

"Nothin'." Benny winked. "I mean, you gotta go through an 'interview'—a formality, that's all."

Jacked hesitated, mulling the offer a final time.

"Let me do this for you, kid," Benny implored. "You're my brother. I owe you."

"You don't owe me anything," Jack demurred.

Benny turned away, as if looking for something off in the distance.

"Okay," he relented. "Maybe it's somethin' I owe myself."

And Jack was struck by that admission, the notion that it wasn't just him who'd be the beneficiary of Benny's offer. By accepting the tugboat job, Jack realized, he'd be giving as much as he'd be receiving. He and Benny would be doing something for each other.

"All right," Jack conceded. "I'll give it a shot."

And he saw his brother swell with a medley of satisfaction and relief.

"You won't regret this," Benny vowed. "And I won't regret havin' ya on the job with me. Ya know, together again, just like when we were kids at 'Tar Beach' . . . you an' me an' Gabriel, up on our rooftop in Williamsburg."

CHAPTER 9

January 31, 1946

Negotiations went downhill fast, opening with distrust before sinking like a stone under the weight of animus, obstinacy, and petty personal differences.

It was more than simply Henry's late arrival, however, that rattled union negotiators. Rather it was his very demeanor: cocky, standoffish, as if he had far better things to do with his time. He offered no explanation for his tardiness. No apologies. Nothing beyond a frosty nod.

If those union pricks have a problem with me, he thought, *they can kiss my ass!*

The unspoken sentiment was reciprocated—in spades.

"Well, well." Benny nudged Tommy Duggan under the table. "Look who the cat dragged in! None other than his royal fucking highness!"

"Pompous asshole," Duggan sneered. "Acts like his shit don't stink."

"Well, maybe we ought to rub his face in it," Benny suggested. "See how he feels then."

"Probably wouldn't like it much."

"You think I give a fuck?"

And with that as a prickly prelude, the collective-bargaining session came to order.

Henry eased into a center seat on the owners' side of the conference table, joining a contingent that personified New York tugboat royalty. Flanking the Gotham Harbor Alliance chairman were George Steele, CEO of Empire Towing, the city's second-largest operator, and Sam Dougherty, principal of Atlantic Marine, the East Coast's premier salvage firm. Bookending the trio were Bertram Phelps, whose company operated a thirty-vessel tugboat fleet, and Harlan Kingsley, the owners' legal counsel.

Facing the owners, like chess pieces in an opening gambit, was the union's five-man negotiating team. United Stevedores Association President Paddy O'Boyle, positioned directly opposite Henry, sat shoulder to shoulder with USA vice president Butch Flanagan and Local 88 treasurer Frank Russo. Benny and Tommy Duggan sat next to one another at the end of the row.

For several nerve-wracking seconds, no one uttered more than a restive cough. The tension was nearly suffocating, the air in the conference room musty as a gymnasium locker, reeking of cigarette smoke, cologne, and nervous sweat.

Proceeding methodically, Henry uncapped his fountain pen and plopped a yellow legal pad on the tabletop. Grinning sardonically, he jotted himself a note—no doubt some nasty dig at the union, Benny surmised. The thought rankled him as much as Henry's aristocratic demeanor. Henry couldn't care less. He knew exactly what buttons he was pushing. Everyone did.

Henry moved with calculation, perfectly aware that every gesture, facial expression, and nuance of body language conveyed a distinct message. Indeed, everything Henry did or said was critical in setting a tone. As the industry's undisputed kingpin, the Alliance chairman wielded prodigious weight among tugboat owners, who all but genuflected in his presence. Nothing was more beguiling to the men than fortune and dominion—and Henry possessed both those things in spades. He also possessed a commanding presence, an innate dominance that asserted itself instantly and demanded deference. It was eminently clear that he spoke unequivocally on behalf of the tugboat owners' coalition—and that the coalition spoke in a single, unified voice.

"I must preface our talks today," Henry said, "by stating, in no uncertain terms, that our alliance believes we've reached a critical juncture in collective bargaining."

"No shit, Sherlock!" Benny muttered, barely under his breath.

Henry hesitated, making it obvious he had overheard the snotty riposte. Benny couldn't care less. Already, he was busting at the seams to lay into the leader of the owners' alliance. There'd be nothing nuanced about it, either. He'd repeat his barb more forcefully, if necessary, to make his feelings known.

Fuck you . . . you holier-than-thou prick, Benny thought, glaring bug-eyed at Henry.

Henry's smirking but unspoken thought was equally dismissive. *Slink back into the hole you crawled from, you grubby cretin.*

And the men exchanged venomous grins.

"As I was trying to say," Henry resumed, "clearly, there's a dire need to reach a contract agreement today. That is . . . if we're to agree to anything at all."

"Our union is well aware of the need to reach an accord," said Local 88 treasurer Frank Russo, a bull-necked tugboat captain. "Midnight's only hours away."

"You mean the deadline to strike?" Henry asked acidly.

"No," Benny snapped. "We mean the deadline to avert a strike!"

Henry bit his tongue. The time to confront Benny Logan, he reasoned, would come soon enough. For now, he'd direct his comments at others in the union hierarchy; Benny would receive no more than a passing glance, Henry's way of implying that the militant shop steward was too trifling to matter.

Benny, equally aware of Henry's disdain, twisted in his seat, ready to pounce, but held his tongue for the moment.

"Well, however you choose to view it, the clock is clearly ticking," Henry said. "The union's midnight strike deadline doesn't leave us time for brinksmanship. Nor does it leave much time to resolve some very substantial differences."

"Frankly, we believe that eight months of good-faith negotiations by our union has been more than enough time," Frank Russo said. "It's a pity we haven't made enough progress to avert the crisis New York is facing."

"Well," Henry said snidely, "it's encouraging to know that at least we're capable of agreeing on something!"

Collectively, the negotiators squirmed. Benny leaned forward, fighting the urge to grab Henry by his throat. Paddy O'Boyle, absent his usual bluster, shrunk in his chair.

As president of Local 88's parent union, the USA, O'Boyle was charged with spearheading negotiations on behalf of the tugboat workers. His silence was conspicuous. Fleetingly, he made eye contact with Henry before abruptly lowering his gaze. Benny caught the subtle exchange and readied a sarcastic comment, but again held back as Tommy Duggan cut to the chase.

Reed-thin, with Macassar-oiled hair and a pockmarked face, Duggan worked in a tugboat repair shop while serving as Local 88's recording secretary. Not only was he Benny's staunchest ally; he was also his closest friend.

"Despite bein' deadlocked in our talks," Duggan said, "our union believes we still have time enough to avert a strike that would surely prove disastrous for our city."

"Well, our side has another opinion," Henry said, haughtily. He tapped a Lucky Strike out of its pack, lodged it between his lips, and touched it to the flame of his gold-plated lighter, snapping the lighter shut.

Once again, Benny fought the impulse to coldcock the Gotham Harbor Alliance chairman. It wasn't simply what Henry said that rankled the union firebrand, but the offhand, callous way he said it: cigarette cradled casually between his fingertips, smirking as he reclined in his chair, the very image of arrogance and power. He personified everything that Benny despised in a man: the aristocratic, snobbish way he carried himself; his elitist, urbane patois; how he belittled people he considered beneath him. More than that, Benny detested the way Henry thought—the way he viewed the world, the opinions he held on most everything.

"Frankly," said Henry, "we believe our negotiations have reached a hopeless stalemate. The fact is, our coalition has made its best, and final, wage offer. In all candor, there's no room for further movement. And to put it bluntly, we don't feel the union has demonstrated a corresponding willingness to reach a constructive and reasonable compromise."

"Well, like most things we've wrangled over," Benny said, keeping his voice quiet but not hiding its contemptuous tone, "we think that's bullshit!"

Instantly, everyone's attention shifted to him. In terms of negotiating protocol, it wasn't Benny's place to speak. Paddy O'Boyle was purportedly the primary mouthpiece for the union. But Benny wasn't taking cues from anyone. He'd air his sentiments whenever the spirit moved him. Didn't matter if protocol was breached, or feathers were ruffled. Not a bit.

"Our side believes there is room for movement by your coalition," Benny continued. "It's our position, as it's been for months, that the city's tugboat owners can accommodate a wage demand that our union believes is reasonable and fair."

"And we," said Henry, "believe that your wage demand is impossible to agree to if the companies we represent are to make a viable profit."

"It all depends," Benny said snidely, "on what you men consider viable."

His own anger building, Henry cleared his throat.

"As we've noted repeatedly," he said, "our companies' profit margins are already razor-thin. Agreeing to the union's wage demand would squeeze those margins beyond reason. We're not just talking about dollars and cents . . . we're talking principle!"

"Principle!" Benny scoffed. "Don't insult us . . . please!"

Henry was taken aback. Benny, again, was unmoved.

"None of what we're discussing is about principle," Benny said. "What drives the tugboat industry, pure an' simple, is love of the Almighty Dollar. The thing is, our side craves money just as much as you men do . . . an' we'll chase after it just as hard!"

As he scanned the owners' side of the table, he continued, "The only difference between our sides is that our members need money to feed an' house their families. You men want it for no reason except to fatten your corporate bottom lines!"

The negotiators were dumbstruck. Henry was aghast. He wasn't accustomed to being addressed in that manner. Nor did he like it. Not in the least.

"Paddy . . . I'm at a loss," he sputtered, turning to O'Boyle. "Aren't you leading the union's charge in these negotiations?"

O'Boyle swallowed hard.

"Yes . . . or no?"

"Yes," the USA president replied, meekly.

"Then I suggest you get your side to approach collective bargaining more responsibly," Henry said. "And frankly, with more deference to those you're negotiating with!"

O'Boyle opened his mouth to reply, but Benny interjected.

"With all due respect to Paddy," he said, "there's more than one voice speakin' for our union these days. And we don't owe any more 'deference' to you than you owe us!"

"Oh—so now we've got to bargain with two parties?" Henry asked. He glared at Benny as though to gauge what deference the union man could possibly expect.

"Put a fair deal on the table," Benny countered, "an' you'll see how unified we are."

"You sure?"

"Try us."

"Gentlemen . . . please!"

Instantly, heads swiveled. Discourse ceased. Paddy O'Boyle, at last, had found his voice.

"Let's all be reasonable," the union president pleaded. "Surely, we can resolve our differences amicably, an' avoid a strike that would be a nightmare to all of us."

He drew a raspy breath, flinty eyes dancing in their sockets. "Do you men wanna see government mediators dragged into these negotiations?" he asked.

"Absolutely not!" Bertram Phelps replied.

A dour presence sporting wire-rimmed spectacles, a jowly face, and owl-like eyebrows, fleet owner Phelps was an old-school operative far more amenable to compromise than confrontation.

"Having lived through contract squabbles before," he said, "I can assure you—government mediators are the last thing any of us want."

"How 'bout politicians?" O'Boyle asked, rhetorically.

"A resounding 'no' to that, too," Phelps replied. "Politicians have no business at a contract-bargaining table. No scruples, either. They'll screw both sides to protect their own interests."

"Our union would also prefer to resolve our differences without involving outside interests," O'Boyle said. "We all agree on that . . . don't we?"

Most of the men nodded. Henry and Benny balked, playing it close to the vest.

"See," O'Boyle quipped. "It's possible for our two sides to agree on something!"

The levity helped. Everyone seemed momentarily calmer.

"But frankly," O'Boyle warned, "if we don't hammer out a deal or make substantial progress today, we're gonna get government mediators shoved up our ass."

His comment gave the negotiators pause.

"Let's face it, the stakes are sky-high," O'Boyle elaborated. "The politicians are gettin' antsy over the prospects of a strike. They're gonna jump in with both feet if our differences aren't resolved soon. An' the Feds don't give a shit about who's 'right' or who's 'wrong.' Their mediators will decide a contract for us . . . an' none of us will be happy about that!"

O'Boyle locked eyes with Henry. "Now, let's get a deal hammered out today!" he implored. "Surely, we can find common ground—cordially an' professionally."

Collectively, the negotiators exhaled.

"Look," said Bertram Phelps, "our coalition needs the union to sympathize with our position. Our wage proposal reflects the harsh realities facing the tugboat trade. Our companies are experiencing intense financial pressure."

"Union members are experiencing financial pressure, too," Frank Russo argued. "The economic knife cuts both ways, you know."

"I'm sure that's true," Phelps conceded. "But tugboat firms in New York can no longer remain viable if our labor costs continue to skyrocket. Union concessions have been achieved at other ports. We've got to do the same in New York . . . or our companies are doomed."

"An' our members are doomed if the cost of livin' continues to rise faster than wages," Tommy Duggan countered. "It's gettin' more expensive for our members to feed their families an' put a roof over their heads."

"That depends on what your families are fed," Henry said with a scowl. "And where they live!"

"They ain't eatin' filet mignon at the Waldorf!" Benny snapped. "How 'bout the fact that some of our members are livin' at the poverty level? At the wage hike you've offered, we're talkin' about barely keepin' pace with the cost of livin', let alone improvin' people's lives. Our men aren't lookin' for a handout—only the opportunity to earn the same livin' wage that most Americans strive for."

"And how," asked Henry, "would you define 'living wage'?"

"It's the idea that a tugboat worker, backed by the right to bargain collectively, can live a comfortable life," Benny replied. "Our members are skilled workers, critical to the welfare of the city. They shouldn't be seen as common laborers."

"And they're not being paid as common laborers," Henry argued. "The average income in America is twenty-five hundred dollars a year. Your members earn far more than that. Besides, the term 'skilled worker' is highly subjective."

Benny glowered. "What's that supposed to mean?"

"What it means," said Henry, "is that your men's 'skills' are being grossly exaggerated. Not to belittle our crews, but all of them can be replaced . . . in some cases, rather easily."

The negotiators squirmed, aware that the contract talks were flying off the rails—a circumstance that neither Henry nor Benny seemed to mind.

"You also used the term 'comfortable' to describe the life your members aspire to." Henry eyeballed Benny. "Exactly what does that mean?"

"It's a life in which a worker can cover the basic costs of raisin' a family," Benny replied. "We're talkin' about the ability to buy basic necessities, an' maybe have somethin' left over for savings. In other words, wages that are fair."

"Well, if 'fairness' is what you're seeking, the offer we've made meets that criterion," Henry said. "There's simply no room for more . . . not without cutting profits to the bone, or raising towing rates to our customers."

"Fine," said Benny. "Then raise your rates!"

"The government has wartime price controls in effect. Remember?" Bertram Phelps said.

"And even if there were ways around those controls," Henry added, "our customers have told us, unequivocally, that they won't accept a rate hike in the current economy."

"What choice would they have?"

"Their choice would be to take their business elsewhere."

"An' where would they go?"

"There are independent tugboat firms still operating in New York, companies that don't carry our overhead," owner George Steele said. "They can undercut us on price and pull the rug out from under us. That's not a risk our members are willing to take."

"Well," said Benny, "maybe your members should demand less of a return. And maybe you should stop pissin' on my leg while tellin' me that it's only rain."

Henry darkened, his blood boiling now.

"Frankly," Benny said, "most tugboat companies are already makin' a healthy profit, if you ask me."

Henry bristled. "That's a matter of opinion."

"Then how about you open your books, so we can see for ourselves?"

Henry drew on his cigarette, fire raging in his gut. *Fucking uncouth lowlife!* he thought, glowering at Benny.

Arrogant, cheap bastard! Benny thought, glaring back.

"Ours are privately held companies, not the corporate 'goliaths' you're painting them out to be," George Steele said coldly. "In almost every case, our profits are modest . . . and our financial results are confidential."

"Or, to put it in language you can understand," Henry growled, "what's on our corporate balance sheets is none of your goddamned business!"

Benny grinned, pleased that he'd gotten under Henry's skin. A single round in a boxing ring with Henry—that's all he wanted. He'd even pay for the opportunity.

"All our coalition is requesting," Bertram Phelps reasoned, "is for your union to acknowledge the financial pressure our member companies are under. We keep conveying that, yet your side keeps pushing for more."

A portly, bow-tied presence, with a vulpine smile and a shock of white hair, George Steele was Henry's closest ally. Invariably, he mirrored the chairman's point of view.

"A four-percent wage hike?" he scoffed. "Really? Don't you think four percent is excessive?"

"Nope," Benny replied. "But we do think your two-percent offer is miserly."

"You may think our wage demands are greedy," Tommy Duggan added. "But the truth is . . . our members are hurtin'."

"And how," asked Henry, "do we distinguish pain from greed?"

"Nothin' we're askin' for is about greed," Duggan said. "We don't feel it's unreasonable for our members to live a middle-class life. We're only trying to protect their interests."

"And we," said Henry, "are trying to protect the interests of companies that employ your members—and without which your members, quite frankly, would be out of a job."

Steele added, "Our position is based on a simple reality: To remain in business, our companies need to turn a profit. If we agree to a four-percent wage hike, it'll swell our operating costs exponentially, and render our businesses unsustainable. Frankly, it's a nonstarter."

Benny glared at the owners. "Well, just like your shareholders are unwillin' to assume greater risks, our members are unwillin' to assume the risk of tryin' to support their families in this economy. In the real world—where we live—people are frightened. The wartime economy is over with. Livin' expenses are chokin' people to death. We'd like to see an understanding of that on your part."

"And what we'd like to see," said Henry, "is a return to a more stable, responsible union leadership—one that demonstrates a spirit of collaboration. That's the way companies grow, unions thrive, and everyone wins. That's how it's been in New York for years . . . at least before the current anti-business sentiment set in."

"So, now we're 'anti-business,' are we?" Benny said.

"That's the impression we're getting." Bertram Phelps tugged on his suspenders. "The union can't achieve what it's looking for by using the threat of a strike as a club over our heads."

"No one is doin' that," Tommy Duggan said. "As we've said repeatedly: a strike is a last resort, the only bargainin' tactic we can resort to in the absence of a negotiated settlement."

"Then," Henry said, "that's a decision your members will have to make."

And with that, the negotiations seemed to hit an impenetrable wall. In less than an hour, collective bargaining had broken down, the chasm between the sides seemingly insurmountable. Intransigence, anger, and acidic haggling had given way to an icy, testy silence. Only one idea seemed to make sense now.

"I think the most constructive thing to do is to take a break," Paddy O'Boyle suggested. "Why don't we take a coupla hours to caucus, grab a bite to eat . . . an' cool off."

No one objected.

"Maybe when we reconvene—say, at three this afternoon—we can stop buttin' heads an' make some much-needed progress," O'Boyle said.

"Only if the union softens its wage demands," Henry offered.

"Only if the coalition sweetens its offer," Benny countered.

And with those parting words, both sides abandoned the bargaining table, battle lines drawn, a potential strike looming, the big gold clock in the Waldorf's lobby ticking off the seconds until America's greatest city would be turned squarely on its head.

CHAPTER 10

June 4, 1945

For as long as he could recall, Jack had tried to draw the two of them together, doing everything in his power to persuade his father and brother to end their pernicious squabble and stitch together the pieces of their shredded household.

Gabriel was dead. Nothing could alter that crushing reality. Nor could anything erase the grievous wounds rendered by Gus's senseless assault on Benny in the wake of the drowning. And yet, Jack reasoned, perhaps there was a way to undo the damage, fix what was broken inside all of them and become a family again. For years Jack nurtured that hope, clinging to it for reasons he could never quite explain. Not, that is, until he'd witnessed the detritus of World War II—seen families forever shattered, lives forever lost. Not until he and Kate had embarked on their own familial journey, married now and soon to be parents. Not until he'd come to understand the need for households to raise themselves from the rubble of their self-inflicted wounds lest they'd never be at peace, never be whole.

So, he tried.

Time and again, Jack leveraged all the wisdom, all the patience, all the resources he could muster, applying those assets to a mission that nevertheless seemed far beyond his reach. Repeatedly, he approached his father and brother about reparation—reasoning, cajoling, pleading with the two of them to reconcile, accept Gabriel's death for the blameless tragedy it was, and finally put their differences aside. At times, he enlisted Agnes in his yearslong quest. Other times, he sought the backing of relatives, family friends, the parish priest. Even his wartime letters home spoke of his fervent wish, should he perish in battle, to go to his grave in peace, knowing that his father and brother had forged a truce.

But nothing worked.

Nothing Jack tried could bridge the cavernous gap between his brother and father. No one could broker a truce. Some people, Jack discovered, would sooner carry their wounds inside of them forever, yielding solely to a spiteful impulse to inflict even more pain. Forgiveness, he realized, was indeed the most elusive of emotions, especially for people bonded by blood. Self-forgiveness, he'd learn in time, was equally hard to attain.

"Just let it go, kid," Benny would say, years after cutting ties with their father. "Nothin's gonna change the way things are."

"I can't let it go," Jack would argue. "Our family has already lost enough. I want to salvage whatever is left."

"That's noble of ya," Benny would reply. "But I got enough family now: a wife, two daughters, you an' mom. Hell, I even got the rank an' file of Local 88. Thirty-five hundred tugboatmen are part of my bloodlines now, every one of 'em my brother."

"That's well and good," Jack would ask. "But what about Pop?"

"Healin' those kind of wounds," Benny would reply, "takes time."

"But it's already been years," Jack would say. "It's time to bury the hatchet."

"That's where you're wrong, kid," Benny would reply. "What happened between me an' Pop will never be over. Too much damage done. Too many differences between us."

"Damage can be repaired, Benny. Differences can be bridged."

"Not the ones between me an' Pop. We're worlds apart, kid. Always have been. Just start with who I am in Pop's eyes . . . an' who I'm not."

Jack knew that argument inside and out. He'd heard it dozens of times, and it wasn't entirely off-base. Indeed, Gus had never offered Benny anything beyond criticism, rejection, and scorn—and that was even before Gabriel died.

"C'mon, kid," Benny would reason. "You know I'm right. You and Gabriel were the 'favored sons,' the ones who made Pop proud. Then there was me: the proverbial black sheep . . . nothin' in Pop's eyes but a worthless piece of shit." He would chuckle then, his laughter tinged with irony and pain.

"An' then," he'd say, "as if to prove Pop right, I flunked the biggest test of all: couldn't save Gabriel when the chips were on the line."

That's when Jack would feel the frustration mount.

"Damn it, Benny!" he'd say. "You did everything you could, trying to save

Gabriel. How long are you gonna punish yourself for what happened that day?"

"Good question, kid." Benny would grin. "I guess sometimes you gotta pay your entire life for one rotten moment."

Jack felt Benny's pain, wanting in the worst way to assuage the torment. Sixteen years later, Benny was still pained to his core by Gabriel's death, burdened with sorrow and guilt, unable to let go of the belief that he had failed his brother. In many ways, Benny's life since that day had been a quest for atonement and vindication, a relentless yearning to fill the gaping hole in his heart.

"You know," he told Jack, "much as I've hated Pop for condemning me, he probably was right. I should have taken better care of Gabriel, shouldn't have let him drown. Let's face it, kid: no matter what I do, I'll never be able to live that down."

"That's bullshit, too!" Jack would bristle. "There's nothing to make amends for, Benny. And the truth is: you don't need forgiveness just from Pop. You need it even more from yourself."

Benny would go silent then, pondering his brother's words. If anyone could reach him, it was Jack. If nothing else, he'd always listen to his sagacious younger brother.

"You gotta patch things up, find room in your heart for forgiveness," Jack would urge him. "If not for your own sake, Benny . . . then for mine."

"Do I?"

"Yeah. If you ever want us to be a family again."

"I already told ya, kid. I got enough family now. Besides, the real differences 'tween Pop an' me have nothin' to do with Gabriel. They go a lot deeper than that."

And indeed, that much was true. In many ways, the crux of the rift between Benny and Gus ran far deeper than the tragic happenstance of Gabriel's death. For years, Benny had been looking for a reason to disown his father. Gabriel's death was simply the moment he had waited for.

*　*　*

When Gus Logan moved his wife and sons from Chelsea to Williamsburg, riding the wave of pre-Depression prosperity lifting New York's working class, the family's financial picture instantly went from dismal to tolerable—thanks primarily to Gus's new job.

The Republic Sugar Company had been the first sugar supplier in America to formally brand its products, applying the trademark name "Dixie Sugar" to tiny, rectangular cubes, then convincing grocers to abandon their traditional method of selling cone-shaped loaves that required a special tool to cut. Republic's marketing ploy of offering it in tiny packets had paid huge dividends.

Americans had always had an insatiable sweet tooth, and refined sugar had long ago established itself as a dietary staple. With sweetened products like candy, soda, and pastry in high demand, sugar was big business—and New York its epicenter. Dixie Sugar, by the turn of the twentieth century, had become the nation's leading sugar brand and one of Brooklyn's largest employers. Some five thousand workers reported in round-the-clock shifts to the company's East River headquarters, a hulking refinery whose neon sign shone like a nighttime beacon over much of Williamsburg.

Gus was a cog in Dixie Sugar's mammoth workforce, his job advantageous in several ways. Aside from representing a palpable upgrade in status from cleaning soiled bedsheets, Gus's new position, at twenty-three hundred dollars a year, offered a significant pay hike from the thirty cents an hour he'd earned at his former job. Just as importantly, Dixie Sugar's complex of rounded-arch-style brick buildings was situated on a ten-acre stretch of waterfront, four blocks from the Logans' apartment. Gus could walk to work in minutes, saving on carfare and commuting time. He could also put in reams of overtime, boosting his take-home pay considerably.

But while Gus's new job afforded distinct advantages, the work itself was far from pleasant. While retaining its original trade name, Dixie Sugar had relocated to Williamsburg from its Mississippi Delta birthplace during a time when New York began shouldering the workload resulting from the destruction of the Civil War. The cavernous Brooklyn refinery looked every bit its age. Machinery was antiquated, floors and ceilings made of highly flammable, creosote-coated wood, and a labyrinth of forbidding, rat-infested tunnels ran beneath the factory, sugar crystals hanging like stalactites from floor-to-ceiling pipes.

Gus's job mirrored that workplace to a T.

Raw sugar, shipped to the refinery by boat, was yellowish-brown in color.

But since the public demanded a snow-white product, sulfur dioxide had to be bubbled through the cane juice to bleach out impurities. The sugar was further purified with phosphoric acid and calcium hydroxide, centrifuged to wash away the coating of raw-sugar crystals, and dissolved to produce syrup.

Charged with those tasks, Gus labored in the clammy, perilous underbelly of the refinery—wearing no mask, no gloves, nothing to shield him from the chemicals and toxic residue of his work. After shifts, he'd arrive home coated in sugar dust, his clothing scented with a medley of sweetness and sweat, the product of processed sugar and factory temperatures that soared at times to more than a hundred degrees.

In time, Gus began wearing his job in other ways, as well. Years of work at Dixie Sugar had rendered his hands gnarled, his shoulders sloped, his urine amber and cloudy. His breathing had become wheezy and labored, too. On the rare occasions when he spoke, Gus hacked in spasmodic fits—especially on raw, wintry days. Laughter produced intense bouts of coughing. And now, at age sixty, Gus tended after waking from a night's sleep to hack up gobs of sputum tinged with blood.

Despite those maladies, however, Gus willingly accepted the pernicious impact of his workplace. Through the years, there'd been myriad attempts at unionizing the refinery—particularly after an explosion of volatile sugar dust killed several workers—but management thwarted each attempt. Union recruiters were barred from company grounds. Employees were bribed to refrain from organizing. The company even threatened to relocate out of state if a union was ever formed.

The result of all that was predictable: Dixie Sugar remained an open-shop employer, working conditions ungoverned, collective bargaining non-existent, all its workers employed at will. There was no recourse for wrongful termination, workplace discrimination, and other abuses. Federally mandated overtime laws, employee benefits, and worker protections were years away. Employees—regardless of seniority, job description, or status—had to fend for themselves. Workers remained employed, earned promotions, and were granted pay hikes solely at the whim of management. The only leverage they possessed was whatever goodwill they engendered. If they climbed the workplace ladder, it wasn't because they held a gun to management's head, were protected by a labor contract, or were backed by a union—it was because they showed up to work each day, busted their ass, and demonstrated unquestioned loyalty to the company. That was the understanding, the implicit pact between management and employee. If someone didn't like the arrangement, they could simply take a hike. And Gus had learned long ago to abide by those requirements.

Others were self-imposed. Despite the rigors of his job, Gus adhered to the same routine since the moment he was hired. Each morning, steady as a metronome, he'd rise before dawn, carry a lunch pail to the refinery, and punch a clock, disregarding inclement weather, ignoring personal conflicts, shrugging off illness or injury. In twenty-six years, other than for company closures, holidays, or paid time off, he hadn't missed a single day's work.

To Gus, his unblemished attendance was a source of pride, a testament to resiliency, fortitude, and dependability—a badge of honor that reflected his core beliefs. Showing up to work was something men were supposed to do. Work, to him, was obligatory, woven into the moral contract binding men to their families. Men were expected to work, expected to support their family. Besides, Dixie Sugar paid him. In exchange for that paycheck, Gus believed, he owed the company nothing less than an honest day's work. No cutting corners. No missing time. And no slacking off because work was tough.

Work was supposed to be tough.

But there was more to Gus's mindset than merely those dictums. For him, reporting to work wasn't simply an act of dedication, commitment, loyalty, or pride. Truth was, he was grateful for the chance to hold a job, happy he was able to work. It hadn't always been that way—for him, or for others like him.

Gus remembered, all too well, how unschooled refugees like him had it when they'd first arrived in America: begging for even the most menial work, juggling two or three jobs at a time, working for a pittance. He remembered what it was like during the Depression, when legions of workers suffered the indignity of queuing up for government relief. Remembered, too, how wartime sugar rationing had brought Dixie Sugar to its knees, forcing layoffs he had dodged only through his record of diligence and allegiance.

No.

Work, for Gus, wasn't an obligation. Nor was it a chore. To Gus, work was a privilege. A blessing. A gift.

He was grateful that even in the hardest of times he'd been able to hold down a job and never beg for a handout. He was only too grateful that he was no longer laboring sixteen-hour days cleaning shit-stained bedsheets; grateful that business was once again booming at Dixie Sugar and he was able to work double- and triple-shifts; only too willing to keep his nose to the grindstone and abide by the rules; only too happy he had the wherewithal to lift his head off the pillow each morning and put in a good day's work.

So what if the Dixie Sugar refinery was worse than a dungeon? Lots of factories were even worse. So he couldn't join a union and bargain collectively for better pay and benefits? His work ethic alone would earn him a raise.

To Jack, Gus's virtues were admirable, counterweights to his shortcomings. Benny, on the other hand, saw their father through a different lens. To his oldest son, Gus's work ethic was hardly a reflection of fortitude or strength, obligation or honor, perseverance or pride: it was a product of weakness, and all about fear.

Men like Gus, Benny believed, were hardly profiles in courage. To the contrary, to Benny they were doormats, cowards, everything he battled against as a union leader. To Benny, organized labor's real enemy wasn't so much corporate management as it was workers' indifference, fear of biting the hand that fed them. To Benny, the real obstacle to success was men like his father.

He resented his father's willingness to cede control of his livelihood to his employer, resented how Gus never made waves, resented how he allowed himself to be victimized because he was too intimidated, too unenlightened, or too apathetic to fight for more. Even as a young boy, Benny had vowed to be different, vowed to fight the workplace injustices that Gus refused to confront, vowed to be everything that Gus wasn't when it came to his job—and to his sons.

"You talk about the differences between you and Pop," Jack would say. "But Pop set a good example for us. Worked his ass off. Never shirked his responsibilities. Did whatever was needed to support our family."

"An' what about the things he didn't do?" Benny would argue. "What about the fact that we hardly ever saw him, or that he never made us feel like he really gave a shit?"

"Maybe punching a clock day in and day out was his way of showing that he cared, the only way he knew," Jack would say. "There's nobility in what Pop did, Benny. Nobility in what he still does."

"Nobility?" Benny would scoff. "C'mon, kid—grow up! The ol' man spills his guts for a company for twenty-six years, never missin' a day's work . . . an' you think that's a badge of honor? Really? When all he gets in return is a coupla weeks' vacation, a measly paycheck, a shithole workplace, an' a cheap gold watch when he's all used up?"

Benny laughed derisively. "An' to top it off, Pop's grateful for that? Grateful for a pat on the back? Grateful if the company throws him a bone? With no union to fight for him, no power to make things better, no choice but to beg for an annual raise, an' take it up the ass if he has a grievance?"

He shook his head. "An' you think that servile mentality—that so-called work ethic—is admirable?"

"Yeah, I do."

"Well, I think it's pathetic! The way Pop thinks doesn't make him a role model—all it makes him is a sucker! An' why? 'Cause guys like him let companies shit all over them an' make a fortune off their sweat. Pop is the 'poor schnook' who works his ass off an' prays that management will like him an' reward him out of pity for his struggles. He's the loyal company soldier. Always doin' the right thing. Strokin' the boss. Happy just to have a job."

"And what's so wrong with that?"

"What's wrong with it is that it makes Pop a pushover . . . an' makes it hard for workers who wanna get ahead. Pop never makes waves, takes whatever his company dishes out. An' why? 'Cause he's got no backbone. 'Cause he lives in perpetual fear of fightin' for what's rightly his. An' you find that kind of groveling self-sacrifice admirable? You think there's nobility in it?"

"At least I don't resent it . . . like you do."

"You're goddamned right I resent it!" Benny would snarl. "Guys like Pop are an impediment to the progress I'm bustin' my ass to achieve. They need to change the way they think . . . or get the fuck out of the way!"

Jack always felt defeated when Benny spoke like that, as if the angry divide between father and son was a black mark that could never be erased. At times, it seemed as if Benny resisted reparation because it would somehow imply that he accepted Gus's perceived shortcomings—or worse, that they were a genetic flaw that he might have inherited. By rejecting Gus, Benny was stating in no uncertain terms that the last thing he wanted was to be a mirror of his father.

In truth, the seeds of Benny's resentment toward Gus had been sown early in childhood. Those of his wrath were planted the day Gabriel died.

Jack would persevere. "So that's what the silence, the distance, the refusal to forgive is all about? The fact that you and Pop see the world differently . . . have different points of view?"

"Seems to bleed into things, doesn't it?" Benny would counter.

"What things?"

"Pop is disappointed in me because I wasn't a better son . . . an' I'm disappointed in him because he wasn't a better father. Whatever flimsy bond we might have had was destroyed the day Gabriel drowned."

"But did it ever occur to you that maybe Pop is disappointed in himself because he wasn't a better father?" Jack would reason. "Did you ever think that maybe Pop saw qualities in you that he secretly admired, qualities he didn't possess but wished he did? Maybe your strength and courage reminded him of his own weakness and fear. Maybe part of him is ashamed about who he is."

"Whoa, kid!" Benny would put up his hand. "You're gettin' way too deep."

"Maybe so. But, in the end, what Pop thinks about himself is something he has to live with," Jack would say. "What matters to me is that you can't let your differences destroy whatever family we have left. To never let go of your anger? Never speak again? Do you really want to live that way for the rest of your life?"

"I live with a lotta things I don't want, kid," Benny would say. "It's part of the journey."

"And you don't want to change it?"

"Whatever need I had to do that died years ago."

"And it doesn't bother you?"

"Not as much as it once did."

"Still—you don't want to make it better?"

"Like I told ya, kid . . . that takes time."

"And what if you run out of time, Benny? What if you and Pop never make peace?"

"Then that'll be unfinished business," Benny would say. "There ain't a person alive who won't carry regrets with them when they go to their grave."

"And that's okay with you? Okay for you and Pop to lose each other forever?"

"Maybe we already have."

"But you can change that. It's never too late. All it takes is a word . . . a gesture."

"Sorry. No can do."

Then, as if amending his thought, Benny would add: "Besides, I got my own way of tryin' to fix things between Pop an' me."

"And what's that?"

"It's got to do with the union."

"The union?"

"Yeah. See, maybe if I handle union business the right way, Pop will come to see me in a whole other light. Maybe if he realizes that I'm fightin' my ass off for poor schnooks like him, he'll be proud of me. You know, kid . . . same way he's proud of you."

He unfurled a crooked grin. "Maybe if I do right by the union, Pop will see that I'm not such a fuckup after all. Who knows? Maybe if I help raise the bar for workin' stiffs like him, he'll come to see me as somethin' more than just a no-good, lowlife piece of shit."

Chapter 11

January 31, 1946

There was nothing Henry learned at that morning's bargaining session that he didn't already know.

Even prior to the meeting, he had a solid grasp on the genesis of Local 88's hardline bargaining stance. He was equally cognizant of the infighting roiling the tugboat workers' union, the local's changing power structure, and how he wanted to handle negotiations through the runup to the threatened strike—and, if necessary, beyond.

Each of those certainties was the product of more than idle guesswork. Indeed, for Henry, exhaustive due diligence had always been a core business practice—and, in this case, that meant getting a lay of the land from a uniquely insightful source. Someone who knew Local 88 inside and out. Someone whom Henry had relied on in previous times of labor unrest. Someone on whose discretion he could faithfully bank.

Paddy O'Boyle.

For the better part of two decades, Henry had nurtured a comfy, behind-the-scenes relationship with the United Stevedores Association president, and days earlier had requested a tête-à-tête with the veteran union leader—his request prompted by a troubling sense that contract negotiations were taking an adverse trajectory in the wake of World War II: less predictable, less controllable, less likely to conclude amicably.

Henry's instincts, as usual, were spot-on. From the very outset of collective bargaining, in fact, Henry had discerned that decades of established order had run their course, and it would no longer be business as usual in dealing with the city's tugboat workers. He could see it in the surly faces of militants like Benny Logan and Tommy Duggan, hear it in their unbridled demands, the way they balked at marching lockstep to the dictates of veteran union leaders. Rank-and-file enmity, Henry understood, involved more than simply saber-rattling now. Something toxic, he suspected, had seeped into the relationship between the city's tugboat owners and their workers. Something equally toxic, he sensed, was brewing inside the union, as well.

He was right on both counts.

Still, Henry felt that he needed to get a precise reading on the situation. Why take chances with something as critical as a labor-contract negotiation? Might as well find out what was going on straight from the horse's mouth.

Henry met Paddy O'Boyle over dinner and drinks at the union leader's favorite eatery, Peter Luger Steak House, a landmark Brooklyn restaurant in the shadow of the Williamsburg Bridge. The setting was all too familiar. The men had dined there numerous times, usually in celebratory fashion.

Bathed in a toasty, amber glow, Peter Luger's was packed with smartly dressed patrons, its brass-and-wood décor scented with a medley of cigarette smoke, pricey cologne, and freshly cooked beef. Tuxedoed waiters and busboys wound their way along sawdust-covered floors amidst the chatter and bustle. Christmas had long since come and gone, but the restaurant's ceiling and walls remained festooned with multicolored holiday lights.

Henry and Paddy tapped glasses as they faced one another in a private nook near the rear of the restaurant.

"A belated Merry Christmas," toasted Henry, nursing a Chivas Regal on the rocks. "I guess we're about to find out if this is still the 'season of giving.' You know, Paddy: peace on earth, good will to men . . . and all that other bullshit."

"Dunno." O'Boyle forced a laugh. "No one seems to have the Yuletide spirit these days."

"How about you, Paddy?"

"Well, you know me. I'm always ready to give."

"And receive?"

"That, too."

The two men shared an easy give-and-take, comfortable in one another's presence despite the rancorous contract negotiations they led from opposing sides. O'Boyle chowed down on a T-bone the size of his plate. Henry picked at a ribeye and fired up a cigarette.

"You know, you shouldn't smoke so much," O'Boyle rasped, his own voice a whiskey-and-cigarettes baritone. "You'll wind up in an early grave."

"You stopped . . . after all these years?" Henry seemed surprised.

"My ol' lady put the hammer down," O'Boyle quipped. "Tol' me it was either the cigarettes or her."

Henry recoiled. "And you chose her?" he said, laughing. "Well, thanks for the sage advice. I'll give it some thought."

But his thoughts, as so often was the case, turned instead to Carolyn. Indeed, cigarettes were a habit that his late wife, too, had warned Henry about. Time and again, she'd urged him to quit smoking, watch his diet, and schedule annual physicals. And time and again, he'd ignored her advice, pointing to his seeming robust health as evidence that her concerns were overblown. In the end, Henry's conviction had proven sadly prophetic. Carolyn had never so much as touched a cigarette, and had scrupulously monitored her health. Yet it was she, not Henry, who had fallen ill. She, not Henry, whom cancer had consumed. And she, not Henry, who had died.

Henry drew again on his Lucky Strike, thoughts of Carolyn swimming in his head. God, how he missed her, more than ever now, more with each passing day. Without Carolyn in his life Henry felt untethered, adrift like a dinghy in a roiling sea. Nothing could fill the cavernous void she had left behind. Not Henry's tugboat dynasty. Not his children. Not his Sands Point mansion, his bank account, or the other tokens of his success. Certainly not his endless, infuriating obsession with the tugboat workers' union . . . which was the subject he turned to now.

"What's worse for me than these goddamned cigarettes," he told O'Boyle, "is what's happening inside Local 88."

"That's not the best thing for my health either," the USA president said.

"So level with me," Henry implored. "I need to know what's going on inside the union . . . and no one knows that better than you."

Henry was right on that front as well. No one was more familiar than Paddy O'Boyle with the inner workings of New York's tugboat workers' union and its parent, the USA. No one was a more expert mover and shaker. No one was more powerful or more connected . . . or more corrupt.

* * *

A fixture for decades on New York's waterfront, Paddy O'Boyle had cut his teeth in Manhattan's notorious Hell's Kitchen neighborhood, starting his career as a "wagon boy" who delivered groceries to the North River docks before landing a longshoreman's job at the age of sixteen.

A strapping six-foot-four, O'Boyle made a reputation for himself as a "sheriff," or bouncer, at a Hell's Kitchen social club, and later as a dock-walloper, strongarming late-paying longshoremen on behalf of loan sharks in the mob-infested United Stevedores Association. After a stint as a union recruiter, and later as a business agent, he'd amassed enough political capital to win election as USA president, a post he'd held for some thirty years—and one that had benefited the union's rank and file as well as O'Boyle's underworld cronies, New York's tugboat owners, and, especially, the union boss himself.

To tugboat owners, O'Boyle was the embodiment of an ideal union leader: convivial, conciliatory, and squarely in the owners' hip pocket. Indeed, throughout O'Boyle's reign as USA president, contract negotiations between New York's tugboat owners and Local 88 had been both amicable and expedient. Never once had there been the slightest glitch in collective bargaining—or a work stoppage, a lockout, or a palpable breach in the relationship between management and workers. As the top dog in Local 88's parent union, O'Boyle had been able, without exception, to provide for labor peace.

There were reasons for that. For one thing, O'Boyle spoke the salty, down-to-earth language of New York's tugboat workers, portraying himself to the men as one of the boys: an earnest, backslapping working stiff who had pulled himself up by his bootstraps and busted his ass for every penny he had ever earned. Affable, garrulous—and highly adept at union politics—O'Boyle held enormous sway over Local 88's rank and file, his outsized personality, powers of persuasion, and mob ties going a long way toward convincing the workers to see things his way.

But O'Boyle could also speak the language of the city's tugboat owners. Utterly compliant, and unshakably self-serving, he and Henry for years had negotiated labor contracts in private, their discussions adhering to a familiar and congenial pattern.

The two men, clad in shower shoes and towels, would open their negotiations in the steamy confines of a Coney Island bathhouse. There, they'd conduct a candid heart-to-heart, swiftly find common ground and, by the time they toweled off, the framework of a labor contract would be in place. There'd be something in it for O'Boyle, of course—and enough to spread around to whoever else needed a taste. Afterward, the men would seal the deal during a round of golf at Winged Foot or over dinner and stogies at Peter Luger's.

Consummating the agreement was equally simple. Once he and Henry had shaken hands on a tentative contract, O'Boyle would go to work selling the deal to a rank and file that would invariably rubber-stamp whatever agreement the union boss put in front of them. Objections to the contract's terms were rare, protests over the nature of the negotiations practically unheard of. If someone squawked, O'Boyle was usually persuasive enough to change their opinion. If dissidents became too vocal, a couple of mob goons would pay them a visit. That usually quieted things down in a hurry.

For decades, each of the principals involved in the collaboration had been happy: tugboat owners, because they'd purchased a year or more of labor peace, usually on the cheap; workers, because their weekly paychecks flowed unabated; the union hierarchy, because Henry's payoffs lined their pockets; and O'Boyle's underworld cronies, because they had a vested financial interest in seeing a steady flow of commerce at New York Harbor.

Henry was happy, too. And why wouldn't he be?

Paddy O'Boyle was, in many ways, the consummate business partner: reliable, discreet, a skillful fixer who delivered unerringly on his promises. Once he and O'Boyle had shaken hands on a contract, Henry could rest easy, confident that the deal would pass muster with the union's rank and file.

But the symbiosis between Henry and O'Boyle extended far beyond negotiating labor contracts. Under O'Boyle's reign as union president, the United Stevedores Association had wrapped its tentacles around not only tugboats, but around barges, dredges, and every other harbor enterprise that was unionized. With Gotham Harbor Alliance members agreeing to employ only union workers on their tugboats—and the owners' coalition thereby gaining control of all available labor—Henry and O'Boyle had effectively denied independent firms access to virtually every substantive revenue stream in New York Harbor. Since that tacit agreement had been struck, the number of non-union firms at the harbor had shrunk to a handful, while the average fleet size of coalition-member firms had soared. Some seven hundred tugboats, each of them union-manned, handled virtually all waterborne commerce in New York now. Independent firms had been stripped of their greatest competitive advantage: lower labor costs and, hence, the ability to charge lower rates. An enemy of both the union and the tugboat owners had essentially been eradicated.

In addition, Henry and O'Boyle had tacitly agreed that, for however long O'Boyle remained USA president, the powerful union would never use its leverage against Gotham Harbor Alliance-member firms. With that assurance, Henry no longer had to concern himself that thirty-two thousand longshoremen would ever lend their support to a New York tugboat strike. He and O'Boyle, in effect, had severed tugboat workers from their parent union. All Henry ever had to contend with was a neutered Local 88, a far more manageable task.

But there was more to Henry and O'Boyle's partnership than simply their mutual thirst for money and power. In truth, Henry had a genuine affinity for the longtime union boss—seeing O'Boyle in many ways as a kindred spirit. Sure, the union leader was uncouth and crass, the flip side of Henry in pedigree and demeanor. And sure, he was crooked as the day was long—picking union members' pockets, bleeding Local 88's treasury, and hobnobbing with mobsters at racetracks, card games, and casinos. Yet O'Boyle, much like Henry, was an operator: a cagey, seasoned insider who wasn't so much an architect of the system as an able functionary within it. Henry appreciated faculties like those—so similar to his own.

But now the longtime alliance between the two men had seemingly gone awry. O'Boyle, as Henry was learning, had committed one of leadership's cardinal sins. Unwittingly, over time, he'd lost touch with his constituency, failing to recognize how the union's rank and file had changed and how his misdeeds had gradually caused his power to erode. Indeed, union members' traditional deference to old-guard bosses like O'Boyle had all but evaporated in the wake of World War II. Many such leaders were now seen as out of touch, over the hill, and hopelessly soiled by corruption and greed. Union members had grown restless, angry, disaffected. Fellowship was no longer easy to coerce or to buy. A growing backlash to O'Boyle's leadership was thwarting his efforts at compliance with businessmen like Henry.

While O'Boyle remained ex-officio figurehead of Local 88 by virtue of his post with its parent union, he had lost much of his clout with the tugboat workers he ostensibly led, a growing number of whom were accusing him of being too submissive, too blinded by self-interests, too comfortably in bed with the enemy. O'Boyle's act had worn thin. Younger, more contentious leaders like Benny Logan had lost patience for wink-and-nod agreements and backroom deals. He and his growing legion of supporters were nowhere near as reticent as the union's old-guard leadership to pick a fight with tugboat owners. O'Boyle no longer spoke a language the men responded to. To most, he was little more than a paper tiger, a tired old bull being ushered to pasture.

"I need to get a handle on this, Paddy," Henry confided to the union leader as the two men ate their dinner. "Are you still calling the shots on our contract talks, or is it Benny Logan and those other insurgent pricks?"

"Well, the men haven't gotten rid of me yet," O'Boyle quipped. "They wouldda bale-hooked me an' drowned me in the river by now if they really wanted me out."

"Who knows?" Henry deadpanned. "They still might."

"Don't joke around like that," O'Boyle said darkly. "It ain't funny."

"All right." Henry relented. "But level with me: what's going on?"

Bathed in the restaurant's muted light, O'Boyle had the appearance of a punch-drunk fighter slumped on his stool: eyes glassy and unfocused, earlobes dangling, bulbous nose glinting like a Christmas-tree ornament.

"What's happenin," he said, "is that it ain't so easy for me to pull strings anymore."

Henry squinted. "How come?"

O'Boyle hesitated, reluctant to admit what was happening inside a union he'd led for decades: a steady, inexorable changing of the guard.

"A new cast of characters is callin' the shots," he finally confessed.

Henry wasn't surprised. For months already, he'd been banging heads with the likes of Benny and Tommy Duggan—angry, headstrong antipodes of the affable, compliant O'Boyle.

"I understand there are hardliners commanding attention," he said. "But I thought the two of us had a deal."

O'Boyle shrugged. "So did I."

The USA president then confirmed what Henry suspected all along. A handshake agreement in which O'Boyle committed the union to a two-year extension of its wartime no-strike pledge in exchange for a modest pay hike had been given a rousing thumbs-down by the rank and file. A second deal, negotiated by Local 88's old-line Wage Scale Committee, had met a similar fate. It was those rejections that had spurred the formation of the union's bellicose Strike Committee, and Benny's emergence as the voice of the insurgents.

"This ain't a typical negotiation," O'Boyle said. "The men are in no mood for conciliation, an' they don't want contracts spoon-fed to them. They're too pissed off."

"Pissed off at what?"

"At me . . . for one thing."

"Why you?"

"Because they think I'm tryin' to sell 'em a bill of goods."

"Really?" Henry feigned surprise. "Haven't the two of us always taken care of them?"

"Guess they no longer see it that way," O'Boyle said.

Henry doused his cigarette. "So, that militant prick Benny Logan is leading an insurgency, huh?"

O'Boyle nodded morosely.

"And the deal you and I agreed to?" Henry asked.

"The men want more."

Henry felt his blood boil. If there was one thing that infuriated him, it was a loss of control. Henry needed to call the shots, always. It was ingrained in him, every bit as integral to his persona as his influence, his ego, his money.

"I recognize that the men want more, Paddy," he said. "It's human nature to want. Just not too much!"

O'Boyle cocked an eyebrow. "What do you consider 'too much'?"

"It's when the line is crossed between need and greed."

"An' who decides where that line is?"

"I do!"

The pair fell silent. O'Boyle poked at his T-bone. Henry pushed his dinner plate aside.

"So, the deal that you and I shook hands on is dead in the water?" Henry asked.

"Normally, it'd be rubber-stamped by now." O'Boyle sighed. "But like I said, these ain't 'normal' times. We're dealin' with a lot of emotion on the part of the men."

"What kind of emotion?"

"The men have waited a long time for a bump in pay," O'Boyle said. "Four years of honoring Uncle Sam's no-strike pledge, sittin' on their hands, workin' their asses off in America's interest."

"We were at war!" Henry said. "Hitler, Mussolini, Hirohito . . . remember them?"

"Of course I remember," O'Boyle acknowledged. "But the war is over. The men wanna make up for lost time. They feel they're owed more than a token raise. An' they ain't signin' off on any kind of no-strike pledge."

"Their demands are out of line!"

O'Boyle stared out through bloodshot eyes. "There's no wiggle room on your end?"

"Our coalition can't go any further." Henry shook his head defiantly.

"Can't—or won't?"

"Both."

Again, the pair drew silent. Henry drew on his cigarette. O'Boyle drained his cocktail.

"So, the deal that you and I struck?" Henry probed again. "It's dead in the water?"

"I'm still fightin' . . . treadin' water till I see which way the tide is headin'," O'Boyle said. "But you can't stop a flood when all you're holdin' is a blotter."

Henry studied the USA president, trying to get inside his head. He'd never seen O'Boyle in quite this light before. Once such a swaggering figure, the union leader seemed shriveled, like a mighty oak whittled to a twig, waffling between competing interests. On the one hand, O'Boyle's every pore tugged at him to do what he had always done: negotiate with Henry, sell their deal to union members, and stroll off with his usual bounty. On the flip side, O'Boyle knew that he could push only so hard in the face of the union's regime change. The union leader was fighting for his political life, reluctant to rock the boat even while being pressured by his longtime benefactor to do just that. At some point, he'd have no choice but yield to the prevailing view of the rank and file. Mirroring the insurgents' negotiating stance was O'Boyle's only way of preserving credibility. Bucking militants like Benny could well put his head in a noose—and he knew it.

"The bottom line," O'Boyle said, "is that the deal we negotiated ain't gonna fly."

"And there's no way," said Henry, "that we can fix things?"

"Whaddaya mean by 'fix'?"

"Well," said Henry, "what if we called in a mediator?"

"Who? City Hall? The NLRB?"

"No." Henry shook his head. "I'm talking about far more persuasive people."

The inference was crystal clear. Underworld associates, several times in the past, had acted as unofficial "arbiters" in waterfront labor disputes, coercing workers to refrain from striking in order to protect the mob's financial interests. Henry was suggesting, none too subtly, that they fulfill that role now.

And his suggestion made perfect sense. Even from its earliest days as a moneymaking enterprise, New York's waterfront had been under the thumb of mobsters who earned a fortune from cargo theft, extortion, kickbacks, protection schemes, and other criminal activities. Dockside hiring, even now, was dictated by mob capos who handpicked longshoremen and other workers based on their willingness to funnel their wages to racketeers. All the while, companies with interests in shipping, warehousing, and other waterfront activities willingly paid higher costs, in essence a "mob tax," simply to keep the wheel spinning, while politicians and other public officials—profiting from contracting, licensing, and other fees—turned the other cheek.

Paddy O'Boyle's covert deals with Henry were merely the tip of the iceberg. In truth, Local 88's parent union was rotten to its core, a criminal enterprise whose leaders prospered by systematically exploiting their members: stealing dues, billing the union for lavish personal expenses, and skimming money from union coffers. In Paddy O'Boyle's USA, elections were rigged, union charters were granted as a form of shakedown, mob cronies held lucrative phantom jobs, and union officials routinely used their leverage to get workers hired and fired.

In exchange for the power he wielded, O'Boyle had, in essence, a single job: keep Local 88's rank and file working, and the money rolling in. O'Boyle was, in many ways, little more than a bagman for his crooked cronies, his union presidency a sham. All the while, Local 88 enjoyed neither palpable support nor genuine independence. Indeed, when it came to New York's tugboat workers, USA's upper echelon couldn't care less. For decades, tugboat workers—their voices squelched, beholden to the men in power—had simply followed the path of least resistance, utterly compliant as O'Boyle and his cohorts ran roughshod over them.

None of this, of course, had ever proven problematic to Henry. To him, corruption was a fact of life on the city's waterfront. Henry hadn't birthed it; nor was it his job to eradicate it. It was far easier to simply reap the rewards. After all, the system worked flawlessly; collusion was good for business. Henry may have seen organized labor as inherently evil, an enemy of corporate America, but he was only too willing to play ball with union leaders when he stood to benefit.

But that, as was suddenly apparent, was proving problematic.

"So, Paddy?" he probed. "How about we get a couple of your waterfront 'friends' to pay Benny Logan a visit, and deliver a message."

O'Boyle flinched. "What kind of message?"

"Something in the spirit of conciliation," Henry said with a cynical look. "Nothing that a couple of broken kneecaps wouldn't convey."

O'Boyle sat slumped in his seat, expression somber, neck folds bulging like bubbles on a threadbare tire.

"The message," said Henry, "would be for Logan to back off: soften his wage demands, cut the strike threats, and stop riling up the rank and file. Or else—"

O'Boyle said nothing.

"What's wrong?" Henry probed. "Isn't that the way union rabble-rousers usually get muzzled?"

"Maybe," O'Boyle said. "But these 'friends' of mine that you're talkin' about? They're layin' low these days. Glare of the spotlight has got 'em spooked."

Even Henry couldn't deny that. New York's underworld had recently come under unprecedented scrutiny amid allegations of racketeering and loansharking. Grand jury probes were underway. Support was even building for the creation of a Congressional commission to oversee waterfront activities.

"I think we're flyin' solo with our negotiations," O'Boyle said.

Henry shook his head glumly. "But where does that leave me?"

"I ain't exactly sure."

It was time for a final tactic now. Something tried and true.

"Would an 'incentive' help?" Henry tapped the breast pocket of his jacket, bulging from an envelope stuffed with hundred-dollar bills. "Same deal as ever, Paddy. Ten large. Yours to spread around, as needed."

The union boss shook his head.

"What's the problem?" Henry seemed taken aback. "Do I need to sweeten the pot?"

"That ain't it." O'Boyle said. "I don't think money's gonna move the needle."

"Well, that's disappointing," Henry lamented.

"For me, too," O'Boyle said. "Believe me."

The two men went silent; the situation was crystal clear.

"So in other words," said Henry, "Benny Logan and his gang of union insurgents are hellbent on playing hardball with me."

"Seems like that's their intent," O'Boyle said.

"Very well." Henry flashed a vulpine smile. "Just be forewarned then that I have no choice but to play hardball, too. And no one plays hardball with more purpose than me."

Chapter 12

June 5, 1945

The interview was a sham, nothing more than a thinly veiled pretense. In truth, Jack had the tugboat job sewn up the instant he'd succumbed to Benny's pitch. Nevertheless, rules were rules. Union dictates mandated that Jack adhere to the hiring protocol for all job candidates, even favored ones: file an application, submit to an interview, and pass muster with Local 88's hiring boss.

So, early on the morning after Benny had sold him on the deckhand opening, Jack met his brother at Local 88's hiring hall, a converted cargo shed at the tip of a dilapidated pier on Manhattan's Lower West Side.

The aging dock and its dreary surroundings mirrored the tawdry, helter-skelter aura of the North River waterfront, hub of New York's tugboat trade. Rust-stained, algae-coated cargo ships hugged dozens of finger piers abutting a miles-long stretch of railyards, freight terminals, and meatpacking plants. Streets were lined with warehouses, workshops, industrial lofts, and seedy gin mills. Traffic rumbled along the cobblestoned viaduct running the length of Manhattan's western flank.

As the brothers approached the hiring hall, however, it was obvious that they weren't alone. A queue of job applicants, including uniformed ex-servicemen, stretched the entire thousand-foot length of the pier. Many, vying for a prime spot on the waiting line, had camped there overnight in sleeping bags, lean-tos, and pup tents.

"Who are those guys?" Jack asked.

"Guys applyin' for the tugboat job who ain't my brother," Benny said.

Jack was shocked. "All those applicants for a single job?"

"Like I tol' ya, kid," Benny said, "jobs are hard to come by these days."

Jack opened his mouth to protest, but Benny would have none of it.

"Pipe down with your 'nepotism' bullshit!" he squawked.

"But bending the rules ... landing a job just because I'm your brother?" Jack said. "It's not right."

"Maybe not." Benny shrugged. "But this is how things are done. What ya know means shit. Who you know? That's different. You happen to know me. So consider yourself lucky."

"But—"

"But nothin'! Just keep your head down an' walk."

Grudgingly, Jack acquiesced, ignoring scattered catcalls and protests while accompanying Benny to the front of the line, where a pair of beefy guards bookended the hiring hall's entrance. Benny winked and one of guards threw open the door.

"Welcome to Local 88, kid!" Benny grinned.

Inside the musty gunmetal shed, several rows of wooden benches, arranged classroom-style, fronted a beat-up metal desk. Chalky shafts of sunlight seeped through twisted Venetian-blind slats. Plastered to the walls were pin-ups of Betty Grable, Jane Russell, and Rita Hayworth, along with racy female caricatures nicknamed "Tail Wind," "Little Gem," and "Lady Luck." Behind the desk, a scraggly, crewcut man sat slurping from a bowl of clam chowder. His name was Carmine D'Amato. He was Local 88's hiring boss.

"Hey, paisan!" Benny called. "How's my favorite dago doin' these days?"

D'Amato wiped a sliver of chowder from his lip. He was far older than Benny, rheumy-eyed and stooped, his face as crusty as the barnacled hull of a derelict cargo ship.

"Glad to see ya, Benny," he grunted.

"Been way too long," Benny said.

"Well, you already got yourself a job," D'Amato chided. "Guess you don't need your ol' pal Carmine no more."

"Ah, don't go spoutin' horseshit like that!" Benny cackled. "I'll always need you, Carmine. Hell . . . you think I'm here today on a goddamned social call?"

D'Amato grinned through a mouthful of crooked, browning teeth. He could have easily been mistaken for one of the scabrous Bowery rummies who drifted to the westside docks each day, scrounging for handouts. Appearances, however, were deceiving. D'Amato wielded prodigious clout within the tugboat trade, doling out coveted jobs, often in exchange for money or personal favors.

Like most gatekeepers, he usually leveraged his import to the hilt, acting callous and hard to get. He was far different in Benny's presence, however: deferential, pliant, like a kid angling for his allowance. Benny, it was obvious, wielded prodigious clout, too.

"Carmine . . . say 'hi' to my brother Jack," Benny said.

D'Amato extended a meaty paw. He and Jack shook hands.

"Jack just landed stateside after fightin' the fuckin' Krauts in Europe," Benny said.

"Did ya now?" D'Amato said. "Well, glad ya made it home."

"Glad to be home," Jack said.

"Where were you stationed?" D'Amato inquired.

"Mostly in England and France," Jack replied.

"Ah, don't let my brother feed that humble bullshit to ya!" Benny interjected. "Jack did more than his part in the war. Christ . . . he was smack in the middle of D-Day!"

"That so?" said D'Amato, eyebrows raised.

Jack winced. He didn't like talking about the war—or worse yet, portraying himself as some kind of hero. Most men who'd seen the war up close were that way. It wasn't simply that people didn't want to hear war stories, though that was often the case. It wasn't even so much that Jack wanted to purge painful memories, though that too was true. But for Jack, the war was over, plain and simple. There were other things to think about now, time to put the war behind him, and get on with the rest of his life. Besides, the real heroes were the men and women who hadn't made it home.

Benny shared no such mindset, however. "Fuck yeah, Carmine!" he boasted. "Jack saw action on one of those LDTs . . . you know, the transport boats that landed our boys on the coast of France."

"Jesus!" D'Amato cringed. "That must have been tough."

"Goddamned right it was tough!" Benny crowed. "An' I'm proud as hell of my brother. Without men like Jack, the Allies would never have made it onto the Normandy beaches. The whole invasion of Europe would've gone to shit. Men like my brother . . . they won us the fuckin' war!"

"Well, thanks for all you've done," D'Amato said humbly.

"We can thank Jack even more," said Benny, "by showing him how much our union appreciates everything he did for Uncle Sam."

Nodding at a list of names clamped to a clipboard atop D'Amato's desk, Benny said confidently, "I'm sure you'll find Jack's name on the applicant list for the McFarland deckhand job. Probably right at the top!"

"Just did!" D'Amato handed a job application and a pencil to Jack, who proceeded to a nearby bench to fill the paperwork out.

"Fuckin' war hero . . . my brother!" Benny said.

"Sure sounds that way," D'Amato agreed.

"An' now that he's home," said Benny, "he's lookin' to jumpstart his life."

D'Amato chuckled. "Ain't we all?"

"Hell yeah!" Benny nodded. "A lotta lives need to get back on track now that the war is over. An' our union is gonna see to it that Jack gets the break he deserves."

"Sure thing," D'Amato said. "What are his plans?"

"Jack's gonna work on a tugboat," said Benny. "An' go to college at night."

"College?"

"Uh-huh." Benny cackled. "Believe that? College man . . . in my family?"

D'Amato snickered.

"Hell," said Benny, "I wish I had Jack's ambition, let alone his half his brains. Me? I'll probably be bustin' my cajónes for the union till it lands me in a fuckin' grave."

"Makes two of us." D'Amato grinned. "Gotta hand it to your brother, though. At least he's got a dream."

Benny cackled. "You had dreams once too, Carmine—didn't ya?"

"Who remembers?" D'Amato said. "I ain't got the time for dreams no more."

"Well, Jack has the time," Benny said. "Hell, he's all of twenty-four. When you're that young, you got time for all kinds of things . . . even dreams."

* * *

Sure, there was still time. Even now, after all the lost years—the detours, the roadblocks, the deferrals—Jack possessed that most precious of gifts: time for a second act, for dreams yet to be devoured by misfortune or chance, dreams so elusive that he couldn't help but wonder at times: why bother chasing them at all? Why not simply let them die and spare himself the disappointment, the folly, the pain?

But dreams for Jack were indefatigable. Dreams had sustained him throughout his entire life, tendered hope through even his darkest of days: the privation, the uncertainty, the personal loss. And especially, the war.

Jack had spent the past four years immersed in the cauldron of World War II, an Army corporal on one of the hundreds of assault-landing vessels that delivered soldiers, equipment, and supplies to the Normandy beaches during Operation Overlord, trigger point of the Allies' effort to liberate Europe from Hitler's Third Reich. Assigned to the Sixth Engineer Special Brigade, a unit of the U.S. Army Corps of Engineers, he had prepared rigorously for the war's pivotal moment, training for eleven months alongside thousands of Allied soldiers, sailors, airmen, and marines.

Nothing had prepared him for D-Day, however. Nothing could have.

The Allies' five-thousand-vessel armada, steaming across the fog-shrouded English Channel, had timed its landing for high tide, in the misty light of dawn. Two beaches along a forty-mile stretch of French coastline had been targeted by the American-manned Western Task Force. Jack's landing craft was assigned to the beach code-named Omaha.

What followed would be assigned to the annals of history.

As Omaha beach came into view, the several dozen infantrymen crammed into Jack's landing craft grew keenly aware that this wasn't simply a routine training exercise. Battle-hardened G.I.s, facing the specter of death, grew hollow-eyed and trancelike. Men were praying, voicing confessionals, crying out to loved ones, pleading for mercy and absolution. Others wept unabashedly, vomited over the side of the landed craft, or soiled their fatigues.

Jack felt wobbly, his arms and legs trembling, his heart tripping wildly, his mind flooding with vivid, disjointed images, like a spool of film gone haywire: splashing through the surf as it washed across a white-sand beach at Coney Island . . . playing stickball on Roebling Street with a group of boyhood chums . . . sitting in the bleachers at Ebbets Field, the outfield grass verdant as a country meadow, the scent of hot dogs and roasted peanuts wafting through the stands . . .

Then all of it suddenly dropped away, as the fury of the beachhead assault came fully into focus: an *ack-ack* sound, muffled at first, then growing louder and soon becoming thunderous. And within seconds, Jack's landing craft was swallowed up in an avalanche of ear-splitting noise: mortar shells, artillery, and anti-aircraft fire bursting in midair; fighter planes and bombers roaring overhead; assault craft battering the cliffside with machine-gun fire; the boom of battleship cannons pounding coastal targets.

To Jack, it seemed as if a biblical Hell had opened its jaws to swallow the landing force whole. The entire channel rocked and quaked with the firestorm of battle. Wind gusts raked the water. Frothy swells battered Jack's landing craft. The pallid sky was peppered with tracer bullets, flares, barrage balloons, and billows of smoke.

Jack was certain that, at any second, he was about to die. He thought fleetingly about his mother, busy with her volunteer church duties, and his father, working double shifts at the Dixie Sugar refinery. He thought about his poor, lost brother Gabriel, the two of them on their Tar Beach rooftop hatching brazen adventures. He thought about Benny, and how his gallant older brother had taught him how to fight: head up, wits about him, using adrenaline as his servant, never his master.

There were other thoughts too, more pious and profound: thoughts about the heartache and insanity of the untethered violence engulfing him; the incalculable loss of human potential; the melancholy realization that nothing in the realm of humanity—nothing—was more inevitable than war, fighting ingrained in man's very nature.

Jack thought about how inconsequential he was in the overall scheme of things, a tiny speck in the sweeping expanse of a war raging across entire continents and oceans. He thought about how fate was so random, death so arbitrary, and if it might be possible to buck the odds and survive. He wondered what it might feel like to die. Would it be painless and swift? Agonizing and prolonged? Dreamlike? Blissful? Eternally dark and silent? He wondered if there was an afterlife, and if so, where might his soul reside? He wondered, if he perished, how he'd be remembered: if people would honor his memory, mourn his loss, view his sacrifice as righteous and noble. He wondered if somehow he could have been better—a better brother and son. A better soldier and friend.

A better man.

Jack wondered, too, how it could be possible that humankind, capable of soaring works of genius—the rise of civilizations, the harnessing of science, the advent of language, the creation of cultural masterpieces—could simultaneously possess such a propensity for annihilation and atrocity, and be so captive to the basest of instincts: hatred and cruelty, prejudice and brutality, jealousy and wrath, conquest and domination. What would God think? How could there even be a God? And where was God now, amidst the chaos and the horror, deaf to so many desperate cries for help?

Jack thought fleetingly about all those things as his landing craft plowed through the frothy English Channel, flush in the jaws of battle. Then it was nearly impossible to think at all. Weather, visibility, and the swirling seawater proved as daunting an obstacle as the enemy defenses. Waves swept over the sides of amphibious assault crafts, soaking soldiers and supplies. Tanks, jeeps, artillery, and other equipment were swamped. Dozens of landing vessels were bottled up by underwater obstacles or destroyed by enemy artillery. Death hovered overhead like a sickly brume.

When the bow ramps of Jack's LDT flew open, soldiers were torn to shreds by artillery shells and gunfire as they struggled to wade ashore through icy, neck-deep water, others pulled downward by powerful undertows, bodies and limbs floating in the blood-red tide. Rifles, helmets, and lifejackets washed in and out with the surf. Jack was spattered head to toe with bone fragments, muscle, sinew, and blood.

And then the carnage worsened.

As the landing crafts beached, assault teams were greeted by land mines, salvos of mortar shells, and fire from machine guns and artillery. Soldiers lobbing hand grenades, unleashing flamethrowers and firing rifles advanced slowly through skeletal, smoking piles of metal. Men dug foxholes and command posts. Medics scattered to triage stations. Wounded, shell-shocked G.I.s screamed for morphine. Chaplains issued last rites. Corpses, along with the smoldering wreckage of tanks and other equipment, littered the scoured, charred killing field. Graves-registration units combed the beach, collecting dog tags, shooing away buzzards and horseflies, removing bodies, and digging mass graves.

Through all his months of training—seaborne excursions, amphibious landings, live-firing drills in daylight and darkness, rolling seas and freezing temperatures—Jack had never envisioned such a surreal, gut-wrenching mélange of mayhem, emotion, and carnage. Through even his grimmest imaginings, he never knew he could be so overwhelmed by sights and sounds and scents: the stench of gasoline and gunpowder, seawater and smoke, excrement and mangled human remains. He never knew he could feel so pummeled by emotions, so focused and hellbent on fulfilling his mission:

Make it to shore and back.

Abet his brothers-in-arms.

Simply survive.

Jack's slow-moving LDT was defenseless, swallowed up by the fury of the coastal assault. But through it all, the shallow-draft amphibious vessel cut a path through the choppy, swirling waters, back and forth from beachhead to ship, delivering troops and supplies, ferrying wounded soldiers to hospital ships anchored off the coast. As time seemingly stood still, Jack and his crewmates persevered in the face of the savagery, working nonstop for forty-eight hours before tying up alongside a transport ship for rations, while infantry and armored units captured the beachhead, carved out footholds, and moved inland over cliffs and through hedgerows and shrub brush, then through flooded lowlands and country towns all the way to Paris and Berlin.

At times, it seemed impossible for Jack to make sense of it all, easy to see how all that he'd lived through could sully or destroy a person, the memories ingrained forever, the wounds never fully healed. It wasn't hard to see how everything he had lived through could test a person's sanity, lead them to succumb to disillusionment, hopelessness, despair. Could anyone who'd lived through all that truly have faith in mankind, or feel hopeful about the future, or believe in a benevolent God? Why had some survived when legions had perished? Was it random? Was it luck? Was there some inexplicable purpose to Jack's life now that he'd made it home safe and sound?

Jack battled his emotions and his unanswered questions as fiercely as he'd battled the Axis enemy. At times, even home again in New York, the fighting at an end, he'd awaken, sweat-soaked and frantic in the dead of night to flashbacks of cannons firing, soldiers screaming, the entire world ablaze. Sometimes, he'd have to consciously remind himself that the war was truly over, and the only way to distance himself from it was to not talk about it, or think about it; to convince himself that his sacrifice had helped preserve a cherished way of life; to learn to live with the scars. There was no other way. Not if he wanted to remain sane. Not if he wanted to be capable of acts and kindness and compassion and love. Not if he wanted to cling to his dreams.

* * *

Carmine D'Amato coughed a gob of sputum into a crusty yellowed handkerchief as he eyeballed Jack's job application.

"Your brother says you're lookin' to go to college at night," Local 88's hiring boss said.

"That's the plan," Jack said.

"Think you can manage that after a full day's work?"

"I hope to try."

"Ain't gonna be easy."

"The way I see it," said Jack, "I've been through worse."

"You sure have." D'Amato grimaced. "What're ya plannin' to study?"

"I'm hoping to become a teacher."

"Teacher, huh?" D'Amato nodded. "Well, that's certainly a noble profession."

Noble or not, it had long been at the heart of Jack's postwar goals. Jack had been a junior at Pace, halfway to a bachelor's degree, when Pearl Harbor came under attack. Two days later, he had lined up with scores of other volunteers at the National Guard Armory across from the family's apartment, answering America's call to arms. At age twenty, he was leaving home for the first time in his life, on his way to boot camp in Georgia, and then to London and specialized training in Inveraray, Scotland.

Yet all through that time, Jack had clung to the same dream he had nurtured prior to the war: he wanted to become a teacher.

To Jack, teaching seemed an especially enticing career. The New York City school system, already the crown jewel of public education in America, was likely to gain even more prominence in the years ahead, Jack believed. Legions of ex-G.I.s were returning home, setting down roots, starting families. Education,

Jack reasoned, would be given heavy emphasis in the postwar era, with an entire generation of parents eager to see their children attain a quality of life that they themselves had been denied. Schooling, they—and Jack—believed, would be the gateway to that upward mobility, a ticket into America's emergent middle class, and teachers would be the primary conduit: coveted, respected, even eligible for benefits like health insurance and a pension after twenty years.

For Jack, attributes like those were nothing to sneeze at. Secure, stable jobs with substantive benefits weren't taken lightly in working-class neighborhoods like Williamsburg. Jack's father and brother could attest to that. Gus Logan had been denied those perks his entire working life. Benny fought for them every waking hour of his.

For Jack, however, there was more to teaching than simply its tangible fruits. As his family's first college graduate, he'd be able to shed the grimy work clothes worn by generations of forebears. He'd be able to rise to the level of white collar, earn a living with his head instead of his hands. As a teacher, Jack wouldn't merely be treading water—he'd be lifting himself to higher ground, validating the notion that, even after all the lost years, there was still a chance to chase his dream.

And now he was getting that chance.

Weeks after D-Day, Congress had passed its landmark G.I. Bill, setting aside billions of dollars to help returning veterans re-enter the job market or reboot their education. Jack gratefully accepted Uncle Sam's endowment: three hundred dollars in mustering-out pay, along with an annual credit for tuition, books, and other costs. And shortly after returning to New York, he'd re-enrolled at Pace, attending classes three nights a week, immersed in the subject he loved more than any other: Mathematics.

For as long as anyone could recall, Jack had possessed an immense fondness for math—an exceptional aptitude too. As a math prodigy, he'd been assigned to a "special-progress" class in junior high school, and promoted a grade above others his age, studying trigonometry and calculus while his fellow eighth-graders were wrestling with algebra and geometry.

But it wasn't simply that numbers came easy to Jack, or that they'd always been a source of excitement and joy. Numbers had been a sanctuary too, a shelter from the storms that had buffeted Jack's life. So much of his childhood had been awash in chaos, fraught with uncertainty, out of his control. The realities of his family's existence were harsh, the Great Depression ruinous, the streets of Williamsburg unforgiving. Gabriel had drowned. Benny had left home. The Logan family had been torn asunder, Jack's childhood aborted, his life turned upside down.

Mathematics had been a counterpoint to all that—an abstraction perhaps, but one that proffered clarity, certainty, solace. Numbers were tranquil, orderly, predictable. There were rules that were consistent and inviolate. One plus one always equaled two; four times four always equaled sixteen; the square root of nine was always three. If you were careful and applied yourself, you'd arrive at the same answer every time. No matter how vexing the problem, you could usually find a solution, a means for establishing order, a way to overlay turbulence with quietude. Jack also found intrigue in math, excitement, the same joy that others found in music, literature, science, and art. The subject had a wealth of practical applications, too. As a boy, it helped Jack calculate the batting averages of his favorite ballplayers, bowling scores for him and his friends. It was certainly a boon in the Army, where the laws of probability aided immensely during friendly games of poker and craps.

Jack was confident that as a high school math teacher he could discover the practical, white-collar benefits he craved as a product of the family that raised him, the neighborhood he'd grown up in, and the era in which he'd come of age. He could show young people how numbers existed everywhere—in nature, science, politics, religion, even poetry—and how math was a language all its own, rife with patterns, relationships, and mysteries to be solved.

As a teacher, he'd find ways to expose his students to the same sense of adventure he'd discovered in math, the delight in solving the seemingly insoluble, the same sense of certainty and peace. Through it all, Jack would strive to buck the shackles of curriculum, the tyranny of exams, and all the other things that sucked the life from the subject. Instead, he'd make his students feel as safe with numbers as he did. He'd delight them, inspire them, help them nurture dreams of their own.

That was the plan, anyway. That was the dream.

In two years, at twelve credits per semester, Jack would earn his bachelor's degree and land a job teaching high school. It was a modest enough dream, he reasoned—nothing too audacious or risky. All he had to do was keep his nose to the grindstone and keep reaching for it before it fell apart or slipped away, unnoticed, over time.

"Your application looks good." Carmine D'Amato grinned. "Report to Pier 53 at five o'clock tomorrow mornin', an' look for the tugboat *Jupiter*. Her crew'll be expectin' you."

"Thanks, Carmine." Benny pumped D'Amato's hand. "I owe you one."

"Sure thing." D'Amato grinned. "I'll find somethin' you can do for me."

Benny chuckled. "I'm sure you will."

"Congratulations!" Benny chirped, as he and Jack exited the hiring hall, the queue of deckhand applicants as long as ever. "You just landed yourself a job!"

Jack cringed, sullied by the process, yet grateful for the opportunity. Benny was right: this was how things were done. You could beat yourself up about it till you were blue in the face, or you could reap the rewards when it was expedient, do what was needed to get by. Jack had pushed aside his reticence, his qualms about nepotism, and his fear about owing Benny a favor. The need for a paycheck had trumped all of that.

"I'm proud of ya, kid!" crowed Benny, slipping a union membership card into Jack's palm. "You're a New York City tugboatman now . . . part of the brotherhood."

"And what does that mean?"

"It means that whatever war tugboatmen are wagin', your brothers will have your back."

"That's reassuring," Jack said. "But what kind of war are you talking about?"

"Who knows?" Benny said. "Somethin' unexpected could rear its ugly head at just about any time."

CHAPTER 13

January 31, 1946

They headed in different directions for their lunchtime recess. It was only fitting. Tugboat owners and union officials had been pulling on opposite ends of the same rope across eight months of failed contract talks. It was hardly a surprise then that their negotiating hiatus led them to starkly different venues—or that the three-hour cooling-off period yielded no movement whatsoever in resolving the collective-bargaining deadlock.

While Benny and his fellow union reps adjourned to caucus at a nearby nickel-a-plate automat, Henry ushered his tugboat-owner colleagues into his private Waldorf-Astoria suite, where the men were greeted by trappings befitting the status of their host.

The penthouse suite, maintained year-round by McFarland Marine Towing, was akin to an exclusive men's club, richly appointed with antique furnishings and deluxe amenities. French doors opened to a plushily carpeted bedroom adjoining a marbled-tiled bathroom, boudoir, and billiards room. A glass-enclosed terrace lined with potted palms afforded a sweeping vista of midtown Manhattan, all the way to Central Park.

"Now, this is why guests flock to the Waldorf!" tugboat owner George Steele gushed. "They come to enjoy the finer things in life . . . not to butt heads with a bunch of rabid union reps!"

Henry grinned. For that was precisely the point.

Indeed, for more than a decade Henry had used the sumptuous Waldorf suite as a feel-good retreat for favored clients, politicians, and others he wished to curry favor with. His top clients—mostly well-heeled shipping magnates from Europe, China, and South America—relished their periodic visits to New York, largely for a taste of the city's vibrant nightlife. And Henry enjoyed hosting those guests in first-class fashion, regaling them with tickets to

Broadway shows, splurging on gourmet dinners, even arranging discreetly for private forms of entertainment when the need arose.

The Waldorf suite, to that end, was a highly coveted perk—and an asset, for Henry, that had paid substantial dividends. Henry's guests appreciated spending their New York sojourns at a world-class hostelry where they could rub shoulders with visiting royalty, celebrities, and society's crème de la crème. Their appreciation was reciprocated in the form of both recurrent business and steadfast fellowship.

New York's tugboat owners displayed a similar kind of fellowship as they gathered around a banquet table heaped with club sandwiches, pastries, condiments, and soft drinks. It was difficult to believe, given the amiable chitchat, that the collegiality being evinced hadn't always existed. But that was very much the case.

For decades, in fact, New York's tugboat owners had fought tooth and nail among themselves, battling each other as fiercely as they'd battled pro-labor political agendas and waterfront unions. It was Henry, however, who had almost singlehandedly put an end to the bitter turf war. Shrewdly, over time, he'd convinced the owners that not only was there enough business in New York for all of them, but that their companies could coexist amicably by taking a cue from the very unions they were battling—in other words, by joining forces and finding strength in unity.

The strategy had succeeded wildly. The formation of the Gotham Harbor Alliance ten years earlier had effectively put an end to decades of predatory business practices in the city's tugboat trade. Members of the thirty-company coalition instantly found both a common identity and a collective purpose. Protocols were established for towing rates other business practices. More importantly, the owners began negotiating labor contracts as a single entity rather than piecemeal, giving them leverage when it came to collective bargaining.

"Before we eat lunch, I'd like to offer a toast," said Henry, emerging from behind a well-stocked bar with a crystal decanter and trayful of matching whiskey tumblers.

"Limited Edition Pappy Van Winkle!" proclaimed Henry, pouring each man a splash of the esteemed Kentucky bourbon. "As synonymous with America as Old Glory herself!"

"And let's not forget good, old-fashioned capitalism!" George Steele rhapsodized. "The values and institutions that make America the envy of the world!"

The men raised their glasses in a toast.

"Hail to the Great American Spirit!" Henry enthused. "To the right for businessmen like us to control our companies' destinies and turn a profit. And to what I believe will be a landmark labor-relations victory here in New York!"

"Hear, hear!" the owners chanted, sipping their whiskey before settling into a pair of leather sofas, lunches set on a cocktail table before them.

"We've toasted to an anticipated labor-relations victory," owner Bertram Phelps said dourly. "But realistically . . . where do our contract negotiations go from here?"

"Likely straight into the crapper!" George Steele quipped.

Laughing uneasily, the owners dug into their lunches.

"Seriously," Phelps said darkly. "I was just thinking—"

And privately, Henry cringed.

Bertram Phelps, to Henry, was the weakest link in the owners' otherwise-resolute chain: flaccid, panicky, and prone to capitulation. Phelps would unfailingly, instinctively, default to appeasement, a mindset that Henry couldn't abide. Henry's admiration was reserved for men whose mindset mirrored his own: bold leaders willing to push the envelope and open new doors. Phelps, to Henry, existed on a lesser plane—as did most other men. Indeed, among the city's tugboat owners, only George Steele and Sam Dougherty were wholly aligned with Henry in viewpoint and temperament, although neither was nearly as cunning or vengeful. Few men were.

"Perhaps," said Phelps, "there's room for movement by our side."

"Movement?" asked Steele.

"Movement," Phelps repeated. "Some way to put our contract negotiations into a more constructive framework."

Once again, Henry cringed. Phelps's suggestion was precisely what the Gotham Harbor Alliance chairman vehemently opposed. Purposefully, however, he remained silent, anxious to gauge where the other men stood. There'd be time enough later, he reasoned, to impose his point of view.

"What are you proposing?" Steele inquired.

"Perhaps we could inch our wage offer up a bit," Phelps said.

"How far?"

"Half a percent maybe."

"You want us to raise the proposed wage hike from two to two-point-five percent?"

Phelps nodded. The other men mulled the idea. Henry remained mum, aching to respond but biding his time.

"Or maybe we can extend the workers' lunch break," Phelps said. "You know . . . throw that on the table, and seek some sort of giveback in exchange."

"You really think the union would go for that?" Steele asked. "Especially if it's tied to a giveback that they vowed would be a nonstarter?"

"Dunno." Phelps shrugged. "It depends, I suppose, on how much the workers want to avoid a strike. Who knows? Even a token hike in our wage offer might get them to soften their position."

After a moment's thought, Sam Dougherty asked, "What would half a percent cost us?"

"Too damned much, if you ask me!" Henry said with a voice like steel. "I say a penny more than we've already offered is a penny too much. The offer we've put on the table is more than fair. I say we hold the line right there!"

As usual, Henry's demeanor set the tone, his viewpoint drawing instant deference. With the tugboat owners, as with most others, Henry usually got his way. He expected it. Was accustomed to it. Often demanded it.

"For as long as I can remember," he said, "our negotiating stance with the union has been one of conciliation. Our companies have bent over backwards to placate our workers, agreed to contract demands that weren't always in our best interests . . . all in a desperate effort to avert a strike."

The owners sat silently. Listening. Thinking.

"And despite our good-faith negotiations, our coddling, our caving in . . . what have we gotten in return?" Henry asked.

"Nada!" Steele replied. "Zilch!"

"Precisely!"

Henry fished through a pack of Luckies and fired one up.

"For decades," he said, "labor unions have ruled the roost in New York—all in a flagrant quest for power!"

No one objected. They all believed it.

"Think about it," Henry said. "The union has won control over hiring, killed proposals to reduce tugboat crews, and tied us in knots with rules and regulations. Hell, I can't even fire a worker—for just cause—without a grievance hearing and union approval!"

"They've certainly driven business costs through the roof," Dougherty griped.

"Claimed towing rights to everything in the harbor," Steele grumbled.

"Driven companies out of business," Phelps added.

"And gotten far too big for their britches!" Henry asserted while, pouring from the decanter, he freshened each man's drink. "To me, unionism has become nothing less than a criminal conspiracy in America, a counterweight to everything men like us have worked all our lives to achieve."

"Amen to that!" said Steele.

"You know, it's laughable when you really think about it," Henry continued. "Organized labor portrays itself as 'heroic' to the working class, and paints business leaders like us as tyrants. But the so-called exploitation of labor— the notion of the 'poor, downtrodden worker' being victimized by capitalist oppression—is nothing but a fairy tale." He glared briefly at each of the others.

"It was capitalism—not labor—that made America great. Businessmen who built the factories, the railroads, and the cities. Businessmen who liberated the 'powerless and the oppressed' from lives that were far worse. In reality, businessmen like us are the true heroes: the thinkers and the doers who invest the money and take the risks . . . who have the ingenuity, the foresight, and the courage to lift society to greater heights!"

He laughed mockingly. "Labor unions? What a joke! Their ranks are populated by malingerers and malcontents—lazy, entitled deadbeats with no vision, no ambition, nothing but an endless litany of sob stories."

"Always pushing for more!" Steele grumbled.

"Forever abusing their power!" Phelps added.

"Bleeding our businesses dry!" Dougherty chimed in.

Confident that he was winning minds, Henry continued his diatribe.

"Our workers," he said, "should be grateful for all that we do for them. They should be kissing our asses for the jobs we've created and the money we put in their pockets! The last thing they should be doing is biting the hand that feeds them!"

"So true!" Steele groused. "Whatever we offer those ingrates, it's never enough."

"Some of them don't even put in an honest day's work, but it's too much trouble to fire them!" Dougherty groaned. "Hearings, legislation, red tape! It's cheaper to keep them on the payroll than to pay their disability."

"Fewer headaches, too," Steele grumbled.

Henry took another long drag on his Lucky. "I'll tell you flat-out," he said, "I'm fed up with hearing labor unions plead poverty . . . fed up with their carping about how 'callous, profit-driven employers' like us exploit them . . . fed up with everything organized labor has denigrated in America!"

"Hear, hear!" the men declared, raising their glasses.

"All the bullshit we hear about employees' rights?" Henry asked rhetorically. "Well, how about employers' rights? Don't we have rights, too?"

At that moment the attorney, Harlan Kingsley, weighed in. "Well," he said, and the others fell silent. "Maybe the pendulum has finally swung in our favor. Anti-union sentiment is peaking nowadays. The public is gagging on all the pro-labor legislation that's been rammed down their throats by Washington."

"Goddamned liberals!" Steele railed. "Every labor law those New Deal assholes have ever passed has been a setback for America! Stripped the courts of their authority! Swelled the size of government! Given unions free reign to run roughshod over businesses!"

"Thank goodness the landscape is finally shifting," Kingsley said with lawyerly moderation. "For decades, organized labor has been calling the shots. But at long last, it's losing ground."

To the owners, that certainly seemed to be the case. If unions were up in arms in postwar America, pro-business forces were fighting back equally hard, having finally gained control of Congress and passed legislation that handcuffed organized labor, including fines for strikes that threatened national security.

"Best news ever!" Henry smirked. "Businesses need protection from these goddamned criminals. Unions strike? I say issue injunctions! Slap them with fines! Jail their leaders!"

Laughing giddily, the owners toasted again.

"Gentlemen," said Henry, "I believe if we play our cards right, we can achieve the goal we want: to help unions beat a hasty retreat, tails between their legs." He dragged again on his cigarette. "Organized labor has had its 'Golden Age' in America. The Knights of Labor? The Wobblies? Unions like those wielded enormous power once, but they're relics of a bygone era now. History relegated them to the scrapheap. And that, I assure you, will happen again."

Henry sipped his bourbon.

"Labor unions have abused their power," he said. "The wave of strikes we're seeing now has turned political and public opinion against them. Mark my words: one day, the unions we're at odds with will be nothing but corpses rotting in a mass grave. And why? Because America won't need them anymore. Their endless greed, their abuse of power, will have prompted their demise."

To a man, the owners nodded. Henry had them believing. Committed. Unified. All they needed now were tactics. And Henry was prepared to supply those, as well.

"Do you think the union's strike deadline is legitimate?" Phelps asked.

"Who knows?" Steele replied. "The workers could simply be bluffing, testing us."

"And that," said Henry, "is something that we may have to test ourselves. When push comes to shove, we may have to call their bluff . . . dare them to strike."

"And if they take the bait?"

"We'll see how they feel about their decision once their monthly rent comes due!"

"Let them feel the pain, huh?"

"That's the idea."

Immersed in thought, the men returned to their lunch.

"But let's not be blind about this," Phelps warned. "A strike will hurt us in the pocketbook too."

"What's your best guess on the hit our businesses would take?" Steele asked.

"A million dollars a day, minimum, in lost revenue," Phelps replied.

"I'd say that's fairly accurate," said Henry, seemingly unruffled.

The other owners didn't seem nearly as blasé. The potential revenue loss from a strike would impact their companies far more than it would Henry's.

"And the loss of good will?" asked Phelps. "What about that?"

"I'm sure we'll take a hit there, too," Henry conceded. "But rather than speculate about uncertainties, let's focus on what we know for certain."

"And what is that?"

"For one thing," Henry said, "we know that the marching orders to Local 88's members are no longer coming from the parent union."

"Paddy O'Boyle's out?" Steele asked in surprise.

"He's still union president," Henry clarified. "But his voice is getting lost in the static."

"But if O'Boyle is no longer calling the shots," Phelps asked, "who is?"

"Dissidents," Henry said. "Militant activists led by Benny Logan."

"Well, that makes things more complicated," said Steele. "Hardliners like Logan are a pain in the ass. Their demands are extortionate . . . and they're stubborn as hell. It's nearly impossible to bargain with them."

"That's why our negotiations are deadlocked," Dougherty opined. "Hell . . . we can't even buy off their leaders these days."

"Speaking of that," asked Steele, "isn't there some way we can 'goose' the right people . . . induce union leadership to view our wage offer a bit more favorably?"

Henry shook his head. "No."

"How can you be so sure?"

"Because," said Henry, "I've already tried."

He shared the insights he'd gleaned during his dinner with Paddy O'Boyle, including how the union boss eschewed a substantial payoff in exchange for a rubber-stamped contract ratification.

"Money is no longer a lever," he said. "Not as long as Logan and his acolytes are calling the shots."

"Well, it wasn't long ago that we celebrated Christmas," Steele said. "Maybe we need to put the 'Spirit of Christ' in those union insurgents."

"I think we need to put the fear of God in them first," Henry said, to laughter from the other men. "What I'm proposing is that we lead the union precisely where it's threatening to go. In other words, bait it into a strike."

"But why?" Phelps asked.

"Economics . . . for starters."

He paced the room, taking the measure of the others, then explained. "I'm convinced that the union can't sustain itself for very long in the event of a strike. Their strike fund, I believe, is limited. Perhaps their resolve is, too. I'm certain the workers can't afford a walkout that lasts more than a few days."

"And how about us?"

"Clearly, we're a lot better off."

That much was indisputable. The Gotham Harbor Alliance, in anticipation of a potential work stoppage, had amassed a strike-defense fund of five million dollars, enough to offset revenue losses for more than a week. Several owners, including Henry, were also covered by private strike insurance.

"A strike is a battle of attrition," Henry said. "By inflicting pain, you gain leverage. Our side, clearly, can afford to outlast the union if their members walk off the job."

"But a million dollars a day in lost revenue?" Phelps all but gasped. "That's a huge price for our companies to pay . . . wouldn't you say?"

"Maybe so," Henry agreed. "But I believe it's a price worth paying."

He poured another round of drinks.

"Let me ask you gentlemen," he said. "How much money are you willing to invest in order to win our war with the labor unions?"

"Invest?" Phelps asked.

"Precisely," Henry replied. "You see, I believe that any revenue losses we might incur in the event of a strike should be seen by us as an investment."

The owners seemed confused.

"What I'm saying," said Henry, "is that while a strike might hurt us in the short term, luring the union into a work stoppage may be the best decision we'll ever make. Ultimately, it could save us millions of dollars . . . and solve our labor problems for good."

"Are you suggesting that we stop negotiating?" Phelps asked. "Declare an impasse and walk away from the bargaining table?"

"Not at all," Henry said. "I think it's critical, for appearances' sake, that we continue bargaining. But we should make it clear that the wage increase we've put on the table is our best and final offer . . . and unless the union agrees to a reduction in crew sizes or a cap on overtime, there's no room for further movement."

"That'll never fly," Phelps asserted.

Henry smirked. "I know."

"So, what's the point?"

"The point," said Henry, "is that it will look as if we tried."

"And as if it were the union," said George Steele, "that was unwilling to make any concessions that might have ended the stalemate . . . right?"

"Precisely!" Henry said as he doused his cigarette. "Now you're thinking like real businessmen. What we're doing, by offering smoke and mirrors, is calling the union's bluff, giving their leaders no choice but to cave in—or to carry through with their threatened strike. Either way, we win."

"No one," said Phelps, "wins in a strike."

"Don't be so certain," Henry countered. "Think about it: A strike will shut down New York Harbor at the worst possible time—the dead of winter."

"That's exactly why the union set the deadline they did," Phelps said. "They're timing their strike for when the city is most vulnerable."

"True," Henry said. "But that timing can easily backfire, and I'll tell you why. If a strike halts fuel and other supplies from reaching the city, it's going to wreak havoc. Homes will run low on heat. Businesses will hemorrhage money. Hospitals, schools, mass transit, municipal services—all of them will be impacted. The public hardship will be monumental."

"So how will that backfire on the union?" Phelps asked. "It sounds like it gives strikers precisely the leverage they want."

"That's a reasonable assumption," Henry said. "But follow my logic: one way or another, the strike will inevitably play out in the newspapers. And the side that successfully rallies public support will surely have the upper hand."

"And the issues underlying the strike?" Phelps asked. "What about those?"

"They won't matter."

"Who's 'right' or who's 'wrong' won't matter?"

"No," Henry said. "The only thing that'll matter is what the public believes. And ultimately, we want the public to believe that we're the good guys, the tugboat workers are the villains . . . and their strike is heresy."

"And how do we achieve that?" Phelps asked.

"Simple." Henry said. "The union will do it for us."

Henry eyeballed his colleagues. "Think about it. The union walks off the job, tugboat service is suspended, chaos reigns. Now, whose 'fault' will that be?"

"The strikers," George Steele replied.

"Precisely!" Henry said. "They'll be seen as a bunch of callous, irresponsible malcontents putting their selfish, petty interests before the public good."

Dougherty chuckled. "The public will think the workers are holding an entire city hostage simply to benefit themselves."

"And how," asked Phelps, "will we come off?"

"We'll come off as the good guys," Henry said. "Responsible. Conciliatory. Open to good-faith negotiations. Concerned about the city and its people."

"Helpless in the face of the union's power play," Steele chimed in.

"Victimized, like everyone else, by a bunch of greedy bastards," Dougherty added.

Henry beamed. "Well, wouldn't we be?"

The owners laughed. Henry did, too. He loved having them eating out of his hand.

"The way I see it," he continued, "sentiment will quickly swing to our side. The newspapers will scream bloody murder. Politicians will point the finger. Public pressure will have the strikers crawling back to work, on our terms, even faster than the impact of lost paychecks."

The owners fell mute, considering Henry's stratagem.

"But isn't the strategy you're proposing a bit, um . . . calculating?" Phelps asked.

"And what's wrong with that?" Henry asked.

"What I mean," said Phelps, "is what about the impact of a strike on people's lives? Shouldn't that matter? Is this battle simply about perception? Don't we have a responsibility to avoid the damage a tugboat strike will cause?"

"I think we have an even greater responsibility," Henry said. "I'm hellbent, quite frankly, on reversing the past abuses of organized labor, punishing unions for their transgressions, and putting them in their place."

"Are you advocating an all-out assault on organized labor?" Phelps asked.

"That I'd love to see." Henry chuckled. "I'd argue against unions' very legitimacy . . . fight them to my dying breath."

"But that's not something you can say publicly," George Steele said.

"No, it's merely wishful thinking," Henry said. "But what I can tell you, off the record, is that it's time we stop labor unions from holding a gun to our heads with their extortionate demands and their strike threats. Enough is enough! It's time we ended our 'charm offensive' . . . time we asserted ourselves and regained ownership of what's rightly ours!"

Henry could feel the owners' attitudes palpably shift. He loved the power of his ability to fuse logic, emotion, and personality as an instrument that could bend people to his point of view. The power was intoxicating. He could never get enough.

"Make no mistake," he said. "World War II is over, but another war is raging now. Businessmen are battling organized labor for control of the workplace. And nothing less than the survival of corporate America—perhaps even the soul of our country—is at stake."

"But why us?" Phelps asked. "Why must tugboat companies be the ones shouldering the burden, assuming the risks."

"Why not us?" Henry replied. "Someone must have the courage to lead the charge. This is our crusade! Our time!"

Henry met the resultant silence head on. "How we act as a coalition can send a powerful message," he continued. "Not simply to workers and companies in New York, but to every industry in America! The message is: We're no longer ceding control to organized labor! We're taking back our businesses! Our companies are ours to manage . . . not the unions!"

"Well," George Steele conceded, "I must admit that your suggestion has its merits."

Henry beamed. "Mark my words. The longer any strike goes on, the greater the opportunity for turning public opinion our way, applying financial and political pressure, and getting the union to soften its demands—or cave in entirely. When all is said and done, we won't have to worry about the union taking a hard line. Ever again!"

The comment drew a satisfied laugh.

"So, it's agreed," Steele said. "We give the union nothing more than smokescreens—innocuous proposals simply to demonstrate, when they're rejected, that it was the union who was unwilling to budge. We give them no choice but to agree to our terms . . . or strike."

Phelps nodded. "I must admit, while all of this seems calculating," he said, "it's also very astute."

"Well," said Henry, smugly, "men like us weren't handed our success, were we? We earned it . . . and not by conducting ourselves like village idiots."

George Steele then proffered a final toast. "Organized labor has declared war on corporate America," he said. "Now we can lead our workers into the strike they've threatened . . . and lash them with the very rod they've had the audacity to fashion."

"In other words," Henry said, smiling, "let's stick it to those union ingrates but good!"

CHAPTER 14

June 6, 1945

Daylight was burnishing a woolly predawn sky when Jack reported to the McFarland docks for his first day on the job. His workday, if nothing else, started early. It'd be hours yet before the sleepy port city would be fully astir, its streets desolate and dark, the inky North River speckled with lamplight.

Jack made his way along a creaky wooden quay, then traversed a narrow gangplank where a tugboat, engine thrumming, was tied to a mooring post. The air was thick with the scents of diesel fuel, oil, and hemp. Even in the dusky half-light, he could make out the bold brass lettering engraved on a nameplate set below a brine-smudged pilothouse window.

Jupiter.

New York was known for its distinctive style of tugboat and, by that measure alone, *Jupiter* certainly fit the bill. Its cylindrical pilothouse, a weatherworn red, loomed high above the tugboat's angled foredeck. Tendrils of blue-grey exhaust leaked from a squat black smokestack. Rubber-tire fenders were strung the entire length of the tugboat's port and starboard sides, their metal railings dented from butting against the hulls of ships. A rope mat lashed across the vessel's bow resembled the droopy whiskers of an old bull walrus.

Appearances, in this case, were deceiving, however. By every measurable yardstick, *Jupiter* was anything but ordinary. Built at the turn of the century to service the waterfront refineries of Charles Pratt's Astral Oil Works, *Jupiter*, at a hundred feet long, was the largest wood-hulled tugboat in New York Harbor. Propelled by diesel-electric power, the latest advance in engine propulsion, the tugboat, even at its outsized length, was capable of an unmatched blend of power, handling, and speed. *Jupiter* could run fast, turn on a dime, and pull hundreds of times her weight. In tugboat terms, she could do it all.

And she pretty much did.

Having acquired the prized vessel shortly after becoming CEO, Henry McFarland had put *Jupiter* to work on literally every harbor assignment imaginable. Prior to World War I, she'd assisted in transporting crude oil, kerosene, and petroleum from Astral's refineries to ports across the globe. During the second war, she'd been requisitioned by the U.S. military to assist in the launch of warships from the Brooklyn Navy Yard. She'd also served during the so-called Golden Age of luxury passenger ships—an era during which New York served as principal port-of-call to the world's most glamorous ocean liners—and had been front and center during numerous occasions of pomp and circumstance. Mere weeks earlier, *Jupiter* had been afforded the solemn honor of docking the *Joseph V. Connolly*, a Liberty ship bearing the remains of slain G.I.s being repatriated from the battlefields of Europe for burial in the U.S.

If Jack had been able to handpick any tugboat in America, he couldn't have chosen a finer, more prestigious vessel on which to work. The flagship of McFarland Marine Towing Inc., *Jupiter* was the undisputed queen of New York Harbor, pride of the city's seven-hundred-vessel tugboat fleet.

Stepping aboard the stern deck, Jack was greeted by a scruffy deckhand sifting through an assortment of towlines, bridles, and chains. The man, clad in a soiled T-shirt and denim overalls, removed a leather glove and extended a calloused, rope-burned hand.

"Pleased to meet ya," he mumbled through a toothsome grin. "The name is Charlie Long . . . but most people just call me 'Shorty.'"

It was easy to see why. Built like a miniature fireplug, Shorty was at best five feet tall. His stocky, compact frame coupled with the juxtaposition of his nickname and surname made for a humorous amalgam that he obviously liked playing up.

"Shorty Long, huh?" Jack, smiling, shook his hand. "Pleased to meet you, too."

"Welcome aboard," trilled Shorty, his ruddy, windburned face leathery yet guileless, almost childlike.

"You arrived just in the nick of time," he told Jack. "We've been down a crewman for about a week now, an' can sure use another hand on deck."

"And I can sure use the work," Jack said. "To be honest, though, I'm green as all get-out. Never worked on a tugboat before."

"Ah, don't sweat it," Shorty pooh-poohed. "You'll learn the ropes in no time flat. Just follow my lead. Before you know it, you'll be a tried-and-true hawsepiper."

"A what?"

"A tugboatman." Shorty grinned. "One of us."

He then escorted Jack to the pilothouse to meet the rest of *Jupiter's* crew.

Dutch Hendrik, the tugboat's captain, sat at the vessel's polished-brass controls, navigational chart and tide table spread across his lap. First Mate Mack Nowak, a thickly muscled ex-sailor, brewed a pot of coffee on a cast-iron galley stove. Chief engineer Luke Huggins, spindly and weathered as *Jupiter* itself, stood at the doorway to the tugboat's engine room. Each man greeted Jack warmly, filling the pilothouse with jaunty banter.

Not for long, though. It didn't pay McFarland Marine Towing for its tugboats to sit idle at their dock. Within minutes, *Jupiter's* ship-to-shore radio was cackling with the voice of a dispatcher rasping a litany of numbered vessels and berths, shorthand for the morning's assignments.

"Two-twenty-four . . . East River. Forty-eight . . . North River."

—Head from a wharf on Manhattan's West Side, coal barges on both hips, for a delivery to a prison hospital on Welfare Island in Queens.

—Haul a loaded flotilla of scrap-metal barges to a smelting facility in Staten Island.

—Escort the RMS *Queen Elizabeth* from the Chelsea Piers passenger terminal through the harbor for its voyage out to sea.

No sooner had Dutch Hendrik recorded the assignments than he was revving *Jupiter's* engine. Luke Huggins moved below deck to the engine room. Mack Nowak exited the pilothouse. Jack accompanied Shorty Long to *Jupiter's* fantail. And within seconds, the tugboat, reversing screws in a reflux of water, was pulling from the dock, rounding into a stiff breeze at The Battery, and steaming toward the steely glint of the East River. Dutch Hendrik, seated at the vessel's steering wheel, barked engine-room commands to Luke Huggins through a metal voice pipe. Nowak checked on the status of the vessel's towing bridle and other equipment. Shorty leaned against a stem post, tossing pieces of chum to a flock of mewing seagulls trailing the boat.

"Headin' Eastbound . . . for the Gate."

Dutch Hendrik barked into the handpiece of his ship-to-shore, piloting

Jupiter to the Hell Gate tidal strait, near the junction of the East and Harlem rivers.

"Will you boys listen to that beee-u-tiful sound!" Mack Nowak yowled as *Jupiter* throttled up, its engine cutting loose with a roar that sent the tugboat rumbling.

"Oooooh, baby!" Nowak quivered. "Can't you just feel that sexy vibration just washin' all over ya!"

Shorty roared with laughter. Jack did too. He'd been on the job mere minutes, but already he felt a palpable kinship with his crewmates and a sanguine connection to *Jupiter*—emotions that he sensed, even then, might well last a lifetime.

"*Jupiter* will never kill you." Shorty cackled. "But sometimes, the way she rattles around on the water, she'll make ya wish you were dead!"

"Maybe so," Mack Nowak shouted over the din. "But come hell or high water, she always finds a way to get us home!"

"Amen to that," Shorty said. "Amen to always finding our way home."

And standing on *Jupiter*'s fantail, sunlight glinting on the water, Jack couldn't help but think how good it felt to have finally made his own way home. Back from a war that had taken such a grievous toll. Back to the city he loved with all his heart. Back with Kate finally at his side.

*   *   *

She was the best thing, by far, that he'd brought home from the war—the only thing that, even remotely, could redeem the horrors he'd lived through, the things that he'd seen.

Sure, there were other things Jack brought home from his four years overseas: a duffle bag stuffed with postcards, letters, and keepsakes from landmarks he'd visited in Europe, and photos of army buddies whose memories he'd honor for as long as he'd live. There were the dog tags that graced his neck since boot camp, dress uniform and fatigues, and campaign medals that honored his service to America. Inside him was an indelible sense of satisfaction, too. Glory in a job well done. Pride in how his unit had proven its mettle in battles against not just a formidable enemy, but against heartache, desperation, and fear.

All those things had shaped Jack, steeled him, made him the man he was now. All of them counted for something. After all, if not for the war how would Jack have ever known that he could persevere through the firestorm of combat, learn from it, and use it as a fulcrum to move forward with his life? How else would he have had the opportunity, at the age of twenty no less, to have journeyed so far, accomplished so much, been part of something as monumental as the War for Democracy, a battle to save the world from tyranny? How else could he have come to understand the fragility of life, appreciate even its simplest joys, and recognize how everything he cherished could be snatched from his grasp so randomly, so suddenly?

How else would he have ever met Kate?

It was the early part of 1942 when the two of them first crossed paths, weeks after Jack arrived in London with the first wave of American G.I.s assigned to the European Theater. Thousands of Allied servicemen were being stationed in England then. Before long, many of them would be headed to the beaches of Normandy, and then into southern France for the bloody slog toward Germany. Until then, there'd be months of training—and plenty of free time, too.

Life in London had been especially arduous in the early years of the war in Europe, the British capital subjected to stringent rationing, the constant threat of invasion, and the fury of Adolf Hitler's Luftwaffe. German bombing raids had ceased by the time Jack arrived, however, and the outsized American presence had lifted spirits in the city. London swarmed now with fresh-faced, fun-loving G.I.s, glamorous in their crisp, tie-and-collar khakis. Dance halls, nightclubs, and underground restaurants swarmed with Allied servicemen. Piccadilly taverns were packed to the rafters. Party girls and prostitutes roamed London's streets and pubs.

Accustomed to a traditional British reserve, and starved of glamour and excitement, London's women were swept off their feet by the impetuous, freewheeling Americans, who had no qualms about violating longstanding social taboos. G.I.s were lavish in their treatment of British women, showering them with nylon stockings, silk scarves, chocolates, and other gifts readily available from PX stores but rationed throughout most of England. It wasn't necessarily smooth sailing, however. While England and America had much in common, including their Axis enemy, the differences in culture, lifestyle, and customs at times made co-existence dicey. Americans were viewed by many natives as cocky and brash, Brits seen as stuffy and aloof. British soldiers—nicknamed "Tommies" and garbed in woolen uniforms and stiff, hob-nailed boots—resented the fact that U.S. servicemen earned several times their pay and often portrayed themselves as heroic crusaders, summoned to save the island nation from certain defeat. Many Brits saw the American presence as akin to a hostile occupation. Conflicts were commonplace, fistfights and quarrels a regular occurrence.

U.S. military brass, anxious to keep a lid on potential squabbling, issued countless directives advising G.I.s how to behave on British soil. The War Department also discouraged American servicemen from becoming involved with British women, warning the G.I.s repeatedly about the dangers of venereal disease, the risk of unplanned pregnancies and backstreet abortions, and the threat of being relieved of their paychecks by canny British gold-diggers.

None of that mattered, however, when Jack met Kate.

No one would have suspected it of the winsome nineteen-year-old, but Kathryn Anne Sedgwick had been pummeled and shaped by a lifetime awash in economic calamity, separation, uncertainty, and war. The only child of a career military officer and an auto-factory worker, Kate had been born and raised in Coventry, a medieval city known then as the hub of the British automotive trade. With successive deployments to India, China, and Northern Ireland, Martin Sedgwick, a colonel in the British Expeditionary Force, had been absent throughout much of his daughter's childhood, while Kate's mother Emily worked full-time at the nearby Daimler Company auto factory. For lengthy stretches of her childhood, Kate had lived in the care of relatives and neighbors, or forced to fend for herself. Schoolwork, household chores, and hobbies occupied much of her time, along with visits to family in the English countryside. Games like hopscotch, hide-and-seek, and jump-rope were interspersed with solitary pastimes like knitting, needlepoint, and reading childhood fables about Winnie-the-Pooh, Raggedy Ann stories, and The Velveteen Rabbit.

Life took a more daunting turn, however, when Kate turned seven.

The Wall Street Crash of 1929 sparked a chain of cataclysmic events across Great Britain. While a Depression ravaged much of America, British banks were failing, unemployment rampant, the country's economy in a virtual freefall. Cuts in military spending thrust Martin Sedgwick into an unexpected early retirement, stripping him of both salary and pension. With Britain's manufacturing sector plunging, Emily Sedgwick was laid off from her job at Daimler. And no sooner had Britain begun a halting recovery, years later, than an even more menacing shadow began creeping across the nation.

With appeasement efforts failing, war with a powerful German enemy was all but inevitable now. Martin Sedgwick was summoned from retirement to help train Royal Air Force personnel at nearby "shadow factories," established by the British government to convert Coventry's auto factories to the production of aircraft, munitions, and tanks. Emily turned to church-sponsored volunteer work. With Jews and other non-Aryan refugees fleeing Nazi-occupied territories in Europe, Kate's mother was soon immersed full-time in rescue operations, housing refugee children in local boarding houses, army barracks, and college dorms. Kate, at sixteen, left school to go to work part-time as a bank teller, while volunteering twenty hours a week as an ambulance attendant. With the war in full swing, however, young British women were required to register for various forms of defense work. Kate decided on nursing, training for eleven months in the nearby city of Birmingham before landing a job at St. Bartholomew's, London's oldest hospital.

By the time Kate arrived in London, St. Bart's was inundated with casualties from battlefields in the Mediterranean, Burma, and North Africa. Gravely wounded Tommies, arriving at the hospital in an endless stream of ambulances and Humvees, were being rolled in on gurneys and stretchers, then assigned to triage stations or operating rooms. Others, caked in seawater and sand, were queued up in blood-spattered hallways and corridors, the stench of misery and death everywhere. Most of the soldiers had suffered blast injuries: shrapnel wounds, second- and third-degree burns, severed limbs, and broken bones. Others were blinded or paralyzed, their bodies mangled and torn.

St. Bart's operating rooms bustled with surgeries all around the clock, seven days a week. Kate worked, nearly non-stop, in eighteen-hour shifts: grading the wounded for urgency of treatment, applying tourniquets and dressings, and assisting surgical teams in candlelit operating rooms. With medical personnel soon being dispatched to Dunkirk and Tobruk, the shortage of nurses grew critically acute. Kate, like others, pitched in however needed. When she wasn't immersed in resuscitation or surgery, she was busy delousing children and caring for patients stricken with diphtheria, hepatitis, dysentery, malaria, and scarlet fever. At other times, she rolled bandages, sterilized instruments, cleaned equipment, disposed of bedpans, prepped dressings, and manned St. Bart's rooftop in fire-watching duties.

Often, the care Kate provided was aimed as much at lifting flagging spirits as healing broken bodies. She treated wounded Tommies to hot tea and buttered bread; read to them from magazines, newspapers, and books; lit their cigarettes; wrote their letters; chatted about wives and sweethearts, parents and comrades, and memories of life before the war. Sometimes, she simply sat with the men, holding their hand as they whispered confessionals and mumbled prayers and wondered if they would live or die. Many of the wounded were shellshocked or delirious, in and out of sleep, or unable to speak. Other simply cried. Still others joked that they must have died and gone to heaven because Kate, in her pristine white uniform and nurse's cap, looked so much like an angel.

And that's how she looked to Jack the first time he laid eyes on her.

He had been wounded during a routine training exercise—nothing major, merely a shrapnel burn—and transported by ambulance to St. Bart's, where Kate was on emergency room duty.

For her, it had been the latest in a series of long, grueling days. Exhausted and frazzled, she was hardly prepared for a potential romantic encounter; nor did she look the part. With makeup strictly rationed, Kate, like other women, had been mixing calamine lotion with cold cream as a base for facial powder and improvising with beetroot juice instead of rouge. With hosiery inaccessible, she sported pencil-drawn seams down the back of her legs, and wore unbecoming, masculine clothing. She had long ago grown accustomed to not looking or feeling her best.

None of that mattered, however. Not to Jack.

To Jack, the slender young nurse who tended to his burn was nothing short of stunning: luminescent in the amber glow of the hospital's lamplight, with sparkling green eyes, radiant skin, and auburn hair set peek-a-boo-style under her nurse's cap.

Kate, much to her surprise, was similarly smitten by her patient: so dashing and heroic-looking in his mud-spattered fatigues; so gracious and courteous, earnest and outgoing, funny and smart.

So American.

Jack, more embarrassed than injured, apologized for landing in the hospital with such a trifling wound. Kate joked that she was shocked he would even bother being treated for so minor an injury. Their chemistry natural and instantaneous, the two of them chatted amiably while Kate dressed Jack's burn. Each felt an inner tinge of excitement. Neither one believed in love at first sight. After all, how could you love someone before you even knew them? The attraction they felt was palpable, however. And far from fleeting.

Jack visited St. Bart's on half a dozen occasions after his release, never failing to bring floral bouquets, scented soap, or tins of coffee—and always asking for a date. It didn't take long for Kate to accept the offer. And before long, the two of them were a bona fide couple.

Falling in love was easy in wartime London, the war a potent aphrodisiac, and intimacy a ready means for coping with the unremitting stress. With times so uncertain, danger lurking around the corner, and people so far from home, conventional social barriers quickly evaporated. Anxious to seize the moment, couples were reaching out to one another, crossing ethnic backgrounds, cultures and religions, willing to take risks they'd normally avoid. No one could be certain, after all, what the following day might bring. No one knew how long they'd live. Legions of G.I.s were courting British women. Almost as many were falling in love—Jack and Kate among them.

The couple, in many ways, were ready sweethearts—compatible in outlook and temperament, viewpoint and sensibilities—and their courtship was both whirlwind and romantic, cobbled together during nightly passes, weekend leaves, and a monthlong furlough during which Jack opted to remain in England instead of returning to the States.

Kate showed her beau all around London: Big Ben, London Bridge, Piccadilly Circus, all the usual tourist sites. The couple attended USO Camp Shows starring Bob Hope, Bing Crosby, and other Hollywood luminaries; danced to the music of Benny Goodman, Harry James, and Tommy Dorsey; attended the cinema to see Clark Gable, Cary Grant, and Vivien Leigh; and sampled Greek, Thai, and Indian delicacies at West End bistros and pubs. Sometimes they'd stroll for hours, holding hands, on the towpaths along the Thames, or on pathways that wound through London's Royal Parks, the air redolent with the scent of spring, the parklands flush with blooming flower beds, palace gardens, and exotic birds.

Their conversations were earnest, heartfelt, and boundless. The two of them spoke of childhood and family, of hometowns and friendships, nursing and soldiering, aspirations they harbored, memories they cherished, apprehensions they shared. Each time they conversed there was a peeling away of layers: a stirring sense of discovery, a deepening bond, an awakening to exciting new possibilities. At times the war seemed almost to vanish, as if it were nothing but a rumor. Other times, Jack could allay his trepidation about the perilous D-Day mission he was training for, and Kate could push aside the haunting trail of broken bodies and mangled spirits she was treating, and the two of them could escape into one another. Confidantes. Best of friends. Lovers now, too. Amidst the chaos, the uncertainty, the immeasurable tragedy of war, they had discovered something joyful and comforting in one another, something that could survive dissemblance and doubt, something that they sensed could last a lifetime.

Kate taught Jack British slang, introduced him to native currency and etiquette, and taught him about the British sports of rugby, cricket, and soccer, foods such as fish and chips, and pastimes like Sunday roasts and afternoon tea. Jack was shocked to discover that Great Britain was so tiny—roughly the size of Virginia—and that London, built on swampy ground and not on bedrock like New York, had no skyscrapers.

More shocking yet was what Jack saw on London's streets. Ravaged by German bombing runs, the British capital was colorless and cold for lack of electricity and fuel. Homes and businesses lay in ruins. Trees were splayed at their trunks, torn apart at their roots. Children played atop mountains of rubble and crawled through bomb craters in search of shrapnel souvenirs. The scent of bomb soot, sawdust, and cordite hung in the air.

"I only wish you could've seen London before the bombs tore it to pieces," Kate lamented. "It was all quite beautiful, really." Then she added, haltingly, "Its women were beautiful then, too."

"They still are," Jack said.

And he meant it. With all his heart.

Kate lowered her eyes, saddened by how overwrought she'd become, embarrassed by the unbecoming, masculine clothing she'd been forced to wear:

long, boxy skirts; drab, colorless blouses; overcoats fashioned from tattered woolen blankets.

"The war has taken its toll," said Kate, her eyes glistening. "It's worn us down, extinguished the light that once shone inside of us."

"You'd never know it," said Jack, "from the way you look."

And he meant that, too. To Jack, Kate was beautiful in every way: her eyes bright and eager; her voice gentle and soothing; her heart generous and giving. And her spirit: so indomitable. So hopeful. So resilient.

So British.

Sixty thousand Brits had perished in German bombing raids, large swaths of London decimated and starved of rations and fuel. You'd never have known it, though, from the way most Londoners went about their lives: refusing to be defeated even in the face of relentless enemy assaults. Jack admired the British spirit, their fortitude, their grit. He felt a palpable kinship to them, too. The Brits, Jack knew, were far from perfect, stained by shameful acts of conquest and pillage, exploitation and genocide, and other sins of the Anglo-Saxon Empire. But no one could argue that they weren't survivors, or that they weren't resourceful and determined, resilient and tough. They reminded Jack, in that regard, of people back home. Reminded him of New Yorkers.

So did Kate's parents. Martin and Emily Sedgwick, staunchly conservative and deeply religious, were wary of Kate's courtship, reticent about encouraging a union between their only daughter and an American soldier. They'd heard plenty of stories, after all: sordid tales about G.I.s looking to sow their seed in England, preying on young women and leaving them heartbroken or pregnant. Kate's parents were fearful that Jack would disappear as quickly as he'd materialized. Even worse to Martin and Emily Sedgwick was the prospect of their daughter's relationship succeeding. The last thing the two of them wanted was for Kate, still in her teens, to get hitched to a G.I. and run off with him to America. And they let Jack know it, too—in no uncertain terms.

A lanky man with thinning hair and a pencil-thin mustache, Martin was decidedly standoffish at first.

"You know what most Brits say about you Yanks, don't you?" he asked.

"You mean that we're 'overpaid, oversexed—and over here'?" Jack took the bait.

"Overdecorated, overstaffed, and overbearing, too," Kate's father said.

Still Jack played along, aware of the common American retort: that British soldiers were "underpaid, undersexed, and under Eisenhower." He refrained from saying that, however, suggesting instead that he could understand why American G.I.s might be difficult for some Brits to accept.

"But you've got to admit one thing, sir," he told Martin. "It's preferable for us Americans to be in Britain than those goddamned, bloody Nazis!"

Martin roared with laughter. The ice had been broken. And things improved steadily from there.

The medieval heart of Kate's hometown, along with much of its industrial infrastructure, had been demolished by Luftwaffe bombing runs. While the Sedgwick's home had been spared, the impact of the German aerial assault was all too evident. Food supplies throughout Coventry were scarce, electrical power intermittent, water tainted by sediment.

Cognizant of the family's limited rations, Jack refrained from eating his fill at dinner, putting Kate's parents at ease with polite, respectful gestures and gentle, sensitive comments. With meat, butter, eggs, sugar, and other staples unavailable, Kate's mother served a bland combination of boiled potatoes, Brussels sprouts, and a stout, acrid-tasting tea. Jack could sense she was uneasy about the offering, so he went out of his way to compliment both the food and the surroundings, noting that after subsisting for months on K-rations—and living in barracks and pup tents—it felt wonderful to be in a real home, eating real food.

From there he continued to assuage the Sedgwicks' concerns. He spoke of his postwar plans to return to college and get a degree; spoke fondly about the Tommies he had trained alongside; spoke of his respect for the British people, their traditions and resolve, their strength and pride. Emily Sedgwick was won over instantly, Martin soon afterward.

By the time Jack bade them goodnight, Kate's parents felt far less queasy over their daughter's burgeoning romance. Like anyone who ever met Jack, they could sense that he was decent and compassionate, courteous and sincere, and possessed of an inherent goodness. They could sense, too, that he was thoughtful and earnest, and that he'd provide for their daughter. They could also tell from the way Jack looked at Kate—and she at him—that the two of them were, truly, very much in love.

Jack's gifts, even on his meager G.I.'s paycheck, grew more personal and lavish as the months wore on: a cashmere sweater, a pair of high heels, an engraved gold locket. His and Kate's conversations grew deeper and more personal, too. For the first time they could recall, they allowed themselves to give their imaginations free reign, and talk about the things they'd do if they were lucky enough to survive the war: marry, start a new life, relish a world at peace. Wasn't that what they were fighting for, after all? A better, kinder, more tranquil world in which they could raise children free of the obstacles and the challenges they had faced; a world that was laden with promise and hope and an end to the terrible, unrelenting uncertainty; a world in which dreams like theirs could really come true.

In time, if things broke right, they agreed, they'd buy a house of their own, furnish it their way, and plant tulips and azaleas, reminders of London's Royal Parks. They'd never fail to count their blessings either. Seize each day. Always look ahead, never behind. Never squander time, or lament things they didn't have, or take serenity for granted. If only they could make it through the wretched, endless war.

If only they could survive.

Before long, Jack was in the final stages of his D-Day training, soon to be transferred to England's southern coast, where thousands of Allied vessels were assembling to transport troops across the English Channel to begin the liberation of occupied France.

The impending invasion was a closely held secret. All anyone knew was that a massive amphibious landing was being planned; no one knew when it would take place, or where. Briefing instructions and maps had yet to be issued. Code references were being used in lieu of place names. Incoming mail was barred, outgoing letters censored, dummy operations staged as a form of deception.

Kate, too, could sense that an invasion was imminent. For weeks, St. Bart's had been receiving massive shipments of antibiotics, equipment, and medical supplies. Nurses and doctors were arriving in droves. Additional beds were being brought in, non-critical patients evacuated to hospitals outside London, to allow for an anticipated influx of casualties.

The countdown to D-Day—the weeks of separation, uncertainty, rumors, and anxiety—was the most challenging time Jack and Kate would ever experience as a couple. Jack's return to London after the invasion was the most jubilant.

When VE Day was declared, London brimmed with unbridled joy. Ecstatic crowds roamed the streets near Buckingham Palace and Number 10 Downing Street. London Bridge was draped in Union Jacks. Bands played, fireworks exploded, church bells tolled, people danced. A week later, Jack and Kate were married at a hundred-year-old chapel outside London, celebrating at a local pub with a handful of Jack's army buddies and a gaggle of nurses from St. Bart's. Emily Sedgwick hand-sewed Kate's wedding gown from the recycled silk of a former RAF parachute, a keepsake that Martin was only too happy to donate. The couple honeymooned for one night, compliments of Kate's parents, at London's five-star Savoy Hotel.

Then it was time for Jack to go home.

A point system had been developed in which a G.I.'s length of service and combat duty yielded a score that either sent him stateside, dispatched him to the Pacific, or remanded him to Europe as part of the Allied occupation force. Jack, who had accumulated enough points for his discharge, sailed to New York in style, one of thousands of G.I.s on HMS *Queen Elizabeth*, requisitioned as a U.S. Army troopship for the war. Kate joined him two months later.

Congress by then had passed the War Brides Act, easing immigration requirements for women whom American servicemen had married during the war. Tens of thousands of war brides, many of them pregnant or accompanied by children fathered by G.I.s, were pouring into the U.S. from Continental Europe and elsewhere. Kate, sailing from Malta on the SS *Argentina*, was among them— though not before a hellish, ten-day voyage at sea, much of it spent in a canvas bunk stacked five deep in the musty bowels of the converted cargo ship.

The North Atlantic was uncommonly rough that spring, the *Argentina* battered by gale-force winds, treacherous waves, and icy squalls. Many of the five hundred women and children aboard the aging vessel became violently ill. Cabins were transformed into sickbays. Medical supplies ran short. Babies were abandoned, in some cases, by seaworn mothers. Nearly a dozen of the forlorn refugees, succumbing to various ailments, were buried at sea.

When the *Argentina* sailed past Ambrose Tower, the string of lightships that served as the sentinel beacon for New York Harbor, the war brides rushed to the vessel's portside railing, huddling in the face of a nighttime chill to catch a glimpse of the Statue of Liberty, its gold-leaf torch aglow against a star-swept sky.

"America the Beautiful" blared through loudspeakers as the women sang along. And Kate was moved to silent, joyful tears, stirred by both the tangible and the abstract—the magnificence of the harbor and everything that it stood for.

It was a snapshot that Kate would remember always: her first glimpse of America; the moment she realized that her perilous voyage across an ocean of chaos and despair, her harrowing wartime existence in Europe, was finally at an end, and a new life in postwar America—a peaceful, happier existence—was about to begin.

There was so much hope to cling to, so many dreams finally within her reach. Sailing through the quiescent harbor, the city's skyline aglitter, Kate felt a wave of gratitude and joy wash over her. New York Harbor, after all, was so much more than the welcome haven she so desperately sought. It was, in many ways, the entrepôt to an entire new world of aspirations, a tangible symbol of longing, survival, and transformation. Kate was safe here, no longer riddled with doubt and fear. Jack was here, too, somewhere in the spangled city. Finally within reach. Looking forward, as she was, to the start of their life together. Waiting to take her home.

Nudged into port by a trio of tugboats, the *Argentina* made a brief stop at a quarantine station before docking in Manhattan. Ferries and fireboats greeted the ship with whistles and horns and water cannons. Bands played. Reporters and cameramen swarmed aboard to interview and photograph the war brides as they disembarked. Then, escorted by a squadron of MPs, the women were whisked through customs and shuttled to Red Cross headquarters in Manhattan, where hundreds of their husbands waited alongside military brass and politicians. There were speeches, tributes, reunions, celebrations.

When Kate and Jack were finally reunited, the two of them embraced as if they'd never let each other go. And Kate saw something she had never seen before. She saw her intrepid, young husband weep, joy and relief etched upon his face. And any doubt she had harbored over her decision to marry, emigrate to America, and tie her fate to Jack's vanished instantly. They had survived the war. Their love had blossomed amidst Europe's ruins, through uncertainty, anxiety, separation, combat, and a universe of differences—their bond strengthened by sacrifice, commitment, honesty, and faith. There was so much to be thankful for, so much to be excited about, so much to look forward to.

When the welcome ceremony wound to a close, the crowd filed from Red Cross headquarters and spilled onto midtown Manhattan's streets. Ex-servicemen escorted their war brides to homes in New York and the surrounding region. Other women were bused to Penn and Grand Central Stations, before dispersing to cities and towns across America.

Jack hoisted Kate's suitcase, as the couple made their way to a Park Avenue train station. Hordes of pedestrians moved in serpentine waves along sidewalks and streets. A cacophony of car horns, police sirens, and jackhammers pierced the air. Subway trains roared from beneath iron sidewalk grates.

"Trust me," Jack shouted over the hubbub. "It's a lot more peaceful in Brooklyn."

"Then let's go home," Kate said. "Peace and quiet is what I want more than anything now, Jack. Peace and quiet and you."

*　*　*

Working on a tugboat wasn't the easiest job in the world, or the most prestigious, or the highest-paying, Shorty Long told Jack after his first day on the job. But the work, said Shorty, had its upside.

The two of them were standing on *Jupiter*'s foredeck as Dutch Hendrik nudged the tugboat into her Pier 53 slip, the glare of an orange-red sun reflecting off a westside Manhattan skyline that seemed to sit atop the gently undulating water.

"For one thing, it's an honest day's work," Shorty said.

"Nothing wrong with that," said Jack.

"Nothin' better than it either," Shorty said. "'Cept the love of a good woman."

Jack smiled. That, he already knew.

"Bein' aboard *Jupiter*," said Shorty, "you get the feel of the open water. There's somethin' about the salt air in your lungs. Cleans the grime off you, makes you feel alive."

"Nothing wrong with that either," Jack said.

"Gets in your blood . . . that's for sure."

Shorty tossed a towline to the dock and leapt off to tie *Jupiter* to a mooring post.

"You get to see the sun rise in the morning an' set at the end of the day," he said.

"That must be a treat," said Jack. "Like a picture postcard, I'll bet."

"Hell, yeah," said Shorty. "Nothin' like sunrise an' sunset over New York Harbor. Reminds you of how peaceful the world can be. Makes you appreciate just bein' alive . . . that whatever heartaches life may throw at you, there's beauty to it, too."

"Not many jobs," said Jack, "can make a man feel like that."

"Not many things anywhere in life," Shorty said.

And within seconds, *Jupiter* was tied fast to the dock, secure for the night. Dutch Hendrik finished up with his paperwork. Mack Nowak and Luke Huggins shook Jack's hand, as his two new crewmates disembarked.

"See you in the mornin', matey," Nowak chirped.

"Sure thing," Jack said.

Shorty grinned. "Hell, even if this job ain't somethin' you'll be doin' for the rest of your life, who knows? Maybe you'll come to love it same way the rest of us 'hawespipers' do. Maybe it'll get in your blood, too."

Jack warmed to that prospect. Maybe Shorty was right, he thought. Maybe, like his crewmates, he would come to love the tugboat trade. Maybe, he thought, the work would get in his blood, too.

CHAPTER 15

January 31, 1946

Union leaders were trapped now between a rock and a hard place: out of bargaining ploys, out of patience, and nearly out of time. With contract negotiations intractably deadlocked, and a midnight strike deadline looming, the city's tugboat owners had backed Local 88 officials into a corner, whittling their options to two: either accept the owners' token contract offer or collectively endorse a strike.

To union leaders, either choice was onerous. Still, both were carefully considered when Local 88's five-man Strike Committee caucused at a nearby Horn & Hardart, seemingly lightyears from where tugboat owners were convening in Henry's Waldorf-Astoria suite, less than a block away.

The automat, one in a chain popular among working-class New Yorkers, was its usual beehive of activity. A steady stream of patrons entered and exited the eatery through revolving-glass doors that opened to a spacious, Art Deco-style cafeteria in which diners queued up at token dispensers, vending machines, and buffet steamers. Mirrored walls and floor-to-ceiling windows made the restaurant seem several times its size.

Strike Committee members, seeking a modicum of privacy, carried their lunches on plastic trays to a picnic-style table, taking seats amidst a hubbub of jangling cash registers, rattling cutlery, and chatter from other patrons. Benny and Tommy Duggan sat facing one another. Paddy O'Boyle and Butch Flanagan, O'Boyle's top lieutenant in Local 88's parent union, flanked Duggan on either side. Local 88 treasurer Frank Russo settled into a seat at Benny's arm.

"These negotiations are goin' to hell in a handbasket . . . an' the clock keeps tickin'," Russo groused. "It feels like the owners are just darin' us to strike."

"That's exactly what they're doin'," Tommy Duggan said.

"Well, if that's their objective, why even bother negotiatin'?" Russo queried.

"Why come to the bargainin' table when all they're doin' is yankin' our chains?"

"The owners are coverin' their asses—that's why," Duggan replied. "In reality, there's no way they want an amicable, negotiated settlement."

"So, what do they want?"

"Capitulation by our union," Benny declared. "Or a strike."

Russo seemed perplexed. "But why would they want a strike?"

"Simple," Benny said. "So they can paint us out as a gang of reckless, greedy hooligans willin' to bring the city to its knees for our own selfish gain."

"But won't people see the owners that way, too?" Russo asked.

"Why would they?" Duggan said. "We're the ones goin' on strike . . . not them."

"But the owners will bleed money too, if we walk off the job," Russo said.

"They're figurin'," said Benny, "that our union will bleed a whole lot worse." Somberly, the men dug into their lunches.

"What about our strike deadline?" Russo asked. "Any logic in extendin' it?"

Duggan and Benny each grimaced, the two of them in lockstep: disenchanted, disgruntled, and ready to take the tugboat owners to the mat. The other men seemed conflicted, rattled by the gravity of the situation. Paddy O'Boyle, quiet as a church mouse, stared morosely at a corned beef on rye.

"What kind of deadline extension are you talkin' about?" Duggan asked Russo.

"A couple of days." The union treasurer shrugged. "Maybe a week."

"What would be the point?"

"A good-faith gesture, maybe," Russo replied. "Who knows? A deadline extension might send a signal that our union is willin' to go the extra mile, give negotiations every possible chance to succeed. Maybe the owners will see it as an olive branch."

"I say we take an olive branch," said Benny, "an' shove it up Henry McFarland's ass!"

The union reps shared a stilted laugh, fully cognizant that the crisis they faced was far from funny. To a man, none of them embraced the prospect of a strike that could potentially halt paychecks, ravage the union, and have a catastrophic impact on the city. Nor were they willing to accept either the measly wage hike that the owners had proposed or the backroom deal brokered by Henry and Paddy O'Boyle.

"I ain't kiddin," Benny said. "Mr. Big has got me pissed-off enough to wring his neck! For months he's been blowin' smoke up our asses, pretendin' to bargain in good faith. He doesn't have a clue, though, what 'good faith' really means. An' now our backs are against the wall. The owners are callin' our bluff. The only thing an extension of our strike deadline would signal . . . is weakness!"

His comment gave the other men pause. Like Henry with the owners, Benny's viewpoint carried enormous weight, as much a product of his fiery personality as his soaring popularity among the union's rank and file. Even Paddy O'Boyle, ostensibly outranking Benny as president of the parent union, didn't buck the rebellious up-and-comer.

At least not yet.

Benny stole a glance at O'Boyle, wondering whether the union boss's silence signaled a surrender to the power shift underway within the union, or if the wily old codger was mulling his own way of ending the standoff—some clever, last-ditch ploy he could pull from his bag of tricks. Indeed, the latter was precisely what O'Boyle was doing—though he wasn't quite ready to show his cards just yet.

"You're probably right about a deadline extension signalin' weakness," Frank Russo conceded. "But if we offer to postpone our strike an' the owners agree, it might buy us time for a breakthrough in negotiations."

"Ain't eight months enough time?" Benny said. "That's how long we've been tryin' to reason with those greedy bastards."

Benny scowled, his balding pate gleaming in the glare of overhead pendant lights. Patrons at nearby tables were eating, chatting, reading newspapers, oblivious to what was being discussed and the impact it would doubtless have on their lives.

"An' talkin' about our strike deadline?" Benny said. "The owners still haven't taken it seriously enough to budge off their single lowball offer. They're just darin' us to strike."

"Benny's right," Tommy Duggan asserted. "The only way to avoid a strike now is to convince the owners that we're not bluffin' . . . that we're willin' to do whatever it takes to get a deal done—even that means walkin' off the job."

"You think they believe that now?" Russo asked.

"Hell, no." Benny sniggered. "I think Henry McFarland sees us as a bunch of gutless buffoons, an' if he pushes us to the brink, our union will come apart at the seams."

"An' the other owners?"

"They're nothin' more than sheep. They'll follow wherever their 'shepherd' leads them. An' now he's leadin' 'em to call our bluff an' force a strike."

Benny's comment sparked a long, troubled silence.

"I stand with Benny!" Tommy Duggan finally said. "There's no reason to extend our strike deadline. We've played by the rules, given collective bargaining eight months to pay dividends. But nothin' has worked. The owners have essentially put one offer on the table, and told us to take it or leave it. If they were gonna up the offer, they would have done it by now. Instead, all we've got from those cheapskates is ungatz!"

The other men drew silent.

"Let's face it," Benny said. "Despite his bullshit, Henry McFarland has never wanted an amicable settlement of our differences. So he cajoled the owners to throw us a bone an' then told us if we don't like the offer to go shit in our hats."

"I agree," Duggan asserted. "The two-percent pay hike they threw on the table is simply a ploy that's givin' McFarland a chance to scuttle the negotiations. The owners are just throwin' marbles under our feet ... darin' us to accept a bullshit deal."

"Or," said Benny, "to show 'em our fuckin' mettle!"

He crashed a fist onto the table, rattling the cutlery and plates.

"There's only one way to deal with schoolyard bullies like Henry McFarland," Benny said, "an' that's to kick 'em in the teeth. Our union is in a street fight now! No holds barred!"

Benny let his words sink in.

"The owners claim they're cash-poor, but that's a crock of shit," he said. "Trust me—their corporate ledgers are bloated enough to grant us the raise we're seekin'. They're just too tightfisted to ante up. I say we show 'em that we're unified, an' that our strike threat is real! I say we show 'em how workin' people in America feel these days . . . the bitterness an' frustration that are eating men like us alive!"

*   *   *

Benny's comments hit a raw nerve with Local 88's Strike Committee. They also mirrored the sentiments being aired at union halls, jobsites, and contract-bargaining tables across America. Indeed, World War II had cost American workers four-plus years of sacrifice, uncertainty, and sweat. New York's tugboatmen were no exception, having gone without a pay hike since the outset of the war.

But there was more to tugboat workers' angst than merely their frustration over government price controls, wage freezes, and no-strike pledges. Something deeply troubling was weighing on the men: a rapidly encroaching fear.

It was hardly a secret by now that New York was molting rapidly in the aftermath of World War II, shedding old layers of skin to make way for an entirely new kind of city. Rising taxes, antiquated facilities, and skyrocketing costs for labor, utilities, and land were forcing companies to shutter their operations, lay off workers, or flee for greener pastures in the suburbs or other states. Middle-class whites, all the while, were abandoning the city in droves as waves of minorities flooded in. An entire new economy was also taking hold, as New York evolved from a manufacturing and wholesaling hub into an international center for finance and other white-collar services. Equally jarring to tugboat workers was how the city's waterfront was evincing the early signs of a stagnant, dying port: outdated docks abandoned and rotting from neglect; longshoremen fretting over anticipated pink slips, tugboat firms mulling a move to more-favorable East Coast ports.

Clearly, the handwriting was on the wall: New York's role as the world's preeminent port would inevitably dissipate in the not-too-distant future. Break bulk cargo would be transported in massive containerships to ports that offered better rail connections and cheaper labor. Commercial airlines would seize the business handled now by passenger ships. Coastal trade would shift from tugboat and barge to railroad and truck.

And that was merely the tip of the iceberg. As cargo ships continued to grow in size and navigation capabilities, fewer tugboats would eventually be needed to help dock the same amount of freight. With natural gas arriving in the city by pipeline, and electricity flowing across power lines, coal would also diminish in importance. All the while, new bridges, tunnels, and roads would enable products to be delivered by truck rather than over water, further reducing the city's reliance on tugboats.

Benny had been cognizant of this budding metamorphosis for several years—sensing, astutely, that all of it was destined to impact the city's tugboat workers dramatically, perhaps threaten their very existence. He recognized the ground shifting beneath the union's feet. With the inevitable demise of the port, he presaged, Local 88's impact would surely diminish. In many ways, the clock was already ticking. The union had to seize whatever contractual gains it could now—before tugboat workers lost their bargaining power, rusted in place, or abandoned the city entirely. Before it was too late.

A work stoppage, Benny reasoned, could well be Local 88's last best hope for survival. Capitulating at the bargaining table, in contrast, would allow tugboat owners to dictate workers' fate—or, worse, force the union's demise. On the flip side, a substantive new contract could carry the union into the foreseeable future, and assure its relevance for even longer.

"These negotiations ain't about just a coupla extra bucks in our paychecks," Benny told the union reps. "We're fightin' for our lives now. Everything's on the line for our union. Everything!"

"Benny's right," Tommy Duggan said. "We're talkin' survival. The tugboat owners will destroy our union if we let 'em . . . stonewall everything organized labor is tryin' to achieve in America."

"Who would have thought it?" Benny said. "We just spent four years fightin' the Krauts an' Nips halfway 'round the world, only to discover that our real enemy—the companies we spill our guts for—are right here in America, waging war against their workers."

The union reps again drew quiet and pensive.

"It's been twenty years of takin' it on the chin," Benny said. "First the Depression an' then the war. Nothin' but scrimpin' an' savin', makin' ends meet or doin' without. I'm sick an' tired of it! It's time for us to collect the fruits of our labor, the sacrifices we've made . . . time for us to put the kibosh on the owners' endgame."

"Their endgame?" Frank Russo asked. "What's that?"

"Like I said!" Benny barked. "The owners are out to bust our union!"

He continued, "To Henry McFarland, these contract negotiations are nothin' less than a personal vendetta. That angry bastard is hellbent on stickin' a dagger in our hearts. He sees the negotiations as his one big chance to make an example of our union, punish organized labor for its supposed sins."

"Benny's right," Tommy Duggan said. "To businessmen like McFarland, unions have gotten too big, too powerful. McFarland is determined to regain leverage, unionize in his own way, with his Gotham Harbor Alliance—and, if necessary, destroy our union in the process."

"I'm sure it'd save the tugboat owners a shitload of money if our union went kaput," Russo conceded. "A shitload of headaches, too."

"Their only problem," said Benny, "is that we ain't goin' nowhere!"

He eyeballed the other men. "Don't you guys see it? If we cave in now, our union will be neutered. The owners'll see us as a bunch of gutless limp-dicks. They'll shit all over us in future negotiations, ram labor contracts down our throat!"

"That's why we gotta put the hammer down now!" Duggan asserted. "No one's givin' us a goddamned thing. If we want somethin' bad enough, we gotta take it . . . by walkin' off the job at midnight, just like we've threatened!"

Again, an ominous pall fell over the conversation. Paddy O'Boyle sat head down, jaw clenched. He'd yet to utter a peep.

"How much pressure can we bring to bear if we strike?" Russo inquired.

"Enough to shut down the harbor," Duggan replied. "Cutting off fuel an' food shipments in the dead of winter should get people's attention."

"You think other unions will honor our picket lines, or stage sympathy strikes?" Russo asked.

"That remains to be seen," O'Boyle's sidekick Butch Flanagan cautioned. "You never know what other unions might do when their asses are on the line."

Benny felt his anger spike. He knew that O'Boyle was behind Flanagan's noncommittal response, using his personal stooge as a mouthpiece to push an anti-strike agenda.

"Then fuck other unions!" Benny declared. "If we've got to, we'll go to war alone!"

Again, the men fell into a long, troubled silence.

"What you're sayin' is well an' good, Benny," Frank Russo finally said. "But a vote to strike can't be taken lightly. We're talkin' about men's livelihoods here!"

"No one's takin' any of this lightly," Tommy Duggan said. "We're all aware that a strike will be tough on our members an' their families, not to mention the public."

More silence. More thought. And still not a peep from O'Boyle.

"Where do things stand with our war chest?" Duggan asked Russo.

"We're sittin' just north of twenty-two grand," the union treasurer replied.

Both the question and its answer were critical. For months in anticipation of a potential strike, Local 88 had been accumulating an emergency strike fund, assessing payments of a quarter of members' hourly wage, on top of their regular monthly dues—a move aimed not only aimed at protecting workers in the event of a work stoppage, but at boosting leverage at the bargaining table by sending tugboat owners a message that the union had the financial wherewithal to weather a strike.

"How much time will twenty-two grand buy us?" Duggan inquired.

"Not a lot," Russo replied, glumly.

The union treasurer informed the committee members that, in the event of a strike, tugboat workers would receive a single payout of three times their regular monthly dues—or roughly thirty dollars—regardless of the duration of the strike. Most of the workers normally earned three to four times that amount per week. Clearly, there'd be a serious financial hardship resulting from a potential strike.

"After a coupla days," Russo said, "our men'll be suckin' wind."

"An' there's no tellin' how long a strike might last," Butch Flanagan warned.

Another long and troubled pause ensued before Russo finally said, "The reality is, any strike we stage can't go on for very long. Our men can't sustain it. Neither can the city. If both sides can't settle quickly, City Hall, or even the Feds, could impose a settlement of their own."

"The tugboat owners," said Flanagan, "could also seek an injunction blockin' any strike."

"I don't think they'll go that route, at least not right away," Benny surmised. "More likely, they'll try to squeeze our nuts . . . let us feel the sting of lost paychecks."

"An' the politicians?"

"My guess is that they'll sit on their hands, at least for the short-term . . . pressure both sides to resolve our differences on our own."

"Why would they do that," Russo asked, "if there's so much at stake?"

"'Cause," said Duggan, "they can't afford to take sides."

Benny nodded. "The politicians have gotta straddle the fence in the event of a strike. They won't wanna piss off organized labor by comin' down hard on our union. There's a lotta workin' people in New York, you know . . . a lotta votes."

"Benny's right," Duggan said. "The politicians won't wanna piss off the city's business interests either, by comin' down on the tugboat owners—not with the ties City Hall has to local corporations."

"Exactly," Benny said. "They've got no choice but to remain neutral, at least for the short term. They won't win popularity contests by takin' sides, or forcin' a settlement."

"They may have second thoughts, though . . . when they see the carnage a tugboat strike wreaks on the city," Butch Flanagan warned.

"Maybe . . . but by then everyone will have had enough," Benny said. "The owners will be as anxious as we will to settle the damn thing."

Butch Flanagan glanced sideways at Paddy O'Boyle, who nodded subtly, as if granting his surrogate a license to speak.

"What about strikebreakers?" Flanagan said. "What if the tugboat owners call in scabs?"

"Companies don't pull that shit anymore," Duggan scoffed. "It's like throwin' gas on a fire."

"I wouldn't put it past Henry McFarland, though," Flanagan said. "That scumbag might try anything to break our strike."

Again Russo was the first to break the men's somber silence. "Who could he bring in?"

"Head-knockers," Flanagan said. "Pinkertons maybe."

"Nah." Russo shook his head. "Pinkertons ain't in the strikebreakin' racket anymore. They gave that up years ago, in the coal mines an' steel mills."

"How 'bout the Bergoffs?" asked Flanagan, referencing brothers Pearl and Leo Bergoff, whose infamous Bergoff Service Bureau had called on local street gangs to thwart several strikes in New York.

"The Bergoffs are outta the strikebreakin' business," Russo replied. "Both of 'em are rottin' in jail."

"An' Boss James Farley?" Flanagan said. "King of the Strikebreakers?"

"Farley kicked the bucket years ago."

"Well," Flanagan said, "there's always coons. Fuckin' niggers will do anything to cop a paycheck."

Abhorrent as his comments were, Flanagan had a point. Black workers, barred from entry to many American industries, had been employed as strikebreakers in prior labor disputes, although they were generally fired the instant the strikes were settled.

"My point," said Flanagan, "is that the owners could call in just about anyone to try an' break our strike. Plenty of men are scroungin' around for a paycheck these days."

"Maybe so," Duggan said. "But even if the owners were ballsy enough to summon scabs, they can't just bring in anyone off the street. Tugboat work in New York requires special skills."

"So maybe they'll call in pros, out-of-work tugboatmen," Flanagan said.

"Then we'll call in scab-hunters," Benny said, "an' we'll run the bastards out of town!"

The men grew somber, the specter of violence exacerbating their sense of dread over the impact a strike would doubtless have. It was only then that Paddy O'Boyle made his play.

"I still believe there's a way outta this," the USA president said. "I still believe we can get the contract we've been lookin' for . . . an' avoid a strike."

"What makes you think that?" asked Benny, barely disguising his disgust.

Benny wasn't sure who he hated more: Henry McFarland or Paddy O'Boyle—the wolf everyone was aware of, or the one in sheep's clothing. Didn't matter. To Benny, both men were repugnant, adversaries he hungered to quash.

"I've negotiated contracts with the owners before," O'Boyle said. "They ain't as tough to deal with as we're makin' 'em out to be."

Benny scowled. "They ain't?"

"No," said O'Boyle. "An' I think I've demonstrated the kind of deals I can negotiate."

"Yeah?" Benny scoffed. "An' what happened to the last deal you brought to the men, Paddy . . . the contract you negotiated privately with Henry McFarland?"

"I still think that deal was solid," O'Boyle said.

"An' our men," said Benny, "thought it was horseshit!"

Benny was busting at the seams to lay into O'Boyle. And the time for that, he reckoned, would come soon enough. The tugboat dispute, it was clear, was no longer simply a case of workers versus management. A battle was heating up inside the union, too. Union officials, until now, had managed a unified front, masking the discord threatening to fracture the rank and file. But that wasn't going to last much longer. Paddy O'Boyle's demise as the union's chief power broker would come. Benny would see to that personally. And soon.

But now the longtime union boss issued one final plea.

"Lemme try talkin' again to Henry McFarland," O'Boyle proposed.

"An' what would that accomplish?" Tommy Duggan asked.

"McFarland an' me speak the same language," O'Boyle replied. "We've worked together before. There's a mutual trust."

"Is that what your relationship with McFarland is all about, Paddy?" Benny snidely asked. "'Talkin' the same language'? 'Mutual trust'?"

"That's the gist of it."

"Nothin' more?"

O'Boyle had his back up now, face flushed, swollen as an overripe melon.

"What are ya tryin' to say, Logan?"

"I think we're all aware that there's more to your dealings with Henry McFarland than simply a matter of trust," Benny said.

"Prove it!"

"Whatever the case, Paddy," Tommy Duggan said. "Do you really believe you can work somethin' out on your own that we can't as a committee?"

"I think it's worth a try."

O'Boyle scanned the other committee members, searching for support. Only Butch Flanagan nodded affirmatively. The other men sat stone-faced and non-committal.

"Let's face it," O'Boyle said, "a lotta money is at stake for the owners if we walk off the job. I can deliver that message . . . an' might be able to get them to offer somethin' our members can feel better about."

"An' what are you gonna offer in return, Paddy?" Benny asked. "Another no-strike pledge? Some other giveback provision that will blindside our men?"

"Nothin' like that."

Benny smiled wryly. "So, let me get this straight, Paddy: Henry McFarland will hike his wage offer to us just 'cause he's done business with you in the past ... an' trusts you?"

O'Boyle opened his mouth to reply. But before he could utter a sound, Benny shot Tommy Duggan a skeptical glance and the pair, in unison, shook their heads.

"Thanks, Paddy," Benny said. "But we're done with backroom horseshit like that!"

O'Boyle slumped in his chair. And just like that, the balance of power within Local 88 had shifted—not formally, but substantively enough to matter. Paddy O'Boyle was still USA president and Local 88's chief negotiator. But he was no longer calling the shots.

"We'd appreciate whatever support our parent union can offer if we strike," said Benny. "But the past is dead. We're conductin' business differently from now on."

Benny's message was definitive: Unless some miraculous breakthrough occurred when the union reps and tugboat owners reconvened at 3 o'clock, a strike was a virtual lock. The only questions were whether it would be USA-sanctioned or led by Benny and other militants; whether it would involve Local 88's entire rank and file or be a wildcat; and whether it would be a unified act of protest or something akin to an insurrection.

Either way, a labor conflagration was brewing, unlike any the city had ever witnessed. It was simply a matter of how long the tempest would rage, and how much damage it would wreak.

CHAPTER 16

September 18, 1945

By summer's end, he was fully settled in. Three months after landing his deckhand job, Jack had navigated the tugboat trade's ineluctable learning curve, bonded with crewmates, and discovered a peaceful, heartening oasis during his mornings on New York Harbor.

Not that the job was free of challenges. Despite whatever contractual victories tugboat workers might have won in past years, the work itself remained taxing and, at times, perilous. *Jupiter*'s crew labored virtually nonstop across nine-plus-hour workdays, pausing only between an endless string of towing assignments and for thirty-minute lunch breaks, usually taken in the vessel's galley kitchen.

As on other tugboats, each crewman aboard *Jupiter* was tasked with a specific job. Dutch Hendrik, as *Jupiter*'s captain, had full authority over the vessel's crew, as well as responsibility for the tugboat's safe and efficient operation. Mack Nowak, second in command, oversaw deck operations, including upkeep of towing hooks and other equipment. Luke Huggins was responsible for operating and maintaining *Jupiter*'s engine and generator, along with its electrical, hydraulic, fuel, and heating systems. Shorty Long handled deck chores. Jack did much the same.

Deckhands, Jack learned soon enough, needed to be proficient in the use of shackles, chains, winches, and other equipment. They had to be equally adept at tossing and tying towlines to mooring posts and bitts on docks and towed vessels. They also had to be capable of leaping from tugboats to barges—and from barge to barge—to secure the vessels in lengthy flotillas. Most importantly, they needed to be able to handle hawsers, the long, thick ropes used for towing.

Mastering those tasks, Jack discovered, required a specialized set of skills. Leaping from *Jupiter* to vessels in tow, often in darkness or choppy water, required balance, timing, and agility. Pulling hawsers required considerable strength. Tossing towlines demanded intense concentration, since the lines had to hit their mark on a single toss, shackles secured or freed at just the right instant. Proficiency in those tasks meant time saved; time saved meant money earned. It also meant that crewmen didn't get hurt, though that was always a distinct possibility.

As if the work wasn't demanding enough, conditions made it tougher yet. Tugboat crews labored year-round in all kinds of weather, including rain, fog, gusty winds, and searing heat. Conditions were also fast-changing. Powerful squalls could sweep across the harbor at a moment's notice, with sudden movements and slippery decks resulting in nasty spills or crewmen being tossed overboard. The improper handling of towlines, winches, and other equipment could also result in debilitating injuries.

New York Harbor was also nowhere near as pristine as it might have appeared from a distance. Canals and creeks reeked of raw sewage, rancid trash, chemical spills, and sludge. Dead fish, animal carcasses, even human remains—the victims of accidents, suicide, and foul play—bobbed on the water's surface. Some waterways were so clogged with toxic chemicals that they blistered the paint on *Jupiter*'s hull.

None of those obstacles deterred the crew, however. Nor did they deter Jack, who learned to cope with the job's challenges the same way he learned its tasks: through observation, repetition, and the guiding hand of crewmates.

Especially Shorty.

Shorty showed Jack how to slather petrolatum ointment on his face to protect it from the wind, and how to smear bootblack under his eyes to cut the glare of sunlight; taught Jack how to toss docking and towing lines lasso-style, so they'd hit their mark unerringly, and how to tie bowlines, figure-eights, and other nautical knots. He taught Jack how to time his leaps from tugboat to barge, how to climb steep ladders on the flanks of passenger and cargo ships, and how to secure *Jupiter*'s hawser in a figure-eight wrap around the horns of the tugboat's H-bitt and stream the pile of thick nylon rope, using a stopper to hold it fast before slowly letting it out. He also taught Jack how hawsers had to be "faked down" after use—carefully packed layer upon layer so that they'd roll off the pile without tying themselves into knots, or unfurling in a dangerous whipping motion.

Jupiter's skipper had an equally important skillset to teach.

A fixture in New York tugboat circles, Stephan "Dutch" Hendrik had mastered his special line of work across a decade-plus as *Jupiter's* captain. At age forty-eight, he was an expert helmsman, known as much for his steely nerves as his expertise in navigation, towing, and seamanship—all of which were critical to his job.

Lying at the confluence of the Atlantic Ocean, Hudson River, and Long Island Sound, New York Harbor was ground zero for the Port of New York, whose system of navigational channels spanned hundreds of miles along the waterfronts of New York and New Jersey. With a double-sea entrance—north through Long Island Sound and south through Sandy Hook—the port was as complex as it was unique. Rivers and streams were interwoven with tidal fingers, canals, channels, inlets, and creeks. Dozens of beaches and port facilities dotted the region. The city itself was an archipelago, a cluster of islands impacted by the twice-daily sweep of ocean tides.

While most New Yorkers were familiar with the city through their interactions with landmarks such as streets and shops, Dutch Hendrik knew New York's labyrinth of waterways like the back of his hand. He knew the harbor's diverse topography, its underwater shape and depth, and the contours of land that bounded it. He knew the location of navigational buoys, islands, and coves that served as steering points; knew where shoreline bends created calm water, how bridges and tunnels could render radio transmissions indecipherable, and where potential hazards like reefs, shoals, and decaying wharves lay hidden beneath the surface.

Hendrik also understood the science of the harbor, a living, breathing entity with daily and seasonal rhythms and cycles. Always moving. Always changing. Always affecting how and when *Jupiter* worked.

Hendrik knew that the commingling of freshwater and saltwater created estuaries, oscillating waterways that flooded as the ocean pushed in and ebbed as the water withdrew. He knew how the harbor behaved at high and low tide, at flood and ebb currents, at various times of the day, and in all types of weather. He knew that tugboats worked to a large degree at the will of the water, captive to currents, tides, and seasonal conditions. He also understood that his goal was to captain *Jupiter* in fair currents and favorable weather, letting nature do much of the work.

Working in concert with dispatchers, tide tables, and nautical charts, Hendrik knew precisely when the tide would turn against *Jupiter*. He knew when wind and current could result in choppy water or abnormal wave heights; knew that the difference between low- and high-tide water levels could be as much as six feet; knew that by timing *Jupiter*'s movement in relation to favorable conditions he could shorten the tugboat's passage between locations; knew that even a gentle breeze could cause a towed barge or ship to overrun its course.

Hendrik was also cognizant of how *Jupiter* was captive to the immutable laws of physics; knew how to employ throttle, rudder, and various gears when currents or tidal surges sent the tugboat sheering to port or forced her sideways toward dangerous shoals; knew how to take advantage of the wind and midchannel currents by allowing them to bring *Jupiter* into favorable positions and maneuver in a way that kept the tugboat and its thow aligned. He also knew the best "hold points," places he could pause to allow *Jupiter* and its tow the time they needed to clear big turns or tight spots.

This storehouse of knowledge paid daily dividends. Operating a tugboat within the confines of New York Harbor—with its narrow channels, craggy shorelines, and shifting currents—was immensely challenging. Vigilance was critical. Dozens of vessels had to be accounted for at all times. Accidents could be costly, even disastrous. Ships could be damaged or lost, hazardous cargo spilled, tugboats run aground or collide with sea walls, docks, and other vessels. If *Jupiter* so much as nicked a propeller, McFarland Marine Towing was looking at thousands of dollars in repairs, not to mention time that was lost in dry dock.

Jack recognized, early on, that *Jupiter*'s operation was a product not simply of expertise, but of highly choreographed teamwork. Each crewman was indispensable; each augmented the other. Dutch Hendrik relied on Luke Huggins to obey throttle-and-rudder commands, relayed from wheelhouse to engine room by a bell-and-gong system. Shorty and Jack relied on Dutch to keep the tugboat properly oriented, while maintaining towlines at proper tensions. Each crewman relied on Mack Nowak to offer expert loudspeaker commands, communicated in a special form of verbal shorthand:

"Come ahead slow!"

"Come ahead full!"

"Easy back!"

"Hard away!"

Shorty and Jack, in a similar manner, were also relied upon to perform their jobs with the utmost expertise: communicating via hand signals; paying attention to tow speed and maneuvers; knowing when to heave or slack off so that towlines wouldn't snap or become tangled in the tug's propeller.

Working a tugboat in New York Harbor, Jack discovered, was a daily test of skills that took years to hone. It wasn't a job you learned by reading a textbook, or qualified for by passing an exam. Instead, you worked the harbor day in and day out; cutting your teeth in daylight, darkness, and all kinds of conditions; following the lead of men who knew the job inside out; admitting to mistakes and correcting them; respecting the job the same way you respected the water.

And Jack did all those things. He learned, soon enough, that water was New York's raison d'être—that, more than any other physical entity, water defined America's preeminent city, bordered it, nourished it, impacted every aspect of its economic and social life. Without its harbor, Jack learned, New York would be just another city. Without its waterways, it would lack the arteries that carried its lifeblood. Without its port, it would likely be nothing at all.

Jack appreciated how *Jupiter's* crew went about their daily tasks: the way they functioned as a cohesive unit, making split-second, problem-solving decisions, often by nothing more than instinct. Dutch Hendrik commanded instant respect. Luke Huggins was a master mechanic, adept at operating everything from towing equipment to bilge pumps. Jack, like the rest of the crew, was awed by Big Mack Nowak, a gentle giant with arms the size of tree trunks. He was especially fond of Shorty Long, with his happy-go-lucky spirit, ineffable smile, cauliflower ears, and penchant for whistling while he worked.

Jupiter's crew was equally fond of Jack. All were veteran tugboat workers, years older than Jack, married with children. All had cut short their formal schooling, forced by circumstance to abandon loftier goals. Jack was the only one educated beyond high school, the only one who'd fought in the war, the only one who wasn't a lifelong tugboatman.

None of that mattered, though.

Jack's crewmates recognized that he was merely a transient, his departure from the tugboat trade tied to college graduation. They embraced him, however, not simply for the hardships and dangers he had faced in the war—the missions he'd undertaken and the sacrifices he'd made—but because he reported to work each day on time, ready and willing to pull his weight; because he listened, learned, and respected the job; and because he tackled his duties without alibi or complaint, doing whatever was required, and never slacking off.

Jack's time in the Army had matured him, taught him discipline, the value of teamwork, and how to handle pressure—all of which came in handy on the job. But even more than his willingness to shoulder his responsibilities, his crewmates embraced him because he shared their commonly held values of civility, accountability, self-sacrifice, and hard work; never boasted about his wartime exploits; and always downplayed his ties to Benny, never once mentioning how he'd gotten his job.

His crewmates were also fond of Jack because, like each of them, he loved *Jupiter* and viewed the tugboat through a common lens: as a steady, reliable workhorse that performed its job day in and day out—routinely, and often valiantly—far from the spotlight cast on finance, entertainment, fashion, and other New York glamour industries.

Jack viewed *Jupiter*'s crew in much the same way: not as unskilled, greedy, indolent malcontents, but as honest, skilled, and prideful men who wanted to be rewarded for the critical role they played in the life of the city. Their impact, like those of other blue-collar workmen, would go largely unnoticed; they'd never achieve notoriety, or accumulate wealth, or amount to anything more than common working stiffs. Like others of that ilk, they'd work as hard as they could, eke out a living, provide for their loved ones, and leave whatever mark they were capable of before retiring and fading into obscurity.

But what else was there? What more could men like them aspire to?

Sure, they wanted a bigger paycheck—but who didn't? Everyone who held a job had their hand out, in one way or another. The fact that tugboat workers wanted a long-awaited, well-deserved pay hike didn't make them greedy—it only made them human. Jack could appreciate that the same way he appreciated how his crewmates went about their jobs, the teamwork and expertise they exhibited, the special bond they shared.

The tugboat industry, like similar blue-collar trades, was insular, its ranks populated by fathers and sons, brothers and uncles, cousins and in-laws who followed one another into the work. Some men had been linked to tugboats for decades, passing their knowledge and passion for the work from one generation to the next. For many, tugboats were in their blood, a source of tradition and pride that created a unique esprit de corps, a palpable bond between men who spoke the same language, faced the same challenges, experienced the same emotions, and worked a job that not only gave them a sense of purpose but, in many ways, defined who they were.

Three months into the job, Jack had become one of them. As Shorty had predicted, he was a bona fide hawsepiper, a tried-and-true tugboatman.

And that was more than enough. Jack had no intention of forging a lengthy career in the tugboat trade; being a crewman on a vessel like *Jupiter* would never be his life's work. But for now, the job was helping Kate and him find their footing and make ends meet as they adjusted to postwar life.

Sweeter yet was the fact that Jack had come to truly love the job. Three months in, he thoroughly grasped the appeal that tugboat work could have, the affinity that crewmen could have for a vessel like *Jupiter*, and the special brotherhood they shared. He liked the raw physicality of the work, the feeling of being out on the open water, the way the job put him at the epicenter of commerce in New York and made him feel he was doing something productive, a meaningful cog in the working-class army that helped the city function. He also liked the fact that, three months into the job, he was in the best shape of his life, his movements nimble and fluid, his body supple and tanned.

Kate liked it, too.

The job had simpler rewards, as well: bananas tossed to *Jupiter's* crew by seamen aboard a Honduran fruit boat; vodka and caviar proffered by sailors aboard a Russian freighter; the way *Jupiter* ended some days by towing the *Lloyd I. Seaman* around the Statue of Liberty, hordes of sick children waving from the deck of the floating hospital ship. Then there were the mornings: unspeakably beautiful; brimming with reminders of life's simple joys, the possibilities of a world at peace, and better things yet to come.

Tugboat work, though taxing, also had its pleasant, unfettered moments. *Jupiter's* crewmates enjoyed a breezy rapport, a lighthearted camaraderie founded on a commonality of backgrounds and interests, every bit a band of brothers with *Jupiter* bonding them, giving them purpose, bringing out the best in them. The men shared stories, traded jokes, listened to ballgames on

Shorty's handheld radio, and bantered endlessly about how hopes ran high for New York's baseball teams now that their star players had returned from the war. Each man was also tendered a nickname, a common blue-collar token of affection. There was Shorty, of course, and Dutch, and Big Mack Nowak, also known as "Moose." Luke Huggins, slight of build, was nicknamed "Slim." Jack's moniker, a nod to his collegiate ties, was "Professor"—or "Prof" for short.

All of them had fun with that. Fun in other ways, too.

Sometimes, as a reward for a hard day's work, the men would toss a metal cage off *Jupiter*'s side and haul in swarms of lobsters that they would boil, slather with butter, and wolf down on the foredeck—bare-chested, sweat drying on their skin, spirits soaring with the lift of the tugboat on the harbor's swells. Hands down, those would be the most memorable meals Jack would ever have, some of the most memorable moments too: the sky boundless and blue; the water rainbowlike in the glare of the setting sun; the city skyline coming into focus as *Jupiter* plowed through the harbor, exuding enterprise, confidence, and pride.

Other than the joyous VE Day celebrations he'd experienced in London, the private moments he spent with Kate, and his boyhood forays with Benny and Gabriel, Jack would remember those moments on *Jupiter*—remember them always—as the very best of times. Three months into the job, there was but a single cloud shrouding the horizon. The tugboat workers' labor contract had expired the previous June, and with negotiations on a new deal deadlocked, concern was heightening by the day. Already, rumblings about a potential strike were making the rounds, ominous as an approaching squall.

"Whaddaya make of the contract snafu?" Shorty asked one day over a couple of beers.

Jack shook his head. "I honestly can't say."

"Well, I figured you might have a window into the negotiations," Shorty said. "You know . . . with your brother in the middle of it."

"We haven't discussed it," Jack said. And, in fact, he had seen Benny only once since he'd begun work. The brothers had been far too busy even to speak.

"Well, things look dicey, what with our last contract kaput an' no new deal in the works," Shorty said.

"I wouldn't be worried about it," Jack assured him. "You know how collective bargaining works: gamesmanship; each side testing the other. Negotiations could take a positive turn at any moment."

Shorty darkened. "But what if there is a strike?"

"I haven't thought that far ahead," Jack said.

"Bet you didn't sign up to get your nuts twisted like that—did ya?"

"Uh-uh."

"Me either," said Shorty. "I can't afford to miss even a day's pay."

"Tell me about it," Jack said. "Kate and I are living with my parents. Our savings account is nothing to speak of. A baby is on the way, too."

"That'll cost you a pretty penny."

"It'll also mean one less paycheck for us."

"Dunno how I could get by . . . bein' out of work for even a few days," Shorty lamented.

"It'd sure be tough," Jack said.

"Well." Shorty brightened. "Let's just hope the two sides find a way to work things out."

"Amen to that," Jack said. "Life these days is going just the way I'd hoped. The last thing I want now is for a strike to come along and muck the whole thing up."

CHAPTER 17

January 31, 1946

There was another subject weighing on Henry now, a matter of equal importance to anything he'd attended to that day.

Finished with his lunchtime caucus, and with time to kill before resumption of negotiations, Henry departed the Waldorf-Astoria under the pretense of urgent business, and had Billy Murdock drive him downtown to his office. The report he'd been awaiting, delivered minutes earlier by special courier, was sitting atop Elena Karas's desk, enclosed in a brown manila envelope marked STRICTLY CONFIDENTIAL.

"Otto Blackburn's report," Miss Karas said, smiling.

She handed the envelope to Henry, knowing he'd be pleased.

He was.

"Did you hear from Mr. Blackburn?" he inquired.

"The courier said he'll call at 2 p.m.," Miss Karas replied.

Smiling, Henry ducked into his office, closing the door behind him.

Two typewritten pages in length, the report in Henry's hands had been prepared by Otto Blackburn, CEO of Asset Protection Corp.—a company, as its name implied, that supplied indemnity, security, and risk-management services to businesses across America. Its insurance arm covered roughly half of Henry's tugboats. Forty of its employees worked as sentries at the McFarland docks.

Those services, however, were merely fronts. In truth, Otto Blackburn's firm provided far more than what it purported to. The labor-relations consultancy was also in the business of assuring "employee productivity" and "workplace harmony"—euphemisms for services that Henry valued highly. Beneath its benign façade, Asset Protection Corp. was a leading procurer of industrial detectives, agents-provocateurs, informants, and other anti-labor personnel. In more common parlance, union busters.

The practice was hardly an alien concept to Henry. To the contrary, the Gotham Harbor Alliance chairman viewed it as something akin to a business imperative, one that ran like a DNA strand through his corporate bloodlines. America's business climate, however, was far different now than when Henry's forebears ran the firm. Federal and state legislation expressly banned the anti-union tactics Aidan and Liam McFarland had employed. An era of "preventive" labor relations had taken hold, its emphasis on more-subtle forms of union busting than coercion or violence.

Unlike his predecessors, Henry wasn't interested in thwarting organized labor by firing union activists, rigging elections, imposing lockouts, or forcibly crushing strikes. His approach was far more nuanced, aimed at quashing labor problems before they came to a head and bleeding unions to death through subtle pinpricks rather than beheading them in one fell swoop.

Henry employed highly trained attorneys, industrial psychologists, and others adept at skirting pro-labor legislation. He utilized sophisticated interviewing techniques aimed at screening out potential agitators, trained supervisors to avoid actions that might spark labor unrest, and encouraged his top lieutenants to interact regularly with tugboat crews, fostering the notion of McFarland Marine Towing as one big, happy family. He even wrote personally at times to his workforce, portraying himself as an earnest businessman striving for labor peace, someone who might seem callous and intemperate at times, but beneath it was possessed of transcendent redeeming qualities: loyalty, family values, and a heart of gold.

All of it, of course, was a ruse.

Similarly contrived were McFarland Marine Towing's hiring practices. Purposefully, Henry's tugboat firm filled its employee ranks with a calculated blend of Irishmen and Italians, Czechs and Poles, Slavs and Swedes. A handful of Blacks and Hispanics were woven into the workforce as well—not so much to promulgate integration or equal rights, but because workforce diversity led to internal factions. To Henry, it was sound business to exploit differences in ethnicity, religion, race, and class. Why not leverage prejudice and mistrust?

Better to have workers squabbling among themselves than fighting with management. Better to have them speaking in feeble, disparate voices rather than a forceful, unified shout.

There were limits, of course, to what Henry could do. He understood that he couldn't legally prevent the tugboat workers' union from existing, or from serving as a contract-bargaining entity for workers. But while he couldn't eradicate Local 88 entirely, he could maneuver for every possible edge. Gaining negotiating leverage by forming the Gotham Harbor Alliance was one such tactic. Buying labor peace through crooked union leaders like Paddy O'Boyle was another. Contracting with Otto Blackburn for a variety of union-busting services—most notably labor spies—was yet a third.

In the latter regard, Henry again was hardly alone. Indeed, union busting was standard business practice throughout corporate America in the 1940s, labor spies rumored to have infiltrated dozens of union locals across the country. Blackburn's firm alone boasted a roster of several of America's leading companies, and generated millions of dollars in annual revenue.

And it was easy to see how the money added up.

A former OSS operative during the war, Blackburn charged a whopping two thousand dollars per week for his services, far more than the salaries of even Henry's top lieutenants. In all, McFarland Marine Towing spent north of a hundred thousand dollars a year with Blackburn, payments that were reported as fees for insurance and security services, so that Henry could cover his tracks legally. Invoices were also split up and sent to separate arms of Blackburn's company, so that each charge fell under the minimum required for reporting to the Securities & Exchange Commission. The IRS and other government agencies didn't have an inkling about what was really going on. The National Labor Relations Board and other labor watchdogs were similarly clueless.

But regardless of how costly Blackburn's services were, Henry considered the expenditure money well spent. Indeed, by Henry's estimate, the fees he paid for Blackburn's labor-spying initiatives saved him more than double that amount over the course of a typical labor contract. Just as importantly, it saved him headaches.

Blackburn's labor spies provided Henry with a surreptitious one-way window into the mindset of his workers, enabling him to identify rank-and-file objectives, bargaining posture, and resolve. By so doing, Henry could anticipate the union's tactics, counter its actions, and beat its leaders to the punch. Not having that kind of intelligence for a contract negotiation, Henry reasoned, would be like rushing into battle without the protection of body armor. And Henry never made a move without putting the requisite safeguards securely in place.

*   *   *

Otto Blackburn, as promised, phoned at 2 p.m., turning immediately to the topic at hand.

"What do you make of my latest report?" the labor consultant inquired.

"Well, if what I'm reading is accurate," Henry said gleefully, "the labor tempest I've set in motion is getting more interesting by the minute."

"More opportune for your side, as well." Blackburn chuckled.

Henry tried to match Blackburn's voice to a face. The pair had met only once in the decade they'd been working together, and that was years earlier. Henry envisioned Blackburn as having aged like a rotting apple, with wormy, narrow-set eyes and an oily, pockmarked face. The image wasn't far off.

But Blackburn's appearance mattered little to Henry. What mattered far more was that Asset Protection Corp. had surreptitiously planted two labor spies inside New York's tugboat workers' union. The spies, high up in Local 88's pecking order, were full-time workers with an unfettered pipeline into the union. The intelligence they provided was invaluable to Henry, especially at such a critical juncture in contract negotiations.

"I take it your moles remain close to the action?" Henry asked.

"Like fleas on a dog," Blackburn said.

"Eyes and ears open?"

"Wide enough to know everything that matters to you."

His confidence wasn't purely bombast.

Paid actors in a very real sense, Blackburn's labor spies went by the pseudonyms of Hollywood luminaries Humphrey Bogart and Jimmy Stewart, drawing their normal salaries plus an under-the-table kicker. Their identities were unknown to both Henry and union members, a fact pivotal to their wellbeing. Local 88's rank and file, like that of other unions, didn't take kindly to labor spies. The key to the informants' very survival was to remain invisible—and they'd done just that for more than a year.

They'd also done their jobs exceedingly well. Each week, Blackburn's sleuths prepared detailed reports, including the minutes of rank-and-file meetings, transcriptions of conversations among union leaders, and negotiating tactics. The reports, mailed to a P.O. box, were then delivered to Asset Protection Corp.'s midtown-Manhattan offices, with Blackburn providing commentary before forwarding the documents to Henry.

Blackburn's latest report provided key intelligence about the lay of the land inside Local 88—affirming, among other details, that that there was a civil war raging inside the local, pitting Paddy O'Boyle and other old-guard conservatives against insurgents led by Benny Logan, the factions differing sharply on how to handle contract negotiations.

"Paddy O'Boyle has always been someone I could rely on when it came to labor contracts," Henry said. "I take it, however, that that's no longer the case?"

"Paddy's heart is in the right place," Blackburn reported. "He'd love nothing more than to keep the wheel spinning and the money rolling in."

"But Paddy is no longer the rank-and-file's 'favorite son,' is he?"

"No," Blackburn said. "From what I hear, the workers have had it up to here with him. A younger generation is calling the shots now."

"What do you think they're gonna do with Paddy?"

"Probably dump him on his ass . . . elect their own president."

"And who might that be?"

"It depends, I suppose, on how events unfold."

"What happens 'til then?"

"In all likelihood, chaos reigns."

Henry laughed. To him, the prospect of chaos in the union ranks was more than welcome. Indeed, chaos was precisely what he was banking on. Chaos bred discord, which led to instability, which resulted in weakness.

"I think you'll see a gradual changing of the guard, a circular firing squad of sorts," Blackburn predicted. "The rank and file will be subject to infighting, dissension, backstabbing."

"Sounds delightful!" Henry said. "They'll devour one another like cannibals."

"I'd say that's quite possible," Blackburn concurred. "Certainly over the short term."

"And what about the long run?"

"That's still uncertain. In all likelihood, you'll have to deal with a new cast of characters, insurgents like Benny Logan. They won't roll over willingly, either. They'll put the screws to you, but good."

"They're certainly more confrontational than the old gang," Henry groused. "Lacking as much in civility as in their willingness to compromise."

"They'll fight you tooth and nail," Blackburn agreed. "And they're deeply dug in."

"Well, so am I!" Henry said. "I'm not budging one iota on my wage offer. A two-percent hike is all those bastards will get! And they should be grateful I'm that generous!"

Blackburn chortled. "I take it you're prepared to test the union's resolve."

"Goddamned right, I am!"

"Sounds like you're on a mission."

"It's more like a crusade."

But Henry was as curious now as he was resolute. "Tell me," he said, "from what your spies have gleaned, how far is the union willing to take their fight?"

"All the way," Blackburn replied.

"Willing to strike?"

"Willing and ready."

Henry was further emboldened. A strike, as he'd informed his fellow tugboat owners, was precisely the preface to the endgame he envisioned: forcing the union's hand, damaging it both financially and in the public eye, and hopefully prompting its demise.

"What can you tell me about Local 88's strike fund?" he asked.

"Sits just north of twenty grand," Blackburn reported.

Henry cackled. "Not much of an emergency kitty, is it?"

"The union will be running on fumes before it knows what hit it," Blackburn said. "From the standpoint of finances alone, it can't sustain a strike for more than a few days."

Blackburn paused. "Of course, there's more than simply finances to consider."

"Like what?"

"Well, there's the issue of the workers' resolve."

"And how substantial is that?"

"Hard to gauge. It depends, I suppose, on how fervently the men believe in their crusade . . . and in the strength of their leaders."

"We'll put both those things to the test," Henry vowed. "Personally, I don't give a damn if those greedy ingrates starve to death. This contract will be settled on my terms, and mine alone."

"Well," said Blackburn, "if your goal is to fracture the union, the new cast of leaders may well oblige you. Their willingness to strike may prove a short-term headache—but, in the long run, it may be the greatest gift they could possibly hand you."

Henry snickered. "So, what you're saying is that while the union's militancy may be problematic, the disarray it's breeding may be something I can exploit?"

"Exactly," Blackburn said. "The union's at war with itself? Fine. You stir the pot, sow even more discord . . . play one side against the other."

"Divide and conquer, of course," Henry said. "The oldest trick in the book. Allow your adversary to destroy itself from within."

"A devious approach." Blackburn chuckled.

"I've been accused of worse."

Henry laughed quietly. He liked the way his ideas meshed with those of Blackburn, how the pair communicated in a common parlance: so cutthroat, so business-savvy, so calibrated to human emotion. Sharing ideas with men like Blackburn reinforced Henry's own mindset—made him feel less sullied, less callous, less alone.

"I believe that due to its limited finances and internal divide, the union will quickly implode under the pressure of a strike," Blackburn predicted. "The men will bicker among themselves. Strikers will cross picket lines. Inevitably, the local will collapse and jump at whatever contract offer you've put on the table."

"I'm banking on that," Henry said. "I'm also certain I can rally support for Paddy O'Boyle in the union's turf war—turn O'Boyle's allies against the militants, pressure Benny Logan and his cohorts to soften their demands, and end any strike they may wage."

"Even if O'Boyle's hands are tied," said Blackburn, "perhaps you can get him to throw fear into the rank and file, convince them that a strike would be a risky—and likely a losing—proposition."

"Not a bad idea."

"You can paint the militants—publicly and within the union—as a bunch of out-of-control rabble-rousers looking to stir up trouble," Blackburn suggested.

"The business community," said Henry, "will eat that up."

"They'll rally behind it, as well," Blackburn said. "You'll have tons of corporate support. Politicians will line up on your side, too. Hell, no politician wants to see a tugboat strike. And the public? They won't give a damn about who's 'right' or 'wrong.' All they'll want is their homes heated and food on the table."

"I couldn't agree more," said Henry. "Nothing rattles the corridors of power more than the absence of equilibrium."

"Or worse," said Blackburn, "a crisis in which they're forced to take sides."

Henry laughed, shifting to a topic of equal interest.

"What can you tell me about Benny Logan?" he inquired.

"What do you want to know?"

"Everything. Especially weaknesses I can exploit."

Blackburn paused, consulting a dossier.

"Well, Logan's a tough cookie," Blackburn reported. "Scrappy. Chip on his shoulder. A real hard-ass."

"And the tough-guy persona . . . is it real?"

"Far as I can tell—yes. Logan's an ex-boxer, you know. Fought semi-pro a while back as a welterweight."

"Was he any good?"

"Won his share of fights."

"Well," said Henry, "he's fighting high above his weight class now."

"In the ring with a heavyweight, huh?"

"Not just any heavyweight," Henry crowed. "The fucking champ!"

The men shared a laugh.

"But I must warn you," Blackburn cautioned. "Logan is also a hell of a politician. Possesses the greatest gift any politician can possibly have."

"What's that?"

"He can muster a crowd," Blackburn said. "Work it into a frenzy, too."

"So I shouldn't take him lightly?"

"That would be a big mistake."

"Even with the whole 'street-urchin' persona?" Henry scoffed. "The cursing. The lousy grammar? The 'Brooklynese'?"

"Whatever language Logan is speaking, I can assure you it's being heard," Blackburn replied. "People listen with their stomach, you know—not their ears. They're driven by the things they hunger for."

"And what do tugboat workers hunger for?"

"Someone who feeds them inspiration and hope," Blackburn said. "Someone who can lead them out of the wilderness."

Henry was intrigued. "So, Logan owns tugboat workers' hearts and minds?"

"Without question."

"And how do you explain the 'magic' he wields?"

"Logan cuts a figure that the rank and file relate to," Blackburn said. "Same blue-collar pedigree. Feisty. Tenacious. Logan comes across as one of the men, only with more moxie and smarts."

"Which of those attributes," asked Henry, "supersedes the other?"

"I guess we'll find out," Blackburn said. "Along with whether he scares."

"What's your sense of it?"

"Well, he's certainly got a set of brass balls."

"And substance?"

"A lot more than that of the foulmouthed gorilla he comes across as."

"Staying power?"

"Eighty percent of the men, I'd estimate, are buying whatever he's selling."

"And the other twenty percent?"

"They can be persuaded either way."

"Populist bullshit!" Henry scoffed. "I hate it when men like Logan paint themselves out as some kind of Robin Hood . . . a patron saint of lost causes."

"Rile enough people up," said Blackburn, "and before you know it, you have a movement."

"That's not something I'm banking on," Henry said. "Unless the 'movement' is mine."

Then he had an idea.

"What if I try to muzzle Logan . . . buy him off?"

"My sense of it," Blackburn replied, "is that he won't take the bait."

"Why not?" Henry asked. "Men like him are always angling for an easy buck."

"Maybe so. But Logan is no Paddy Boyle. I get the feeling he's in the fight for reasons other than money."

Henry laughed. "What other reasons are there?"

"I sense," said Blackburn, "that Logan has something to prove."

"To whom?"

"To the world. Maybe to himself."

"And what would that be?"

"That he can absolve some deep-seated inferiority complex . . . trade punches with men in high places."

"Can he?"

"I suppose we'll find that out, too."

Henry was further emboldened. If he were to square off against someone in a high-stakes labor war, he reasoned, it might as well be someone worthy of the fight, an adversary he'd take delight in squashing. Benny Logan qualified on both fronts. Henry relished the thought of putting the union militant in his place.

"Tell me more," he asked. "What about Logan's education?"

"Two years of high school," Blackburn reported.

"That's it?"

"You don't have to be an Ivy Leaguer to be savvy," Blackburn said. "Never underestimate what a man can learn on the streets of neighborhoods like Williamsburg."

"The proverbial school of hard knocks, huh?"

"Teaches street smarts like nowhere in the world," Blackburn said. "Don't let Logan's background or demeanor fool you. Men with 'gutter wisdom' like that can be dangerous. They don't know their limits, or the rules by which the game is usually played."

"Duly noted," Henry said. "What about family?"

Blackburn shuffled through his dossier.

"Logan is married," he reported. "Father of two daughters. Lives in a public-housing project somewhere in the Bronx."

"Military service?"

"Five years Merchant Marine, prior to the war. Still has family in Brooklyn—including a brother, Jack—who, coincidentally, is on your payroll."

Henry couldn't place Jack's name. McFarland Marine Towing employed more than a thousand workers, most of whom Henry wouldn't know if he tripped over them. He preferred it that way. Better not to know them, not to get too close.

"Is there anything to know about Logan's brother?" he queried.

"All I know," said Blackburn, "is that he's an ex-G.I., recently home from the war. Works as a deckhand on your tugboat *Jupiter*."

"Tied at the hip to his brother?"

"Well, blood does tend to bind most men."

"Understood. But does Logan's brother play a substantive role in the union?"

"He's a rank-and-filer," Blackburn said. "A nobody."

"What about Logan's personal life?" Henry asked. "Credit problems? Criminal record? Gambling debts? Any dirt we can dig up to discredit him?"

"Nothing I know of," Blackburn said. "Honorable discharge from the Merchant Marine. No legal issues. His entire existence is tied to the union. It's life and death to him."

"How high up on the food chain is he?"

"He's currently Local 88's shop steward. Apparently, though, he's destined for bigger things, the odds-on choice to become the local's first elected president. Probably depends how he handles contract negotiations and leads the men in the event they strike."

"What about his politics?"

Blackburn hesitated, uncertain over what Henry was driving at.

"Any 'Red' ties we can pin on him?" Henry elaborated.

Blackburn snickered. "None that I'm aware of."

"Well, see if there's anything your spies can dig up."

"Real or imagined?"

"Either."

Both men laughed.

"If I can make the case that Communist radicals have infiltrated the local," Henry said, "it would knock the legs out from under the workers . . . fast."

"Couldn't agree more," Blackburn said. "There's nothing worse these days than being a Communist."

"It's even worse," said Henry, "than being a Democrat."

They shared another laugh.

"Well, nothing you've told me about Logan really concerns me," Henry said. "I can undermine his strengths, paint him as a screamer, an irrational troll with an axe to grind—a carnival barker who tempts the crowd with hints about what's inside the tent."

"Think of him as a modern-day Sisyphus," Blackburn said. "Trying to push a boulder uphill, but destined only to fail."

"Precisely," Henry agreed. "We can chip away at his credibility, convince the men that he's a false prophet luring them on a fool's errand with empty promises—and, in the end, betraying them because it's inevitable that if they strike, they'll lose far more than they'll gain."

"And Paddy O'Boyle?"

"Him we can paint as mature, reasoned, responsible."

"Statesmanlike?"

"That'd be a stretch." Henry laughed. "But you get the idea. If we play our cards right and undercut Logan—using O'Boyle as a foil if we must—rank-and-file unanimity will dissipate. It won't take long for the men to start second-guessing Logan like the Israelites did Moses."

"Well," Blackburn cautioned, "Moses did lead his people to the Promised Land."

"Maybe so," Henry said, laughing, "but Logan won't have forty years."

Blackburn chuckled, as Henry's own laughter inducing a hacking cough. When he finally found his voice again, he laid out his goal.

"If Logan is the captain of this insurgency, I'm going to help him run it aground. Charisma wears thin when times get tough. Power, on the other hand, is retained with cunning. In the end, I'll rip the bark off Logan's back, skin him alive . . . show him who's really running this city."

"I'm certain you will," Blackburn concurred.

"Okay," said Henry. "Let's continue to keep our eyes open and our ears to the ground."

"That's the plan," Blackburn said.

Henry was pleased, his bases covered, hands firmly on the wheel.

"You know, it's a dirty business . . . battling these unions," he said.

"You gotta bend the rules," Blackburn said. "Hurt them any way you can."

"It does gets nasty. But still, there's times I rather enjoy it."

Henry grinned, eyeing a lineup of photos set on a credenza alongside his desk. Ancestors and descendants lined the surface: a daguerreotype of company founder Aidan McFarland, posed amidst a bevy of square-riggers in nineteenth-century New York; next to him, his sons, Patrick and Paul, both Princeton grads, firmly ensconced in the family business, standing alongside a McFarland tugboat; beside them, his daughter Sallie Ann, a junior at Smith, standing at the helm of a forty-foot sloop christened in her name.

And off by itself, a candid shot of Carolyn: luminous, smiling, seated on a vintage stool alongside her Bösendorfer Grand piano.

With a return of his frequent melancholy, Henry thought about his late wife, subconsciously aware that something inside him had gone interminably dark in the aftermath of her death. He recognized, without conscious thought, how ephemeral fulfillment was; with laughter and love absent from his life, darker emotions set within him now like blocks of stone.

"The strike you're angling for should be a barrel of laughs," Blackburn said.

"You're right," Henry said. "Making life miserable for the union is about as much fun as I can possibly imagine having these days."

CHAPTER 18

December 8, 1945

But even with the specter of a toxic labor war looming, there remained a tranquil, heartening rhythm to Jack's life as year's end approached, a pervasive feeling of optimism and hope.

Jack's tugboat job, as from its outset, continued to yield a welcome source of income, gratification, camaraderie, and pride. Nighttime classes at Pace were equally fulfilling, providing the pathway toward upward mobility that Jack and Kate so desperately craved. Best of all, the couple was making their marriage work, every bit as much in love in postwar New York as in wartime London, every bit as determined to forge joyful, conjoined lives.

Not that marriage, like the day-to-day work grind, was always smooth sailing.

For Kate, like other war brides, adjusting to life in America was fraught with challenges. Indeed, most of the foreign-born women who had married American servicemen had never set foot outside their native country, let alone in an alien nation thousands of miles from home. Many of the women found themselves desperately homesick, struggling to keep their marriages afloat. Others faced even greater challenges: vicious forms of xenophobia, segregation, rejection, and isolation. New York's tabloids were rife with sorrowful tales about despondent war brides living in squalor at welfare hotels, abandoned by husbands who'd had a sudden change of heart. In many cases, the women were the ones having second thoughts, their wartime romances withering in the face of postwar realities.

It was easy to see why.

American G.I.s may have seemed heroic, even larger-than-life, in wartime, risking life and limb to battle a fearsome enemy. Things were jarringly anticlimactic, however, in the aftermath of the war. Many ex-servicemen, their uniforms closeted for good, were shorn of all glamour now, their shortcomings and frailties evident, the trauma of the war laid bare. Former high-ranking officers labored now in lowly, poor-paying jobs, or struggled to find work at all. Daring wartime missions were supplanted by humdrum daily tasks. Starstruck war brides from major foreign cities found themselves living on ranches and farms in the middle of nowhere, vying for acceptance by hostile in-laws and others. Couples wrangled over money, children, domestic duties. Relationships soured. Divorce rates soared.

Martin Sedgwick, envisioning that marital outcome for his daughter, had wired three hundred dollars to a bank account he had opened in New York, so that Kate could have money to fall back on should her marriage hit the rocks. But the bank account was never tapped—at least not for its intended purpose. Kate's marriage was hardly floundering. To the contrary, it was flowering.

Married life, Jack and Kate found, suited them far better than they'd ever dare imagine. After agonizing periods of separation and uncertainty in war-torn Europe, the couple relished being together in postwar New York, exultant in the lambency of peace, and the feeling that they were finally building the life they'd pined for. Grounded, prudent, both of them mature beyond their years, each recognized that marriage wasn't a product merely of passion, or even love, but a sacred covenant that required nurturing and commitment, and thrived on a foundation of communication, compromise, and respect.

Jack, for his part, also recognized that Kate had made a valiant leap of faith, investing her future in their union, while leaving a cherished part of herself in England. He accepted that reality, however, never feeling threatened by it or belittling it, but recognizing it was a void that needed to be filled, in large part by striving to make Kate feel at home in her adopted city.

As Kate had done during their London courtship, Jack escorted his wife on weekend excursions to New York's major attractions: the Empire State Building, Statue of Liberty, Chinatown, and other popular tourist sites. Just as importantly, he ushered Kate to landmarks tied to the city's spiritual heart, places that gave New York its singularity and character, and tied Jack to emotions and memories he'd always associated with home.

He took her to Coney Island, where they strolled the boardwalk, visited the arcades, and feasted on hot dogs and cotton candy. He took her dancing at Roseland, on hansom cab rides in Central Park, and on picnics to Prospect Park; took her to see the Rockettes at Radio City Music Hall and *Annie Get Your Gun* on Broadway; took her to Ebbets Field to see the Dodgers play, and to the Brooklyn Botanic Garden, a flowering oasis reminiscent of London's Royal Parks. There were more-modest sojourns, too: to roller-skating rinks and pizza parlors, soda shops and beer gardens, movie houses and other childhood haunts.

To Jack, it wasn't so much a matter of familiarizing Kate with New York as in having her connect to the city, understand its ethos, and embrace it as a living, breathing entity: teeming and tumultuous, grandiose and petty, virtuous and deplorable, spectral and enticing; a vast, audacious, densely layered assemblage of soaring superlatives, sordid depravities, and jarring contradictions— triumphs and tragedies, sinners and saints, dreamers and deadbeats, and lives that rose and fell, ebbed and flowed, blossomed and withered.

Jack wanted Kate to see New York through the same lens that he did, as more than simply a mecca for tourists, but as the most human of all cities; a complex amalgam of races, cultures, ethnicities, religions, ideologies, languages, and lifestyles fueled by imagination and intellect, aspiration and yearning, transformation and hope; a monument to America's enterprise and energy, the nation's passion for things large and great; everything that Jack had risked his life for in the war; everything that he lived for now.

Even more, Jack wanted Kate to see New York as a permanent nesting place, a city in which the two of them could nurture their bond, tend to their dreams, and become the people they'd always dreamed of being. At the same time, he wanted Kate to feel reassured, to rest easy over her decision to follow him to America, to feel confident that all the promises he'd ever made came straight from the heart: that his life could be her life, his country her country, his city her city.

Before very long, it was. Living in New York took some getting used to, Kate discovered, but nothing that she couldn't handle. Shortly after her arrival, she discovered that most of the clothing she'd brought from England was unsuitable for both summer and winter—and nearly her entire wardrobe had to be scrapped. It also took time to grasp the nuances between England and America in terms of culture and lifestyle, language and customs, pastimes and foods.

Living in postwar New York was challenging on other fronts as well. While wartime rations on gasoline, consumables, and most household staples had been lifted, shortages nevertheless lingered. The paucity of affordable homes was as acute as the dearth of jobs. Many returning G.I.s, starting from scratch, and short on cash, found themselves forced to double-up with relatives and friends, or to reside in basements, attics, and other makeshift quarters. Homes were cropping up in the suburbs, but those were beyond the reach of many young couples. The G.I. Bill, with its guarantee of low-interest mortgages, would doubtless come in handy one day, but Jack and Kate weren't ready to assume that kind of commitment yet. Like legions of other couples, they had little choice but to move in with Jack's parents—a living arrangement that, while opportune, was far from ideal.

The Logans' Williamsburg apartment was dreary, cramped, and hardly befitting a pair of newlyweds. Privacy, let alone intimacy, was virtually non-existent. The apartment's closet-sized bathroom—with its leaky faucet, runny toilet, and clawfoot tub—was devoid of all amenities. The kitchen contained little more than a tiny icebox, a row of white steel cabinets, worn linoleum floor, and four chairs set around a circular table. Jack and Kate were forced to sleep on twin beds pushed together in the bedroom Jack once shared with his brothers.

Money was hard to come by, too. Like many young postwar couples, Jack and Kate were bereft of nearly all possessions, owning not much more than the clothing on their back. As a dowry, Martin and Emily Sedgwick had given Kate an heirloom tablecloth and tea pot with matching cups and saucers. The only other items she'd brought to America were her ill-suited wardrobe and her mother's recipe for Yorkshire pudding.

Yet, somehow, all of it seemed all right.

In many ways, it was a given that Jack and Kate didn't possess much in the way of worldly goods. They'd never had much to begin with, after all, and needed to grow up fast. Besides, they were hardly alone. Like legions of others who had lived through the Depression and the war, they'd long ago grown accustomed to scrimping, sacrificing, and banking on little more than faith. Like others of their generation, they accepted their humble lot in life and counted their blessings—lucky that they'd made it this far, grateful that things weren't worse. Besides, how could they possibly complain? Circumstances, in many ways, were palpably better now than at any time they could recall. And even better days lay ahead—or so they thought.

It was nearly impossible not to get caught up in the floodtide of optimism washing over much of New York. The long and bloody war, like the economic calamity that preceded it, was over at last. Americans had worked diligently, sacrificed mightily, suffered grave losses. But now it was time to turn the page, emerge from beneath the yearslong shroud of hopelessness, hardship, and despair, a time for recovery and hope. All the energy that had been poured into winning the war had shifted to people's personal lives. Couples were getting married, starting families, buying appliances, TV sets, and cars. Pundits were predicting a "Golden Age" for America, a nation on the precipice of unprecedented affluence, promise, and power.

Best of all, Jack and Kate were truly together now, heady with hope, their bond becoming richer, more layered, more substantive, and mature. So what if circumstances weren't ideal? So what if the two of them didn't possess more? Given all they'd been through, the challenges they faced now seemed inconsequential, almost laughable. By nearly all measures, they were doing just fine.

Agnes and Gus Logan readily embraced their new daughter-in-law, far too overjoyed to have Jack home from the war to quibble over his choice of a wife. Moreover, Kate was eminently likeable: soft-spoken, charming with her British accent, willing to pitch in when it came to cooking, cleaning, and other domestic chores. Jack's parents were enthralled by her mere presence. Agnes paraded her all around Williamsburg, introducing her to storekeepers, neighbors, and friends. Gus treated her like the daughter he'd always wished for: he was more accessible and conversant than he'd ever been with his sons, more willing to convey emotion; more like a real father.

Kate, too, felt surprisingly at ease with the living arrangements in Williamsburg. The congested, threadbare enclave was nothing like the glitzy New York that Kate had seen portrayed in British magazines, tabloids, and movies—nothing like Manhattan, with its upscale ambience, its museums and theaters, nightclubs and hotels, restaurants and retail shops. But Williamsburg possessed a quality that, for Kate, transcended mere glitz.

To her delight, the bustling blue-collar enclave reminded her of home.

Williamsburg's hulking landscape of factories, warehouses, and tenements bore more than a passing resemblance to the grimy industrial landscape of Birmingham, where Kate had trained as a nurse. The neighborhood's streets—glutted with trolleys, retail outlets, and places of worship—sparked fond memories of the working-class enclave where she'd resided in London. The immigrant populace, including survivors of European pogroms, shtetls, and Nazi death camps, shared similar tales of dislocation and despair, renewal and hope. Even the East River, visible from the building's rooftop, evoked a welcome sense of familiarity. To Kate, it closely resembled the Thames, a heavily trafficked, working waterway with tidal channels that wound their way through the urban habitat and left Kate feeling settled and secure.

Living in Williamsburg, even under less than ideal circumstances, suited Kate just fine—as long she had Jack, and he had her, and the two of them had a plan.

Which they did. The pharmaceutical firm Charles Pfizer & Co., located mere blocks from the Logans' apartment, had recently purchased a former icemaking factory that contained the refrigeration equipment needed to convert it into the world's first manufacturing facility for the mass production of penicillin. With her nursing background, Kate had no problem securing a full-time, thirty-dollar-a-week job on Pfizer's penicillin-production line. And now that Jack had landed his fifty-four-dollar-a-week tugboat job, the couple could meet both their financial obligations and savings goal—banking forty dollars a month, even after contributing to household expenses. By December, their joint savings account, including the untapped money Martin Sedgwick had wired Kate, totaled nearly four hundred dollars, a nest egg that would no doubt come in handy—especially now, with Kate in her pregnancy's third trimester, and preparations for the imminent arrival well underway.

Martin and Emily Sedgwick, having already assisted with the purchase of maternity clothes, had pledged a baby carriage and a layette. Gus and Agnes Logan had committed to a basinet, a crib, and Benjamin Spock's bestselling guide to pregnancy and childcare. Jack and Kate had their sights set on something even more substantive. Saving every penny they could, they'd live with Jack's parents until their baby was born. By then, they calculated, they'd have saved enough to rent an apartment of their own. It wouldn't be much to speak of, of course, but at least it would be theirs—to live in and furnish the way they wanted. A step-up.

A start.

One day, with Jack a teacher and Kate pitching in part-time, perhaps they could afford a house of their own, something in one of Brooklyn's newer neighborhoods or even the suburbs. Long Island was the coming thing, people were saying. That's where the future lay for young families like the one they envisioned: affordable homes; modern schools; abundant shopping; open spaces where children could play freely, and people could breathe fresh air. A bright new chapter in their blossoming love story. A whole new life.

All of it seemed possible now, finally within reach. Jack's tugboat job, though fulltime, enabled him to clock out early enough to travel home, shower, and change clothing. Kate could arrive home in time to fix the two of them supper. Jack could then hop on the BMT's L Line for three stops, arriving in time to attend classes at Pace in downtown Manhattan.

Even that was working out well. Fueled largely by ex-servicemen who'd returned to college, enrollment was soaring at Pace, its classrooms, laboratories, and lecture halls crammed with older, working students—more serious, more mature, and far more appreciative than traditional undergraduates of the opportunity they had been handed. Many of them had lost their innocence— and, in many cases, a whole lot more—on the killing fields of Tarawa, Guadalcanal, Anzio, and the Ardennes Forest. Compared to that, the demands of term papers, lectures, and final exams could hardly be considered a hardship, even after a hard day's work.

To Jack, being back in college symbolized, as much as than anything, a palpable return to normalcy, the sense that he was truly picking up where he'd left off prior to the war. Bathed in the nighttime glow of classrooms, laboratories, and lecture halls, he felt grounded and safe, emotions that augmented the buoyant symmetry of his postwar life.

Kate shared those emotions, along with the growing sense that everything they were feeling now might truly last. Maybe, the two of them thought, the hard times were truly over now. Maybe the miserable lot their generation had been forced to endure wasn't a lifetime sentence, after all. Maybe, after everything they had lived through, there was something better on the horizon, a rainbow in the wake of the storm.

Why couldn't that happen? Why couldn't it be their fate?

The Depression had ended, the war was over, the trials and tribulations endured. Jack and Kate weren't in Europe anymore, engaged in combat, tending to casualties, riddled with uncertainty, sorrow and doubt. America was their home now, New York an irrepressible backdrop of boundless energy and glowing possibilities. Maybe here, they thought, they could rekindle their lives, unfettered and unafraid, threads in the city's variegated mosaic, happy to have come this far, hopeful of going even farther.

Maybe, they thought, their time had finally come.

Yes, it would mean hard work and sacrifice, but that much was assumed. Jack could live with the notion of keeping his nose to the grindstone—working and studying, scrimping and saving—because the future wasn't just about him or Kate anymore. Their children would be the beneficiaries of their hardship, their sacrifice, their work. Their children would be the ones with the better life.

Kate, too, could live with that notion. Just as she was happy that legions of women had abandoned their traditional roles to help win the war, she was proud of her time as a nurse, having discovered a sense of liberation and achievement in the wartime role she'd played. But while some women battled the notion that they'd passively stand down from their wartime roles, Kate had no problem turning her attention now to family and home. If peace and optimism were the tradeoffs for liberation and equality, they seemed well worth the price—especially now that she and Jack were finally together, charged with the unbridled joy of impending parenthood, a testament to their enduring love.

There was no forgetting everything they'd lived through: the memories, the wounds, the scars. But maybe there was a silver lining to that, too. After all, even in the face of its heartache and loss, the war had brought the two of them together and helped them see life in a way that they otherwise may not have: as a precious gift they could cherish, cling to, and share.

Now that the war was over, maybe they could finally live the dreams they had harbored for so long, and find a way to live with the scars—as long as there were no more untoward roadblocks, no enduring setbacks, no injurious conflicts.

Maybe, for the first time in their lives, they could allow themselves, finally, to trust the fates. Maybe things would turn out all right—as long as they stayed together and there was a semblance of peace, and they could cling to the notion that somehow, some way, they could always manage to be this happy.

CHAPTER 19

January 31, 1946

Negotiations ended almost immediately after they resumed. It was inevitable.

By now a deathlike pallor, months in the making, had settled over the contract talks. No longer was collective bargaining a rational, dispassionate exchange of ideas. Nor did it resemble, even remotely, a bona fide effort at compromise. To the contrary, the negotiations had descended into some place somber and vengeful, little more than a relentless volley of bellicose outbursts and personal attacks, a vivid reminder that while the focal point of the contract dispute was ostensibly power and money, its roots, as with most conflicts, lay somewhere in men's hearts. Henry McFarland and Benny Logan had brought their animus, their obstinance, their personal histories, into the fray. Driven by the same primal urges, the same dark emotions, the same sense of anger and loss, the two key principals in the labor dispute had made the squabble all about themselves.

And so the pivotal bargaining session, the final one scheduled before the union's threatened strike, was caustic and brief. Henry, adhering to his goal of sabotaging the negotiations, immediately set a confrontational tone. Armed with the intelligence he had gleaned from Otto Blackburn's labor spies, and buoyed by the growing divide in the union's ranks, he marched his fellow tugboat owners back into the Waldorf-Astoria conference room. And no sooner had the union reps settled into their seats than the Gotham Harbor Alliance chairman cut loose with a hostile opening salvo.

"Gentlemen, our coalition has gone as far as possible in our collective-bargaining efforts," he said. "The gulf between our sides is simply too wide. As we've said throughout our negotiations, we view the union's wage demand as excessive and unreasonable. In contrast, the wage offer we've put on the table is, in our view, equitable and fair."

"An' that leaves our negotiations . . . where?" Local 88 treasurer Frank Russo sputtered.

"At an impasse," Henry declared. "A hopeless deadlock."

The negotiators squirmed in their seats. Henry lit a cigarette, casually brushing a particle of lint from the lapel of his suit.

"As we've noted repeatedly," he said, "our employment costs have skyrocketed."

"By 'employment costs,'" Benny interrupted, "are you talkin' 'bout pay?"

"That's precisely what I'm talking about."

"Well, if 'pay' is what you mean," said Benny, "why don't you just call it that? We can't conduct a negotiation if we don't even speak the same language!"

"I've been voicing that very sentiment," said Henry, "for the past eight months."

Henry drew on his cigarette, enjoying the truculent repartee. He knew where he wanted the bargaining session to go—straight into the toilet—and he relished the notion of tweaking Benny in the process. Benny reveled in the tit-for-tat as well. He too understood that the negotiations were falling apart. Might as well take Henry along for the ride.

Scowling, jaws taut, the two men locked eyes. There was little pretense about their mutual disdain, only a weak attempt at professional courtesy.

That arrogant cocksucker is going to blink first, Benny thought.

I'm going to tear that scruffy gorilla's heart out, Henry mused.

"Well, regardless of nuances in language," Henry said, "your union claims that wages are essentially flat, and that your members, given cost-of-living increases, are effectively going backward in real income. And our coalition believes that claim is nothing more than funny math."

"I assure you our members don't find the math 'funny' at all," Benny snarled. "An' they don't find it funny that tugboat companies seem obsessed with their bottom line, to the detriment of payin' their workers a livin' wage."

"That's a claim I find funny," Henry growled. "And one that I resent!"

Henry took another contented drag on his Lucky. Benny felt like stuffing the cigarette down Henry's throat. Again, the men exchanged frosty glares.

"You see," said Henry, "despite the dire picture you paint, tugboat workers are not exactly indentured servants, shackled by chains. And contrary to your opinion, our coalition believes that Local 88 members make a damned good living. Union leadership has seen to that, through years of amicable negotiations. And frankly, so have I."

"Our members make a good living?" Benny asked, facetiously.

"Damn right, they do!"

"An' I suppose we should be beholden to you for that?"

"Me and my fellow coalition members!"

"An' how would you possibly have any clue what our men think or feel?" Benny said. "Do you ever talk to any of them? Can you even see your tugboats from that ivory tower you call an office?"

An ominous pall hung over the conference room now. Negotiations were going off the rails, and neither Benny nor Henry seemed to care.

"You may find this hard to believe," said Henry, "but I'm not unacquainted with the notion of financial struggle. My Irish-immigrant family wasn't always so privileged, you know."

"Maybe not," Benny said. "But your family's challenges are ancient history. Our men live theirs in the here an' now."

And that's where the caustic repartee came to a screeching halt. Henry had had enough. Benny had pushed him to the limit of his patience.

"I believe it's fruitless," Henry said, "to try and bridge our differences any longer."

He took the measure of the other tugboat owners. No one dissented.

"The bottom line," said Henry, "is that no amended wage offer will be forthcoming. Our coalition is done negotiating. And, given the union's midnight strike deadline, it's obvious that the window to achieve an amicable settlement has essentially closed. Frankly, if Local 88 doesn't soften its demands, there's nothing left to discuss."

The negotiators plunged into a cavernous silence.

"Well, if that's your position," Frank Russo said, "then our Strike Committee has no choice but to call for a rank-and-file vote. An' we're prepared to recommend that our members reject your wage offer . . . an' ratify a strike."

"That's regrettable," tugboat owner Bertram Phelps lamented. "There hasn't been a New York tugboat strike since 1920. It's a shame that our negotiations have come to this."

"The real shame," said Benny, "is that there's such an unwillingness on management's part to sympathize with our members' needs."

"And that there's an equal unwillingness on the union's part," Henry countered, "to issue a wage demand our side can live with."

The two men exchanged menacing stares, their enmity coursing like an electric current through the conference room: each with a bone to pick; each firmly entrenched in his position; each possessed of an iron will, their standoff akin to rivals stranded in a desert, ready to battle over a single grain of sand.

I could strangle that arrogant prick, Benny thought.

I'd like to squash that foulmouthed SOB like a bug, Henry mused.

And that's where the negotiations effectively ended, an impenetrable wall separating sides that, captive to the mindset of their principals, were holding firm. Bitterness and obstinacy had trumped reason and compromise. Only divine intervention, it seemed, could prevent a calamitous strike. And deities, like nearly all civility, were nowhere to be found.

"We hope your union reassesses its position, and postpones any strike in the interest of the public welfare," said Phelps.

"Like I said," Frank Russo replied, "our members will put it to a vote."

"Please be certain to remind them, prior to any vote," said Henry, "what a strike will mean to them and their families, as well as to our city."

"I think they're already aware," Benny said.

"Then let me remind you, Mr. Logan." Henry doused his cigarette. "The strike that your union is threatening will effectively close New York Harbor at the most inopportune time—crippling the city, costing untold sums in revenue and wages, and creating immense hardship for millions of innocent people."

"You can blame your coalition for that," Benny said.

"More accurately," said Henry, "your union can blame itself!"

"We can point fingers all day," George Steele said. "But regardless of who's culpable, please recognize that our companies have a fiduciary responsibility to our customers, our shareholders, and non-striking employees."

"An' what is that supposed to mean?" Benny asked.

"What it means," Henry replied acidly, "is that our companies have a mandate to operate, by any means necessary, in the event of a strike."

"Should we interpret that as some kind of a threat?"

"Interpret it however you want. It simply means that every available option, bar none, will be considered to keep our tugboats operational."

"An' your side should be equally aware," warned Benny, "that in the event of a strike, every tactic our union has at its disposal, bar none, will be considered to assure that your tugboats remain idle at their docks."

The testy exchange nearly sucked the air out of the room. Henry wasn't finished, however. Paychecks covering the past two workweeks were due February 1, the opening day of the threatened strike, he reminded the group. Those paychecks, he said, would not be issued in the event of a work stoppage, nor would they be granted in the form of back pay when or if a strike was settled. In other words, tugboat workers would effectively lose two weeks' pay the instant they walked off the job. Adding to the duress, Henry declared, all benefits—including accrued vacation, pension contributions, and family medical coverage—would be suspended throughout the duration of any strike.

"There'll be a steep price for union members to pay if they walk off the job," Henry warned. "And that price will heighten dramatically by the day."

No one from the union's side uttered a word.

"In addition," said Henry, "our coalition can offer no guarantee that the same jobs will exist for Local 88 members when any work stoppage ends. Although workers cannot be fired for striking, permanent replacements can be hired in their stead. In other words, a strike—regardless of outcome and duration—may effectively cost your members their employment."

"We're aware of that," Tommy Duggan said.

"Very well," said Henry. "Then there truly is nothing left to discuss."

And with that, he capped his fountain pen, gathered his belongings, rose from the table, and marched from the conference room, the other owners trailing him like a gaggle of geese. Benny and the other union negotiators quickly followed suit.

A divisive new chapter in the contract dispute was about to unfold. The conflict, fought solely behind closed doors until now, would quickly spill onto the most public of stages. Collective bargaining had collapsed. Eight months of verbal haggling, toxic exchanges, theatrics, and saber-rattling was about to erupt into full-blown labor war, its battleground the sprawling canvas that was the City of New York.

CHAPTER 20

January 31, 1946

It didn't take long for the burgeoning crisis to assume an ominous new shape. Within minutes after the collective bargaining impasse was declared, word of the impending strike was conveyed to City Hall, where antsy public officials met in an emergency session to map contingencies. Shipping firms, coal suppliers, and other tugboat customers were notified about imminent service disruptions. Passenger-ship lines prepared for cancellations. Waterfront businesses girded for closure. Police Department officials planned deployment of cops to likely picket sites.

Amidst the harried preparations, tugboat owners and union leaders met in separate sessions to plot their next move. While union leaders summoned Local 88's rank and file for a strike-ratification vote, Henry convened an owners' meeting at Gotham Harbor Alliance headquarters, a century-old mercantile building on Manhattan's East Side, where representatives of coalition-member firms gathered in a conference room abuzz with the nervous chatter of businessmen facing a watershed moment for their companies.

From his seat at the end of an oval conference table, Henry informed the tugboat owners that the likelihood of a strike had risen exponentially with the collapse in negotiations. An amicable contract agreement, he told the men, was seemingly out of reach, the gulf between the warring parties too wide. Complicating matters, he added, was the fact that Paddy O'Boyle had effectively lost control of Local 88 to a group of disgruntled, unruly zealots who were virtually impossible to bargain with.

"If we're going to have a strike," Henry said, "I lay the blame at the feet of the defiant, misguided renegades now calling the shots for the union. While these so-called 'labor leaders' issue outlandish demands and refuse to compromise, our coalition has done everything humanly possible to avert a strike."

Henry conveyed the lie straight-faced, matter-of-factly. "We've planted our flag exactly where we want," he said. "Now we'll see if the union's strike threat is real, or simply a shot across our bow." He paused. "And if the workers do strike, we'll see how they feel about it after missing a paycheck or two."

Indeed, the entire city was about to find that out. For even as Gotham Harbor Alliance members convened at their Manhattan headquarters, Local 88's membership was gathering to either ratify or reject the work stoppage their Strike Committee was prepared to endorse.

The polling place for their vote, the Loews Kings theater, in the heart of working-class Brooklyn, seemed wholly incongruent to its intended purpose. The landmark theater, stately as an Old-World opera house, was the borough's glitziest movie palace, a popular venue for Hollywood blockbusters, stage shows, and high school commencements.

This evening's bill of fare, however, was far different than the usual pair of celluloid features—as was the mood inside the theater, smoldering with the powerful, thinly veiled emotions of the nearly three thousand tugboat workers who filled the cavernous auditorium to its rafters.

Local 88 members were perched on a perilous ledge now, facing a decision that could just as easily prove catastrophic as triumphant. The men were swimming, too, in uncharted waters. Indeed, except for a handful of old-timers, most of the city's tugboat workers had never assembled for a vote of such magnitude. A strike of even a brief duration, the men were aware, would likely have dire consequences. Two weeks of wages, at a minimum, would instantly be sacrificed, benefits suspended, jobs potentially lost, businesses closed, workers' families endangered, millions of city residents impacted. Government officials could issue injunctions, impose fines, and order arrests. The union itself could rupture at the seams if its rank and file proved intractably split.

Weighing just as heavily on the workers was the fact that opinions about a potential strike remained sharply divided. While most workers seemed prepared to ratify a walkout, a sizeable number were still angling for a last-ditch settlement, with many of the men prepared to endorse the sweetheart deal Paddy O'Boyle had negotiated with Henry. Because of this divide, the stakes were heightened dramatically. In effect, the strike vote would serve as nothing less than a referendum on union leadership—old-liners versus new-age members, conservatives versus renegades. The current state of Local 88, as well as its future, would be put to the test.

All this only served to ratchet up the tension as the workers—clad in peacoats, flannel work shirts, ivy caps, and union windbreakers—nervously awaited the start of the meeting. Onstage, union leaders sat like mannequins on wooden folding chairs. Benny and Tommy Duggan, flanked by fellow Strike Committee members, chatted with officials from the United Stevedores Association. At center stage, Paddy O'Boyle, gavel in hand, stood behind a wooden lectern, poised to call the meeting to order.

"I wonder where all of this is headed," said Big Mack Nowak, stuffed into a plush velvet seat alongside the rest of *Jupiter*'s crew.

"Only the Good Lord knows," Shorty Long intoned. "An' He ain't sayin'."

"I just hope wherever it's headed," Dutch Hendrik said, "that no one gets hurt."

The specter of violence loomed menacingly, especially if non-striking workers crossed picket lines or, more ominously, if strikebreakers entered the fray. That thought sent a shudder through Jack. For him, far more than simply the union's fate was on the line. His brother's fortunes—his reputation, his union standing, perhaps his very life—were at stake, too. Not only was Benny up to his eyeballs in a labor conflict that could rock the city, but he'd placed himself squarely in the crosshairs of both tugboat owners and union rivals alike. Henry McFarland and Paddy O'Boyle weren't the kind of men it it was wise to be pitted against in a battle over money and power. Even more menacing were people on the fringes of the squabble, shady villains who lurked in shadowy corners with sharp and ready knives.

Jack faced his own risks, too. Linked by blood to the union's strident leader, he would hardly be viewed as a neutral party in the sharply divided union. Who knew what kind of trouble that could spell? Benny's enemies could come after Jack—and perhaps other family members—as targets of retribution. Such things had happened before. In labor wars, no holds were barred.

No sooner had Jack's trepidation settled in the pit of his stomach, however, than Paddy O'Boyle rapped his gavel onto its wooden stand, the amplified thwack reverberating like a rifle shot through the theater.

"All of you know why we're here," O'Boyle rasped, as the assembled throng came to order. "So, I'll cut to the chase."

O'Boyle spoke as if through a mouthful of gravel, his garbled words at times indecipherable. His sentiments, however, were crystal clear.

"New York tugboat workers haven't walked off the job since 1920," he said. "That's a quarter-century of union leadership successfully negotiatin' contracts that have provided Local 88 members with a decent, steady paycheck."

He had the workers' attention. The veteran union boss may have lost a step or two with age, but he'd retained more than a semblance of his political chops. He plied those talents now.

"Many of you were kids—or a gleam in your daddy's eye—the last time our union went on strike," O'Boyle said to a smattering of laughter. "But I'm sure the old-timers here tonight remember that strike very well."

The comment sent an ominous buzz through the crowd.

"It was eighteen days of hell!" O'Boyle reminded the men. "Picket lines! Fistfights! Open warfare on the harbor! Tugboats were firebombed. Marines had to be called in to put a lid on the violence."

O'Boyle's face grew twisted, sweat running down his forehead and cheeks.

"An' how did the strike end?" he barked. "The same way all strikes end!"

He shot a sideways glance at Benny, who sat stone-faced mere feet away.

"Unlike some union leaders here tonight," he continued, "I know firsthand 'bout the carnage a strike can render. Lives are ruined. Careers are destroyed. Men go beggin' for work anywhere they can find it, just to scrounge a buck."

O'Boyle's eyes swept the theater, silent as a graveyard now.

"An' that ain't the worst of it!" he said. "Management will resent you, too. Think you'll ever sniff a penny of overtime if you strike? No way! Promotions? Forget that, too. Once you walk off the job, your company will have it out for you. The bitterness can last years . . . sometimes forever!"

One man, hip flask in hand, slurred a response, and O'Boyle quickly stared him into silence.

"In the 1920 strike, our union won some concessions, sure. But the owners won some too. When all was said an' done, both sides got the deal they probably would've got at the bargainin' table . . . if they'd only compromised instead of stubbornly standin' their ground."

He glanced again at Benny, more openly this time.

"But instead of an amicable settlement, tempers got out of hand, egos got in the way, an' both sides came to their senses only when the situation got bloody!" He paused, to a smattering of applause, and then continued. "My point is that no one wins in a strike! Everyone pays a price!"

His next comment seemed aimed at Benny alone.

"See, it's one thing to issue threats," O'Boyle resumed, "but it's another to walk off the job. Union 'brotherhood' is commendable," he continued, turning toward the audience, "but there's a hefty price to pay when you choose principle over a paycheck, an' you're forced to defend 'union solidarity' to your wife an' kids when you can't pay the rent. An' if the strike lasts? Think you can ever heal the wounds you opened, or recoup the paychecks you lost?"

Red-faced, drenched in sweat, O'Boyle groped for his closing argument.

"The union brothers who walked off the job in 1920 sacrificed for our local. Their loyalty an' commitment will never be forgotten. But there's a saner way to handle things. I'm askin' you men to push your anger an' frustration aside, let reason prevail, an' see negotiations through. Your parent union has always done right by you. I've always done right by you. Gimme a chance to reach a responsible, negotiated settlement! I ask ya, again, to ratify the contract I've put in front of you, or extend our strike deadline an' authorize your Strike Committee to continue with collective bargainin'."

Hammering the gavel for emphasis, he shouted over growing murmurs and whispers, "Now let's get this goddamned dispute settled . . . without ruining men's lives!"

With that, the union boss abandoned the lectern to a tepid mix of applause, catcalls, and boos. And mostly an awkward silence.

Now it was Benny's turn. Jack's heartrate quickened as his brother ambled to the podium with the same cocksure bravado he'd carried into the boxing ring: chin jutting, head held high. The theater grew hushed as he twisted the microphone's gooseneck arm, adjusting it to his height. This was his winner-take-all moment, his one big chance.

"You men just heard Paddy make a powerful argument against a strike," Benny began. "An' I'm here to tell you . . . Paddy is right!"

The audience seemed thrown off-kilter, bewildered. But not for long.

"Paddy told you that a strike will mean hardship an' sacrifice . . . an' he's right!" Benny said. "He told you that ratifyin' a walkout might be as tough a decision as you'll ever have to make. An' he's right about that, too!"

Benny eyeballed the audience, sitting silent and rapt.

"Paddy also said that you men should vote to accept the owners' so-called 'final offer'—negotiated by him and him alone—or give your Strike Committee more time to reach an acceptable deal," Benny said.

"Well . . . I say Paddy's wrong about that! Dead wrong!"

The audience seemed stunned by the force of Benny's words. The workmen leaned forward in their seats, mesmerized, silent.

"For eight brutal months," Benny said, "your Negotiatin' and Strike Committees have been beatin' their heads against the wall, bargainin' in good faith. We've made reasonable demands, offered compromises, an' busted our nuts to avoid a strike. In return, the tugboat owners haven't budged! Not a goddamned inch! They've put one offer on the table an' tol' our union to either shit or get off the pot . . . that was the only offer we were gonna get!"

"Tell it like it is, Benny!" a worker exhorted. "Tell 'em what they can do with their bullshit little offer!"

A burst of applause riffled through the theater, rising slowly in volume. Paddy O'Boyle and his USA allies squirmed in their chairs. Benny waited for the rumble to die down.

"The owners," he said, "believe we're a bunch of limp-dicked pawns they can push around at will. They think they can get rich off our sweat . . . back us into a corner an' watch us cave in like frightened little kids!"

"Bullshit!" someone bellowed.

And, in unison, the audience began chanting.

"Bullshit! Bullshit! Bullshit!"

Benny let the chant deepen.

"You're right!" he bellowed into the mic. "An' I'm goddamned sick of it!"

More chants, an ear-piercing din that rattled the theater's chandeliers now.

"Paddy bragged about how he never led our union into a strike, an' that's true," Benny said. "But to me, not goin' on strike all these years ain't somethin' to be proud of! Not goin' on strike only means that we've rolled over at the bargainin' table, lost our fire an' our guts . . . an' become lambs who eat whatever crumbs the owners toss us!"

A murmur spread through the theater, building in volume like an approaching tsunami.

"That ain't who we are!" Benny shouted. "Is it?"

"Hell, no!" the men shouted.

Again, they began chanting.

"Hell, no! . . . Hell, no! . . . Hell, no!"

The tugboat workers leapt to their feet, whooping, shouting, pumping their fists. Jack could feel a wellspring of pride bubble up as he watched his brother command the audience. Rally them. Inspire them. Lead them.

"Is goin' on strike a risk?" Benny asked. "Damn right, it is. But so is gettin' up each mornin' an' climbin' aboard a tugboat. The question is: is it a risk that's worth takin'? I say yes!"

More shouts. More cheers. More applause.

"I say we send the tugboat owners a different message than the one Paddy proposed," Benny said. "I say we tell 'em we've had enough of the crumbs they've been feedin' us! I say we let 'em know that we're the ones holdin' the hammer . . . that four years of sittin' on our hands while we helped America win a war is enough!"

"Goddamned right!" someone shouted, and the crowd burst into wild, unbridled applause.

"I say we tell the owners we're fightin' to get what's justly ours!" Benny exhorted. "I say we tell the owners we're sick of workin' our asses off while they reap the rewards! I say we tell 'em to take their so-called 'final offer' an' shove it up their asses! We're worth more! We deserve more! We demand more! We're done negotiatin' . . . done rubber-stampin' backroom deals!"

A thunderous ovation rocked the theater.

"We got no idea how strong our union is," Benny said, "because we never had the guts to test ourselves! We've always taken the easy way out, relied on leaders who treated us like sheep!

"I say all that changes tonight!" Benny demanded. "I say we show the owners how important we are to their businesses an' to this city. I say we show 'em that we can't be bullied or taken for granted! I say we stand united! Talk in a single voice! Take our battle to the picket line!"

"Strike!" someone shouted.

And the men, fists raised, roared in unison.

"Strike! Strike! Strike!"

The audience was electrified. Men were whooping, hollering.

"Benny . . . Benny . . . Benny . . . Benny!"

Everyone was on their feet now, applauding, rushing the stage, reaching out to touch Benny and shake his hand. Paddy O'Boyle was escorted offstage to a chorus of jeers. New York's tugboat workers had repudiated their old-guard leadership. What had begun as a fledgling reform campaign had morphed into a full-blown insurrection. Benny's time had come.

So had the time for a vote. Previous contract proposals had been subject to paper balloting. Not tonight. A voice vote, it was decided, would suffice. The proposed contract negotiated by O'Boyle and Henry was offered for ratification. "Yeas" were barely audible, overwhelmed by an avalanche of "nays."

The vote to ratify a strike was equally decisive, the audience erupting in cheers when the proposal was overwhelmingly approved. O'Boyle's supporters had no recourse but to affirm their support for the decision. The workers—shaking hands, clapping one another on the back—cut loose with a rousing, ear-splitting chant.

"Strike! Strike! Strike!"

The next two hours were spent on housekeeping. A General Strike Committee was named to oversee the work stoppage. A picketing committee was charged with picket-line assignments and sign-making. A finance committee was given responsibility for budgeting, recordkeeping, fundraising, and strike-fund disbursements. A publicity committee was charged with press relations and internal communications. Strike captains were assigned as point men.

Union officials then informed the workers about their rights and legal obligations, including the need to conduct themselves in a peaceful, orderly manner. A rented storefront near the Chelsea Piers on Manhattan's west side would serve as strike headquarters, the men were told, the strike fund dispensed on a schedule to be announced.

"Now, let's stand together an' fight!" Benny exhorted as the workers filed from the theater, pausing under its darkened marquee before drifting off into the night, ready to traverse the dark and troubling road that doubtless lay ahead.

CHAPTER 21

February 1, 1946

Dawn broke sullen and unsettled on day one, as if morning itself was uncertain when to begin. The strike, however, was already in full swing, with scores of workers manning picket lines at the North River piers where the city's major tugboat firms docked their vessels.

If union leaders had purposefully timed their work stoppage for the height of winter, when the city was most vulnerable to a harbor closure, their timing could not have been more impactful. Temperatures, as if on cue, had plunged overnight to the single digits, with intermittent snow showers laying an icy carpet over docks and quays. A blustery wind roiled the river, its gunmetal waters bucking with feral swells.

Undaunted by the elements, striking workers went about their dual mission: halting harbor traffic while publicly conveying their contract grievances. Bundled in mackinaws, wool caps, and layers of cold-weather gear, they marched in an orderly single file, their breath visible in vapory spurts. Other men huddled for warmth around trashcan bonfires that lined the waterfront like torches. A cordon of police in long blue overcoats and earmuffed caps maintained a wary vigil as the striking workers filed past, their handwritten messaging conveyed on cardboard placards nailed to broomsticks:

NY TUGBOAT WORKERS ON STRIKE!

NO CONTRACT, NO WORK!

Support LOCAL 88 in It's FIGHT 4 a LIVING WAGE!

Benny and Jack, having hardly slept, reported to the waterfront at their normal 5 a.m. start time. Their schedules throughout the work stoppage would be anything but normal, however. Benny, as he would early each day, met with union officials at the converted grocery store under the West Side Highway overpass. Jack fell into line with his *Jupiter* crewmates and other picketers at the nearby entrance to the Chelsea Piers, a row of pink-granite buildings that served as New York's primary passenger-ship terminal.

Although still early in the work stoppage, the strikers' primary objective seemed well within reach. With passenger-ship service indefinitely suspended, and cargo vessels immobilized, the normally bustling harbor was eerily still. Other than a smattering of fireboats, police cruisers, and commuter ferries, literally nothing moved on the city's waterways. Dozens of idled freighters, oil tankers, and railroad-boxcar floats sat moored to their docks. Garbage scows heaped with trash rested in their slips. Incoming ships were already being diverted to other ports, or dropping anchor in a miles-long queue that stretched to the mouth of the harbor. What hours earlier had been the world's busiest port had been rendered virtually dormant.

Despite the harbor's closure, however, the strikers' messaging had garnered little attention thus far. The bulldog editions of the city's daily newspapers had gone to press too early to carry strike coverage. Radio broadcasts conveyed only sketchy details. Most New Yorkers were still unaware of the unfolding drama, or the impact it would have on their lives.

But that would quickly change.

Seeking to short-circuit the budding crisis, mayoral officials summoned tugboat owners and union leaders to an impromptu "peace parley" at City Hall, where representatives of the warring parties voiced sharply divergent views about what had sparked the work stoppage. Grievances were aired, positions defended, emotions vividly on display. At one point, the meeting became so heated that Henry and Benny had to be physically restrained and dispatched to separate rooms.

Reluctant to take sides in the labor dispute, the Mayor's Office urged a brief cooling-off period and a timely resumption of negotiations. City officials, stressing the utmost urgency in reopening the harbor, issued appeals for civic responsibility and offered their assistance in resolving the stalemate. The meeting, with little resolved, lasted roughly an hour. Minutes afterward, New York's mayor convened a press briefing to address the unfolding crisis.

Nicknamed "Irish Eddie" by the city's saucy tabloids, Edmund Flannery was a former Bronx clubhouse politician who had assumed New York's mayoralty a scant three weeks earlier. Inexperienced as an administrator, and ill at ease in the public spotlight, the gawky, scabrous-faced Flannery seemed flummoxed by the city's unexpected plight, overwhelmed by the phalanx of reporters and photographers crowded into City Hall's Blue Room.

Stating that he didn't want to unduly alarm the public, Flannery did precisely that, acknowledging the potential impact of the strike by estimating that some eighty percent of the city's coal and fuel-oil shipments, along with half its food and medical supplies, could potentially be disrupted by the walkout. Pressed by reporters, Flannery noted that essential services—including the city's transit system, hospitals, and public schools—had roughly one week's worth of coal reserves. On the flip side, the mayor admitted, a prolonged strike could prove enormously damaging, given the critical role tugboats played in the city's daily life. Prompted by advisors, Flannery refrained from answering the resultant flurry of questions, ending the briefing by pledging that city officials would work diligently to return normalcy to the harbor quickly as possible.

But normalcy, at this point, seemed like little more than wishful thinking.

Indeed, no sooner had Flannery concluded his briefing than presses began rolling at New York's galaxy of newspapers, each one splashed with wall-to-wall coverage of the walkout. Reporters, photographers, and radio-broadcast crews fanned out to interview striking workers. Press conferences were convened at police headquarters, Sanitation Department offices, and the city's Board of Health. Tugboat owners and union leaders also met separately with reporters.

Greeting newsmen at Gotham Harbor Alliance headquarters was a sumptuous breakfast buffet: heaping platters of scrambled eggs, along with mountains of French toast, an array of pastries, and urns of hot coffee. Instantly, the reporters gravitated to the bountiful spread.

"Give reporters a good hot meal and you'll own them body and soul," Henry said to fellow tugboat owner George Steele, a sloe-eyed ally with a jowly face and perpetual sneer.

"I can buy any one of those worthless hacks for nothing more than a two-dollar steak," Henry boasted disdainfully.

And he believed it, too.

To Henry, New York's press corps was nothing more than a rabid flock of indolent lapdogs who blindly accepted whatever pabulum they were fed. Most reporters, in his view, were inherently on the take, exchanging favorable coverage for cordiality or cash. Few, he believed, worked diligently or aspired to the truth. Fewer yet were muckrakers or crusaders. Rather they stalked the city's streets in a ravenous pack, hungry for an eye-catching headline, a spellbinding scoop, a provocative quote—and a path to the nearest watering hole.

As for the newspapers that employed them, most, to Henry, were equally contemptible, the tabloids nothing more than scandal sheets trafficking in mayhem, gossip, and sex, and the broadsheets effete rags that blew with the prevailing political winds and pandered to whatever special interests paid the freight. Their only value to Henry was how he could use them.

And now he would try. The city's newspapers, Henry knew, would line up on either side of the tugboat dispute. *The Daily News, New York Post, Mirror*, and *Journal-American*—all with extensive blue-collar readerships—would surely be sympathetic to the striking workers. *The Herald Tribune*, unofficial voice of the Republican Party, would just as assuredly condemn the strikers, as would the staunchly conservative *New York Times, World Telegram*, and *Wall Street Journal*.

Henry called the press briefing to order from behind a chest-high lectern. Instantly, the reporters abandoned the buffet. Notebooks and pencils emerged. Camera flashbulbs popped.

"The tugboat strike that we're witnessing is highly regrettable," said Henry, reciting a statement he had scripted with the aid of a public-relations firm he kept on retainer.

"Our coalition believes that the union's decision to effectively close New York Harbor was both premature and avoidable," he said. "We further believe that timing this strike for the height of winter is the product of ruthless calculation. Our city, clearly, is most vulnerable at this time of year. The decision to strike now is irresponsible, vindictive, and displays a flagrant disregard for the welfare of New York and its people."

Henry paused as the gaggle of reporters scribbled notes, photographers cocking and releasing the shutters on their bulky Speed Graphic cameras.

"The Gotham Harbor Alliance has negotiated in good faith," Henry declared. "We've made a very liberal wage offer, and have done everything possible to avert a strike. Our goal has always been to seek an amicable resolution to this contract dispute. Union leadership, in contrast, has been unreasonable and disingenuous."

Henry controlled the timbre of his voice, his verbal pacing, facial gestures—anything he could—to look appear measured and sincere. All of it was calculated, carefully rehearsed—and phony as a wooden nickel. Nevertheless, it seemed impactful. Dutifully, the reporters recorded every word.

"Tugboats have been critical to New York's daily life for decades, and the companies that operate them have been essential to our city's economy," Henry continued. "We're sorry for any hardship this strike may cause, and we'll do whatever is possible to assure those hardships are minimized. We hope the union will similarly act in the public interest, and not continue to turn its back on the city."

Then he opened the floor to questions.

"What are the key issues spurring this dispute?" a reporter asked.

"I'd rather keep the specifics confidential," Henry replied. "But a key issue, as you might imagine, is money. There's a substantial difference between what the union is seeking for a wage increase and what tugboat owners can offer, given the current economy."

"How wide is the difference?" the reporter asked.

Henry deferred a response. Other questions, however, came in rapid succession.

"Would you say the two sides are far apart?"

"The short answer is 'yes."

"Has any progress been made toward a settlement since negotiations began?"

"Not enough to avoid the situation we're in."

"Are there any bargaining sessions scheduled?"

"Not at this time."

"Are you open to resuming negotiations?"

"Tugboat owners will do whatever it takes to reach a quick and amicable settlement."

"Do you envision the strike being a lengthy one?"

"I suggest you direct that question to union leaders. After all, they're the ones who've decided to deal this punishing blow to our city."

"But what's your sense of it?"

"Well, we certainly hope the strike doesn't last long. We'd like to get the dispute settled quickly, and we'll try to maintain services as we work toward that end. Our docks remain open. Work is available under the wage-and-benefit package contained in our final offer to the union. Any tugboat worker willing to work is welcome to do so."

The next question had a decided edge.

"Strike leaders have implied that your coalition is engaged in union-busting," a reporter from the pro-labor *Daily News* said. "How would you respond to that?"

"I'd say that the charge is patently false," Henry stated. "Frankly, if I were involved in union-busting, I must not be very effective. Union power has proliferated for decades on the city's waterfront. I can also state, unequivocally, that McFarland Marine Towing is a union shop that's been in business for nearly a century . . . and we've always been fair in our employment practices."

Then he planted the seed he most wanted to.

"You should also know that there are differing opinions regarding the strike within the union itself," he declared.

"Can you be specific?" the *Daily News* reporter pressed.

"What I mean," Henry replied, "is that it's my understanding that the union is riddled with dissension. A militant, rebellious faction has been pushing for this strike. A more moderate—and, frankly, more reasonable—faction is willing to accept our wage offer or at least continue negotiations."

Henry waited for the reporters to catch up with their notetaking.

"My point," he said, "is that I don't think the union's longtime leadership believes we're trying to 'bust' the union. Nor does its parent, the United Stevedores Association. If you want confirmation of that, ask USA president Paddy O'Boyle. He's a responsible union leader who has worked for years in negotiating equitable contracts and avoiding strikes."

"Isn't Paddy O'Boyle who you're negotiating with now?" a reporter asked.

"Not entirely." Henry grinned. "Other people are involved."

"By that, do you mean Benny Logan?"

"Precisely."

"And what's your opinion of him?"

"Next question," said Henry, to a smattering of laughter.

"What about the Wagner Act?" a reporter asked. "What's your opinion of that?"

Signed into law a decade earlier, the Wagner Act barred companies from interfering with unions, guaranteeing workers the right to organize and engage in collective bargaining.

"Some people call the Wagner Act organized labor's 'Bill of Rights," the reporter said. "Do you agree?"

"I'm as politically conservative as anyone alive," Henry said, "but even I believe that workers' rights to join a union is fundamental to our democracy, and that unions have helped workers avoid exploitation. The problem is that unions have also helped workers exploit employers."

Henry paused, to be sure he was being quoted correctly.

"What tugboat owners are opposed to is not unions per se, only irresponsible actions by extremists who are hell bent on holding America's greatest city hostage as a means of achieving outlandish demands. We don't believe unions should use strikes as leverage in labor disputes. Conflicts need to be resolved at the bargaining table, not on the streets."

"Are you an advocate, then, of Taft-Hartley?" the *Daily News* reporter probed.

The recently enacted Taft-Hartley Act, a major blow against organized labor, enabled federal officials to pursue injunctions barring strikes believed to endanger the public wellbeing.

Henry nodded. "I'm an avid supporter of that legislation."

"But unions charge that Taft-Hartley is anti-labor," the *Daily News* reporter said. "Labor leaders call it a 'slave-labor' bill. What do you call it?"

"I call it fair," Henry said.

"You don't consider it punitive to organized labor?"

"Not at all. To be perfectly candid, organized labor brought Taft-Hartley on themselves," Henry said. "For years, the playing field in America has tipped too far in workers' favor—too many abuses, too much power, one strike after another crippling America. Our country needed a law like Taft-Hartley to put the same limitations on unions that are in place for employers."

"Do you believe Taft-Hartley should be invoked for this strike?"

"Well, it certainly can be argued that a tugboat strike endangers the public wellbeing, but I think government officials should delay invoking Taft-Hartley," Henry replied. "As I said, I'd prefer to see a negotiated settlement prior to the government seeking an injunction against strikers. After all, these men are valued employees . . . and I wouldn't want to see them hurt."

Pledging round-the-clock availability, Henry ended the briefing by informing reporters that he'd be conducting similar sessions each day of the strike. Press releases, he said, would be available to assist in the preparation of stories. The breakfast buffet, he added, would be accessible all morning.

"I anticipate you'll be accurate in your coverage," Henry told the press corps. "And, of course, fair to our side."

Then, smiling broadly, he gestured toward the breakfast buffet.

"Now, why don't you boys help yourself to some coffee and a bite to eat."

He pointed outside, where a flurry of snow showers was being tossed about by howling gusts. "I wouldn't blame you one bit," he said, "if you'd rather not venture into that godawful cold."

* * *

One hour later, Benny and Paddy O'Boyle addressed the same group of reporters at strike headquarters on the west side of Manhattan.

Union officials, guarded in one another's presence, had agreed in advance that O'Boyle would serve as Local 88's primary mouthpiece—that is, Benny warned, for as long as the USA president perpetuated the myth that Local 88's rank and file was fully in lockstep over the decision to strike. Benny had also made it clear that he'd monitor O'Boyle's every word, jumping in instantly if the union boss failed to mask his objection to the walkout. Regardless of intra-union fissures, Benny said, there'd be no perceptible crack in Local 88's public stance. O'Boyle, as skilled in self-preservation as in union politics, had agreed.

At least for now.

"Welcome to our humble abode," the USA president quipped, as reporters squeezed into the storefront's tiny rear office, gathering before a desk behind which O'Boyle and Benny were seated. Other union officials stood somberly alongside. Rows of empty shelves lined the walls of the former grocery store. A coal stove, embers aglow behind a metal grate, threw a blanket of heat across the barren space.

Unfamiliar with New York's press corps, and unknown to them, Benny was somewhat unnerved by their presence in such numbers. Nevertheless he introduced himself as the head of Local 88's Strike Committee, deferring to O'Boyle for comments. The USA president began by confirming that the two sides in the labor squabble were far apart on the terms of a contract, with no further negotiations scheduled.

"What brought this conflict to a head?" the *Herald Tribune* reporter inquired.

"Our union is seeking a contract that would compensate workers fairly for the vital contributions they make in the operation of the harbor," O'Boyle said.

Though nowhere as erudite or polished as Henry, O'Boyle—seasoned by years in the public spotlight—was nevertheless skilled at manipulating the press, primarily by nurturing the notion that he was a living, breathing embodiment of the "Average Joe"—an honest, humble union figurehead seeking nothing more than a fair shot at a living wage for the powerless, downtrodden working man. That image, the USA president reasoned, would resonate with reporters. After all, most of them were Average Joes, too.

"It's not our goal to inconvenience or injure the public—an' if our actions cause that, we're truly sorry," O'Boyle said.

With his forlorn expression, skin dangling like a dewlap beneath his puffy jaw, O'Boyle looked every bit like a cuddly basset hound: humble, sincere, and contrite.

"The public, we believe, would be supportive of our union if they knew the facts," he told reporters. "Like our members, most New Yorkers are average workin' folks, just lookin' to care for their families."

Satisfied with the comment, Benny nodded, though ready to jump in if O'Boyle wandered off-script.

"The union is being painted as irresponsible in its decision to strike," a reporter asked. "How would you respond to that?"

"I'd say that our side has done everything possible to avoid a strike," O'Boyle replied. "But everything we tried in collective bargaining failed."

Benny, less enamored with that response, waded in.

"The tugboat owners presented us with a single offer—an' basically told us to take it or leave it," he said. "As far as we're concerned, their offer would set us back years. We've tried to negotiate in good faith, but the owners brought this to a head by refusin' to budge. Striking was our only real choice."

O'Boyle, biting his tongue, grinned wryly. Already, Benny was getting riled.

"The tugboat owners say it would be more productive if the strike had been postponed, and negotiations continued," the *Herald Tribune* reporter said.

O'Boyle opened his mouth to reply, but Benny beat him to the punch.

"Eight months of collective bargainin' have gotten us zilch!" he said, sharply. "Our members are tired of bein' jerked around."

Benny and O'Boyle, seated in tandem, drifted apart like similar poles on facing magnets. And now they took turns fielding questions, their disparate opinions increasingly apparent with each response, their rift more thinly veiled.

"The owners are blaming the union for making unreasonable demands and timing the strike for the height of winter, to inflict maximum damage to the city," a reporter said. "What's your response to that?"

O'Boyle answered quickly, "Our union bargained responsibly. Our demands were not excessive, given that our members haven't had a raise in four years."

Benny said, "The timin' of the strike is because no progress was bein' made at the bargainin' table. We've been 'negotiatin' since last summer with no progress. The winter had nothin' to do with it."

"What are the prospects for a speedy resolution?"

O'Boyle said gruffly, "We're hopin' that cooler heads prevail an' the strike ends soon."

Benny retorted, "Our members are prepared to remain outta work for as long as it takes to achieve a fair an' equitable contract."

The gathering felt more strained now, the union leaders' body language and verbal tone suggesting that the pair was at odds. The *Times* reporter, in particular, seemed to sense that—and tried to light a fire.

"We've heard reports that the union is deeply divided, with different factions wishing to resolve the dispute in different ways," he probed. "Is that true?"

O'Boyle answered suavely, "Debate is healthy. So are differences in opinion. This is a democracy, after all—ain't it?"

"Everyone in Local 88 is singin' out of the same hymnal," Benny said, then continued. "Our men speak with one voice."

"Is the parent union behind this strike?" the *Times* reporter pressed. O'Boyle's and Benny's responses kept the reporters looking back and forth at them like a metronome.

"The USA is working hard to broker an agreement."

"We anticipate our parent union's full support."

"Are you saying we can expect USA longshoremen to walk off the job in support of the strike?" a reporter asked.

"Nothing like that is in the works. We're trying to resolve this dispute at the local level. The USA is involved only in aiding with negotiations."

"Nothin' is off the table. Our parent union can jump in at any time."

"Would the union accept a wage hike in exchange for a reduction in crew size?"

"We're open to anything in the interest of negotiation."

"Absolutely not. There are no givebacks that we'll agree to."

"Do you believe the owners are engaged in union busting?"

"No. Our Local, under my leadership, has successfully negotiated many contracts with the owners, who've always shown the utmost respect for the union."

"Henry McFarland claims his owners' alliance doesn't oppose unions, but their actions suggest otherwise. Union busting? I wouldn't put it past them."

"Does your side trust Mr. McFarland?"

"Certainly . . . an' we have for years."

"Mr. McFarland has his interests to protect. We have ours."

O'Boyle cringed. Benny seemed more resolute than ever.

"Would your union welcome outside support in helping to achieve an acceptable contract?" a reporter asked.

O'Boyle answered, "Anything constructive from outside parties is welcome."

Benny laid down the stipulation, ignoring O'Boyle's sidelong glare. "As long as the outside involvement favors neither side."

"Where do things go from here?" the *Herald Tribune* reporter inquired.

"That remains to be seen," O'Boyle said. "We're hoping that negotiations can resume, with or without intervention, an' we can hammer out a deal."

"Right now, we're on strike," Benny declared. "The harbor has been effectively closed. The interests of the city will be served once a settlement is reached, an' that'll take a more concerted spirit of compromise on the part of the owners."

"Sounds like you'll need more than mudslinging to resolve this," a reporter said.

"That may be true, but mudslingin' is all we've got for now," Benny said. "It ain't possible to shake hands on a deal, you know, when the other side is extendin' nothin' but a clenched fist."

CHAPTER 22

February 1, 1946

The impact of the strike may have been slow to sink in for most New Yorkers, but it hit home immediately for Jack, who returned to Williamsburg weary and frazzled at the close of day one, barely in time to shower and scarf down supper before heading to classes at Pace.

For Jack, the past eleven hours had been both toilsome and troubling. Rather than attending to his daily assignments aboard *Jupiter*, he'd spent the entire day walking picket lines in the teeth of the brutal elements. The unrelenting freeze, whipped about by biting gusts, had gnawed its way through thermal gloves, fleece cap, and multiple layers of outerwear. Jack's joints were achy and stiff, his arms and legs tingly, his feet so blistered he could hardly walk.

The soreness and exhaustion, debilitating as that was, wasn't the worst of it, however. Simply being on strike was far worse. Like most of his crewmates, Jack had never been called upon to navigate the treacherous crosscurrents of a high-stakes labor war. Never had he witnessed the dogged resolve of common workmen, bound solely by the mucilage of their union brotherhood, sacrificing paychecks—and perhaps their livelihoods—for something as amorphous as a principle. Never, outside the firestorm of combat, had he seen a band of brothers so riddled with trepidation and hope, determination and fear. Bearing witness to that had been both heartbreaking and inspiring.

Now he'd retreated to the sanctuary of the family's apartment, and Kate greeted him with a warm embrace, a change of clothes, and a home-cooked meal.

"You look like you've been through another war," she said.

"Feels that way, too," Jack said, through chattering teeth.

"Rough day, huh?" She gently stroked his flaky, wind-burned face.

"Rough as they come," he groaned.

He was hardly a complainer. But he had to admit that being on strike was far more taxing, in a multitude of ways, than putting in a normal day's work.

"It drains the life from you," he said. "In every possible way."

"I'm sure," Kate said. "But now you're home, with me."

Kate's words alone warmed Jack. So did a hot shower, a set of dry clothing, and the supper Kate had prepared: pot roast, baked potato, her special blend of English tea, and a helping of Yorkshire pudding.

"Maybe this will help," Kate said about the pudding, Jack's favorite.

"An end to the strike," said Jack, "would help a whole lot more."

"Well, maybe that will come sooner than anyone thinks," Kate offered. "Sometimes people need to take a step backward in order to move forward."

"I hope you're right." Jack plopped wearily into a chair at the kitchen table. Kate sat beside him.

"So tell me . . . what was your day like?" she asked.

Picking at his meal, Jack recounted the past eleven hours, most of it consumed by bone-chilling stints on the Chelsea Piers picket lines. The strike was mere hours in duration, but already Jack desperately missed work: the banter of crewmates; the gratification; the tranquil, buoyant feeling of New York Harbor at the break of day.

"I guess it's true that you never know how much you love something," he said, "until it's gone."

"Well, I know how much I love you," Kate said, smiling, "and you're still here."

"Thanks, darling." Jack squeezed her hand. "I love you, too."

And he did. More than ever.

Even now, still so early in their union, Jack felt his marriage to Kate growing more substantive by the day. There was solidity to the relationship now, a sturdy foundation that inspired a growing sense of confidence. In England, their bond, while palpable, had always seemed unnervingly fragile, overlain with anxiety and months of nagging doubt. Would the Allies emerge victorious? Would Europe be spared? Would their relationship survive the war? Would they?

But all those questions had been answered now. Fear and trepidation had dissipated. A sense of certainty had taken hold, magnified by the joy of impending parenthood. It wasn't simply that Jack and Kate were very much in love, it was the abiding conviction that they would be there for one another without question or fail—that, with any challenge they'd ever face, Kate would be at Jack's side and he at hers, to lean on and confide in, comfort and love. An anchor. A beacon. An ally and companion to help weather life's storms.

"Look on the bright side," said Kate, ever the optimist. "Maybe something good will come from all the uncertainty and disruption. Maybe, in the end, things will work out for everyone."

"One can only hope," said Jack, reaching for a ray of sunshine but plunging, instead, into a pool of dark, disquieting feelings. Familiar ones, too.

Here he was, having accepted the tugboat job solely as a financial stopgap— and solely at Benny's behest. The last thing he'd expected was to become embroiled in an emotionally charged labor dispute. Yet now he was smack in the eye of the storm, with nowhere to hide and no way out. Bad timing? A rotten break? Or was there something more to it?

Sometimes, Jack couldn't help but feel that the latter was the case—that circumstance, more so than free will, was dictating the course of his life, rendering him a hostage to the whims of fate, an unwitting victim doomed by a preordained destiny. Hadn't that been the case, after all, for as long as he could recall? The same confounding pattern? The same succession of unwanted storms? None of it his doing. None of it his choice. All of it yielding turmoil and hardship, ambiguity and doubt.

Being trapped as an indigent young boy in the jaws of the Great Depression. Bearing witness to Gabriel's death, Benny's egress and exile, his family's rupture. Then being forced to do battle in a once-in-a-lifetime war. And now, being thrust unwittingly into an aberrant labor conflagration, spearheaded in large part by his brother.

How could the sum of those occurrences not make a man feel doubtful and cynical? How could it not make him feel that everything he was reaching for would forever be beyond his grasp, that he'd spend an entire lifetime bucking some irrevocable, predetermined fate? If that were the case, Jack thought, why bother to hope? Why harbor dreams? Why aspire to anything beyond what was already written in stone?

Sometimes, Jack was left only with questions, unsure if he truly owned his life, or if that belief was merely delusional. Sometimes, it seemed as if even the simplest of pursuits was futile. That alone was troubling. A man could grow despondent carrying thoughts like those around. Even the most sanguine of men could abandon all hope.

"Tell me," Kate asked. "How do you feel about the strike. I mean . . . really?"

It was a loaded question. Nor was it one to which Jack could frame a ready response. His jumbled emotions were difficult enough to decipher. Explaining them was harder yet.

"To be perfectly honest, I have mixed feelings about it," he finally confessed.

"Mixed? How?"

"Mixed in the sense that my heart tells me one thing, and my head says something else."

"Tell me what's in your heart," Kate said.

Hands clasped at the waist, Jack leaned forward in his chair.

"Well, my heart is with the workers," he replied. "Especially my crewmates."

"They're not the greedy malcontents they're being portrayed as, are they? Not the reckless hoodlums wreaking havoc for their own selfish gain?"

"Far from it," Jack said. "I see most of them as decent, hardworking men fighting for a better life, willing to make sacrifices and put their asses on the line. I sympathize with them and the challenges they face. I face those same challenges too."

"Are all the men so pure of heart."

"To be perfectly honest, no. I've come across plenty of rotten apples in the union: men who are violent and twisted, leaders who've corrupted their power, deadbeats who've never worked an honest day in their life."

"The union has its share of warts, doesn't it?"

"It's a group of people. All kinds. Nothing more than a reflection of its rank and file."

"So you're fully involved in the strike now, following your heart," Kate said. "But what does your head tell you?"

"My head," said Jack, "tells me that the issues behind the strike aren't as black-and-white as they're painted out to be . . . by either side."

"What does that mean?"

"It means that the strike is being fueled as much by emotion as it is by reason."

"What kind of emotion?"

"Anger. Bitterness. Frustration. Greed."

"On whose part?"

"Everyone's."

He picked listlessly at his supper.

"I guess what I'm trying to say is that the real issues behind the strike have become obscured by rhetoric and posturing," he explained. "Sure, the union is fighting for a pay hike that the owners are bucking. But money isn't what this strike is really about."

"What is?"

"Power. Ego. Greed. Exerting leverage. Exacting revenge."

Jack paused to gather his thoughts.

"I mean, collective bargaining is supposed to be a negotiation, a civil exchange of ideas," he said. "But instead, it's become an outlet for grievances, an opportunity for each side to bash the other side's brains in. Both sides have become unyielding, deaf to one another, convinced that the other side is out to destroy it. Both are seeking capitulation."

"Well if that's the case," said Kate, "why support the union?"

Jack grinned wryly. "Because when push comes to shove, Kate, all of us must choose a side. I'm a union man, duty-bound to adhere to a collective will. It's the same as being a soldier. You do what your side needs you to do."

"Even if you don't agree with the path you're being asked to walk?"

"My personal feelings," said Jack, "don't matter as much as other factors. I'll honor the covenant I pledged to abide by when I joined the union. The union is on strike. To cross our picket lines would mean betraying a brotherhood I vowed to support. Like it or not, I have no choice but to honor the strike."

"We always have choices," Kate said.

"Of that," said Jack, "I'm not so sure."

There it was again: the gnawing feeling that life made all the choices, and men like him were powerless in the hands of fate, captive to the agendas of others— that even after all the obstacles and all the setbacks, there was yet another hurdle to overcome, another hardship to endure, another battle to fight.

"The fighting never really ends for us, does it?" Kate asked. "Even if all we're looking for is shelter from the storm."

Jack sighed. "What you and I are looking for, Kate, doesn't seem to matter much in the larger scheme of things."

Then he added: "Besides . . . there's Benny."

Kate seized on that. "Benny's role in the strike makes things far more complicated for you, doesn't it?"

"What do you think?"

"I think," said Kate, "that you feel trapped . . . that even if you can't bring yourself to wholeheartedly endorse the strike, there's no way you'd ever take sides against a brother to whom you owe both loyalty and gratitude."

"Well," Jack said, smiling, "you sure figured that one out . . . didn't you?"

Jack pushed his dinner plate away, his meager appetite sated. Kate wasn't finished, however.

"Tell me about Benny," she probed.

"What about him?"

"What kind of brother has he been?"

"A damned good one, I'd say."

"How so?"

"Benny always looked out for Gabriel and me," Jack said. "He was our guardian, our role model, and idol. Benny has a hard, impenetrable edge to him, but that's only a mask . . . the kind that he's been wearing his entire life."

"What kind of mask?"

"Whatever kind was needed. A mask in school to hide his learning deficiencies. A mask in the boxing ring to hide his fear. A mask at the bargaining table to hide his insecurities."

"And when it comes to you, Jack? What mask is he wearing then?"

"When it comes to me, there are no masks," Jack said. "I know Benny for who he is, underneath the façade, at his core. I know he's softhearted, devoted to the people he cares about most. He'd give me the shirt off his back if I needed it. Always has."

"Your father never had much to do with him, did he?" Kate asked.

"Our father never had much to do with any of us," Jack replied. "Never had the time."

"Do you think that's all there was to it—in Benny's case?"

"No," Jack said. "In truth, Pop and Benny never saw eye to eye."

"Why?"

"Just grated on one another, I guess."

"Or maybe," suggested Kate, "they disappointed one another?"

Jack was struck by the insight. It was one of the many qualities he loved about Kate: her ability to see inside people's hearts.

"To Pop, Gabriel and I were always the 'favored' sons," Jack said.

"And Benny?"

"Let's just say Pop never cared for the way Benny conducted his life."

"But Benny craved your father's approval, didn't he?"

"What young boy doesn't?"

"You think Benny resents your father for withholding it?"

"I'm sure he does. But I also think that's a big part of what fuels Benny. In many ways, he's still just a kid desperately trying to show our father—and the rest of the world—that he's worthy of recognition, redemption, and respect."

"The things that people need most," said Kate, placing a hand gently on Jack's arm, "they search for their entire life. Maybe Benny wasn't the problem your father painted him out to be . . . but just a boy who needed a better father."

Maybe, Jack thought.

"Gabriel's death hurt Benny deeply, didn't it?" Kate asked.

"It hurt all of us," Jack said. "But Benny took it hardest. Sixteen years later, he's still tormented by it. All his life, he'd sworn to take care of Gabriel and me. I'm sure he still questions whether he did everything possible to save Gabriel's life . . . or if Pop was right and he could have done more."

"Humiliated too, I'm sure," said Kate, "for having fallen from his pedestal as the benevolent Big Brother?"

"Probably."

"Hasn't forgiven himself for what happened that day, has he?"

"No."

"How could he . . . if forgiveness isn't offered by the person he needs it from most?"

"I dunno," Jack said. "All I can tell you is that I've done everything I can think of to pull Benny and Pop together. The wounds run too deep, though. I'm not sure there's any way to ever make things right."

"There's always a way," said Kate, "as long as people are alive."

Jack chuckled. "Well, maybe you can teach me that trick."

"And maybe," said Kate, "you'll learn it on your own."

Jack looked away, empty, devoid of certainty.

"Whatever the case," he said, "that's even more reason I owe Benny my support. When it comes to family, he's already lost enough. I don't need to add betrayal to the mix."

"No," said Kate. "If anything, you probably want to be there for him at all costs. Protect him as he always protected you. Free him from his torment."

"I only wish I could."

Jack checked his watch. It was nearly time to leave for his classes.

"More importantly for now," said Kate, "is whether Benny is the right man to lead the union through this strike."

"That, I'm far more certain about," Jack said.

"How so?"

"The union craves a leader who's passionate and committed. The men are fed up with the old regime—cronyism, betrayal, and sweetheart deals."

"Benny's different?"

"Benny would sooner throw himself on a hand grenade than sell the men out," Jack said. "In that regard, he's exactly the leader the union needs."

"He may be incorruptible," Kate asked, "but will he bend?"

"We'll have to see."

"Are you saying that his 'fighting spirit' could be a chink in his armor?"

"Maybe," Jack said. "Problem is, it's hard for Benny to give ground. In some respects, he equates compromise with weakness. The contract negotiations are like a prizefight to him. He's seeking capitulation. I'm afraid he's made the conflict a personal tug-of-war between him and Henry McFarland, the tugboat owners' ringleader."

"So what you're saying," said Kate, "is that this entire dispute, in many ways, has boiled down to two stubborn, headstrong leaders going head-to-head?"

"I'm afraid so."

"Isn't that dangerous?"

"It's no way to settle a dispute," Jack said. "But regardless, I've got to stand with Benny. I owe him, Kate. He's always been there for me."

He rose from his chair and carried his dinner plate to the sink.

"How long do you think the strike is going to last?" Kate queried.

"Hard to say. Reaching an accord will take a lot of work, by both sides."

"You mean it might take days, if not weeks?"

"Uh-huh."

"And it could get ugly too?"

"Labor disputes have a way of doing that." Jack sighed. "A lot of people could get hurt."

"Including us?"

"I'm afraid so."

"So, what do we do?"

"We weather the storm, best as we can."

"But how can we make ends meet without your paycheck?"

"We'll have to figure that out. The union has a strike fund, though it's not much. And we still have your paycheck."

"Thirty dollars a week," said Kate, "won't get us very far."

"Then we may have to tap our nest egg."

"There isn't much there to tap. Most of what we've 'saved' is the money my father set aside for me. You've already lost two weeks' pay and the strike has barely begun. Whatever we've saved will quickly disappear. And our moving plans? What about those?"

"We'll have to put all those things on hold."

"Well, we sure know how to do that, don't we?" Kate said wryly. "Sometimes, it seems as if putting our plans on hold is all we've ever really been able to do."

CHAPTER 23

February 2, 1946

The newspapers feasted on the story. A strike of such enormous magnitude—unbridled labor war at New York's most critical commercial hub—was nothing less than front-page fodder. Kindling, too, for a firestorm of equal intensity.

Just as organized labor and corporate interests were locked in a bitter power struggle in the wake of World War II, big-city newspapers were engaged in a pitched battle of their own. New York's bevy of daily papers, battling one another for readership and advertising dollars, lusted like junkies for a palpable buzz. Some published as many as three editions a day, excluding EXTRAS hawked by newsboys at street corners, bus stops, and subway stations. Newsstands bulged at their seams with periodicals vying for the most evocative photo, the most arresting scoop, the splashy headline known in newspaper circles as "wood."

The tugboat strike, viewed in that light, was a veritable forest of ready-to-fell timber—a breaking news story riddled with conflict, controversy, a compelling cast of characters, and major import for America's preeminent city. The stakes, in many respects, couldn't be higher: fuel and food deliveries threatened by a harbor-crippling work stoppage; passenger and cargo ships unable to dock in port; legions of citizens facing workplace closures; political and social divisions being stoked; and the potential for the crisis to heighten by the day, stretching the news cycle interminably. In other words, for the city's press corps, nothing short of a perfect storm.

The story particularly struck home for millions of Americans. Labor unrest, after all, wasn't confined solely to New York, or merely to the tugboat trade. A battle for workplace supremacy was raging now across much of the nation. For while America had emerged from World War II as a military and economic powerhouse, many workers, scarred by the aftermath of the First World War, dreaded a reprise of the Great Depression. Postwar inflation was rampant, wages stagnant, jobs at a premium. While wartime salary freezes and no-strike pledges had officially expired, collective bargaining on new labor contracts had yet to begin in many industries. Frustrations that had festered throughout the war were reaching a boiling point now. In the past year alone, some five million American workers had staged strikes in protest over wages, benefits, and work conditions. Mere weeks earlier, striking teamsters had made headlines by halting truck traffic on major U.S. highways, while a strike by railroad workers left thousands of travelers stranded, and a work stoppage by coal miners brought the nation's economy to a virtual standstill. Similar fault lines were being laid bare in automaking, steel, petroleum, meatpacking, even public education. And now the strike wave, the largest in America's history, had washed ashore on the most public of stages, home to nearly every major journalistic enterprise in America. New York Harbor had become the front line in the war for control of the nation's workplace. The tugboat strike was major national news.

New York's press corps jumped on the unfolding drama like a pack of hungry wolves. Strike coverage was splashed across the front page of each of the city's nearly dozen daily newspapers, in languages from English and Italian to Polish and Yiddish. EXTRAS flew off the presses. Bold-faced headlines, some of them dripping in blood-red type, heralded the news:

TUGBOAT STRIKE HALTS CRITICAL FUEL, FOOD SHIPMENTS!

PORT CRIPPLED BY TUGBOAT WORKERS WALKOUT!

NEW YORK HARBOR STUCK IN DIVISIVE DEEP FREEZE!

The labor conflict—pitting the Average Joe against Corporate America, the scrappy underdog against the privileged elite—also lent itself to passionate, widely disparate viewpoints, including intonations of a class war that threatened to tear at the fabric of the city. Reporters and editorial writers, pandering to their disparate readerships, instantly lined up on opposite sides of the dispute. The city's working class bibles published editorials supporting the striking tugboatmen while condemning tugboat owners for failing to engage constructively in collective bargaining. The pro-business papers all portrayed the strikers as rebellious and irresponsible, demanding that they return to work immediately so that negotiations could resume and damage to the city be minimized.

Media coverage, however, was only just revving up—as was the impact of the work stoppage, its theatrics, political fallout, and the tactics aimed at coping with it.

Throughout day two, hordes of reporters roamed the corridors of City Hall, hounding public officials for updates and opinions about the work stoppage. Others stood vigil at the offices of the Gotham Harbor Alliance, the North River tugboat docks, and Local 88's strike headquarters. Striking tugboat workers were photographed as they manned picket lines against the backdrop of a listless New York Harbor. The phone in Henry's office rang off the hook with interview requests. Union leaders were besieged by similar inquiries.

But contact with the principals, at least for the time being, was virtually impossible. Henry was purposefully laying low, content to let the impact of the work stoppage fully sink in. Local 88 officials were doing much the same.

Not everyone at the center of the labor tempest enjoyed the luxury of silence, however. At his second press briefing in two days, Mayor Edmund Flannery echoed the sentiments of most New Yorkers—terming the strike "regrettable," renewing his plea for a resumption of negotiations, and offering the resources of City Hall in brokering a settlement.

The mayor then went a major step further. Describing the strike as potentially the gravest threat ever faced by the city, Flannery unveiled the most radical mayoral action in peacetime history: a rationing plan aimed at addressing what, almost overnight, would become an acute shortage of fuel.

Flannery's hastily-cobbled-together edict permitted the distribution of coal and fuel oil exclusively to public utilities, hospitals, nursing homes, schools, police stations, firehouses, and other locations deemed critical to the public wellbeing. Deliveries were banned to all non-essential sites, including office and apartment buildings, restaurants, hotels, theaters, taverns, retail shops, houses of worship, and places of amusement. Public transportation was ordered to operate on limited weekend schedules. Heat was reduced in the electrified cars of subway trains and trolleys. Private homes, apartment buildings, offices, and factories were ordered to lower their temperatures to no more than sixty degrees.

Flannery also affirmed what had already become eminently clear: the ripple effect of the strike, he warned, could well represent the greatest disruption to New York's daily life since protestors of Civil War draft laws staged racially-charged riots in Manhattan nearly a century earlier. There simply was no precedent for what was unfolding, Flannery said, no way to forecast how profound an impact the strike might have.

And it was easy to see why. New York's appetite for fuel oil and coal was voracious. Nearly every office building, factory, hospital, school, and residence relied on steam heat, electricity, and gas. The Consolidated Edison Company, the city's primary utility, required thirty thousand tons of coal a day to ensure its normal output. Upwards of four million gallons of fuel oil was consumed daily by other utilities, including the New York Steam Company, whose electric-generating stations and network of underground steam mains, the largest in the world, served nearly eight million customers.

With tugboats out of service, Flannery said, the critical fuel needed to operate these energy-generating utilities would be unable to reach its intended destinations. Starved of that fuel, the mayor added, major utilities would cease functioning within days. And the timing of the fuel cutoff, Flannery noted, would only exacerbate matters. Indeed, weather forecasts were calling for a protracted cold snap and additional snowfall, with temperatures expected to remain below freezing and demand for fuel soaring. In another words, the mayor said, things might get far worse before they got better.

"The public," Flannery warned, "should prepare for that contingency."

And that was all the city's press corps needed to hear. Scrambling to out-scoop one another, reporters raced to rows of telephones to call their stories in. Editors groped for provocative angles to plumb. Newsrooms produced reams of copy. Linotype machines cranked out slugs of lead type that were set into composition blocks in the form of pages. Bundles of newsprint were wound onto presses whose collective roar rumbled like an earthquake through the city.

By midday, virtually every New Yorker and metro-area commuter was cognizant of the burgeoning crisis facing the city. Most—shaped by social standing, political affiliation, and employment status—would have sharply differing opinions about the strike. Most would be hoping that the conflict, regardless of resolution, would end quickly. Most would find themselves praying, with good reason, for that very same outcome.

CHAPTER 24

February 3, 1946

Henry woke from a patchy sleep early on day three, excited as a kid on Christmas morning.

Indeed, orchestrating the strike, to this point, had been as titillating an endeavor as Henry could recall across his thirty-plus years in business. Sticking it to the tugboat workers' union had been a long-held goal, payback for the heartache organized labor had dispensed for decades. Unions like Local 88 deserved a damned good whipping, Henry reasoned. Who better to administer the punishment than him?

But there was more to Henry's ebullience now than merely quenching a thirst for retribution; making life miserable for the tugboat workers' union was, in some aberrant way, fun. Bringing militants like Benny Logan to heel would do nothing less than caulk the anguish wrought by Carolyn's death. Schadenfreude, in many ways, was Henry's only real pleasure these days. Reveling in other people's pain was the only way to assuage his own.

But Henry didn't dwell for very long on either his motives or his emotions. Instead, he hurriedly dressed, wolfed down a muffin and coffee, and summoned Billy Murdock for the forty-minute drive to his office, the pair stopping first at a Wall Street newsstand where Murdock jumped out of Henry's limo to scoop up an armful of newspapers.

Henry could barely contain his exuberance when Murdock deposited the newspapers on his lap. Indeed, just as he had predicted, each of the city's major dailies had published wall-to-wall coverage of the tugboat strike. Editorials, op-ed pieces, and columnists addressed the economic, political, and social implications of the work stoppage. Arguments on both sides of the dispute were aired. Henry was quoted extensively, sounding lucid and conciliatory. The hospitality he'd proffered to the city's press corps the day before had seemingly paid dividends. Strike coverage seemed, at worst, balanced—if not tilted slightly in the tugboat owners' favor.

"I've never seen coverage this extensive about a labor dispute in New York," Billy Murdock exclaimed. "From the way the papers are playin' it up, you'd think another war has broken out!"

"It has," Henry said. "Believe me, it has."

Murdock stole a peek at his boss through the rearview mirror.

"This is no run-of-the-mill strike, is it?" the ex-cop inquired.

"Hardly," Henry replied.

"Stakes are high?"

"High as they can possibly get."

Murdock shook his head ominously.

"How long do you see the strike playing out?"

"I'll know more," said Henry, "once the workers miss a paycheck or two."

Murdock nodded. "Past-due bills can change men's thinking, huh?"

"So," said Henry, "can skittish wives."

The two of them shared a laugh as Murdock headed toward Gotham Harbor Alliance headquarters, where Henry was scheduled to meet with his fellow owners.

"What's your take on Irish Eddie's feelin's about the strike?" Murdock asked.

"I think his gloom-and-doom forecast," said Henry, "is right on target."

"Things could get dicey, huh?"

"It won't take long," Henry said, "for the entire city to unravel."

"What happens then?"

"Public hardship. Mass chaos. Panic in some quarters, I'm sure."

"Sounds ominous."

"With good reason," Henry said. "New York has never faced a crisis like the one that's about to unfold."

"And Flannery's fuel-rationing plan?" Murdock asked. "What about that?"

"Ill-advised and premature." Henry sneered. "Our new mayor has his head squarely up his ass. I suspect he's in a full-blown state of panic already."

Henry relished the prospect of New York's chief executive floundering in the face of the strike. He made no secret of his disdain for Flannery, a left-leaning political hack who'd soundly defeated Henry's GOP choice in the recent mayoral election.

"It's a long way from the Bronx clubhouse to the corridors of City Hall," Murdock said. "Irish Eddie is swimming in the deep end of the pool now."

"Drowning is more like it!" Henry crowed.

Murdock chuckled. He didn't care much for Flannery, either. Typical Democrat, to the ex-cop's way of thinking. Way too soft on crime.

"I'm sure he didn't expect a crisis like this three weeks after getting sworn in," Murdock quipped. "The poor sucker hasn't even had a chance to get his dick wet yet."

"Tough shit!" Henry declared. "Crises do come with the mayoralty, however."

He reclined comfortably in the plush rear seat. Sure, it was still early in the strike; and a lot could happen to alter the course of situations as volatile as this. But Henry had fired a successful opening salvo. By dragging his feet at the bargaining table, eschewing compromise, and convincing fellow tugboat owners to mimic his position, his blueprint was firmly in place. Local 88 had been lured into a potentially damaging strike. The city was in peril, the media in an uproar, public officials seemingly clueless about how to address the budding crisis. It was precisely the scenario that Henry had angled for, ripe for exploitation.

To Henry, chaos, at least for the time being, was welcome. Indeed, if city officials bungled matters badly enough, he reasoned, they could exacerbate the very crisis they were trying to contain. The balance of Henry's plan could then seamlessly unfold. The strike would evoke widespread disorder, the union would be held culpable, public and political pressure would mount, and a divided, cash-strapped Local 88 would be forced to capitulate. If things broke right, the entire balance of workplace power in New York could swing in management's favor. With any luck, the tugboat workers' union might be eradicated entirely, militants like Benny Logan led to a public pillory. Henry might even attain a result akin to moral larceny—winning contract concessions simply because he could. That would be the sweetest outcome of all.

So far, so good, he reflected.

Murdock dropped him off at Gotham Harbor Alliance headquarters where, unnoticed by picketers out front, he slipped in through a rear loading dock and minutes later was presiding over a meeting of tugboat owners, along with their legal and public-relations teams.

Henry polled the owners regarding the status of the strike. Nothing untoward was reported. Most tugboat firms were either shuttered entirely or being operated on a shoestring basis by management personnel. Picketing was said to be peaceful, organized—and seemingly impactful. Virtually no movement was reported on the city's waterways.

"New York Harbor is shut tighter than a nun's ass," the white-haired George Steele said. "I suppose, from the union's perspective, the strike is having its desired effect."

"It's having its desired effect from our perspective, too," Henry offered. "Believe me: what's happening now is precisely what we want."

As always, Henry controlled the tenor and direction of the owners' discourse, his viewpoint giving the other men food for thought. Long as he could keep the other owners believing in his crusade, Henry was sure, he could retain their support. Some ventures, he knew, even he couldn't undertake alone.

"The union is achieving its goal for the short term, but their actions will quickly backfire," he said. "Mark my words: if union leaders think a strike will win public support, they're woefully mistaken. Exactly the opposite will occur."

"Are you certain?" asked Bertram Phelps, skeptical as always.

"I'm as certain," said Henry, "as the day is long."

Henry used his thumbnail to spin the striker on his lighter, firing up a Lucky he shook from its pack.

"Public sentiment is shifting in business's favor these days, and this strike will further tip the scale," he said. "What we've set in motion, gentlemen, is the beginning of the end for labor unions in New York—and perhaps elsewhere. Believe me: someday organized labor will be nothing more than a spent force . . . an appendage to business in America."

He took a long pull on his cigarette.

"Strikes like the one we're seeing," he said, "are going to be the death knell for labor unions, render them a victim of the power they've abused. And you know what? Their wounds will have been self-inflicted. Labor unions will have earned their demise."

Exhaling a puffy plume of smoke, he added, "Now we need to convey our own message in the strongest possible terms."

"And exactly what is that?" Phelps asked.

"It's that we've drawn the line, once and for all, against organized labor," Henry said. "And we're determined to halt unions in their tracks before they destroy our country!"

He drew again on his cigarette. "I believe we have a chance, at this pivotal moment, to set an example for businesses across America, and plot a favorable course for future relations with all unions."

"And now that we've baited them into this strike," Phelps asked, "what next?"

"We step on their neck . . . exploit the one weakness I believe is fatal."

Henry then divulged the telephone conversation he'd conducted with Otto Blackburn, who had since agreed, for a hefty fee, to supply daily reports from his union sleuths. Henry never referenced the labor consultant directly; nor did he reveal that he'd planted a pair of spies inside the union. That admission, he guessed correctly, would be poorly received. But armed with Blackburn's latest intelligence, he expressed confidence that he had an accurate read on the infighting wracking Local 88.

"We know for certain," he said, "that Paddy O'Boyle has shaken hands on the deal that he and I negotiated, and which he still believes he can sell to the striking workers. Right?"

Coalition members nodded their assent.

"We also know that the work stoppage is being spearheaded by insurgents who are bucking O'Boyle, and have won over the rank and file."

Again, the owners gestured in affirmation.

"To me," Henry said, "this signals that the union may be fatally split—militant supporters of Benny Logan backing the strike and old-line O'Boyle partisans willing to accept the deal we privately struck. I believe that's the weakness we can exploit . . . that the union, under the pressure of the strike, will come apart rather quickly at the seams."

"How quickly?" Phelps asked.

"Within days."

"And then?"

"I see Local 88 dissolving into chaos, if not imploding entirely, and settling on the contract terms we've proposed . . . terms we'll be able to dictate for years to come. I also see a return to union leadership by Paddy O'Boyle."

"And Benny Logan?"

"I envision him being tossed out on his ass."

"And what if union capitulation takes longer than a few days?" Phelps asked.

"I believe," said Henry, "that we can hasten the process."

"How?"

"To that end, I propose a three-part strategy. One: attempt, as always, to win the public-relations battle through the newspapers. Two: continue to solicit Paddy O'Boyle's support in undermining union hardliners. And three: try to induce strikers to cross picket lines."

"How do you suggest we do that?" Phelps inquired.

"By offering incentives."

"What kind?"

Henry tapped his pants pocket. "The kind that get results."

Phelps recoiled. "But won't that prove costly to us?"

"I'll personally pay the freight," Henry vowed.

That pledge seemed to allay any concerns.

"I suppose we could also petition Congress to invoke Taft-Hartley," attorney Harlan Kingsley suggested.

"Think the Feds would do that?" Steele asked.

"I'm confident they would," Kingsley opined. "Clearly, a cutoff of fuel and food to a city like New York represents a serious threat to the public wellbeing."

The owners mulled the tactic. Henry, however, had something else in mind.

"Look," he said, "no one loves Taft-Hartley more than me. But seeking to invoke it is a card we can play later. I think it's more advantageous, for now, to keep the Feds at arm's length from this dispute . . . make them believe that the two sides can resolve it on their own."

"And why is that?"

"I think our leverage would be seriously undercut by government intervention," Henry reasoned. "The Feds will force us to settle at terms we've rejected all along. They'll ram a contract up our asses, just to end the strike."

"So, what are you proposing instead?" Phelps asked.

"I say we let the strike play out. The longer it runs its course, the stronger our side becomes."

"Stronger?" Phelps recoiled. "Even as our companies bleed money?"

"Yep. Absolutely."

Henry then detailed the specifics of his plan. He suggested that the coalition's public-relations firm draft a letter to strikers, claiming that the walkout was being fostered, contrary to the workers' interests, by a handful of renegades bucking the conciliatory stance of responsible union leaders. The letter would state that tugboat owners were anxious to return to the bargaining table in a good-faith effort to reach an equitable settlement. It would further pledge that any employee who returned to work could resume his job, at overtime pay and without prejudice; that lost wages would be restored; and that the returning workers, in contrast to strikers, would run no risk of losing their jobs.

"Sounds like a potent incentive to cross picket lines," Steele said.

"But at overtime pay?" Phelps balked.

"Again . . . on my dime," Henry pledged.

Within seconds, the owners concurred.

"I think what we've achieved as a coalition thus far is nothing short of miraculous," Henry said. "Think about it: our companies have put past enmity aside and linked arms in a mutually beneficial effort. It's essential that we stand firm. No cracks in our ranks!"

To that, too, the owners agreed.

"Good!" Henry grinned. "Now, let's see if we can induce strikers to cross picket lines. If we can get enough of the men to return to work, and cut Benny Logan's nuts off in the process, we can end this strike quickly and set the union back years—perhaps for good!"

CHAPTER 25

February 3, 1946

While tugboat owners mulled their next move, union leaders were busy mapping tactics of their own.

Local 88's strike headquarters bustled like an anthill. Strike captains feverishly worked the phones, issuing directives, fielding queries, and receiving updates from picket sites across the city. Union supporters—mostly the wives and children of strikers—sprawled across the floor, stenciling slogans onto placards and nailing them to broomsticks. Striking workers seeking respite from the frigid temperatures outside, milled around bridge tables set with urns of hot chocolate, coffee, and baked goods.

Activities of a far different sort were underway in the office at the rear of the former grocery store, where Local 88's Strike Committee had gathered for their morning meeting. The cramped office, furnished only with a bridge table, folding chairs, and a potbelly stove, was barely large enough to contain the union's six-man brain trust, which included Benny, Tommy Duggan and Local 88 treasurer Frank Russo, along with Paddy O'Boyle and two of O'Boyle's sidekicks from the United Stevedores Association.

The rough-hewn assemblage, reflecting decades on the front lines of organized labor, mirrored the entire spectrum of rank-and-file sentiment about the strike. Crammed into the tiny office were union officials who enthusiastically backed the walkout and others who vehemently opposed it: staunch allies of both Benny and O'Boyle, along with others whose nebulous allegiances could be bought or sold for a pittance. Such was the nature of union politics. Internecine rivalries were commonplace, backstabbing par for the course, allegiances shifting at the drop of a hat.

"What're the newspapers sayin'?" asked Lou Grimes, a cigar-chomping O'Boyle sycophant stuffed into a shabby double-breasted suit.

"All the anti-labor rags— the *Times, Herald Tribune, Wall Street Journal*— are rippin' us new assholes," replied Eddie Cooper, a crusty USA official. "Most are callin' our members irresponsible, rebellious, greedy. They're sayin' we got no business walkin' off the job when we should be negotiatin' . . . that we're leavin' the city in the lurch."

"Don't they know how the tugboat owners have been yankin' our chains at the bargainin' table?" Grimes asked.

"I guess they print whatever bullshit Henry McFarland sells 'em." Cooper shrugged.

"Ah . . . who reads that highbrow crap anyway?" Grimes chomped on his stogie. "What's the *Daily News* sayin'? The *Post*? Papers that regular people read?"

"They're pullin' for us," Cooper said. "The *Daily News* called us 'champions of the workin' class.' Said we deserve every penny we earn for the important work we do."

"An' the *Post*?"

"They said that the tugboat owners are out of touch with workin' people, that they've declared war on blue-collar New York."

"See!" Grimes exulted. "There are people on our side . . . plenty of 'em!"

The union leaders seemed assuaged. Like Henry, each man understood the import of public opinion. Winning popular support for the strike, they recognized, was perhaps the most critical card the union could hold.

"We gotta walk a fine line, though," Tommy Duggan said. "We can't come across as a bunch of greedy radicals lookin' for a handout, even if the public be damned."

"That's exactly what Henry McFarland's paintin' us out as," Grimes said.

"Is that what people think?" Eddie Cooper asked.

"It's too early for most people to be thinkin' anything yet," Benny said.

"They'll form opinions soon enough, though," Duggan added.

"That's what scares me," said Grimes. "Let's face it: this strike is gonna wreak havoc on a lotta lives. The public may put up with the hardship for a while, but people have their limit. It ain't gonna take long for 'em to get angry an' start pointin' fingers."

"An' if they point at us," said Cooper, "we're screwed!"

The strike leaders grew pensive, the office scented with woodsmoke, the hiss and pop from the potbelly stove the only sound. O'Boyle seemed especially pensive, and with good reason: he was in a serious bind. Despite his role as USA president, he'd been reduced to little more than a figurehead, a toothless tiger being pushed aside by a new breed of rebellious leadership. While he retained a cadre of hardcore supporters, he had no choice now but to play ball with Benny and other militants, or lose whatever waning support he retained. It was an unnerving situation for the longtime union boss, who sat forlornly on his chair, as if longing to either flee the city or find some way to turn his fortunes around.

In truth, he was doing both. And Benny knew it. Benny trusted O'Boyle not at all—suspecting, correctly, that the union boss was in cahoots with Henry McFarland and doing the tugboat owners' bidding. Indeed, other than Tommy Duggan and Jack, Benny wasn't sure whom to trust on a waterfront crawling with opportunists, connivers, and backstabbers.

O'Boyle and his cronies, Benny was convinced, would stab him in the back without thinking twice, the moment the opportunity arose. Betrayal, he believed, was less a question of if than of when. Worse, the longer the strike lasted, the greater the likelihood that O'Boyle could work to undercut Benny's leadership, short-circuit the walkout, and rally supporters for a return to power. On that, Benny would bet his life.

In many respects, he was doing exactly that.

"What's happenin' on the front lines?" he asked now.

"Everything's goin' as planned," Tommy Duggan replied. "Picket lines are peaceful, unified, an' organized."

"What about the harbor?"

"Dead as a doornail."

"An' the men?"

"Spirits are holdin' up. They're just freezin' their nuts off out there."

Benny turned to Eddie Cooper. "Can we bring in parkas, blankets, gloves?"

"Already on the way," Cooper reported.

"How 'bout wood for the trashcan bonfires?"

"We're burnin' wood scraps, Christmas trees . . . whatever we can get our hands on," Cooper said. "What we really need, though, is a fuckin' heat wave."

"Well, that ain't in the cards," Benny said. "Winter is what we wanted. Winter is what we got."

That much was for certain. Weather forecasts were calling for conditions to worsen considerably over the next several days, a potential nor'easter forming off the coast.

"Could be a blizzard," Lou Grimes said ominously. "All the winter we ever wanted!"

The men laughed apprehensively. Cold weather was a double-edged sword. On one hand, it strengthened the strikers' leverage by increasing the city's appetite for fuel oil and coal, supplies of which were unable to enter port. On the flip side, the wintry conditions wreaked havoc on both picketers and an increasingly antsy public.

"Well, there's nothin' we can do about the weather," Benny said. "Our men'll just have to tough it out."

"Our men are tough as nails," Grimes said. "But even they have their breakin' point."

"Men can do the impossible," Benny observed, "if they believe in what they're doin.'"

"Then we'll just have to keep 'em believin," Grimes said.

"Leave that part to me," said Benny.

He turned again to Duggan. "How about crossovers?"

"None . . . as far as I know," Duggan said. "Not yet anyway."

That, of course, could be a problem. Nothing could cripple a strike faster than defectors crossing picket lines, abandoning the fight and returning to work.

"Think we can keep our picket lines intact?" Benny asked.

"We'll give it our best shot," Duggan replied.

"Let's face it," Grimes warned, "some men are gonna cross the lines. Lost paychecks, family pressure, public backlash—those things are gonna eat away at the men's resolve."

"Incentives might do the trick, too," Duggan said. "Promises of back pay, money under the table . . . the owners are gonna try every trick imaginable to break the strike."

Benny turned to Eddie Cooper. "How 'bout the politicians? City Hall? The Feds?"

"They're payin' attention . . . that's for sure," Cooper replied. "Politicians are pussies, though. They blow with the breeze. For now, they're sittin' on their hands, tryin' to nudge both sides toward a settlement. They're gettin' antsy, I'm sure . . . but stayin' neutral."

"Which way do you think they'll lean if the strike continues?"

"Hard to know," Cooper observed. "Each side is critical to their interests. They don't wanna step on anyone's toes—either the business community or blue-collar voters. Who knows what they'll do? Principle don't matter to those assholes. The only thing that matters is what's in the ballot box."

"Well, one way or another, the politicians can't sit on their hands for much longer," Benny said. "They gotta do whatever's needed to reopen the harbor. There are no votes to be had if food an' fuel are runnin' low, businesses are closed, an' people are out of work. For now, I say we let the politicians feel the heat an' hope they jump into the fray soon as they really start sweatin'."

Benny's comment mirrored a core belief. Unlike Henry, who resisted outside intervention at this point in the strike, Benny was certain that the union's best chance for a favorable settlement hinged on luring government officials as quickly as possible into the fray, to help jumpstart negotiations, or even broker a deal.

"The politicos have their asses on the line," Benny said. "They can't afford to let a strike continue to cripple the harbor—or worse, to see it spread."

"City Hall's gotta be shittin' bricks about the possibility of contagion," Duggan said. "Imagine other unions jumpin' into this dispute, shuttin' down the entire goddamned city?"

"That'd end the strike real fast," Eddie Grimes predicted. "In our favor, too."

"Maybe so," Benny said. "But City Hall can't allow that. The Feds can't, either. It won't be long before they're tightenin' the screws, on both sides, to end the strike."

"But won't we get our nuts clipped if the politicians jump in?" Grimes asked.

"Maybe so," Tommy Duggan replied. "But at least we'll come out of the fight in one piece. We won't survive at all if Henry McFarland has his way."

The men fell into a troubled silence.

"Okay, then," Benny finally said. "Let's limit picketin' to thirty minutes per man, an' get our guys indoors as often as possible. Keep the bonfires burnin'. Bring in whatever's needed to battle the cold. Whatever we do, the harbor's gotta stay closed. The longer we can manage that, the greater our leverage."

"I'm sure the owners feel the same," Grimes said. "No doubt they're gonna try to wait us out, an' squeeze our nuts."

"Let 'em!" Benny said. "We'll squeeze theirs just as hard."

Everyone seemed in concurrence, at least on the surface. For the union, there really was no choice but to hang tough and muster as much public support as possible.

"Speakin' of support," said Benny, turning to O'Boyle. "How's our appeal goin' for help? Anything cookin' with other unions?"

"Workin' on it," O'Boyle said, noncommittally.

"I'll bet you are," Benny replied facetiously.

The two men exchanged frosty, malevolent glares.

"An' how 'bout the USA comin' across with a coupla greenbacks?" Benny pressed.

"Workin' on that, too," O'Boyle said.

Sure, you are, Benny thought. *And I bet there's a bridge you'd like to sell me, too.*

The strike leaders agreed that Benny and O'Boyle, revealing no sign of their rift, would continue to deal jointly with the press. Lou Grimes and Tommy Duggan, it was decided, would focus on soliciting the support of other labor unions. Frank Russo would serve as chief emissary to City Hall. Picketing would continue unabated.

There was but one final piece of business for Benny to attend to. Late that day, he summoned Jack to strike headquarters, pulling his brother aside as soon as he walked in.

"I need you to handle somethin' for me, kid," Benny told his brother. "It's a critical job . . . an' one that you're especially suited for."

A four-man committee was being established to administer the strike fund, a job that involved precise calculations, monetary disbursements, and, most importantly, oversight. The committee consisted of Tommy Duggan and Frank Russo, two of Benny's closest confidantes, as well as Paddy O'Boyle's righthand man, Butch Flanagan, whom Benny trusted as much as he did O'Boyle himself.

"I want you to be part of that committee," Benny said. "An' it ain't just 'cause you're a genius at math."

"Why, then?"

"I need a set of eyes on the strike fund. Someone I can trust." Benny paused, then continued. "Let's just say there's been some 'fiduciary lapses' in the past regardin' union finances. Money has a funny way of disappearin' around here."

That, as any union insider knew, was a gross understatement. In truth, union finances, for decades, had been subjected to gross improprieties by the crooked hierarchy of the United Stevedores Association. Financial records were finagled, and bookkeeping was shoddy. Embezzlement and fraud were rampant, with members' dues siphoned off whenever money flowed into pension funds, insurance, lobbying efforts, and other accounts. Paddy O'Boyle, as union president, was formally on the books for a twenty-thousand-dollar annual salary, but earned several times that through a litany of financial shenanigans—not to mention the bribes he pocketed from Henry. Most USA higher-ups were similarly on the take.

"How long has this been going on?" Jack recoiled.

"Long as there's been a union," Benny replied in a blasé tone.

"Where does the money go?"

"Who knows, kid? No one ever goes lookin' for it. Sure as hell not our rank an' file."

"The union has never conducted an internal audit?"

"Are you kiddin'?" Benny burst out laughing. "Why would it? Everyone who's anyone has their hand in the till."

Jack shook his head forlornly, feeling deflated, embarrassed that he'd closed his eyes until now to the union's seedy side. He had wanted so badly to believe in something above board, something more virtuous and worthy of the tugboat workers' faith.

"Look," Benny said, "I hate to bust your bubble, an' I ain't certain that there's gonna be hanky-panky, but we don't have a lotta money in our strike fund to begin with . . . an' you can never be too careful."

Jack pondered his brother's comments. Clearly, he was getting an education, his eyes opening to the union's sordid underbelly. He hated what he was seeing— hated, just as much, that his forthright brother was forced to swim in such a slimy cesspool. Equally troubling to Jack were his growing concerns that he was being drawn deeper each day into the slimy morass—captive, as throughout his entire life, to powerful forces he could neither resist nor control. When would he finally change that calculus? Chart the course of the life he wanted? Decide his own fate? Those were questions he couldn't answer now.

"So whaddaya say?" Benny prodded. "Can you give me a hand with my problem?"

Jack was troubled by what was unfolding around him, and the reason his brother needed him. Benny wasn't simply spearheading a labor movement; he was bucking a deeply entrenched system, potentially taking money out of people's pockets. In fact, he was playing with fire, and likely as not, he could get seriously burned.

"You okay?" Jack asked.

"So far, so good." Benny grinned. "Then again, ya never know when a little 'Irish confetti' might come flyin' my way."

"Irish confetti?"

"You know, kid—a passel of bricks tossed from a rooftop."

The attempt at humor fell flat. To Jack, nothing about the situation was even remotely funny. A lot of powerful, connected people had a stake in the tugboat strike. Some played by their own rules, others by no rules at all. It wasn't farfetched to think that any one of them could try to protect their interests in some untoward way. Nor was it farfetched to think that Benny, as the strike's figurehead, could pay a hefty price.

"I'll be perfectly frank," Jack said. "I'm scared for your wellbeing, Benny. You don't need to be a martyr on the union's behalf, don't need to get yourself injured or killed."

"I appreciate the sentiment, kid." Benny waved his brother off. "But I can take care of myself. Always have."

He glanced around suspiciously.

"The problem 'round here," he said, "is that the walls have eyes an' ears. You never know who's your enemy or who's your friend. Every one of them wears a disguise."

"But there are people that you trust, right?" Jack asked. "Tommy Duggan?"

"Tommy is a trouper." Benny nodded. "I'd trust him with my life."

"Frank Russo?"

"A straight arrow."

"Others?"

"A handful, maybe. But regardless . . . I still need a trusted set of eyes on the union's strike fund. An' there's no one in the world, kid, that I trust more than you."

Benny slung an arm around Jack's shoulder and pulled him close.

"So, you'll do this for me, huh?"

Jack had a queasy feeling in the pit of his stomach. This was precisely the kind of request that had made him reluctant about accepting Benny's job offer in the first place: a fear of obligation, of having to repay a favor he wasn't sure that he could. Still, how could he say "no" to his brother? Especially after everything Benny had done for him. Especially now.

"Sure," Jack acquiesced. "I got your back."

"Thanks, kid." Benny shook his brother's hand. "Shit, if nothin' else, you can ride the strike out here at headquarters. Consider it a favor, from me to you."

"A favor?"

"Sure." Benny winked. "It'll be a hell of a lot easier managin' our books indoors than freezin' your nuts off on those goddamned picket lines."

CHAPTER 26

February 3, 1946

It didn't take long for the strike to have a marked corrosive effect, its stranglehold on the harbor triggering a growing state of paralysis across the stagnant, glacial landscape.

With most of the city's tugboat fleet moored to their docks, and non-striking personnel unable to fulfill towing assignments, the harbor remained for the most part eerily still. Police Department cruisers made their daily rounds, fireboats delivered fuel for emergency equipment, and military tugs handled the movement of warships. Little, beyond that, moved on the city's waterways. Passenger liners, cargo ships, oil tankers and other vessels languished in their slips, or sat at anchor. Docks and other waterfront facilities were deserted, commerce at a standstill, tens of thousands of workers idled.

But those were merely the overt signs of the strike. Far more damaging was the impact the work stoppage was having on the city and its populace.

Across the North River, on the New Jersey waterfront, thousands of tons of coal sat heaped on barges, unable to be delivered as a source of power, electricity, and heat. Garbage scows swarming with rodents and seagulls lined waterfront piers and waste-transfer stations, unable to be towed to ocean dump sites. Tankers carrying millions of gallons of fuel oil remained similarly immobile, unable to reach distribution facilities and refineries. To make matters worse, lingering wartime shortages meant that the city had only limited reserves of those precious commodities. And those were being depleted rapidly.

Impacted, too, were food supplies. In Jersey City and Hoboken, carloads of livestock were rolled onto barges that couldn't be shipped to stockyards across the river. Perishable produce sat rotting in the cargo holds of ships. Freight trains loaded with wheat, grain, and other bulk cargo were backed up for miles, as were shipments of canned goods, beverages, frozen foods, and medical supplies.

Increasingly panicked by the growing crisis, city officials hastily summoned representatives of Local 88 and the Gotham Harbor Alliance to an emergency meeting with Mayor Flannery's chief labor advisor, Desmond Quinn, assigned as a mediator in the dispute.

A respected long-time bureaucrat and a master conciliator, the courtly, silver-haired Quinn seemed not only eminently qualified for the role he'd been assigned, but unruffled by the prospect of dragging the warring parties back to the bargaining table or brokering a contract settlement on his own—despite the several key obstacles that stood in the way. First, while government officials could encourage the opposing sides to resolve their differences, they lacked the legal authority to formally impose a settlement. Nor were they anxious to dictate terms and face a potential backlash from either the city's labor or business interests, both of whom were vital to political fortunes.

An even greater obstacle, Quinn soon discovered, was that negotiating positions were so entrenched, and bitterness so ingrained, that representatives of the opposing sides could barely be coaxed into the same room for a civil discourse. After nearly coming to blows during their prior City Hall meeting, Henry and Benny had separately rejected Quinn's proposal for a face-to-face meeting. Now communication between the strike's two key principals was being relayed strictly through intermediaries. Surrogates had also been designated to participate in a factfinding mission overseen by Quinn, the delegations led by Tommy Duggan and Frank Russo for the union, and George Steele and Bertram Phelps for the tugboat owners.

"This situation has got to change if there's any hope of resolving this stalemate," Quinn informed the negotiators. "Leaders can't refuse to meet and exchange ideas. Disputants can't settle their differences unless they truly want to. The question is: Do you want to?"

"Speakin' for the union," Russo said, "I'd say . . . that depends on the tugboat owners offering more than nonstarters."

"And our coalition," countered Steele, "feels that the union needs to return to reality on the issue of a wage hike."

"Reality?" Duggan scoffed. "How about the reality that our members are facing?"

"And how about the reality our companies are facing?"

"But we—"

"And we—"

Both sides were talking over one another now, no one listening, no one giving ground.

"Gentlemen—please!" Raising a hand until, slowly, the negotiators quieted, Quinn said, "Success in resolving conflicts like this depends on compromise, each side bending on their demands in order to achieve a greater good."

Calmly, the mediator tamped a pinch of tobacco into a corncob pipe, and lit it with the strike of a wooden match.

"No one in a labor dispute gets everything they want," he said. "Both sides need to stop thinking of resolution as 'victory' for one side and 'capitulation' for the other. The only 'victory' we're seeking is one of compromise over coercion. In the end, both sides need to win."

With his calming, unflappable demeanor—and a natural talent for being conciliatory yet tough, demanding yet fair—Quinn had the negotiators' attention. He would need that, and a lot more, to solve the conflict that City Hall had lain at his feet.

"Our common goal, ending this strike, is far more important than any differences you have," said Quinn. "The responsibility for making collective bargaining work rests upon both management and labor. You must all be willing to engage one another if we're to reach an accommodation that satisfies everyone."

The negotiators sat silent, listening.

"But instead of trust and respect," Quinn scolded, "we've got leaders who hurl incendiary comments at one another, send proxies to meetings, rip each other in the press, and seem hell-bent on destroying one another rather than working cooperative in the public interest."

No one could argue with that. Indeed, even as Quinn chastised the negotiators, Henry and Benny sat in separate rooms. Left to their own devices, they'd remain apart another all day, unable—unwilling—to contain their animus, stubbornly making their point rather than acceding to the need to negotiate.

The city couldn't wait for that, however. Neither could Quinn.

"Now, let's put the rancor aside and start a constructive discourse," said Quinn, requesting a clear and thorough explanation of the issues that had spurred the strike.

George Steele defended the owners' offer of a two-percent wage hike on a one-year contract; Frank Russo justified the union's demand for a four-percent raise. And Quinn, listening patiently, pondered the depth of the impasse, and talked common sense.

"We've got to find a way to work creatively, and fairly, to bridge the gulf between both sides," he said. "Despite your differences, you need to unite in a common cause: to keep New York Harbor functioning."

"We've been tryin' that for eight months," Tommy Duggan said.

"Then you've got to try harder," Quinn said matter-of-factly.

"The gap between our sides," George Steele argued, "seems insurmountable."

"No gap is insurmountable," Quinn said. "Even the most spiteful rivals can put aside destructive rhetoric and get a deal done. Now, let's get to work!"

Quinn stroked a silky mustache, his steely tone voicing the need for a swift, no-nonsense approach.

"Regardless of your differences, the city needs the harbor open," he said. "While City Hall is resolved for the time being to remain neutral, we insist that both sides find a solution to this impasse! Is that understood?"

All the negotiators nodded their assent.

"Now exactly what is needed to get this strike settled?" asked Quinn.

"It may seem like our union is asking for the moon," Frank Russo began, "but World War II cost our men four years of salary increases. Our union endured a wartime wage freeze, suspended our rights to collective bargaining, and supported the government's no-strike pledge because it was more important to do our patriotic duty than to win a pay hike."

"That's commendable," owner George Steele said. "But the war should have no bearing on these negotiations. We're trying to go from Point A to B—not from A to D. A four-percent wage hike is patently unfair. And frankly, the money is just not there."

"And we believe otherwise," said Russo. "The war has everything to do with our wage demand. For four years, our men played by the rules—made every sacrifice asked of us and patiently sat on our hands. All we're asking with a four-percent raise—in effect, one percent for each of the last four years—is to make up for lost time and reap the rewards of our loyalty and sacrifice. The two-percent raise that's on the table doesn't even cover the cost of inflation. In effect, our men are being asked to go backward."

"Wages may have been frozen during the war," Steele countered, "but tugboat workers made out like bandits with overtime and hazardous duty pay."

"Tugboat firms didn't make out so poorly either," Tommy Duggan said. "War profiteering had its share of rewards."

"That's a crock of shit!" Steele charged.

"Is it?"

But in truth, each side had a point. With half of America's troops and one-third of overseas supplies passing through New York Harbor during World War II, waterborne traffic had soared to record heights, with tugboat firms posting hefty profits. Union members had profited as well. Work during the war had been plentiful, overtime pay abundant. Assignments for the towing of munitions had also drawn hazardous duty pay. And with tugboat firms shorthanded due to the military draft, many crewmen had performed double duty, earning the salaries of more than one worker.

"It's disingenuous, in light of that, for the union to plead poverty," Steele said. "Local 88 has no justification for making the wage demand it has."

"And we feel that we have every justification imaginable," Duggan said.

Back and forth the negotiators went, nonstop for two hours. Quinn listened intently, asking questions, taking notes, gaining a grasp of the issues and the personalities involved in the conflict. In closing, he proposed a resumption of negotiations, subject to non-binding mediation by City Hall. Both sides agreed to consider the idea, although union leaders rejected a proposal for a temporary, good-faith suspension of the strike while the owners balked at a suggestion that the dispute be submitted to government arbitration. And shortly before noon, the negotiators emerged from behind closed doors into a crush of reporters, whom Quinn informed there was nothing of substance to report.

News was being made on other fronts, however. Even as Quinn convened tugboat owners and union leaders, city officials were cobbling together a sweeping plan to cope with the strike. A Disaster Control Board—comprised of police, fire, housing, energy, health, sanitation, and school officials—was charged with spearheading a response to the crisis. Tighter rations of fuel to public utilities, transit services, hospitals, nursing homes, and food-distribution outlets were mandated. Police officers were posted at bridges and tunnels to prevent fuel deliveries to unauthorized users. Board of Health emissaries began inspecting office and apartment buildings, issuing summonses for violations of the sixty-degree heat ceiling.

And then the lights went out. With fuel shortages looming, an embattled Mayor Flannery issued a mandate that a blackout, beginning at dusk, be imposed across the city. Outdoor electric signs were ordered extinguished. Streetlamps and traffic signals had their wattage reduced. Lights in office buildings were ordered turned off or dimmed.

As nightfall descended, New York was plunged into a state of near-total darkness. Bridges and landmarks faded to black. Homes and buildings became silhouettes against a moonless sky. Even Con Ed's headquarters, a midtown-Manhattan building topped by a glittering tower of light, had its power cut.

As did Times Square. Just months earlier, the bawdy epicenter of nightlife in America—symbol of New York's energy and heat—had welcomed tens of thousands of revelers gathering for VJ Day, shouting, singing, and embracing as they marked the Allies' wartime triumph over Japan. Mere weeks earlier, more than a million celebrants had gathered in a shower of music, strobe lights and confetti, flooding Times Square with the wave of optimism sweeping across America while ushering in the New Year, a long-awaited era of prosperity and peace.

But now . . . nothing. Times Square's giant "spectaculars" no longer flashed their glittering, multi-colored neon brilliance. The signboards, facades, and marquees of nightclubs, dance halls, burlesque houses, and movie theaters were extinguished across the entire Great White Way. The Motograph News Bulletin known as "The Zipper" ceased scrolling headlines from its location at One Times Square. The G.I. on the Camel cigarette billboard no longer exhaled wispy entrails of smoke. New York's vibrant hub—the landmark site where crowds gathered to celebrate presidential elections, military victories, World Series games, and other major events—lay dormant and deserted, its electric glow dimmed, its effervescence drained.

Across the length and breadth of the city that never slept, New York had fallen into a dreamlike repose, its millions of inhabitants in a seeming state of suspended animation. In many ways, the drumbeat of everyday life had been silenced, as if America's greatest city, invaded by some baleful, insidious disease, stood on the brink of death.

CHAPTER 27

February 3, 1946

As daylight dissolved to night, a heightened sense of dread enveloped New York, vast sections of the sprawling metropolis rendered virtually invisible by the citywide blackout. Manhattan's skyline, cloaked in darkness, was visible only in silhouette. Pedestrians toting flashlights and lanterns wandered ghostlike along shadowy, deserted streets. Entire neighborhoods seemed tilted from their axis, dreamlike and menacing even to longtime residents.

Having retreated indoors like most people, the Logans gathered for an early supper, their evening routine as disjointed as the city itself. Agnes puttered about the candlelit kitchen in an overcoat and mittens. Gus and Kate, home due to workplace closures, sat forlornly at the kitchen table, bundled in sweaters. With nighttime classes suspended at colleges throughout New York, Jack had joined the family for a rare meal together.

Not that their meal was in any way pleasurable. With steam heat off in their building, the Logans' apartment was nearly as frigid as the snowbound landscape outside, warmed only by the open gas burners of their stove. Cast-iron radiators sat like useless sculptures. Newspapers had been stuffed into window joints and door frames, but howling gusts still managed to seep through cracks. Gus and Jack sat forlornly at the kitchen table. Kate, wrapped in a quilt, rocked silently in her chair.

"You all right?" Jack asked his wife.

Smiling wanly, Kate nodded. But clearly, she was not. Not in the least.

"P-p-p-please forgive me," she sputtered like an untuned engine. "I don't mean to upset anyone . . . but I need a few minutes to myself."

With that, she abruptly rose from her chair and retreated to the bedroom she shared with Jack. She was seated at the edge of their bed, trembling like a newborn fawn, when Jack arrived seconds later at her side.

"What's troubling you, darling?" He slipped an arm around her and pulled her close.

Kate raised a quivering hand.

"I'm . . . sorry," she stammered, groping for an explanation. "I didn't mean to upset anyone. It's just that I—"

But there was hardly a need for an explanation. Jack knew instantly what was evoking Kate's distress. It was the darkness enveloping the city. The blackout.

"I can only imagine what you must be feeling," Jack said, sidling up to Kate as she sat quaking under her quilt.

But even imagining the emotions pummeling Kate was impossible for Jack. How could he comprehend his wife's distress, or know what she was feeling? He'd never lived in London during the early part of the war. He had never experienced the unmitigated terror wrought, even six years later, by the simple onset of darkness.

But Kate had. Having worked in London through most of 1940 and '41, she had lived through the city's most terrifying days—and its darkest, most hellish nights.

Much of Central Europe had already fallen by then to Adolf Hitler's war machine. Germany had occupied the Low Countries and invaded France. With America yet to enter the war, England was standing as the last bastion of Allied resistance to the Nazis. And Hitler turned to a never-before-used weapon of intimidation and fear.

For eight unrelenting months, the German Führer ordered thousands of warplanes across the English Channel, a tactical move aimed at crushing the British spirit prior to an all-out invasion of the island nation. Night after night, the fury of the Luftwaffe was unleashed upon the British capital. Night after night, air-raid sirens pierced the silence, Londoners ran for cover, and the Royal Air Force scrambled its fighter planes to defend the city from the ferocious aerial assault. And night after night, London was plunged into darkness, blackouts swallowing all semblance of light, engulfing the city in terror, and setting the stage for Hitler's Lightning War, the London Blitz.

"Six years later and it's still so terrifying to me," Kate sputtered. "It's as if it happened only yesterday . . . as if it will happen again tonight."

As she cowered in the darkened bedroom, in the blackout engulfing New York, Kate couldn't help but recall the ghastly nights she had endured in London, couldn't help but relive them either.

"My God," she sniffled, fighting back tears, "it was so terrifying, what we lived through then. All the things that I remember . . . all the ways that I was afraid."

"Tell me about it," Jack said.

"It's so hard," Kate stammered. "All of it is locked up . . . deep inside me."

"Try to let it out, darling," Jack coaxed. "It's okay. You're safe with me."

And haltingly, in fits and starts, Kate began opening herself up to the abject terror she was feeling, recounting what she always tried to hold at bay—all of it bubbling to the surface, washing over her in a floodtide now.

* * *

The bombing runs always began as a rumbling sound, like a swarm of bumblebees flying into England from the channel coast of France. Windows would start rattling, shards of plaster shaking loose from walls and ceilings; dishes and cutlery tumbling from cupboards and tables. Then the wail of air-raid sirens would pierce the darkness, and you could hear the thump-thump of heavy bombs exploding in the distance and the muffled boom of anti-aircraft cannons and the rat-tat-tat of machinegun fire, and the roar of RAF fighter planes.

Kate remembered peeking out from behind the blackout curtains at St. Bart's, and seeing jagged spears of light bursting over London's East End, then curtains of smoke billowing out from under a canopy of fiery explosions, the nighttime sky aglow in orange and red, as if the sun was setting behind banks of bulbous, feathery clouds.

She remembered how gun-and-searchlight crews would scurry to the rooftops, and hordes of people would race to bunkers and underground railway stations and makeshift shelters in backyards and cellars. She remembered how cars packed with fleeing Londoners would clog the roads to the countryside, how children were herded aboard outbound trains and sandbags were piled in front of government buildings and soldiers manned machinegun nests and everyone donned grotesque rubber gas masks.

Kate remembered, too, how monstrous walls of fire rolled over buildings and factories, railyards and munition plants; how firehoses slithered like giant serpents from riverside water pumps, and how firefighters and air-raid wardens waded through blizzards of ember and spark, and how streets gushed with black water and acrid clouds of smoke sucked the breath from people's lungs.

And suddenly, six years later, sheltering in another blacked-out city, all of what she had lived through somehow seemed real again, as if the Blitzkrieg was happening all over and Kate was trapped inside of it, captive to her terror, awash in a torrent of flashbacks and fear.

"Tell me about it," said Jack, knowing that opening herself up to it was the only way Kate could push through the thicket of terrifying emotions.

"It's hard," Kate stammered, and began to cry.

"Try, darling."

And slowly, she did.

For fifty-seven nights in a row, Kate recalled, London, like other British cities, was targeted by the Luftwaffe bombing sorties. Kate remembered how the German bombers, painted black to avoid detection, peppered the sky in waves. She remembered how they dropped incendiaries to illuminate their targets and timed their bombing runs so that the Thames was at low tide and fire-quenching water in short supply. She remembered the whistle and the shriek of the V-1 rockets, the buzz bombs and the Doodlebugs and the other weapons of Hitler's war machine. She remembered how shipyards and factories and military installations were targeted at first, but how bombs soon began falling on all quarters of London: homes flattened, schools and churches destroyed, streets littered with dust squalls, shards of metal and mortar, pools of water, sawdust and brick. She remembered the acrid scent of leaking gas and burning wood, of gunpowder and burnt flesh, and the sight of mangled bodies and the sound of people crying out for help.

She remembered waiting, too. Simply waiting.

Waiting, terror-stricken, as the bombs plummeted to earth and then went quiet in a heart-stopping lull, before pounding their targets. Waiting, breathless, for the bombing runs to stop and for St. Bart's walls and ceilings and windows to stop spewing clouds of plaster, concrete, and glass. Waiting anxiously for the air-raid sirens to sound the all-clear, the RAF fighters returning to their bases in victory rolls, and the lights of the city to flicker back on.

Never before or since had Kate felt as terrified and lonely as she had during those interminable, pitch-black nights in London. Never had she felt so hopeless or vulnerable or surrounded by misery and death, drowning in the sadness and the insanity of it all. Night after night bombs fell on London, swallowing the city and its people in uncertainty, anguish, and fear. There was no escaping it. Nowhere to hide. Nothing to shield Kate and the others but blind luck and the grace of God.

The rooftop of St. Bart's, like that of other hospitals, was painted with a red cross on a white-square background, the medical symbol aimed at warding off enemy bombers. But that didn't halt the onslaught. Time and again, the hospital was struck. Walls erupted. Ceilings caved in. Windows were blown to bits. Operating rooms, laboratories, and equipment were obliterated. Shrapnel, glass, plaster, and other debris was scattered about. And as the bombs rained down around them, St. Bart's patients were placed on mattresses beneath their beds while Kate and other nurses lay atop them as human shields, singing songs, whispering prayers, tuning in to the BBC to learn if the bombing runs had ceased and they'd live to see light again. Candlelight. Lamplight. Daylight.

Light of any kind.

But light, for the most part, was nowhere to be found during those harrowing nights in London. In its place, darkness reigned, spirits dwindled, terror and despair stalked the city. Night after night, the bombs fell and London went dark, and the victims flooded into St. Bart's: dazed and bloodied; crying and aggrieved; filling emergency wards, operating rooms, and corridors with the smell of burned flesh and mangled bodies, and glassy-eyed survivors roaming hospital wards in a desperate search for loved ones.

Tons of explosives fell on London. Thousands of people were injured and killed. Two million were rendered homeless. Yet somehow, the city survived.

But while Kate had survived the Blitzkrieg, the harrowing assault in many ways had never truly ended for her. And now, with a new curtain of darkness cloaking New York, warnings of food and fuel shortages on the radio—she was once again experiencing the searing flashbacks, the jarring emotions. Her bottled-up terror had once again reared its ugly head, the blackout a trigger, a jarring reminder not only of the Blitzkrieg but the gnawing realization that she had yet to fully distance herself from the nightmarish trauma of the war. And that perhaps she never really would.

"You can't imagine the terror that—even all these years later—a blackout can evoke," Kate whimpered. "The feeling of helplessness, of being at the whim of fate, of waiting for everything you cherish to be obliterated at any moment."

Kate's face was waxen. Droplets of sweat beaded her brow.

"It's impossible for me to describe how a blackout like tonight's can symbolize heartbreak and destruction," she said, "and how the simple presence of light can mean survival and hope."

Jack pulled her even closer, and kissed her forehead gently.

"During those blackouts," Kate said, "we hungered for even the tiniest speck of light. But all we had then was darkness, destruction, and terror. It's impossible for anyone who didn't live through all that to ever truly understand."

"You've never spoken about any of this," Jack said.

"I've never wanted to," said Kate. "I've only wanted to forget."

"I understand." Jack nodded. "But maybe it would help if you talked about it sometimes."

"Why?" Kate asked. "Do you talk about all the things you saw and felt during the war? Do you talk to anyone about D-Day?"

Jack shook his head. Of course he didn't. What he'd seen and felt was impossible to put into words, so why even try? Besides, not talking about it meant not dwelling on it, and that was the only way he knew how to move past it. Talking about it made all of it real again. Pushing the memories and emotions aside made them disappear, at least most of the time.

Not tonight, though. Tonight, there was no ignoring what Kate had lived through. No pushing it aside. No forgetting.

"Maybe I'm being naive," she said, "but I've wanted to believe that the world was finished with blackouts, wanted to believe that once the war ended the lights would come on and they'd never be extinguished . . . ever again."

Kate glanced out the window at the blacked-out city, the East River invisible but for a solitary bell-buoy, twinkling like a fallen star.

"You know," she recalled, "the first thing I saw when I arrived in New York, Jack, were the lights of the city reflected in the waters of the harbor. I'm sure it was just my imagination, but the light seemed, in an odd sort of way, to be beckoning me, drawing me closer, welcoming me to my new life, a life with you, Jack."

She smiled tepidly, bravely. "I'll live with that moment forever," she said. "You see, light was how I knew the war was truly over. The lights of the city, Jack . . . that's how I knew I was close to you again, how I knew I was truly safe, and the two of us could begin our lives together. Light meant everything to me, darling. It still does. Light means fulfillment of a dream. It means hope. It means you."

Jack felt his eyes welling up.

"Was it misguided to feel that way?" Kate asked.

"No."

"Am I being childish? Foolish?"

"Not at all."

"Yet here I am," said Kate, "feeling as if, at any moment, bombs will start falling and buildings will crumble, and people will die. I'm in New York now— not in London. I recognize that the war is over, and I have no reason to feel the way I do. Yet tonight I feel as if I'm back where I was six years ago. Just as vulnerable. Just as frightened. Just as alone."

"But no longer in London," Jack reassured her. "No longer at war. And not alone," he whispered, pulling her close.

Perhaps he hadn't undergone precisely what she had, but Jack, too, had memories he couldn't purge, ghosts he couldn't exorcise, wounds that would never heal. For him, too, the war would never be completely forgotten. Never truly be over.

"Tonight's blackout is nothing like what you lived through in London," Jack said. "It's simply a kneejerk reaction to the tugboat strike, a misguided effort to conserve fuel."

"It's a reminder," said Kate. "That's enough."

"I understand," Jack said. "But what's more important to remember is that London is in the past. So is the Blitzkrieg. So is the war. No one is dropping bombs on New York tonight, Kate. No one is dying."

Kate smiled bravely, her midriff straining against her maternity dress. She looked so vulnerable, so fragile just then. It hurt Jack to see her like that. He'd do anything to allay her fear and assure her that he was there for her, that he'd always be there.

Kate, smiling wanly, curled up in his arms. "Who would've thought that something as harmless as a blackout could have such a powerful effect?" she said. "I guess the war is not truly over—at least not for me. It feels as if all of it just crawled up inside me to reside there forever, deep in my soul."

"The war may never truly be over for any of us," Jack said. "The fighting may've ended, but some battles, I suppose, will rage inside us forever. Maybe we just need to distance ourselves from all of it, allow time to heal the wounds, find a way to live with the scars."

"How?" asked Kate. "How can we ever forget what we've seen and felt. Make sense of it all? Shoulder the weight?"

"Maybe we can't forget," Jack said. "But time can heal the wounds, darling. Time can help us learn. Maybe the way we move past it is simply by being together . . . by living and dreaming and making plans and carrying on and striving for the things we've never had . . . by looking ahead, not behind, and drawing on the strength we have inside us."

"Strength?" Kate chuckled. "Just look at me, as frightened by the darkness as a child."

"Being frightened doesn't make you weak," Jack said. "It only makes you human. And being human, Kate, is the reason I love you. All of us get frightened sometimes, but true strength means refusing to cave in to your fears. It means surviving. And that, you've done."

"Have I?"

"Of course. You've survived because even your worst fears never defeated you, didn't make you succumb to hatred, anger, and remorse. Your spirit was never broken, Kate—and you never lost your capacity for joy and hope. You've survived because you can move past all that's happened. Because you can dream. Because you can love." He ran his fingertips tenderly across Kate's midriff. "And that same strength of spirit, that same resilience, will see you through the tugboat strike . . . and every other obstacle the two of might ever face."

Jack smiled. "See, there's always light, darling, even in the darkest night. That's because true light comes from within. The light is inside of us, Kate. All we need to do is remember that it's there."

"So tell me," Kate sniffled, "will life ever get easier for us, Jack? I mean, we've lived through a Depression, a war, decades of hardship. And now we're in the middle of this dreadful strike. And I'm wondering: when will the battles finally be over? When will the hardships finally end?"

"Maybe never," Jack said.

"Never?"

"Maybe not. Maybe we just need to find our own little island in the middle of the heartache and the chaos, somewhere where we can find peace simply by being together."

Smiling, he rubbed Kate's belly, feeling movement, like the fluttering of a sparrow's wings.

"That's what we have live for now, Kate," Jack said. "Our unborn child, and all the dreams we can help our children realize."

"Yes." Kate smiled. "Children who we can give the kind of life the two of us have never been able to have."

"Happy, hopeful children," Jack said. "Children who'll be loved, and who'll have the courage and the wisdom to cope with life's challenges. Just as you have, darling. Just as I'm trying to do now, too."

"Is any of that possible?" asked Kate.

"I'm certain that it is," Jack said. "Just as I'm certain that the lights of New York will come back on, and that I'll be here to comfort and reassure you if they're ever extinguished again."

Kate smiled.

"You'll see. Before long, this strike will be over, and we can get our lives back on track. Believe me, darling. Our time will finally come."

"Our time?" she asked, still skeptical.

"A time," said Jack, "when we can live the life we're trying so desperately to live. When we can finally feel that setbacks aren't inevitable. When we can believe, once and for all, that our dreams can really come true."

"Sometimes I wonder if we'll ever get to that place," Kate said. "Sometimes, I think it might be easier if we didn't dream at all."

"I never want to stop dreaming," Jack said. "Sharing dreams with you, Kate, is the only thing that keeps me going."

He kissed her on the cheek, his face splaying into a playful grin.

"Now, maybe we can make tonight memorable . . . in another kind of way."

"What do you mean?"

"Well, the setting is perfect." Jack winked. "The lights are out. We're stuck at home. There's nothing for us to do now but go to bed."

Hand on her belly, Kate giggled self-consciously. "What you're hinting at may be a little tricky, given the state I'm in."

"Then maybe we can just hold one another," Jack said. "Be warm and safe and close. Wait for morning. For daylight to come."

"So that we'll know that we're still alive?"

"And that a new day has dawned, and everything in our world is intact, and the two of us are still together, just as much in love as ever."

"That'd be nice." Kate smiled.

"There's nothing I can think of," said Jack, "that could possibly be nicer."

CHAPTER 28

February 4, 1946

Winter pummeled New York for a fourth straight day. Even as the tugboat strike continued to cripple the harbor, a fierce nor'easter buffeted the city and its environs, with frigid temperatures, foot-high snowfall, and howling winds putting a hammerlock on most services. Telephone communications, public transportation, and mail deliveries were disrupted, schools and businesses closed, several million residents trapped inside their homes. Worse yet, the arctic-like conditions magnified the public's appetite for heating oil, firewood, and coal, the scarcity of which only served to exacerbate the citywide crisis. Emergency reserves of fuel had already dwindled precipitously, and by noon Con Edison announced that it could no longer supply gas and electric service to nonessential customers. The New York Steam Corp. was similarly forced to reduce the availability of steam heat to many apartment and high-rise buildings. Several smaller utilities providers suspended service entirely.

Public officials, all the while, seemed utterly baffled about how to cope with the worsening dilemma. Mayor Flannery's fledgling administration, caught flatfooted by the harbor closure, was riddled with infighting and indecision, as advisors and councilmen dithered and battled among themselves about how to handle the quandary, succeeding—through a combination of callowness, ineptitude, and political paralysis—only in exacerbating the very dilemma they were struggling to contain.

Already drawing heavy flack for his muddled, kneejerk response to the strike, New York's embattled mayor took a different tack. Attempting to appear in control in the eyes of a disgruntled and skeptical public, Irish Eddie not only doubled down on his citywide blackout edict, but announced he had no choice anymore but to declare a formal State of Emergency over the city.

One step shy of martial law, Flannery's latest fuel-saving directive permitted the operation solely of public utilities, medical facilities, transportation services, media outlets, banks, and food-processing plants. Ordered closed were all non-essential businesses, including most factories, wholesale operations, restaurants, and retail outlets, except for grocery stores, gas stations, and pharmacies. Sporting events were cancelled. The New York Stock Exchange was ordered to halt trading. Parks and recreational facilities were shuttered, along with libraries, museums, theaters, and tourist attractions.

But Flannery's latest edict proved quickly to be another major gaffe. Indeed, rather than mitigating public concern, as intended, the directive had precisely the opposite effect—fueling a heightened sense of chaos, confusion, and frustration that was bordering now on mass hysteria. Workers brave enough to defy the elements wandered the streets aimlessly, or congregated in parks, before padlocked office buildings, and at vacant construction sites. Police officers dispatched to subway stations, bus stops, and ferry terminals urged bewildered commuters to return to their homes. Millions of people awaited instructions on what to do next.

But no one, it seemed, knew what to tell them. Public officials, flailing helplessly at the dilemma, seemed as flummoxed as the citizenry. Every decision they rendered seemed ill-advised. Every action they took underlined their seeming impotence. City Hall's pleas to end the strike were met on both sides with public posturing, finger-pointing, empty rhetoric, and acerbic exchanges. Contract proposals were nixed, peace offerings rebuffed, government mediators, consultants, and third-party experts sent packing. Henry and Benny continued their refusal to meet face-to-face, communicating instead through intermediaries while rejecting efforts at substantive dialogue. Even Desmond Quinn, as seasoned an arbitrator as he was, seemed flummoxed by the degree to which both sides stubbornly clung to their respective positions.

"Personalities have gotten in the way of progress," Quinn told negotiators. "Concessions and compromise have become impossible now because both sides are focused more on voicing their antipathy toward each other than they are in addressing issues on their merits."

His brow puckered, drawing deliberately on his pipe, he scolded both sides.

"Collective bargaining is an adversarial process, but it's not a game in which there's winners and losers. "What we should be aiming for is 'win-win bargaining,' a collaborative effort whose goal is mutual gain. In the end, reasonable people make reasonable agreements. Each side should help the other side win."

Then his expression turned dark.

"I can tell you this with certainty," he warned. "The powers-that-be are losing patience. They will not stand idly by while America's greatest city spirals into the abyss. New York Harbor will be reopened one way or another—and soon. That's not a threat. It's a promise."

But even Quinn's most forbidding warnings were falling on deaf ears. And although the strike had captured the attention of politicians in both Washington, DC and the statehouse in Albany, government officials continued to eschew forceful intervention, fearful of ruffling feathers and risking a backlash from either organized labor or the business community. Despite the gravity of the public crisis, resolution of the strike was nowhere in sight at the moment. No one—not the most-seasoned mediator, political operative, or government functionary—had ever witnessed a labor dispute on this scale: its impact so damaging, its price tag so enormous, its principals so confrontational and dug in. No one had shown either the wisdom or the political will to resolve the standoff. No one, it seemed, knew what to do—except bear witness as the city continued to quickly unravel at the seams.

* * *

By mid-afternoon on day four, the snowstorm having run its course, striking tugboat workers returned to their picket lines, reinforced by donations of blankets, cold-weather gear, portable toilets, and other supplies. Deliveries of firewood and random debris rekindled the trashcan bonfires lining the North River waterfront. Hot chocolate, canned foods, soup, and other provisions were dispensed at strike headquarters.

Tugboat owners, in the meantime, escalated their anti-strike offensive. A volley of press releases crafted by Henry's PR minions lambasted Local 88 for its "destructive and irresponsible" walkout, and questioned union leaders' integrity, motives, and loyalty to America. Henry also intensified his personal attacks by purchasing full-page newspaper ads and radio spots, their messaging attributed to a fictional "Citizens Welfare Committee" purportedly representing an angry populace fed up with the strike.

Redoubled as well were Henry's efforts at shaping public opinion through his daily press briefings, aimed not only at the city's press corps but at media outlets across America, through stories planted with the Associated Press and other wire services.

"What we're witnessing in New York is a shocking commentary on the ruthlessness of organized labor," Henry was quoted in newspapers from coast to coast. "America's greatest city is literally being held hostage by a greedy, rabid group of union militants exercising a vicious form of mob rule!"

He added, ominously, "It's my duty to warn every corporate leader that the future of capitalism in America is at stake with this strike. Business leaders, government officials, and responsible citizens must rally together to stop it. We cannot allow irresponsible, power-hungry radicals like those leading New York's tugboat workers' union to continue to have a chokehold on our city!"

Nor did he limit his messaging solely to his public-relations barrage. He'd also begun soliciting the support of allies who could reinforce his battle cry.

Henry telephoned sympathetic newspaper reporters, editors and publishers, requesting a new round of editorials denouncing the strike. He appealed to shipping firms, maritime associations, and waterfront businesses to rally against alleged union abuses; lobbied associates in the retail, banking, and real-estate communities to strongarm pro-labor newspapers by threatening to withhold advertising; reached out to civic and legislative allies, requesting that they pressure other labor unions to not stage sympathy strikes. He even contacted friendly religious leaders, asking that they deliver sermons containing none-too-subtle back-to-work pleas.

Within hours, Henry's entreaties were yielding palpable results. Almost on cue, the city's Chamber of Commerce characterized striking tugboatmen as hotheaded agitators whose walkout was nothing short of an insurrection aimed at undermining America itself. A coalition of businessmen—buttressed by the American Legion, VFW, and other veterans' groups—joined the anti-strike chorus, calling on "responsible and patriotic" labor leaders to expunge "subversive influences" from the union's ranks. Editorials in pro-business newspapers bemoaned the economic carnage being wrought on the city.

Demonstrations at Wall Street and other sites reinforced the messaging.

All this buttressed Henry's determination, energizing him even more. Four days into the strike, the Gotham Harbor Alliance chairman could not have been any more pleased with the way events were unfolding.

Admittedly the work stoppage was proving costly—two million dollars in lost revenue, thus far, for McFarland Marine Towing alone. And some of Henry's towing customers were carping over the disruption to their businesses. They'd get over it, though, he reasoned. So would Mayor Flannery, and Desmond Quinn, and the media and the politicians. As for the impact the strike was having on the city's populace, that was simply collateral damage, an inconvenient byproduct of the labor war he'd been forced by union leaders to wage.

The public, Henry reasoned, would forgive and forget. The media hysteria would subside, the politicians spin the story to their benefit, and the city revert to its normal state the instant the strike ended. It was merely a matter of clinging to his strategy, viewing his personal losses as acceptable—an investment in his anti-labor crusade—and holding out, for as long as necessary, to bring the tugboat workers' union to its knees.

The important thing, to Henry, was that events were playing out precisely as he had scripted. Not only had he forced Local 88 into a debilitating strike, but he was rallying support enough to defend his actions. Henry occupied a national platform now, his shadow extending far beyond the confines of New York. Influential people were supporting the anti-labor movement he was spearheading. Momentum was on his side. And if he was bleeding money, the union and its members had to be hemorrhaging.

By Henry's estimate, it would only be a matter of time before attrition took its toll and his strategy won out. He was confident it wouldn't be much longer before rank-and-file unity evaporated, union leaders capitulated, and a bankrupt Local 88 ruptured at the seams, hordes of strikers crossing picket lines, begging for whatever labor contract he was magnanimous enough to proffer.

Behind closed doors in his office at the end of day four, Henry sat gazing across the smoke-gray panorama outside his window. Bands of snow swirled across a backdrop of brooding clouds and lifeless, ice-encrusted waterways. The entire harbor seemed inert, frozen under a hard white sky, cargo vessels at anchor, passenger ships idled in their slips, tugboats moored to their docks.

Struck by the enormity of his power, the scope of his guile, Henry couldn't help but feel a profound sense of self-approbation. For decades, the tugboat empire he ruled had helped birth the city, stimulating commerce, creating jobs, forging a legacy, and earning Henry dominion and wealth, adulation and fame. And now, his mastery of events had brought all of it to a standstill—as if he alone controlled the city's pulsebeat, its life force, its fate.

Henry had led tugboat workers precisely to the precipice he wanted, using the strikers as foils in the anti-labor battle he wished to wage. And now he'd squeeze the workers until he won the battle outright, crushing Local 88—and perhaps other unions, as well.

"Those insolent labor unions had no clue who they were dealing with when they launched their nasty little war," he muttered to himself. "Maybe now they'll realize there's hell to pay when they have the gall to fuck with me."

CHAPTER 29

February 4, 1946

Even as tugboat owners tightened the screws, strike leaders moved to fight fire with fire.

Defiant in the face of the growing business opposition, strikers broadened their picketing from waterfront sites to the offices of *The New York Times*, *Wall Street Journal*, and other anti-strike newspapers. Benny and Paddy O'Boyle, maintaining their pretense of unity, granted interviews to the editorial boards of the *Daily News*, *New York Post*, and other supportive papers. Rallies were staged in Union Square and other symbolic locations. Sympathetic merchants and other union supporters stepped up deliveries of clothing, food, and other provisions to picket sites. Strike leaders, all the while, redoubled their efforts to court allies even more powerful than Henry's: the city's other labor unions.

For union officials, leveraging the power of the city's working class was a prudent strategy, given the battleground on which the tugboat strike was being waged. Indeed, while the popular perception of New York was that of a city whose workforce consisted primarily of white-collar elitists, the fact was that postwar New York, at its heart, was a working-class city. Tens of thousands of blue-collar workers labored in its factories, warehouses, construction sites, and retail establishments. Legions more worked as deliverymen, mechanics, repairmen, and in various forms of manual labor and skilled trades. Hundreds of thousands alone were employed at the Port of New York.

Taken individually, New York's working class amounted to relatively little, their impact negligible, their voice a mere whisper. Collectively, though, it was a far different story. Collectively, New York's blue-collar workforce comprised the vast bulk of the city's population, electoral rolls, and tax base. Collectively, blue-collar workers had built the city from the ground up with their muscle and sweat, lifting New York on their shoulders to help it earn its standing as the world's most important city. Collectively, they possessed both a resonant voice and prodigious political clout. Indeed, while New York may have been ruled by a wealthy aristocracy—a political, intellectual, and corporate class of power brokers like Henry McFarland—the city possessed a distinct blue-collar sensibility. A century after organized labor had established a foothold in the city, unions were at the height of their power in New York. In many palpable ways, they ran the city.

Benny was keenly aware of that, having been surrounded by blue-collar workers his entire life. Williamsburg was in many ways organized labor's very backyard, a breeding ground for Benny's union constituency. The South Bronx, where he resided now, was much the same—a microcosm of the patchwork of working-class enclaves dotting the boroughs outside Manhattan.

Benny may have been a new breed of labor leader, rebellious and scornful of old-guard union bosses, but he clung to two of organized labor's core tenets. One, he believed that labor unions, regardless of stature or affiliation, shared a commonality of interests, values, and goals. And two, he believed that unions, whether industrial or craft, should honor other unions' picket lines. No equivocation. No exceptions. No questions asked.

"If we can get other unions to walk off the job in support of our strike, we can bring the tugboat owners back to the bargainin' table, beggin' for a settlement," Benny told strike leaders at their day-four meeting.

"Benny's right," Tommy Duggan said. "The adage still holds true: 'The longer the picket line, the shorter the strike.'"

"In other words," said Benny, "the greater the leverage we assert, the quicker the strike will end in our favor. Just imagine: thirty-five thousand workers—instead of thirty-five hundred—marchin' on picket lines! Imagine a hundred thousand! Or even more!"

Benny shot a withering glare at Paddy O'Boyle, who sat head bowed, arms crossed at his chest. "Let me put it this way," Benny said. "If we mobilize the kind of support we should be getting from our so-called friends in organized labor, we can shut the entire city down!"

And that was no exaggeration. Indeed, the nature and breadth of organized labor in New York gave it access to a multitude of pressure points that, if applied simultaneously, could literally cripple the city. A sympathy strike by any one of the city's major unions, let alone a slew of them, could instantly shift the balance of power to Local 88, ratcheting up the pressure on tugboat owners, spurring political intervention, and ending the strike in the union's favor.

Seemingly little was cooking on that front, however. While several small unions had begun honoring tugboat workers' picket lines, support was, at best, scattershot. And nothing in the way of palpable backing had been proffered by larger, more powerful unions, whose leaders, while sympathetic to the tugboatmen, were leery about committing their members to a strike.

Not that Local 88 leaders weren't working hard to change all of that. For several days, delegations led by Tommy Duggan and Frank Russo had been soliciting the support of labor leaders tied to shipping, warehousing, and other enterprises at the Port of New York. Leaflets imploring myriad workers to honor the tugboat strike were being distributed at shipyards, cargo piers, dockside taverns, and union halls. Personal favors were being called in left and right.

"So, where do things stand?" asked Benny, polling Local 88's brain trust.

"The Harbor Masters seem willin' to support us," replied Tommy Duggan, referencing the officials who enforced city and state regulations at port facilities.

"That's a start," said Benny. "How about dispatchers?"

"Maybe."

"Dock builders."

"Them, too."

"An' maritime pilots?"

"Nothin' for certain, but it seems possible," said Duggan, of the skilled mariners who guided oceangoing vessels through the river mouths and shoals of New York Harbor.

"How many men are we talkin' about?" Benny inquired.

"Couple of dozen, at the most."

"We need more! Hundreds!" Benny said. "Bigger fish, too!" He turned to Frank Russo. "How about civil servants?"

"Uh-uh." Russo frowned. "Their hands are tied. As public employees, they're banned from striking."

"Construction workers?"

"No commitments yet."

"Barge workers? Warehousemen?"

"They say they'll support us . . . but only verbally."

"What does that mean?"

"It means they'll issue a statement saying they're sympathetic to our cause."

"An' beyond that?"

"We'll have to wait an' see."

Benny scanned the room. "Anything else?"

"A lotta unions say they're thinkin' about supporting us, but are holdin' off for now," Russo reported. "They don't want to commit to anything."

"What's stoppin' them?"

"Most are catchin' heat from political interests," Russo replied. "Plus, let's face it: our union is small potatoes. The bigtime unions an' labor federations like the AFL and the CIO don't owe us shit. This ain't their fight. Most of 'em want to see us settle the strike on our own, so they don't have to put their asses on the line."

"Paychecks over principle," Tommy Duggan said, sourly.

"Some unions are also scared that, if they strike, they'll be slapped with injunctions, fines, maybe even jail time," Russo said. "They're not certain they've got the legal cover."

"Is that legit . . . or just some cockamamie excuse?" Benny asked.

Russo shrugged. "Who knows?"

Benny turned to Paddy O'Boyle. "How 'bout the USA?"

It was a loaded question. Support from Local 88's parent union would provide an instant, immeasurable boost to striking tugboat workers. There were thirty-two thousand longshoremen in the United Stevedores Association. A sympathy strike by even a handful of them could cripple shipping along the entire Eastern Seaboard. It could literally make or break Local 88's walkout.

"Still workin' on it," said O'Boyle, aware that Local 88's Strike Committee had no clue about the tacit deal he'd struck with Henry to never involve USA members in a New York tugboat strike.

"You're workin' on it?" Benny asked, dubiously. "How hard?"

"Hard as I can," O'Boyle said.

Benny snickered. "I'll bet you are."

"What're you implying, Logan?" O'Boyle snapped.

"What I'm sayin'," said Benny, "that you've gotta work harder . . . or let someone else handle the job!"

O'Boyle stiffened. In his younger days, as a dockside head-knocker, he would have gone after Benny right then and there. Would have been a helluva brouhaha, too. But all the union president did was lean backwards in his chair, grinning like a Cheshire cat. It was obvious he was also doing next to nothing to rally USA support for a strike he'd never endorsed in the first place.

"An' long as we're talkin' about support," Benny continued facetiously, "how about the USA kickin' in a coupla bucks to aid our strike fund? Whaddaya say, Paddy? Our parent union can afford to help us out, can't it . . . what with its deep, fuckin' pockets?"

"Workin' on that, too," O'Boyle said stoically.

Benny could feel his insides churn. It was all he could do to keep from reaching out and grabbing O'Boyle by the throat. Benny couldn't stomach the sight of the crooked union kingpin: his florid, pockmarked face; his braying laugh; the scent of the Old Spice he wore in excess, as if to mask the stench of something rotten at the core.

"I guess our piddlin' local ain't important enough to the Big Boys at the USA, huh?" Benny said. "Or maybe, Paddy, you got other interests to protect?"

O'Boyle, fists balled, sprung abruptly from his chair.

"C'mon, Paddy!" Benny egged him on. "Wanna see what I think of you an' your fuckin' leadership?"

O'Boyle hurled a wad of spit at Benny, who lurched toward the USA boss. Quickly, however, the other union reps intervened, pulling the two apart.

"All right," Tommy Duggan said, breaking a protracted silence. "Let's get back to the subject hand. Any other unions we can bank on for support?"

"Nothin' solid," Frank Russo replied. "But the signs ain't all bad."

"What do you mean?"

"Every union I've contacted is takin' a wait-an'-see approach. None of them will commit their support, but none have completely ruled it out, either."

"I guess," Duggan said forlornly, "that leaves us holdin' our dicks in our hands."

"What about City Hall?" Benny inquired. "How long do you think the politicians will continue to sit the strike out?"

"They're too busy chasin' their tails at the moment," Russo replied. "Those halfwits don't know whether to shit, fart, or whistle. Never had to deal with a crisis like this before."

"That'll change soon, though," warned Duggan, fresh off a meeting with Desmond Quinn. "City Hall can't afford to let the strike continue much longer. Any minute now, they'll be jumpin' in with both feet."

"What happens then?"

"They'll twist arms to get both sides to settle. Might even impose their own settlement, in the interests of public safety."

"The government has that authority?"

"That and more," Russo replied. "The Feds have the power to declare a national emergency, issue injunctions, and mandate a settlement on whatever terms they dictate. They can also fine our union an' jail our members if we don't abide by the sanctions they dictate."

After another long and troubled silence, Benny said, "Let's say the government imposes a settlement. Is that necessarily bad? I mean . . . who comes outta this a winner then?"

"Hard to say," Duggan replied. "Both sides probably take it in the shorts."

"Or maybe," Benny suggested, "we don't lose at all."

"How do you figure?"

"Well, if the government settles the strike," Benny said, "you gotta believe they'd force a deal at a wage that's more favorable to us than what the owners have thrown on the table. They sure as hell won't force us to swallow a two-percent pay hike. That'd be a kick in the nuts to every worker in America."

"Could cost 'em a lotta votes," Russo observed.

"Exactly." Benny nodded. "So, if the politicians jump in, it's likely that our union would make out better than we would have at the bargainin' table. We might not get the four-percent bump we've been seekin', but we've gotta do better than the two-percent from Henry McFarland."

No one objected to the logic.

"We just gotta continue to hang tough," Benny said, "an' hope this breaks our way."

He turned to Duggan and Russo.

"Let's turn up the heat on other unions regarding support," he said. "Remind 'em that we're in this fight together, an' we've got their back if they ever need our support. Remind 'em, too, that this strike ain't about just our local. It's about every union in America . . . every worker in this country, an' the brotherhood we share."

Then he glared at Paddy O'Boyle. "An' if our parent union ain't gonna have our back, Paddy . . . you tell USA leadership that I said to go fuck themselves."

He wagged his finger at the union boss. "Remember this, too, Paddy. I've got a long memory."

O'Boyle snickered. "That some kind of threat?"

"No. It's more like a promise."

"A promise of what?"

"A promise that I'll remember who was willin' to stick their neck out for us—an' who wasn't—when I run into 'em somewhere down the road."

"Yeah?" O'Boyle snickered. "An' when will that be?"

"Who knows?" Benny said. "The next time I cross paths with your union cronies, Paddy . . . I might even be in your job."

CHAPTER 30

February 5, 1946

Steadily, insidiously, the affliction wrought by the strike continued to mushroom, metastasizing like a deadly contagion as the city sank further into a deep, dark hole.

Fallout from the five-day-old work stoppage was evident by now in most quarters of New York. With loaded garbage scows unable to access ocean dumpsites, mounds of snow-encrusted trash, scavenged by rodents, were now piled along sidewalks and curbs. A growing number of homes and apartments lacked electricity and heat. Long lines of vehicles queued up at the dwindling number of gas stations offering fuel. Food shortages were also becoming acute, grocery shelves stripped bare by panicky shoppers stocking up on shrinking caches of bread, milk, eggs, and other staples. Dwindling supplies of meat, vegetables, fruit, and fish were being sold by some merchants at prices tantamount to gouging, or were being offered solely to preferential customers in something akin to a burgeoning black market.

Pilloried by the press for allowing the city to sink to such depths, a bedeviled Edmund Flannery had become little more than the butt of jokes, criticized as cowardly, clueless, and overwhelmed by the crisis ravaging the city. Editorials ripped his administration for its indecisiveness and ineptitude. Political cartoons depicted him as a hapless, flustered bureaucrat cowering beneath his desk at City Hall as New York's skyline crumbled to bits.

Attempting to blunt the condemnation and rally a dispirited public, the mayor took to the airwaves, urging citizens via a series of radio broadcasts to remain calm, shelter indoors, and conserve food and fuel however possible. In an abrupt policy reversal, he rescinded his citywide blackout edict, admitting publicly that the directive was a misguided, kneejerk reaction to growing fuel shortages. Streetlights were restored to full power, city landmarks illuminated, and outdoor electric displays turned back on. The Manhattan skyline, Flannery said, could once again cast its radiance upon the city. Nighttime would no longer be as terrifying or as dark.

But at the same time, Flannery announced a plethora of new restrictions that his administration deemed necessary. Municipal buildings, except for police precincts, were ordered closed. Government services were suspended, court calendars scrapped, social agencies shuttered. With fuel supplies at critically low levels, the city also unveiled a priority system for allocating coal and heating oil, rationing emergency reserves through the issuance of certificates distributed to businesses and institutions deemed essential.

But that decision quickly backfired, too. Responding to Flannery's latest rationing plan, building landlords, homeowners, tenants, and merchants flooded police precincts to file applications for fuel certificates, often waiting hours to procure the documents. Bureaucrats wrangled about who was eligible to receive supplies, and who wasn't. Bribes and favors were exchanged for fuel consents. Rejected applicants argued among themselves.

All of which led City Hall to rescind the rationing plan shortly after it was announced, while issuing its most dire warning yet.

"If this strike continues," Flannery told the press, "New York's residents face the specter of continued hardship—and, God forbid, even loss of life."

That was all the press corps needed to hear. Instantly, radio stations halted scheduled programming to broadcast special bulletins. Afternoon newspapers and EXTRAS hinted at imminent cataclysm. Word-of-mouth rumors fueled the growing panic.

But Flannery's warning seemed far more than simply an idle threat. Indeed, even amidst the growing municipal chaos, signs of a public-health crisis were looming.

With the cold snap at its height, and indoor temperatures being maintained only at levels needed to prevent water pipes from freezing, complaints of insufficient heat were pouring into the Board of Health, landlords being lambasted by angry, frightened tenants suffering from the cold. Hospital rooms were also filling up with influenza patients, amidst forecasts of a potential epidemic. An additional plunge in temperature, health officials warned, could spell grave peril. A drop to zero degrees, they said, could well prove disastrous.

But New York's populace was losing far more than merely its sense of wellbeing. By now, it had lost nearly all manner of patience.

Initially divided over their opinions regarding the strike—or, in many cases, ambivalent—the public was unanimous now in its view that the walkout needed to end immediately. Weary of the hardships they'd been forced to endure, people were pointing fingers in all directions, lashing out at both tugboat owners and union leaders, lambasting politicians for their hapless efforts at mitigating the crisis, and clamoring for state and federal officials to impose a settlement. Local 88 strike headquarters and the offices of the Gotham Harbor Alliance were bombarded with irate phone calls. Protestors staged rallies at City Hall. Cordons of police officers were dispatched to put a lid on the growing disorder at picket sites.

Despite all this, no end to the strike seemed even remotely in sight. Proposals to submit the dispute to binding arbitration were rejected by both sides. Henry and Benny continued to disparage each other in the press. Desmond Quinn, joined now by state and federal mediators, worked feverishly to broker a settlement, though attaining only minor concessions.

"This appalling strike is a reminder of how a tiny gang of ruthless, greedy individuals can recklessly cripple the economy and endanger the wellbeing of an entire city for their own selfish gain," Henry told reporters.

Benny countered: "This strike isn't about ruthlessness or greed. It's about what's long overdue and well-deserved by skilled and dedicated workers who love this city."

Henry charged, "Striking workers are exhibiting a vindictiveness that ignores all appeals for public sympathy. They have an obligation to return to work, stop holding the city hostage, and alleviate the suffering caused by their irresponsible actions."

Benny fired back. "The city's tugboat owners are more anxious to attack our union than to negotiate responsibly. We know what their objective is. They want to bust the union, an' we'll be damned if we let 'em!"

Yet even in the face of the hardship and rhetoric, seemingly nothing of substance was taking place to end the ordeal. No apparent movement toward a settlement. No meaningful government intervention. No sign of respite for the weary, fractured city.

New York was in wholly uncharted waters now. Not even in the darkest days of the First or Second World Wars had America's preeminent city witnessed such a dramatic chain of events. Not even in the depths of the Great Depression had it experienced such painful austerities. Not even in the most fabled of natural disasters had it been so completely immobilized, so wracked by uncertainty, so broken and troubled and torn.

CHAPTER 31

February 5, 1946

B ut if the city's residents were getting hammered by the strike, tugboat
workers were bearing the brunt of the pain. It was easy to see why.

Unlike the owners, who could wage their battle from the comfort of
boardrooms and offices, strikers were forced to take their fight to the picket lines,
squarely in the teeth of the hostile elements. That alone was daunting. Weather
conditions had deteriorated even further, with temperatures plunging to the
single digits and swirling gusts whipping snowdrifts chest-high in spots. Even
with picketing capped at thirty-minute stints, legions of workers were being
kayoed by exposure to the glacial terrain. Dozens were hospitalized with cases of
hypothermia, windburn, and dehydration. Several lost fingers or toes to frostbite.
Still others fell victim to the outbreak of flu spreading across the city.

Even more debilitating than the elements, however, was the impact of lost
wages. Like most working-class New Yorkers, the majority of Local 88's rank
and file lived paycheck to paycheck, with little if any savings to fall back on, and
nowhere to turn for help. Finances, in many cases, had been stretched to the limit
even prior to the strike; they were far more tenuous now. Indeed, with wages
having been withheld for the two-week pay period preceding the strike, another
five workdays lost to the walkout, and emergency pay yielding only a fraction
of their normal salaries, tugboat workers had gone payless for what amounted
to nearly a month. With liabilities mounting swiftly, cash-strapped strikers
found themselves being harassed by creditors, and bill collectors, including
landlords threatening eviction. A growing number were being forced to find
second and even third jobs, moonlighting as taxi drivers, janitors, and night
watchmen. Others were pawning valued keepsakes—often at a fraction of their
real or sentimental worth—or borrowing from relatives, friends, and exploitative
money-mongers. Without medical insurance, strikers were also being forced to

pay out-of-pocket for health care, or refrain from seeking such care entirely.

Exacerbating the workers' duress was a pervasive sense of uncertainty. With contract negotiations suspended indefinitely, and efforts to end the strike fruitless, it was impossible to predict how financially devastating the walkout would ultimately prove—or what impact it would have on livelihoods and families. No one knew how great a hardship strikers could endure before caving in to the need for a paycheck. No one knew if the ratcheting tension might erupt into something even more pernicious.

By day five of the walkout, the impact of the strike on workers had become all too evident. A growing number of the men had grown exhausted, overwrought by the pressures they were facing. Verbal squabbles and fistfights were erupting on picket lines. Relationships, even among longtime crewmates, were becoming fractured or frayed. Fissures were opening inside households as well, with strikers being pressured by anxious wives to either cross picket lines or push union leaders for an expedited contract settlement.

Union leaders, cognizant of the mounting strain, worked overtime to keep spirits from waning. Strike captains redoubled their efforts at supplying picket lines with warm clothing, firewood, and other provisions. Soup kitchens and carpools were established to provide sustenance and transportation. Volunteer doctors and nurses attended to strikers' medical needs. Discount vouchers from select groceries and pharmacies helped defray the cost of food and medicine. Workers were also supplied with form letters to forward to creditors, requesting leeway in meeting their obligations.

Acceding to Benny's request, and despite his trepidation, Jack also found himself an increasingly vital cog in the strike's daily machinery, having assumed a role on the union's Strike Fund Committee. It was an effort as complex, and as wrought with emotion, as it was critical.

Working in assembly-line fashion, each committee member was tasked with a specific role. Frank Russo, Local 88's treasurer, served as committee chair, supervising activities, and personally cutting emergency paychecks. USA vice president Butch Flanagan—Paddy O'Boyle's eyes and ears—maintained a detailed financial ledger, signing off on the document each day before securing it overnight in a bank vault. Tommy Duggan, Benny's trusted wingman, helped disburse funds and prepare a daily financial summary.

Jack's role on the committee was specifically tailored to his aptitude in math. His job was to calculate how much strike pay Local 88 members—at various pay grades, seniority levels, and job classifications—were entitled to receive. Entitlements varied considerably. Tugboat captains, who earned between $130 and $145 per week, were eligible to draw a one-time payment of between $85 and $98. Mates, who earned between $105 and $118, were entitled to anywhere from $72 to $80. Allowances were similarly allocated for deckhands, dispatchers, and others.

The system, despite its potential for malfeasance and mistakes, functioned remarkably well. Workers, designated alphabetically by surname, received their strike pay in staggered shifts between 7 a.m. and 7 p.m., so that picket lines could be manned without interruption and the Strike Fund Committee wouldn't be overrun by workers arriving randomly. Strikers, for the most part, adhered to the prescribed schedule. Committee members performed their tasks adroitly. Jack was flawless in his calculations, drawing nary a protest over the emergency pay being doled out.

The strike fund, a sacrosanct lifeline for union members, was also managed with the care and scrutiny it warranted. Pay levels, after computation by Jack, were entered by Butch Flanagan into the financial ledger, which workers initialed in ink when they collected their emergency wages. Reserves were closely monitored. At the end of each day, Tommy Duggan updated his financial summary, sealed it in a brown manila envelope, and left it atop his desk at strike headquarters for union officials to review at their morning meeting.

Jack, again at Benny's behest, also kept an eye peeled for potential improprieties, although nothing underhanded, as far as anyone could tell, had reared its ugly head. Every penny of the strike fund was accurately calculated, properly disbursed, and scrupulously accounted for—a process that was both daunting and tedious, especially for Jack.

Working with only a clunky adding machine, scratch pad, and carpenter's pencil, Jack began his duties each day before dawn, working virtually nonstop till after midnight. Meals were eaten at his desk. Sleep was minimal, as was contact with Kate. For the past five days, Jack had seen his pregnant wife only fleetingly, when the couple awoke, dressed for work, and left the family's apartment with little more than a peck on the cheek.

But daunting as Jack's duties were, they paled by comparison to the burden being shouldered by other striking workers, especially those manning union picket lines. Jack witnessed firsthand the physical toll the work stoppage was having on the workers as they trudged in to strike headquarters each day to collect their emergency pay. Some men—icicles clinging to their whiskers, bodies caked in ice and snow—seemed on the verge of collapse. Others, eyelids and mouths frozen shut, could barely see straight or utter a coherent sound, their words slurry and indiscernible as they fumbled about for their meager strike pay.

Jack had seen faces like theirs before. Seen them on the D-Day assault vessels that stormed the beaches at Normandy. Seen them in the hobo jungles and bread lines of the Great Depression, at the Brooklyn docks during morning shapeup, and in late-night bars after factory layoffs. Always the same wary, frightened mien: glassy eyes and hollow cheeks; masks of incertitude and trepidation; faces as fallow as droughted farmland, weathered and old before their time.

Tugboat workers were generally a rugged, hardy breed, calloused by a lifetime of manual labor, setbacks, and misfortune. Life, for most, had rendered its share of wounds. Trial by fire was nothing new. The strike, however, was a wholly different kind of test, a strange new battle laced with thorny, aberrant demands, and an emotional impact as lethal as bullets. Livelihoods were on the line, finances stretched to the breaking point, relationships under duress, futures tied to leaders with nebulous, divergent agendas. And time was every bit as daunting an adversary as the tugboat owners the workers were battling.

Indeed, the financial reports that Tommy Duggan compiled each day had grown increasingly dire as the strike wore on. The United Stevedore's Association, under Paddy O'Boyle, had withheld any semblance of financial support, and the five-day work stoppage had almost entirely consumed Local 88's paltry war chest. The union had money enough to pay striking workers for only two more days; after that, the men would be running on empty, their financial status weakened dramatically. Perhaps fatally.

Every member of Local 88 was feeling the pinch—including Jack.

On the fifth day of the walkout, when his name appeared on the roster of workers eligible to collect their strike pay, Frank Russo cut Jack a check for twenty-seven dollars, half his normal weekly wage and barely enough for him and Kate to purchase groceries, let alone meet their other household obligations. The reality the couple faced was frighteningly evident now: nothing beyond Kate's trifling paycheck was in the pipeline for the foreseeable future. Already, the two of them had begun tapping the precious savings account they'd worked months to accumulate. Who knew how long their financial freefall would last? Who knew how much of a setback it would ultimately prove? Who knew anything anymore?

Then there was Benny. As the strike's linchpin personality, and equally its spiritual leader and driving force, Benny was paying the steepest price of anyone. For the past five days, Local 88's combative figurehead had emptied himself unflinchingly into the conflict, moving about the city like a whirling dervish, juggling a relentless onslaught of demands: plotting tactics with union officials; convening with government mediators; addressing New York's press corps; leading the charge on picket lines.

To Jack, his brother's daily regimen was reminiscent of the savage brawls Benny had waged years earlier as a prizefighter: as grueling, as ferocious, and just as much a test of fortitude, moxie, and will. But for Benny, as for the city's tugboat workers, the strike was a different kind of fight than any he'd ever waged. Nor was it merely a personal proving ground of physicality, moxie, and skill.

Leading the strike was, far and away, the toughest battle of Benny's life— the adversary more daunting, the pressure more intense, the outcome more meaningful. No less than the fate of the tugboat workers' union—perhaps the future of organized labor in all of New York—hung in the balance. Benny, by virtue of his union stewardship, had been cast in the most glaring of spotlights, every word scrutinized by business and labor leaders, every decision subject to supposition and second-guessing, every action picked apart by politicians, pundits, and the public.

Nor, unlike in his boxing sorties, was Benny in the ring alone. Thirty-five hundred tugboatmen were in the fight with him, men for whom he'd assumed the mantle of leadership, men who'd bequeathed to him their faith and trust. For Benny, nearly everything he valued in life was squarely on the line: his principles, his reputation, his future, a union brotherhood that he considered as nothing less than family.

Perhaps his very life.

But Benny wasn't some wild-eyed, bogus zealot fueled by a radical political agenda or by the writings of sophists and labor theorists. Concepts like industrial democracy and alienated labor meant little to him. Nor did he view capitalism as an economic system that needed to be eradicated. For Benny, the biggest problem with capitalism was that power brokers like Henry McFarland pocketed most of the money while working stiffs like Benny got screwed. And the only way to shift the balance of power, Benny was convinced, was for men like him to link arms, becoming stronger in tandem than they could ever be alone.

Benny's motives might have been complex—a byproduct of his background, personality and character—but there was little doubt that those motives were pure. The fight Benny was waging wasn't as much about chasing a buck as it was about putting an end to a culture of passivity among the workers he led, and emerging from under the thumb of greedy Brahmins like Henry McFarland and feckless union leaders like Paddy O'Boyle. To Benny, the strike was nothing short of a refusal to be belittled, taken for granted, and victimized. And toward that end, he was succeeding wildly, commanding fierce loyalty even in the face of enormous hardship.

In leading strikers through the cold, dark winter of their discontent, Benny had won the hearts and minds not only of New York's tugboat workers, but of tens of thousands of blue-collar workers across the city. In taking a defiant stand against the status quo, he had given voice to a bottled-up yearning, and had become the tugboat workers' inspiration, the embodiment of their fighting spirit—imbuing them with courage and strength, helping them believe they could triumph in a battle that had always seemed unwinnable. Prior to Benny's emergence, tugboat workers had had no substantive organization, no coherent message, no intrepid spokesman. They'd been rudderless, voiceless, wholly at the whim of more powerful interests. Prior to him, there'd been no fight—only a painful status quo, a festering disaffection, and whatever labor contracts were rammed down the workers' throats.

But the past was no longer prologue. Under Benny's stewardship, there'd no longer be acceptance of the status quo, a blind allegiance to bankrupt leaders, or a pervasive sense that union members were powerless in determining their fate. Under Benny, tugboat workers would no longer be lambs—they'd be lions. If he could muster the courage to make a stand, so could they. If he could summon the will to fight, so could they. And success or failure would ride as much as anything on Benny's stewardship. He'd rather die, it seemed, than fail to honor the covenant he shared with his union brethren. Win or lose, he was in the fight for everything he was worth.

But Benny, too, was paying a grievous price for his role in the strike, its impact mirrored in his changing countenance. Indeed, the burden of union stewardship had carved deep gullies into Benny's cheeks, dark pockets beneath his eyes, and wisps of gray in his thinning hair. Five days into the labor conflagration, his grizzled, unshaven face had grown haggard and ghostlike, his voice hoarse, his shoulders sloped. Too busy to eat, too strung out to sleep, he'd lost nearly twenty pounds and appeared as if he'd aged ten years.

It was impossible to know if his careworn countenance was merely a reflection of uncertainty and fatigue, or the early signs of resignation and surrender. Like everything else about the strike, time alone would tell.

CHAPTER 32

February 5, 1946

Tugboat workers and the public weren't the only ones facing the hardship wrought by the strike. Businesses were feeling the pinch, too—tugboat firms included.

Indeed, for each day that the harbor remained closed to commerce, Alliance firms were bleeding three million dollars in lost revenue, a shortfall that had been grossly underestimated by their owners—who were also discovering, to their dismay, that their strike-defense fund had been depleted far sooner than anticipated and strike insurance wasn't nearly covering their losses. With their cumulative shortfall at fifteen million dollars and counting, Gotham Harbor Alliance members were wincing from the pain. Several were now questioning their hardline bargaining posture as well. While no one was willing to openly buck Henry—at least not yet—a handful of the owners were dropping strong hints that they no longer had the stomach to adhere to their leader's hardline approach, suggesting instead that they soften their negotiating stance and accede in part to the union's wage demands. Some were even voicing the belief that winning the strike on Henry's terms could ultimately prove more costly than losing it, becoming a pyrrhic victory that they'd pay for in terms of diminished morale, lower productivity, and a loss of good will. If the union was forced to capitulate—or if it imploded entirely, as Henry desired—the resultant bitterness among their workers could last for decades, some owners reasoned. Tugboat firms, they feared, could be irrevocably damaged, even destroyed.

Henry denied, or ignored, any such possibility, reluctant to give an inch. To him, victory was all that mattered—making an example of Local 88, and striking a crippling blow against organized labor. Five days into the strike, he clung fervently to the belief that it was simply a matter of time before the tugboat workers' union imploded, handing a pivotal labor-relations victory to corporate America. Even now, he wanted not the slightest display of weakness, surrender, or division.

But pressure was mounting on Henry, too. McFarland Marine Towing, with the coalition's largest revenue base, was bleeding money more profusely than any other tugboat firm, and Henry's chorus of unhappy customers, joined now by corporate fiduciaries, was growing increasingly vocal. Much to his dismay, Henry had been phoned several times in recent days by bankers and asset managers, all of whom warned of dire consequences if he didn't stanch the financial bleeding. More ominous warnings yet were emanating from sources outside the city's legitimate business channels. Indeed, with the spigot from harbor-related commerce closed for nearly a week, countless waterfront businesses—including more than a few with underworld ties—were getting financially bludgeoned. Word was being relayed now to Henry through backchannels: New York's crime lords were growing antsy. They, too, wanted the strike ended—soon.

But those weren't the only problems that Henry was suddenly facing, nor were they even the most pressing. Henry's campaign to rally public support, so impactful at its outset, had also begun to fizzle. Waterfront firms weren't the only companies getting financially hammered by the work stoppage. With businesses throughout New York forced into varying degrees of closure, the city's commercial machinery had ground to a virtual halt. Millions of dollars in revenue were evaporating, untold numbers of workers facing layoffs. The public by now was thoroughly fed up with the strike, newspapers clamoring for a settlement, public officials pushing harder than ever for resolution. A government-imposed end to the walkout was also said to be looming, a prospect that had tugboat owners quaking in their boots.

Circumstances had grown even more dire with the arrival that morning of a confidential communiqué from a source inside the Sanitation Department. With its tugboats idled for the past five days, McFarland Marine Towing had been unable to fulfill the terms of its contract to tow the city's garbage scows to their offshore dumpsites. The Health Department, already swamped with complaints about unheated homes, was also being bludgeoned over potential health risks tied to rotting litter. Sanitation officials were getting hammered by protests over mounting piles of trash. Now word had reached Henry that city officials were mulling legal action against his company for alleged breach of contract.

A potential lawsuit on those grounds was nothing to sneeze at. Henry's financial exposure, already considerable, had increased exponentially with the threatened legal action. The liability stemming from his company's inability to fulfill its trash-hauling contract could potentially cost McFarland Marine Towing millions of dollars, not to mention even more in lost business if the city turned to another tugboat firm for future disposal of its trash. This was a gut shot that Henry hadn't foreseen, something that needed to be addressed immediately.

An unexpected noose tightening around his neck, Henry fumbled for a cigarette and reached for the telephone, seeking to contact whatever lifelines he could. In quick succession, he phoned the heads of both the Sanitation and Health Departments, assuring officials that he'd find a way to expedite his company's trash-hauling efforts, despite the absence of striking tugboatmen. He then reached out to the city's Corporation Counsel, begging for time to resolve his labor issues, requesting that legal action be shelved.

By the time he was finished with his phone calls, Henry was sweating profusely, chest aflame. He coughed a gob of sputum into a handkerchief dappled with phlegm, and then fortified himself with a shot of bourbon from a decanter he stashed in a desk drawer.

By now, there was but one last-ditch call to make. Thumbing through his Rolodex, Henry dialed an unlisted number, and a wall phone rang at a smoke-filled social club in the cellar of a South Bronx apartment building. Folding his hand, Paddy O'Boyle rose from his seat at a pinochle game to take the call.

"This gotta be more than just a social call, especially in times like these," the union boss mumbled into the handset of the phone.

"It's times like these," said Henry, "when friends are needed the most."

"Friends?" O'Boyle snickered. "We're on opposite sides of this labor war . . . remember?"

"Then I guess I have no problem consorting with the enemy," said Henry, growing quickly serious. "I'm calling, Paddy, because I need your help."

O'Boyle cupped the handset of the phone to muffle his voice.

"I've already told you, there's no way I can resurrect the deal that you an' I shook hands on," he said. "That horse left the barn the instant the workers voted to strike."

"I'm well aware of that," said Henry.

"An' there's no way that I can strongarm the workers into believin' that the strike is a losin' proposition," O'Boyle said.

"I'm aware of that, too."

"Then how on God's earth can I possibly help?"

Henry could sense a palpable anxiety, as if the union boss was spooked by the mere hint of impropriety. Which he was.

"You know, I shouldn't even be talkin' to you," O'Boyle said. "My ass is on the line."

"I appreciate the thorny position you're in," Henry said. "Sleeping with the enemy isn't as easy as it used to be."

"It's a lot more dangerous, too," O'Boyle said. "I can get my nuts clipped just for takin' your phone call. We can't do business together . . . not with the way things stand now."

"But we've never stopped doing business Paddy," Henry said with false cheer. "We've just had an inopportune hiatus in our partnership."

"A hiatus?" O'Boyle seemed even more puzzled now.

Henry cut to the chase. "I have a proposal that I'd like you to consider."

"What kind of proposal?"

"The kind that I believe you'll find well worth your while."

The phone line went silent, except for the rasp of O'Boyle's breathing.

"You certainly have nothing to lose by listening," Henry said.

O'Boyle's reticence dissipated, the scent of an easy buck too tempting to resist.

"Where do ya wanna talk?" the union boss asked.

"Sands Point," said Henry. "Sit tight. I'll have my driver pick you up."

"An' this'll be worth my while?"

"You know me," said Henry. "I always take care of my friends."

*   *   *

O'Boyle was greeted at the door of the North Shore estate by his longtime benefactor, clad in linen trousers, brown loafers, a pink golf shirt—and the brightest of smiles.

"Glad you found the place," Henry quipped.

"Well, Sands Point is a long way from the Bronx . . . in more ways than one," said O'Boyle. "Your driver found it without a problem, though."

"That's why I pay him the big bucks." Henry chuckled.

"Well, money is like magic," O'Boyle said. "Makes problems disappear."

"My thoughts exactly." Henry grinned. "And that's what I called you to discuss: my money, our problems."

"I'm all ears," O'Boyle said.

"That," said Henry, "is what I was hoping to hear."

He ushered the union boss into a richly appointed drawing room, tastefully furnished with expensive sculptures, artwork and collectibles, much of it purchased at Sotheby's and other leading auction houses. A fire crackled in a massive stone fireplace bordered on either side by shelves full of calfbound books. Sitting catty-corner at the far end of the room was Carolyn's Bösendorfer grand piano, its music rack empty and housing clamped shut.

Henry slipped behind a cocktail bar and fixed O'Boyle a whiskey straight up. He poured a splash of bourbon over ice for himself. The pair then drifted toward the fireplace, over which oil portraits of Henry and Carolyn hung in matching frames.

"She certainly was a beautiful woman," O'Boyle said, wistfully.

"That she was . . . in every possible way." Henry sighed. "I was lucky to have had her in my life for so many years."

"It helps when you look at things that way," O'Boyle said sagely. "Makes personal loss easier to take . . . if you dwell on the good times."

"Maybe," said Henry. "There are times, though, when I'm not so sure."

Henry's candor took him aback. Stoicism, after all, had always been a reliable mask. It wasn't often that Henry opened a window to his inner self. Oddly, though, he felt on safe ground with O'Boyle. While the two of them could hardly be considered true friends, they nonetheless shared a special bond, not uncommon among longtime business allies.

"My belated condolences." O'Boyle crossed himself solemnly, nodding at Carolyn's portrait. "May your late wife's soul rest in peace."

Henry again was touched. In the cutthroat world in which he resided, it was easy to forget that people were capable of conveying emotions such as empathy and sorrow. It was harder yet to distinguish sincerity from deceit.

Opting for the former, Henry was moved by O'Boyle's sentiments.

"Thanks, Paddy." He raised his glass. "And here's to memories of simpler times."

"Yeah." O'Boyle swigged his drink. "Things were a lot easier for us back then."

Henry felt a tinge of nostalgia. Indeed, things had been a lot easier in the years preceding the war, certainly when it came to negotiating contracts with the tugboat workers' union: dealing with a complaisant O'Boyle instead of butting heads with a hostile rank and file; buying labor peace on the cheap instead of paying through the nose at the bargaining table; focusing on productive business matters rather than being bogged down by baseless worker grievances and unconscionable demands—not to mention strikes. There was clarity in the old way, simpler ground rules, fewer headaches. Henry's payoffs to O'Boyle were viewed simply as overhead, a necessary cost of doing business. O'Boyle pocketed the money and did whatever was needed to get a deal done. No pushback. No questions. No bullshit.

"Too bad things are so convoluted now," Henry lamented.

O'Boyle shrugged. "Yeah . . . too bad."

Henry grinned. "But I didn't bring you all the way to Sands Point, Paddy, simply to reminisce. Truth is, I can use your help in bringing the tugboat strike to a satisfactory resolution."

"Satisfactory to who?"

"To both of us."

"I already tol' ya." O'Boyle grimaced. "I've done everything I can. Lobbied for the deal we shook hands on, put my ass on the line. Ain't easy, though, dealin' with the men these days. They're marchin' to a different drumbeat."

"And how, may I ask, are the men holding up?"

"I'd say, for the most part, they're hangin' tough."

"But a growing number of them, from what I understand, sorely miss their paychecks," Henry said, slyly.

"I warned 'em about walkin' off the job," O'Boyle said. "Now they're learnin' there's a price to be paid."

"Tell me, Paddy, are enough of the men looking for a way out?"

O'Boyle shrugged. "Could be."

"And what does that mean?"

"It means that the men have their limits . . . an' anything can happen with just the right push."

"So, what you're telling me," Henry said, "is that the rank and file can perhaps be 'nudged' in a direction that's advantageous to the two of us?"

"Anything is possible," O'Boyle replied. "Whaddaya have in mind?"

Henry tinkled the ice in his glass. "Before I address specifics, tell me, Paddy: what are your feelings about Benny Logan? Do you like him? Respect him? Want him to get what he's gunning for?"

"To be perfectly honest," O'Boyle said, "part of me wouldn't mind seein' the rank an' file land a decent contract. I am a lifelong union man, after all."

Henry let the bullshit slide. O'Boyle would sell out Local 88's members in a heartbeat if he could make a buck. No two ways about it.

"Sure, Paddy." Henry grinned. "But what about Logan?"

"Feisty bastard . . . real pain in the ass," O'Boyle replied. "Part of me admires the sonofabitch, though."

"Why is that?"

"He's in the fight for all the right reasons. Reminds me of myself, when I was idealistic an' full of piss an' vinegar."

Henry chuckled. "But you aren't idealistic anymore, are you Paddy?"

"No," O'Boyle said. "I'm a coldhearted pragmatist . . . just like you."

"No need to apologize for that." Henry laughed. "Most of us were idealistic when we first started out. But eventually we grow up, adapt to realties. Problem is, Logan hasn't learned that lesson yet. He refuses to adhere to rules about how things are done in the world you and I live in."

"That's why the other part of me," said O'Boyle, "wouldn't mind rippin' his heart out."

"Let's focus on that part," Henry said.

And the two men shared a laugh.

"For me," said Henry, "Logan is a pain in the ass who's costing me headaches and money. But for you, Paddy? Hell, he flat-out picked your pocket. Robbed you of power, prestige, control. And the money you were capable of earning? Logan robbed you of that, too . . . didn't he?"

O'Boyle nodded. "An' your point?"

"My point," said Henry, "is that you and I have a mutual interest when it comes to Benny Logan. Both of us would like to see him disappear. Frankly, I wouldn't mind seeing him leave town in a pine box. And I'm sure you wouldn't mind slapping him around for the heartache he's causing you."

"It's possible," O'Boyle said coyly.

"And I suppose it's also possible," Henry said, "that you may want to take back what once was yours: leadership, control, earning power. Am I right?"

"That's possible, too."

"Okay," Henry said, "so now we know where the two of us stand. You never wanted this strike, and I want to end it on my terms. You want the workers to get the deal the two of us negotiated, and for Logan to get his nuts clipped, and so do I. Isn't that about the size of it?"

"I suppose," O'Boyle conceded.

The men sipped their cocktails.

"Men like Benny Logan," said Henry, "are like wolves tearing at the fabric of the status quo—a longtime, successful status quo, I might add."

"I've seen his kind before," O'Boyle agreed. "Bomb-throwers. Out to change the world."

"Thinks he can bend reality to his principles," said Henry. "Hasn't learned that reality will bend him instead."

"Well, maybe he'll learn," O'Boyle observed.

"And maybe," said Henry, "we can teach him that, when push comes to shove, equilibrium usually prevails, and rabble-rousers disappear. Sometimes, they leave by their own free will. Other times, they're shown the door."

"How do you mean?"

"What I'm suggesting," said Henry, "is that you and I work to take Logan's legs out from under him. The result? Equilibrium gets restored. The two of us get the labor contract we want, end a strike that's causing both of us heartache, and you earn enough money to make you—and a lot of other people—very happy."

"Sounds possible." O'Boyle smiled.

Henry then laid his cards on the table, telling the union boss exactly what he was seeking—and how much he was willing to ante up.

"That's a boatload of money," said O'Boyle, bowled over by Henry's largesse.

"To me, it's worth every penny," Henry said. "Besides, think of it as a loan,

Paddy—one that can easily be forgiven."

"An' the collateral?"

"The most important asset you possess. Ties to the right people."

O'Boyle mulled the offer.

"So," Henry asked. "Think what I'm asking for is possible?"

"How far do you want me to go?" O'Boyle asked.

"As far as necessary."

"Things could get ugly."

"Think I give a shit?"

The two men, laughing, shook hands.

"How soon can you set the wheels in motion?" asked Henry.

"Is tonight too soon?"

Henry beamed. "I was hoping you'd say that."

The two men ambled to the bar, where Henry filled a pair of brandy snifters, then opened a mahogany humidor, withdrew a pair of Partagás, and sheared off the tips with a clipper. He lit O'Boyle's cigar, then his own.

"Here's to the good ol' days, Paddy," Henry said. "And to restoring the status quo."

Smiling, the men savored the brandy and drew on their Cubans. Henry then handed O'Boyle an envelope, the same one he'd proffered during their dinner at Peter Luger's, only twice as thick.

"Consider this a down payment," Henry said. "Spread it around, so that the people we need get a taste of the action. The balance of what we've agreed to is payable if we get the results we want."

"Not if," said O'Boyle. "When."

Henry, grinning, showed the union president to the door.

"Nice to be doing business with you again, Paddy. Bedfellows . . . just like old times."

"The pleasure's all mine," said O'Boyle, stuffing the envelope into the pocket of his topcoat as he slid into the rear seat of Henry's Packard for the ride back to the Bronx.

CHAPTER 33

February 8, 1946

Another two days, caustic and divisive, gutted the embattled city, the strike-bred crisis deepening as it languished through the weekend business hiatus and advanced into its second week.

As throughout most of the maddening labor tempest, the hostile elements continued to ravage both strikers and the public. All day Saturday and well into Sunday, another fierce storm buffeted New York, piling windblown snow hillocks across much of the city. Streets and sidewalks were slippery as glass. Skeletal, ice-laden trees sagged like weeping willows. Frozen water mains burst, sending geysers shooting skyward.

With blizzard conditions putting a hammerlock on municipal services, the crisis enveloping the city heightened even more. Stores for the most part remained shuttered, streets impassable, factories, schools, and office buildings deserted. Wary citizens hunkered down in homes and apartments short on heat, hot water, and electricity. The entire cityscape seemed in a state of suspended animation, a still-life frieze on a desolate snow-swept canvas.

The strike, by now, was also no longer the exclusive domain of New York's headline-starved press. In contrast, the eight-day work stoppage had become a major national story, having captured the attention of business leaders, union officials, politicians, and workers across the entire country. Newsreels documented the schismatic saga on theater screens from coast to coast. Newspapers, magazines, and radio commentators dubbed it "The Great American Strike," the costliest labor conflict in U.S. history. Television stations broadcast bulletins on the nation's three major networks: CBS, NBC, and DuMont. *Time* and *Newsweek* portrayed the work stoppage as a pivotal tug-of-war between organized labor and corporate interests, a litmus test for public officials seeking an equitable balance of power in the postwar workplace. *Life*, *Look*, and *The Saturday Evening Post* each published multi-page pictorials, including profiles of Henry and Benny, portrayed as the dogged antagonists spearheading the historic labor conflict.

But the headstrong personalities of its principals weren't the only reasons for the strike's uncanny staying power. Civic incapacity, government inertia, and political inconstancy were contributing factors as well. Even now, with the work stoppage entering its eighth day, no one in the corridors of power could devise a way to effectively cope with the crisis. Officials at all levels of government had yet to mobilize a coordinated effort to halt the acrimonious dispute.

Both sides were going for the legal jugular now, too. In the past twenty-four hours, union lawyers had filed a formal protest with the National Labor Relations Board, charging tugboat owners with bad-faith bargaining. Firing back, the Gotham Harbor Alliance filed a request in federal court for an injunction to prevent strikers from picketing, simultaneously petitioning Congress to invoke Taft-Hartley legislation, forcing tugboatmen back to work under the threat of fines and imprisonment. White House aides, facing mounting congressional pressure, issued a dire warning that if the strike were allowed to continue, its impact on shipments of fuel, food, and medical supplies would soon threaten the wellbeing of literally everyone in America.

"This is no longer simply a dispute between workers and management," the White House said. "It has now become an assault against every citizen in the U.S., and it will no longer be tolerated."

Reinforcing those warnings, government officials by the middle of day eight had cobbled together a contingency plan for delivering limited fuel shipments to New York, contracting with a handful of public utilities to tow coal and fuel-oil barges through the harbor. Food supplies, delivered by private charter, had also begun trickling in. But they too were running into roadblocks. Although other labor unions had yet to strike in support of tugboat workers, a rebellious cohort of sympathetic longshoremen had begun honoring Local 88 picket lines, blocking the movement of supplies between New York Harbor and nearby warehouses. In effect, little of substance could leave the waterfront, even if the supplies were able to be docked. Bales of produce lay on piers, alongside freight pallets, steamer trunks, and sacks of mail. Precious cargo sat in the holds of idled ships.

Worse yet, an element of violence had crept into the toxic mix. Sometime after nightfall on that Monday, several of Henry's tugboats were vandalized at their docks, sustaining damage to their wheelhouses, bows, and hulls. In separate incidents, equipment was stolen from a work shed, bricks hurled through a window at Gotham Harbor Alliance headquarters. While no suspects were implicated in the transgressions, Henry pointed the finger at alleged militant unionists, charging that a violent, lawless element was governing the union now, while demanding that strike leaders be prosecuted and jailed.

Benny was equally perturbed. Though uncertain about the lawbreakers' identities, he disavowed their actions, while voicing appeals for striking workers to refrain from violence or criminality. He also went on the offensive, suggesting that the criminal acts may well have been staged, aimed at compromising the integrity of the union. Henry's charges were denounced as devious forms of slander. At this point, however, no one knew where the truth ended or the lies began. It didn't matter. Both sides in the conflict were paying a hefty price, their integrity undermined, their actions suspect.

With the risk of sabotage running even higher, security was tightened at tugboat docks and corporate offices, reinforced by a court order prohibiting picketing within three city blocks of company property. A gag order further barred both sides from public discourse about the strike. Police, fearful of civil unrest, were posted at fuel depots, warehouses, and docks. Henry doubled the number of watchmen at his docks, equipping his tugboats with steel cages to protect their wheelhouse windows.

The entire city was poised now on the precipice of something more incendiary than anyone could ever have imagined. And no one, it seemed, had the slightest inkling about how to defuse the powder keg—or prevent it from blowing sky-high.

Chapter 34

February 8, 1946

They came after Benny hard. No sooner had Paddy O'Boyle departed Henry's estate, cash in hand, than the phone in Benny's Bronx apartment began ringing off the hook with a flurry of anonymous calls warning of dire consequences if the union's rebellious firebrand didn't persuade tugboat workers to either soften their contract demands or end their strike. A crudely written note stuffed into Benny's mailbox conveyed, in graphic terms, how previous waterfront reformers had wound up swimming with the fishes or buried alive in the Jersey Pinelands. Another missive threatened the wellbeing of Benny's wife, daughters, and other family members—including Jack and Kate.

The harassment campaign, however, was only just beginning. Paddy O'Boyle's sway over Local 88's rank and file may have waned in recent years, but the union kingpin still controlled a sizable contingent of strongarm men willing to go to any lengths to earn a buck. The latest deal struck by Henry and O'Boyle was at once ruthless and cunning, aimed at both terrorizing Benny and sparking a mutiny to oust him from power, all of it culminating in a favorable contract settlement for Henry, and a hefty payday and return to power for O'Boyle. The primary tactics were for O'Boyle, operating covertly, to withhold financial support from Local 88's parent union, keep longshoremen at arm's length from the work stoppage, and mount opposition to the strike not only from the public, politicians, and the press, but from within the union itself.

Already the first tranche of money Henry had proffered, twenty thousand dollars in cash, was tucked securely in a secret O'Boyle bank account. Thousands more were promised. And O'Boyle, after pocketing his share of the bounty, and distributing a liberal dose to accomplices, was making damaging inroads through a variety of dirty tricks.

Within hours of Henry's deal with Paddy, mob gunsels—conspicuous in their leather overcoats, fedoras, and zoot suits—were lurking in the vicinity of both Benny's apartment building and the public school his daughters attended. Private investigators bankrolled by O'Boyle were simultaneously combing through Benny's personal history, in a scheme to lodge damaging charges. An NYPD detective financed by Henry's money falsified a report alleging past arrests for shoplifting, vagrancy, and other petty crimes. Benny's tax returns were rumored to contain gross improprieties, his Merchant Marine record marred by a dishonorable discharge. Other attempts at character assassination quickly followed. Benny was alternately labeled as a womanizer and drunkard, a child abuser and petty thief. When he wasn't being slandered, he was being portrayed as an irresponsible, wild-eyed radical whose leadership was leading strikers on a path to certain ruin. Benny was also convinced by now that his home and office telephones had been bugged, and that at least one spy with a pipeline to Henry had been planted inside the union.

But even as Paddy O'Boyle sowed the seeds of discord and doubt, Henry's covert anti-strike offensive was taking on new forms. Early on day eight, City Hall began being bombarded with phone calls from O'Boyle loyalists masquerading as irate citizens demanding an immediate end to the strike. A puppet group of supposed "loyal company men" launched a word-of-mouth campaign denouncing the work stoppage. A melee erupted at the Chelsea Piers picket lines when strikers were baited into a fistfight with O'Boyle loyalists and arrested by police working in cahoots with Henry. O'Boyle, for the first time, also began showing up at picket sites, suggesting that strikers ratify the contract he and Henry had privately negotiated.

"You men are to be lauded for your commitment," O'Boyle told picketers. "But you've sacrificed enough. It's time to end this strike, and get your families back on their feet!"

O'Boyle, as was his wont, cleverly played both sides, never formally breaking ties with Benny but rather portraying himself as a responsible, conciliatory leader sympathetic to the plight of both strikers and tugboat owners alike.

"It's time for a return to reason," the USA boss said. "Enough pain has been inflicted. You men should return to work, let negotiations resume, and accept the idea of a reasonable compromise."

Emboldened by the O'Boyle-inspired discord, Henry ramped up his own anti-strike efforts—charging, falsely, that out-of-control union members were responsible for the recent sabotage at his docks. Company emissaries were dispatched to workers' homes to convince the men that their strike was collapsing, and a back-to-work movement was underway. Rumors of union capitulation, spread by anti-strike collaborators, ran rampant. Henry even staged a theatrical event at which the gates to his docks were opened so that claques of paid actors could march through, in a supposed return to work.

By day's end, Local 88 was reeling. It didn't help, of course, that the union was running on financial fumes. By now, all of the striking workers had collected their emergency pay, siphoning off virtually every penny of the union's strike fund. No longer did the tugboatmen have an emergency kitty to draw from, or a safety net to break their financial freefall. Nor was there seemingly any way to reverse the downward spiral. Efforts to augment Local 88's war chest through bake sales, raffles, and other fundraisers had proven futile. Pleas for public donations fell, for the most part, on deaf ears. And nothing in the way of financial support was being provided by Local 88's parent union which, at Paddy O'Boyle's behest, had left its tugboat-worker members high and dry.

To Benny, none of what was occurring came as either a shock or a surprise. From the instant it kicked off, Benny suspected that the latest iteration of the anti-strike campaign was being orchestrated by Henry in cahoots with O'Boyle.

"That double-dealin' bastard," Benny raged. "It ain't hard to see what O'Boyle's up to—maintainin' a false front while cuttin' the legs out from under our men. An' all of it for a goddamned buck!"

"That scumbag has been in Henry McFarland's pocket for years," Tommy Duggan groused. "He's a goddamned Judas who doesn't give a shit about anyone but himself."

"Wouldn't surprise me one bit," Benny said, "if the crooked bastard is also behind the sabotage at McFarland's docks . . . tryin' to turn the public against the union by paintin' us out as a bunch of violent hoods."

"Try provin' it," Duggan said.

His point was well-taken. For while Benny's conspiracy theory was squarely on target, there was no way O'Boyle could be fingered for the sabotage. Nor could Benny do much to combat the union boss's shadow campaign, except by redoubling his efforts at rallying strikers—which he did, to a point of sheer exhaustion.

Keeping the work stoppage from unraveling, however, was becoming increasingly difficult. While striking workers continued for the most part to hold their ranks, solidarity was withering. All that night, rogue elements of the rank and file, ignoring pleas for unity, continued to disrupt the strike. Anonymous threats were telephoned not only to Benny, but to other strike principals. Gunshots from a passing car were fired at the homes of several strike captains. Strike headquarters was targeted by a bomb threat, its windows boarded with plywood after being shattered by a volley of bricks.

The union, it now seemed, was coming apart at the seams. Members were squabbling among themselves, pointing fingers at real or imagined traitors to the cause. Others were arming themselves with ax handles, baseball bats, and other makeshift weapons, while traveling solely in packs. With the city refusing to provide formal police protection, the union took matters into its own hands, posting sentries in the vestibule of Benny's apartment building and assigning armed escorts to accompany him everywhere he went. Other bodyguards were assigned to his wife and daughters, who were squirreled away to live at Tommy Duggan's Pocono Mountains cottage. Sentries also kept a watchful eye on the entrance to the Logans' Williamsburg apartment, cognizant of the potential threat to Benny's extended family, including Jack and Kate.

All of this only served to exacerbate the strike's grievous toll on the workers. Its financial coffers depleted, its leadership under siege, its rank and file riddled by infighting, Local 88 seemed now on the precipice of defeat, its strike teetering on the verge of collapse.

Chapter 35

February 9, 1946

But it wasn't only the tugboat workers' union that was imploding now—or even the city itself. The Gotham Harbor Alliance was imploding as well, staggering under the weight of the strike. No longer was it heartening to New York's tugboat owners that the labor union they were battling seemed on the verge of collapse. Fissures within their own ranks were threatening to swallow the owners too.

"This strike is costing us a bloody fortune, and bringing my company to its knees!" Bertram Phelps griped at the owners' day-nine meeting.

Phelps looked as though he'd aged a decade in the past two weeks, his pallor ghostlike, his brow as deeply furrowed as a freshly plowed pasture. He had never wanted a strike in the first place and had tried to resist Henry's scheme to force the union's hand. But, like the other owners, he'd followed Henry headlong into the fray. And now, like the striking tugboatmen, the owners were being pummeled in the wallet, excoriated by both the public and the press, and suffering from decisions meant to punish their adversary.

"Your company is not the only one facing financial ruin," fellow owner Sam Dougherty told Phelps. "All of us are hurting . . . badly!"

Privately, Henry cringed. Discord within the ranks was the last thing he needed now. Unanimity had always been his ace in the hole, the edge he'd tried most scrupulously to preserve. But unanimity was withering rapidly, as was the owners' resolve. Indeed, several of the owners seemed primed for a graceful exit—and were no longer reticent about making their feelings known.

"The money my company is losing is not even the worst of it," Dougherty lamented. "The strike is also costing us an arm and a leg in terms of good will. We're losing public support, political capital, and credibility. Before long, we'll be losing customers—maybe even our entire businesses!"

"What do you mean before long?" Phelps grumbled. "I've already had customers void their contracts because of the strike. They're taking their business elsewhere."

"Where to?" asked Dougherty.

"Across the river . . . to Elizabeth and Bayonne."

"Jersey?"

"What can I say?" Phelps threw up his hands. "At least they can dock their ships there. They can't dock 'em anywhere in New York. Their businesses, like ours, are crippled!"

The men lapsed into a lengthy, troubled silence. As if potential financial calamity wasn't troubling enough, the owners were facing an equally grave threat now. With economic carnage mounting, high-level mediation machinery had finally been put in place. Hours earlier, a team of Labor Department functionaries had been dispatched to assist the conciliatory efforts of Desmond Quinn. Even more forceful intervention was also in the works. For several days, U.S. transportation officials had quietly been drafting plans for forcibly reopening New York Harbor, including seizure of the city's tugboat fleet and an injunction against the striking workers. Those plans were ready to be implemented.

"Who knows what'll happen if the Feds seize our tugboats?" Phelps bemoaned. "That could destroy our businesses!"

The owners grew pensive, their silence a pall.

"The damage from this strike, I'm afraid, could last for years," Dougherty warned. "People have long memories, you know."

"People on both sides," Phelps said. "No one will ever forget the hell we've put our city through. There'll be scars—anger, resentment, bitterness— regardless of how the strike plays out."

"I'm not sure our relationships with our customers, or our workers, will ever be the same," Dougherty added. "And we'll be left to wonder: was the strike we angled for worth the heartache and chaos? Did we really have to put ourselves through all of this?"

The resultant silence made it eminently clear that no one could answer those questions affirmatively. It was only then that George Steele, until now Henry's most ardent ally, voiced what was on everyone's mind.

"We've got to put an end to this madness!" Steele asserted. "Now!"

Instantly, the other owners concurred. Henry struggled to mask his dissent, reluctant to alienate allies who, until now, had granted him uncontested proxy to act on their behalf. But their support—even Steele's—was swiftly evaporating, Henry's leadership fraying at the edges. He could sense it. Everyone could.

"There comes a point in any dispute where both sides have to agree that they've simply had enough," Steele said. "I believe we've reached that point. I'm sure the union has, as well."

Henry hadn't reached that juncture, however. Not when he was seemingly so close to ending the strike on his terms, so close to exorcising his anger and his grief, so close to winning.

Sitting at the head of the owners' conference table, he groped for a way to sway his colleagues and swing momentum back to his side. Yet he could find neither the opportunity nor the words. For once, he was flummoxed. He couldn't risk divulging the details of the covert anti-strike deal he'd struck with Paddy O'Boyle, or the spies Otto Blackburn had planted inside the union, or the dark money he secretly was pouring into his union-busting efforts. Indeed, he couldn't say or feel much of anything beyond a growing sense of isolation, vulnerability, and helplessness.

At last he said, his voice less forceful than normal, "I still believe strongly that our side can't afford to signal weakness or duress. Damn it, we've fought too hard . . . sacrificed too much."

But the men around him seemed unmoved.

"I implore you men," Henry declared. "Stay the course!"

There was desperation in Henry's voice now, a diffidence he'd masked behind a magisterial, commanding countenance. Suddenly, his words were devoid of their usual fervor, tinged by an encroaching panic that the others could discern.

"What you're saying may be true," Bertram Phelps said. "But we simply can't afford additional losses. Most of us don't have your deep pockets, Henry. The reality is that our companies are facing financial ruin if we don't stop the bleeding now!"

"But we're not the ones facing ruination—the union is," Henry stammered. "They're the ones losing this battle . . . not us!"

"You're wrong, Henry," George Steele countered. "It's not just the union that's losing . . . everyone is. Our alliance. Our employees. The people of New York."

Henry felt as if he were climbing a mountain of loose pebbles, struggling for a foothold but slipping. Tumbling backward. Falling.

"But look what's happening," he pleaded, reaching for a cigarette and lighting it with trembling hands. "The union is being ravaged by dissension. Strikers are crossing picket lines, their emergency fund is depleted, the local hasn't received an iota of support from its own parent, let alone other unions."

"And your point?" Phelps said.

"My point," said Henry, "is that the victory we've been fighting for is within our reach. Local 88 is going to collapse at any moment. Organized labor will be neutered. We'll have our businesses back! We'll have the unions exactly where we want them!"

Again, a wall of silence. And then a voice rang out from the far end of the conference table.

"And tell us, Henry . . . where, exactly, do we want organized labor to be?"

The question was provocative, its tone confrontational. Unwillingly, Henry looked down the table at a tugboat owner named Mike Sturgis, seated as far from Henry as possible—a position less coincidental than symbolic, as it instantly became clear.

Sturgis, who with several partners had recently purchased a smallish tugboat company, was among a cohort of youthful postwar entrepreneurs possessing a management approach diametrically opposed to that of Henry. Reticent to assert himself until now, he had grown increasingly skeptical as the strike wore on. And now he seemed ready to make a stand.

"Is everything we've done—dragging our feet in collective bargaining, refusing to compromise, and provoking a strike—aimed at winning a favorable contract?" Sturgis asked. "Or is it aimed at breaking the union's back?"

Henry was caught short. "Both," he blurted—realizing, too late, that he'd been baited. "And if we can kill two birds with one stone," he said defensively, "what's wrong with that?"

"What's wrong with it," Sturgis replied, "is that we're in the tugboat business—not the union-busting business. And if we're to succeed, we need to work together with our employees . . . not try to annihilate them."

Sturgis had the floor now. And Henry could feel something familiar and precious slipping from his grasp: the sway it had taken decades to accrue, the power that had always been an obsession, an opiate.

A flicker of panic comingled with his ever-present anger. *Who is this wet-behind-the-ears whippersnapper, and what does he know about running a tugboat business?* Henry thought. *Why the hell am I ceding the floor to him? And why is anyone listening?*

"I think it's safe to say that we view our workers very differently," Sturgis said.

"And how so, young man?"

Sturgis brushed aside Henry's snide reference to his inexperience.

"You view employees as adversaries—necessary evils who should be compensated as minimally as possible," Sturgis said. "I see them as assets, partners in a very real sense."

"Partners?"

I can't believe this bullshit. This jerk must have read this management crap in some business-school textbook, Henry told himself. Aloud, he continued, "You'd never be spouting this nonsense—calling your employees 'partners', for God's sake—if you'd been through the meat grinder with these unions as long as I have."

Sturgis, however, wasn't backing down.

"I think, to be up to date, our companies need to take a more progressive, collaborative approach to doing business than they've done in the past."

"Collaborative?" Henry asked, mockingly. "What is that supposed to mean?"

"It means that companies should hold their workers in higher regard than they have traditionally. Capitalism and organized labor can co-exist. We need to work in tandem with unions, do what's right for both sides—not simply management."

Sturgis glanced at the other owners. He had their attention, much to Henry's dismay.

"We can no longer afford to have our workers view management as tyrants interested solely in our company's bottom line," Sturgis said. "We need to have not just a labor contract, but a 'social contract' with our workers."

"A social contract?" Henry laughed. "What the hell is that?"

Sturgis met the challenge head-on.

"It's an informal, unwritten pact that communicates a corporate empathy," he said, "a willingness on our part to put ourselves in our workers' shoes, an understanding that we're in this together—even if it means sharing profits and seeking employee input about how our businesses should be run."

Will you listen to this crock of shit? Henry thought. *Is this what business is coming to in America?*

He snapped back, "Pardon me, but nobody is going to tell me how to run my company. And no one is going to share in my company's profits."

He glared at Sturgis, searching for signs of assent. The other owners were non-committal, however. And Henry felt himself sweating, flailing, groping for words.

"You may not have learned this yet, being so new to the corporate world," Henry said snidely, "but it's customary for the lion's share of profits to go to the people who own the business, not to employees."

"But that's exactly my point," Sturgis dissented. "I don't see my company as strictly 'mine.' Sure, I may own it. But businesses are the concern of employers and employees. Our interests are mutual. My employees have as much stake in my company as I do."

"Well," Henry snorted, "that's not the way those of us who've succeeded in the tugboat trade have modeled our businesses."

"That business model," Sturgis said, "may be an anachronism."

"An 'anachronism,' I should note, that yields millions in annual profit," said Henry.

Sturgis sighed. "No one can argue with your company's success, Henry. The point I'm trying to make, though, is that to continue to prosper we've got to adopt a different approach. This is a new era for business, after all."

"A new era?"

"Yes." Sturgis nodded. "It's an era in which management can no longer be as antagonistic toward employees as it has. Workers grow frustrated and hostile when they're forced to live under financial duress or sense management's contempt. They become resentful when they feel their employer is taking advantage of them, manipulating them, viewing them as supplicants."

Henry scoffed. "So, you're saying the traditional approach of management no longer applies?"

"What I'm saying," Sturgis said, "is that the traditional approach hurts companies as much as it does workers, and yields resentment, a lack of productivity, even abuse of corporate assets."

"I have a company to run, the goal of which is to turn the greatest possible profit," Henry argued. "I'm a businessman . . . not a benefactor."

"That much I recognize," Sturgis said. "But when it comes to labor relations, it can no longer be 'us versus them.' Our workers shouldn't be viewed as the 'enemy.' Nor should we be the 'enemy' to them. Being liked by our employees, being generous of spirit, shouldn't be seen by management as a weakness."

"How should it be seen?"

"As if we're their advocate, as well as their bosses," Sturgis replied. "As if we're all on the same team."

"Well, with all due respect, young man," Henry scoffed, "I think you're living in a fantasy world."

"And with all due respect to you," Sturgis said, "I think you're living in the past."

And with that singular, terse exchange, something inside the Gotham Harbor Alliance had shifted irrevocably. Everyone could sense it. Henry McFarland, the all-powerful business czar who'd led the tugboat owners' coalition throughout its existence, shaping its tactics and its strategy, and standing as its defining force, was no longer calling the shots. No longer did he enjoy his exalted status among his peers. No longer was he the puppet master, pulling the strings.

Unanimity among the tugboat owners had all but disintegrated, the taste of the labor war they'd orchestrated growing all too bitter in their mouths—just as it had for the striking workers, public officials, and the eight million people who lived or worked in the crippled, strike-torn city.

CHAPTER 36

February 10, 1946

By now, the strike had assumed an ominous new dimension, far beyond finger-pointing and mudslinging, gamesmanship and political theater.

No longer was the pernicious work stoppage merely a high-stakes drama being acted across a public stage by a sundry cast of heroes, villains, and bit players. Nor, to New Yorkers, was it merely a piddling annoyance, a bureaucratic hot potato, or a skein of catchy headlines. In contrast, the labor imbroglio was cast now in the most deeply personal terms, a scourge that bled into every nook and cranny of the wounded, desolate city. No neighborhood was beyond its orbit. No one who lived or worked in New York was immune to its ruinous grip.

Including the Logans.

Benny, as he had since day one, maintained his grueling, nonstop routine: under blistering attack from Paddy O'Boyle's lackeys; countering Henry's anti-strike offensive; up to his ears on everything from tactics and negotiations to bucking the growing chasm within the union's rank and file.

The latter task was nearly a full-time job. Infighting among strikers, thanks to O'Boyle's shadow campaign, was spreading. Seduced by payoffs, fearful of reprisals, and succumbing to financial pressures, dozens of strikers were undermining the walkout now, crossing picket lines while clashing in many cases with strike loyalists. Benny had his hands full trying to stanch the bleeding: begging the allegiance of tottering strikers, shoring up crumbling picket lines, doing everything in his power to prevent Local 88 from imploding and its strike from collapsing like a house of cards.

The rest of the Logan family was also trying desperately to shoulder the weight—victims, like every New Yorker, of the pernicious walkout.

Jack, despite his trepidation, had been drawn even deeper into the labor conflict, a product of his allegiance to Benny. Like his brother, Jack too was busy eighteen hours a day, helping to manage the remnants of the strike fund, guarding against improprieties, and joining his *Jupiter* crewmates on picket lines. Once again at Benny's behest, he was handling a slew of fiscal responsibilities, including the creation of Local 88's "bargaining book," a multi-layered costing model that shed light on how potential one-, two-, and three-year labor contracts—at disparate job classifications and pay grades—would be impacted in terms of potential wage hikes, overtime pay, benefits, and other factors.

Jack's computations, based on self-taught actuarial principles, was enabling Local 88 negotiators to provide City Hall mediator Desmond Quinn with fact-based arguments in lieu of suppositions—and to counter tugboat owners' claims of an inability to bear added labor costs. Jack, working pro bono, was also saving the union thousands of dollars that otherwise might have been spent on actuaries, accountants, and other financial advisors.

All the while, Agnes, Gus, and Kate were doing everything in their power to cope with the strike-induced ordeal. Williamsburg, like most neighborhoods throughout New York, had effectively closed in on itself in recent days, its ice-clogged streets nearly impassable, its shops and businesses shut, its services virtually nonexistent. While Mayor Flannery's blackout edict had been lifted, sections of the neighborhood were subject to scattered brownouts and power outages. A fresh barrage of snow had rendered the Logans, like other residents, virtual prisoners inside their apartment.

Not that indoor living conditions were pleasant, either. By now, coal and fuel-oil deliveries to the family's apartment building, along with trash collection, had been suspended for nearly three days. Home deliveries of milk, bread, and other perishables were similarly postponed. Refrigerated food had either been discarded or placed on fire escapes to prevent spoilage. Piles of uncollected trash sat heaped in the building's vestibule, hallways, and cellar. With their apartment devoid of heat and hot water, and indoor temperatures hovering near freezing, the Logans puttered about the residence bundled in winter clothing and subsisting mainly on vegetable broth and hot tea. At night, they had few options other than to retire early, shivering under piles of blankets and trying to close their minds to the unremitting hardship.

As if all of this wasn't forbidding enough, family finances had grown tighter than ever. Jack, of course, was no longer drawing his regular salary, his strike-fund allocation having evaporated the instant the check was cut. Gus, out of work for days with the closure of the Dixie Sugar refinery, had missed paychecks normally allocated for utilities and rent. And with potential sewing customers hoarding cash, piecemeal work had also dried up for Agnes. All of which left Kate as the family's sole breadwinner—and only because the city's Health Department mandated that essential businesses, including pharmaceutical suppliers like Pfizer, remain operational even in the face of the strike.

But Kate, too, was facing an imminent loss of income—along with concurrent issues.

Now in its final trimester, her due date mere days away, Kate's pregnancy had proceeded without a hitch, key milestones normal, prenatal screenings and exams routine. Kate had also managed to dodge symptoms such as morning sickness, mood swings, and fatigue, her pregnancy proving to be a source of profound exhilaration, a joyous, transformative experience that opened an entirely new dimension to her identity as a woman. The anticipation of meeting her child and experiencing the bond of motherhood had filled Kate with a sense of fulfillment and purpose unlike anything she'd ever experienced, a welcome counterpoint to her feelings during the war. Her marital bond, at the same time, had also been strengthened, Jack proving to be a dedicated and steadfast partner. Preparing for the new arrival with the setup of a makeshift nursery in a corner of their bedroom had only magnified the couple's sense of excitement and joy.

But the course of Kate's pregnancy had changed markedly in recent days. For one thing, Jack, immersed in strike-related duties, was absent for the most part now, leaving Kate to navigate the final stages of her pregnancy without her primary means of emotional support. And unlike in prior trimesters, Kate was riddled now with back pain, abdominal cramping, and pronounced swelling of her ankles and feet. In the past two days, she had also begun experiencing cervical contractions accompanied by blood-tinged vaginal discharges.

Given those developments, Kate's obstetrician had become concerned that her full-time workload at Pfizer, coupled with strike-related stress, could lead to complications. He was advising Kate, in the strongest of terms, to quit her job and confine herself to the family's apartment, a prospect that she and Jack could ill afford. Already, the precious savings account the couple had cobbled together had been seriously dented. An additional loss of income would put a further crimp on their post-pregnancy moving plans, especially considering the additional expenses tied to birthing and raising a child.

But something even more ominous than all those things had reared its ugly head. Kate had also become a target of the harassment campaign aimed at undermining Benny. In one instance, an anonymous note taped to her locker at Pfizer warned that grave harm would befall Jack if he didn't abdicate his behind-the-scenes role in the strike. In another instance, a missive threatening the welfare of the couple's unborn child was passed to Kate at work. In both cases, Kate, the consummate English Iron Lady—a model of perseverance, fortitude, and faith—bravely kept the threats to herself, determined to tough it out, and hold her emotions in check. Jack, she reasoned, already had enough on his mind. He didn't have to be unduly worried about his pregnant wife, too.

Usually so upbeat, always seeing the bright side of things, Kate suddenly seemed melancholic: fearful, overwrought, burdened by the demands of her pregnancy, the potential for prenatal complications, the health of her unborn child, and fallout from the strike. With ties to her homeland all but severed— transatlantic phone calls not yet feasible, teletype costs prohibitive, news reports sketchy, overseas letters taking weeks to arrive—Kate found herself desperately homesick as well, pining for the presence of her parents and longtime friends. For the past several days, she'd virtually stopped eating, and had retreated into a self-imposed cocoon. At night, desperately missing Jack, she routinely closed the door to their bedroom, covered herself with a pile of blankets, and cried herself to sleep.

And now an even more pressing problem had reared its head: Gus had gotten sick.

For the past few days, Jack's father, who'd missed not a single day of work due to illness in twenty-six years, hadn't been feeling himself. True to character, he'd sloughed his malady off, consenting only to sporadic doses of aspirin and Kate's English tea. But the home care hadn't helped. To the contrary, the course of Gus's illness had grown progressively worse. What began as a seeming cold had become flu-like, with symptoms that included fever, shortness of breath, coughing, and fatigue.

Gus had spent the past two days bedridden, stubbornly opting to ride the illness out rather than see a doctor, assuming, plausibly enough, that he'd contracted the flu. In fact the city's influenza outbreak, exacerbated by the widespread lack of indoor heat, had become a full-scale epidemic. Hospitals, flooded with patients, were reporting shortages of drugs and other supplies. School gymnasiums were being employed as makeshift communal shelters. Police officers and other public servants were donning surgical masks to minimize contagion.

In Gus's case, however, there was more than the usual cause for concern. As his illness progressed, Gus's cough had become raspy and persistent, forcing up gobs of blood-tinged mucus. His skin appeared dusky and purplish. His heartbeat was accelerated, his body wracked with chills. Dull and lethargic, he could barely pull himself from bed.

By the time Agnes persuaded him to see the family doctor, Gus's fever had spiked at a hundred and three degrees, and he could hardly breathe. A chest x-ray and blood work conveyed the alarming news: Gus didn't have the flu. His illness, unlike the epidemic sweeping across New York, wasn't viral. Nor was it routine. Instead, he had contracted a case of bacterial pneumonia.

And there were complications. Years of exposure to sugar-dust fumes at the Dixie Sugar refinery had compromised Gus's respiratory system, reducing his body's defense against bacteria. Already, there was an ominous buildup of fluid between his chest wall and lungs. A secondary infection was affecting his digestive system and threatening to enter his bloodstream. Within minutes of seeing his doctor, Gus was in an ambulance enroute to Williamsburg General Hospital, where he was intubated, administered intravenous doses of penicillin, and scheduled for lung surgery. His condition, doctors said, was grave.

By the time the news reached Jack, Kate and Agnes had already spent several hours at Gus's bedside. Benny, immersed in contract negotiations at City Hall, was clueless about what was transpiring—until Jack dispatched a messenger to summon his brother to strike headquarters.

"They told me it was a family problem," said Benny, upon arriving at Jack's side.

"It's Pop," Jack informed him.

"Pop?"

Benny narrowed his eyes, as if trying to comprehend something beyond the scope of his intellect, unsure what to feel or say. It was always that way when it came to Gus—always the same awkward silence, the same jumble of emotions and thoughts.

"What's goin' on?"

Benny plopped into a chair as Jack conveyed the news.

"Shit!" Benny shook his head, his voice quaggy, devoid of its usual edginess. He listened intently as Jack detailed Gus's illness, seeming concerned although guarded, as if he had the urge to convey alarm but was constrained by his complex, dysfunctional relationship with his father. Nothing, Jack thought, was more convoluted than family. Nothing was even close.

"How sick is the ol' man?" Benny inquired.

"The doctors are trying to contain his illness," Jack said. "But it's not good."

Jack, while candid, was matter-of-fact. He didn't want to come off as alarmist—or worse, manipulative. But he wasn't pulling punches. Benny needed to know that their father's condition was touch and go.

"So, what do the doctors think?" Benny asked.

"They're concerned."

"How concerned?"

"To be honest, Benny, they're not sure Pop is gonna make it. Pneumonia is serious enough by itself. But there are complications."

"Complications?"

"Pop's infection can damage his lungs and cause internal bleeding," Jack said. "It can enter his bloodstream and spread to his kidneys and other organs. Pop's age is working against him, too. So are other factors."

"What do you mean by other factors?" Benny raised an eyebrow. "Is it 'cause of all those years Pop worked in that goddamned refinery . . . breathin' in sugar dust an' other shit?"

"That's part of it."

Jack tiptoed around his response, knowing it would add fuel to Benny's fire—another reason to be angry at Gus for laboring in a non-union workplace devoid of protections, allowing management to call the shots, fearful of pushing for more.

"I don't want to fight about Pop," Jack said. "Not now."

Benny backed away. "So, how are the doctors dealin' with this?" he asked.

"Heavy doses of antibiotics. They're trying to clear Pop's lungs, stop his infection from spreading."

"Can they?"

"They're not sure. What they're doing may, or may not, be enough. At the very least, Pop will need surgery."

Then Jack laid it on the line. "To be perfectly frank, Benny, the mortality rate is extremely high for pneumonia in cases as acute as Pop's. I'm afraid we might lose him."

"Fuck!"

Jack saw a peculiar expression creep across Benny's face, as if his brother's mulish, tough-guy patina was melting and he was marshaling every ounce of willpower to resist yielding to dormant emotions—compassion, regret, forgiveness—and all the years of ignoring Jack's pleas to mend fences with their father.

"Listen," Jack said. "I'm heading to the hospital now."

"Is anyone there?"

"Mom's keeping a vigil. Kate is there, too."

"How's mom?"

"Sick, too. With worry."

"An' Kate?"

"Her situation is dicey. The doctors told her she had to leave the hospital as soon as possible, to cut the potential for exposure to illness. Soon as I get there, I'll get her home."

"Mom's gonna be by herself?"

"I've got no choice."

Benny seemed shell-shocked, his head bowed, his unshaven face a sickly gray. Jack had never seen his brother look so exhausted and overwrought. Benny was usually so guarded, hiding his vulnerabilities behind a patina of callousness and grit. Jack felt sorry for him—sorry for the burden he was bearing, the pressures he was facing, the conflicts and heartache that governed his life. For all of Benny's bluster, all his moxie and strength, Jack saw his brother as a tortured soul who mirrored the enormity of everything he struggled to contain—violence, rage, recurring cycles of guilt and remorse, an unending quest for redemption, exculpation, and respect. Jack felt grateful to be free of that torment—respecting Benny, loving him, wishing he could help him, but happy he was nothing like him. At least not in that way.

"Sure, kid." Benny sighed. "Get to the hospital. Do whatever you can."

"And you?"

"What about me?"

"Why don't you come with me?"

Benny shook his head. "No can do."

"Why not?"

"Well, for one thing, I'm caught in a shitstorm. Gotta get to City Hall for a mediation session, then to the waterfront to stop men from crossin' our picket lines. Besides—"

"Besides what?"

"Fuck . . . do I gotta spell it out?"

Jack nodded. He wasn't letting his brother off the hook that easy.

"I haven't seen Pop—haven't so much as said a word to him—in sixteen years," Benny said. "So, now you want me to make a grand entrance? Under these circumstances?"

"Why not?"

"The time ain't right."

"The time," said Jack, "may never be more right."

"Maybe so." Benny exhaled. "But I ain't ready."

"Not even if you might be running out of time?"

"Uh-uh."

"Not even if this may be your final chance to make things right between you and Pop?"

"Afraid not."

Then Benny paused and exhaled deeply. "You've been tryin' to pull me an' Pop together for a long time . . . haven't ya, kid?"

"Ever since the day Gabriel died."

"That's a lotta years."

"Way too many, if you ask me."

Then Benny offered a gesture Jack had never seen from his hard-as-nails brother. Sentiments he'd never heard, either.

"Don't stop," Benny said. "It may not seem like it, but I'm listenin'. An' maybe one day, all your tryin' will finally pay off."

"I don't intend to stop," Jack said.

"Good." Benny placed a hand on his brother's shoulder. "Thanks for bein' there for me in every possible way, kid. I'll always love ya for that . . . always be grateful."

Then he rose to leave.

"In the meantime," he said, "relay a coupla messages for me. Tell mom I'll call soon as I can. An' tell Kate to take care. We need that baby of yours."

The final message was more difficult to convey. But somehow Benny managed.

"Give Pop a message, too," he said. "Tell him to hang in there. Tell him that I'm thinkin' about him . . . pullin' for him, too."

"That'll mean a lot to him," Jack said. "I know it means a lot to me."

Warmly, the brothers embraced. Then Benny left to attend to union business and the rank and file he thought of as family. And Jack left for the hospital to attend to his.

CHAPTER 37

February 10, 1946

There was no choice anymore but to plumb every possible angle, pull out all stops, even march to the finish line alone if that's what it took to triumph in the labor tempest he had set in motion.

Henry was unraveling now, foundering in the maelstrom battering the city, the past two days as excruciating as any he had experienced across his three-plus decades in business. Not only was his company's revenue shortfall mounting, his personal bank account dwindling, and his tugboat owners' coalition coming unglued, but he was also plunging ever more precipitously from the lofty mantle he'd occupied for decades as a business titan of nearly unrivaled status and clout.

Support for Henry's unflinching anti-union stance was dissipating like a wisp of smoke, his leadership fraying, his motives, tactics—even his temperament—being impugned by the likes of weak-kneed Bertram Phelps and upstart owner Mike Sturgis. His long-time ally George Steele had replaced him as Gotham Harbor Alliance figurehead in contract negotiations with government mediators and union officials. Even his most ardent supporters were jumping ship, anxious to see the strike settled, willing to accede to union demands that Henry couldn't abide. None of them possessed Henry's obstinance, arrogance, or anger. None had ventured into such a spiteful and malicious place in their heart.

Henry would cut ties with the Gotham Harbor Alliance if that's what was called for, he had decided, battle the union his way—live or die by his own decisions, his own rules of engagement.

"Fuck the union and the owners' coalition!" he fumed. "To hell with them both!"

And that was the baleful sentiment that jolted him from a restless, storm-tossed sleep in the early hours of day ten, the tugboat strike having lasted to a point once thought unimaginable.

Absent by now was any semblance of the giddiness Henry had felt in the early stages of the work stoppage, when the labor war he had orchestrated was going precisely as planned. Now he was despondent, wobbly, even afraid. Propping himself up in bed, he groped atop his nightstand for a pack of Luckies and a tin of antacids to quiet his drumming heart, quell the fire in his gut—and initiate what had become an all-too-familiar ritual.

For as long as he could remember, Henry had been captive to not much more than fitful, ghastly patches of sleep. All those corporate demands: business meetings, fiduciary responsibilities, political wrangling, contract negotiations. How could anyone with burdens like those not be deeply troubled? All the ulcer flareups, the heartburn, the panic attacks. How could anyone with ailments like those possibly get a good night's sleep?

But Henry's sleep had only worsened since the outset of the strike. Now there were night terrors, as well—frightful dreams about majestic passenger ships bedecked with gleeful revelers sailing blithely into New York Harbor and drawing Henry's tugboats beneath their massive hulls, before shearing the tugboats with the turn of their mighty propellers as Henry cowered below deck, just as he'd done as a boy on his father's vessels.

In recent days the nightmares, like Henry's wakefulness, had grown more recurrent, more harrowing, their symbolism easy enough to decipher: all of Henry's valued public assets—his corporate empire, his business cachet, his role as a titan of industry—attacked by powerful, unchecked forces; his tugboats' essential role in the city's commerce ignored by a blasé public; and water—the very element that had bestowed upon Henry unchecked political power, vast wealth, his essential self-image as a man of consequence—now wresting even those treasures from his grasp.

Where was Carolyn now, when he needed her the most? Whom could he turn to for comfort, guidance, support? Why should—how could, he agonized—a man so prosperous, so celebrated, so powerful, feel so threatened, so vulnerable, so alone?

Henry thought about how some nights, when Carolyn was still alive, he'd nestle alongside her as she slept, finding solace in her rhythmic breathing, her unfettered spirit, her faculty for distancing herself from the tumult that governed his life. That alone would bring him comfort, help him sleep. But

Carolyn was absent now, and the nights were so much thornier: a shot or two of bourbon to blunt his insomnia; a capful of antacid to quell his raging gut; a sleeping pill to knock him out. And even those antidotes couldn't halt the tossing and turning, the palpitations and cold sweats, the patchy intervals of sleep, recurrent fits of coughing, and the dark, disturbing dreams.

Sometimes, on the worst of his nights, Henry would sit awake in bed for hours, thinking, calculating, plotting. Other times, he'd wander the halls of his dreary, sterile mansion, plunking himself onto his drawing-room couch and staring at Carolyn's portrait, reminiscing, weeping, calling her name.

Even now, eleven months after her death, Henry couldn't accept that he'd been dealt such a nasty, untoward hand: to live the rest of his life alone, bereaved, bereft of the only person who'd ever made him feel valued and loved. Nor could he accept the fact that life held serendipitous twists and turns that made him feel so ineffectual. So powerless. So ordinary.

Even now Henry could smell Carolyn's perfumed fragrance on his bedsheets, his pillowcase, the closetful of her clothing he couldn't bring himself to discard. Even now he could envision her as she once was: vivacious and ebullient; full of laughter and music and song; energetic and passionate and alive.

But Carolyn was gone now. Gone! All that remained were snippets of the life they'd had, memories that slipped like sand through Henry's fingers, and the crushing weight of her loss: an aching, unremitting loneliness that felt like a fathomless hole he couldn't climb out of. All that and his anger too: smoldering, white-hot, stoking the bonfire that burned within him day and night.

He'd never been this angry, Henry thought, when Carolyn was alive. Never this vindictive, abrasive and bitter. Never so consumed by such a naked, unkempt rage. Never so governed by the exigent impulse to lash out at others, so they could feel as empty and cheated as him—so that they, too, could feel his pain.

Maybe if Carolyn were still alive, Henry thought, things would be different. Maybe he wouldn't feel as hostile as he did toward the tugboat workers' union. Maybe he wouldn't be so ruthless, or callous, or have conspired to provoke a labor war that was threatening to destroy the corporate empire he'd built, along with the city that housed it. Maybe Carolyn would have taken him on their sailboat, played her piano, escaped with him to someplace where he could rekindle his spirits, cool the fever that consumed him, rediscover the better angels of his nature.

But Carolyn was gone. She wasn't there to extinguish the inferno that burned within Henry, or to quell the rage he felt compelled to unleash as an expression of his interminable, maddening anguish.

No one was there.

Companionless, aggrieved, deprived of love's most precious fruits, Henry was capable of only the basest of human emotions now. No one was there to console him or appease him or halt him from exacting revenge for the bitterness that consumed him, from making Benny Logan and Local 88 punching bags for his loneliness and his heartache. And the Gotham Harbor Alliance? The coalition that was his brainchild? The alliance of tugboat owners who were suddenly bucking his tactics, resisting his stewardship, standing in his way?

They can go fuck themselves, too!

Untethered from his nightly torment, Henry rose from bed and drifted downstairs, pouring himself a shot of Pappy Van Winkle, emptying another pack of Luckies, and plunking himself on his drawing-room couch. And just like that, it dawned on him what he wanted to do next, the guileful tactic he'd deploy in his pernicious war against the tugboat workers' union.

"This will shake those bastards up," he told himself, smiling grimly at the thought of the union having to deal with the body blow he was prepared to unleash now.

*   *   *

It was 8 a.m., still in time to meet the deadlines for the city's p.m. newspapers, when Henry met with reporters, launching into a rambling diatribe vetted by neither the city's tugboat owners nor their public-relations flacks.

Flailing, he threatened to fire his entire tugboat workforce, claiming he'd sooner shutter his company entirely than capitulate to union demands. Then he announced that he'd be filing formal protests with the National Labor Relations Board, attempting to get the work stoppage declared illegal and the strikers jailed. Then he lodged the charge that he thought would really resonate.

"I'm convinced that we're no longer dealing with reason on the part of union leaders," he told reporters. "I believe the strike that's crippling our city is being dictated more by passion than by rational thinking . . . and by a political agenda fueled by hatred for the institutions of this country!"

"What are you implying?" asked a reporter in Henry's pocket.

"I'm not implying anything," Henry said. "What I'm stating, unequivocally, is that there's reason to believe that the men leading this strike have motives beyond winning a new contract . . . motives that are not only anti-business, but anti-American!"

The declaration sent a shudder through the press corps. But Henry was just beginning. Until now, his attacks on strike leaders had been merely innuendoes. Until now, he'd merely tiptoed around the charges he was about to level.

"Strike leaders call themselves champions of workers' rights," he said. "But I'd call them something else. I'd call them radicals! Fanatic, leftist agitators!"

Frantically, the reporters scribbled notes.

"Are you saying," a reporter asked, "that Local 88 is being controlled by individuals with subversive intent?"

"Let's just say I believe that treasonous elements have infiltrated the tugboat workers' union, using it as a front for subversive ideas aimed at stirring political unrest."

"What leads you to level that charge?"

Henry arched his eyebrows. "Are you asking if I can substantiate my claim?"

The reporter nodded.

"To that," Henry said, "I'd answer with an emphatic yes!"

"What does your evidence suggest?"

"Direct ties between tugboat union leaders and radical agitators who likely are remnants of the American Workers Party and the Communist League of America."

Henry waited for the reporters to catch up with their notetaking.

"Are you charging that anarchists—Socialists, Communists, or Communist sympathizers—are behind the tugboat strike?" Henry's reporter asked.

"Should anyone be surprised?" Henry said, "given all that's happening in America?"

Again, he paused as the reporters feverishly took notes.

"I'm sure all of you are well aware that card-carrying Communists have found America's labor movement fertile ground for advancing their treasonous ideology," Henry said. "I'm sure you've seen how labor unions across the country have been infiltrated by Bolshevik extremists seeking to eradicate capitalism . . . or worse."

"What do you mean by worse?"

"Gentlemen," Henry said wryly. "Do I really have to spell it out?"

No, he didn't. Not in the current political climate. Not in New York, or anywhere in America for that matter. Communist fears for months had been running rampant throughout much of the country, heightened by suspicions that America faced a grave threat from a Soviet Union growing more powerful and hostile by the day. Even as Henry spoke, Cold War tensions were ratcheting up, a Red Scare creeping like a plague across America.

"I think we're facing a threat tantamount to what we faced in World War II," said Henry. "Our country is being undermined by a gang of subversives, a fifth column who masquerade as the 'common man' but instead are looking to perpetrate violence and destroy our way of life! We need to mobilize against these agents of anarchy and revolution!"

"What do you mean by 'mobilize'?" a reporter inquired.

"We need to make the case to patriotic Americans that the labor unrest we're witnessing in New York is likely being instigated by radical agents of the Red conspiracy—Marxists, Trotskyites, and Socialists whose goal is to throw our nation into turmoil, undermine our capitalist system, and take control! We need to halt the current tyranny of strikes, along with workers' treasonous rhetoric . . . and put these labor insurrections down!"

"How do you suggest the public should react?" Henry's shill inquired.

"They should not only be alarmed," Henry said, "but they should help galvanize support for America's businesses, if we're to protect our most valued institutions. Then government authorities should investigate these so-called 'union leaders' regarding their true intent . . . and they should be arrested and jailed for treason!"

Henry ended with a flourish. "I think the people of New York will be safer, and this threat to our way of life ended, when the enemies from within are thrown in jail, where they belong!"

And that was all Henry needed to say. He had set a match to a tinderbox with the expectation that the resultant explosion would rock the city.

Stories in the afternoon dailies and EXTRAS trumpeted Henry's innuendoes:

ANARCHIST LINK CHARGED IN TUGBOAT WALKOUT!

LEFTIST RADICALS SEEN LEADING HARBOR STRIKE!

TUGBOAT KINGPIN HINTS THAT COMMIES RULE UNION!

The allegations hit the union like a sledgehammer. Indeed, no sooner had newspapers reached newsstands than Benny and other union leaders were sent scrambling, forced to defend the integrity of the strike.

"Anyone who calls us Commies, or questions our motives and patriotism, is nothin' but a goddamned liar!" Benny told reporters at strike headquarters, draped in red-white-and-blue bunting, a trio of American flags draping the doorway, "God Bless America" blaring from loudspeakers.

"Most of our men don't have the slightest clue what a Socialist is," Benny said. "They're American as apple pie. The only card they carry is their union-membership card!"

Gathered strikers let loose in a full-throated cheer.

"America! America! America!"

"Are you familiar with Communist Party principles?" a reporter asked.

"Only to the extent that I think they're a crock of shit," Benny replied.

"Do you read *Das Kapital*? *The Daily Worker*?"

"Only the *Daily News* an' the *New York Post*," he said to raucous laughter. "And I dare anyone who even hints that union members are radicals or agitators to say it to my face! Claimin' there's an anti-American agenda on our part is a bald-faced lie. No one in our union is tryin' to overthrow the government. The last thing we are is Pinko sympathizers or Commies-in-disguise."

"If the charges are false," a reporter asked, "what's motivating them?"

"The motive is simple," Tommy Duggan said. "It's the oldest anti-labor trick in the book: tying management's interests to patriotism, while painting union leaders as un-American outsiders bent on revolution. It's the owners' way of sparking hysteria . . . of getting the public to turn against us."

"In other words," said Benny, "it's character assassination, a truth-be-damned tactic to cast doubt about our motives."

"Are you saying, then, that the charge is a lie?" a reporter asked.

"You're damn right I am. I'm sayin' that it's pure deception, part of a smear campaign to divert attention from the real issues behind the strike," Benny said. "Henry McFarland thinks that if he keeps us busy denyin' his charges, or tryin' to weed supposed 'subversives' from our ranks, he'll turn people against us, an' get us to lose focus on the legitimate grievances we're tryin' to remedy."

Benny continued, "The tugboat owners wanna paint us as 'agitators' an' themselves as 'defenders of the American Way'. But they're the ones who are the real 'agitators'—by denyin' workingmen the right to be compensated fairly for their work. We believe in a day's pay for a day's work, and Henry McFarland won't even pay these men for the work they did back in January! Rather than tryin' to defend the American Way, they're the ones bent on destroyin' it."

Strike leaders spent the next few hours refuting Henry's charges, but the damage had been done. By late that afternoon, his red-baiting tactics had sparked a citywide furor. Self-styled patriots condemned "radical" tugboat workers for threatening the social order and corrupting a way of life that Americans had spilled blood to defend in World War II. Pro-business commentators charged that the strike was orchestrated by subversives bent on mayhem and revolution. Calls were issued for strike leaders to be arrested and charged with treason.

Then things got ugly. Shortly after nightfall, across the city, leaflets were distributed describing the tugboat strike as a Bolshevik Revolution. Gangs of anti-Communist crusaders raided the Union Square headquarters of the Communist Party, destroying equipment and breaking windows. Vigilantes roamed the campuses of Columbia University and NYU, vandalizing property, roughing up students, and painting hammer-and-sickle symbols on the walls of buildings and lecture halls.

The crisis facing New York had assumed a toxic new narrative, opinions about the tugboat strike no longer defined by peaceful, reasoned debate. America's greatest city seemed riven, at war with itself, ruled by hysteria, violence, and fear.

CHAPTER 38

February 10, 1946

Somehow Benny rallied. It seemed at times miraculous, the way the strike's dauntless steward managed to tap into a seemingly bottomless wellspring of courage and grit, summoning the toughness and the wisdom needed to bear the burden of leadership. Even as union solidarity diminished, political pressure escalated, and the personal attacks mounted, he remained indomitable. Each time he was knocked to the ground, he rose to his feet stronger and more resolute than ever. Each time he seemed on the precipice of defeat, he dug deeper, seemingly impervious to the weight on his shoulders.

By now, it was apparent that Paddy O'Boyle's covert efforts at submarining the strike, while injurious, were hardly proving fatal to the union's cause. Neither were the surreptitious probes into Benny's personal life, or the attacks aimed at undercutting his leadership. Benny's military record and credit history each proved squeaky clean. No evidence was found regarding personal peccadillos or run-ins with the law. The scurrilous charges aimed at the union firebrand all seemed farfetched, even laughable. Most strikers sloughed them off. Even the mob-backed harassment campaign wasn't proving to be a meaningful deterrent. Within minutes after the threatening calls began, Benny's home and office telephones were taken off the hook. His wife and daughters remained safely under wraps at Tommy Duggan's Pocono Mountains cottage. And although requests for formal police protection continued to fall on deaf ears, the cadre of union bodyguards accompanying Benny was tighter than ever. He went nowhere in the city now without a team of armed escorts watching his back.

Equally apparent was that Benny's stature among the union's rank and file had risen to heights akin to that of a Bunyanesque folk hero, an exemplar of the passionate, headstrong leader New York's tugboat workers had always craved. Veteran tugboatmen, hat in hand, approached to shake his hand and express their gratitude for all he was doing on their behalf. Organized labor officials from across America phoned to convey their admiration and support. Pro-union politicians hitched their wagon to his rising star.

But the rewards Benny was proffering to tugboat workers were being reciprocated in spades. For just as the strikers drew fortitude and courage from Benny, he was drawing those same strengths from the men, feeding off their fellowship and respect. Even as he kindled the spirits of striking workers, they in turn kindled his—made him more committed, more unassailable, a better leader.

So, in many salient ways, did Jack.

The past ten days had seen Jack assume an increasingly pivotal role in helping Benny navigate the strike, reversing the roles they'd played as young boys and becoming a confidante, a de facto advisor, and a pillar of strength for his brother. Jack's job in flawlessly calculating emergency strike pay had lent order and credibility to a potentially chaotic function. His role as watchdog over potential fiscal shenanigans had eliminated a major source of concern for Benny. His creation of the union's bargaining book had provided Local 88 officials with critical ammunition to rely upon in negotiations with tugboat owners and government mediators. Most importantly, Jack had become an integral part of Benny's inner circle, a trusted sounding board and counselor, ballast to his brother's hotheaded intransigence.

For his entire life, Benny had clung to the notion that toughness and bravado were the qualities that best defined a leader, and that his unyielding stance in contract negotiations would produce the best of all outcomes for the union. But Jack, by virtue of his unflappable demeanor and innate wisdom, had persuaded his brother to view the labor conflict through a very different lens, while shining a light on a more enlightened approach.

Even as Benny confronted his darkest and most challenging moments, Jack was emerging as a calm voice of reason, providing Benny with balance and perspective. Gradually, purposefully, he'd convinced Benny that the capacity to compromise was hardly a reflection of acquiescence or weakness, but rather an intelligent, constructive means to an end. True strength, he'd assured Benny, lay not in bullheaded obstinacy but in a willingness to yield as well as to demand, to listen as well to speak, to give as well as to take. Success, he'd convinced his headstrong brother, could be achieved through means other than brute force.

That counsel had made a palpable difference to the union and the strike. Thanks largely to Jack, Benny had become not only more effectual as Local 88's overseer, but more insightful and conciliatory, tempered and mature—not only a better leader but, more importantly, a better man.

"You know, it hurts me to the core, puttin' the city through this kinda pain," Benny confessed one night. "I just hope people realize that our union had no choice but to strike. We never could've got the contract we deserve at the bargainin' table. Henry McFarland wasn't gonna let that happen, an' Paddy O'Boyle is too crooked to give a shit. Walkin' off the job was the only way our men were gonna get out from under the thumb of those weasels."

Benny wasn't wrong. Jack was able to see that now. The past ten days, torturous as they were, had opened his eyes to the cutthroat realities of collective bargaining, and allowed Jack to see how powerful, unscrupulous men would go to any lengths to advance their narrow self-interests. Jack, for the first time, was seeing that regardless of whatever misdeeds labor unions perpetrated, they were the only means to meaningful social power for people like Benny. Ideology was secondary, principles beside the point. But leverage? Leverage was irrefutable, all that really mattered. Henry McFarland understood that full well. For decades, he'd used his money and cachet as levers to cultivate alliances, peddle influence, and build an empire. Benny understood it too, using his passion and his commitment to inspire tugboat workers to put their collective asses on the line for a common cause, for something better.

"You know," Jack admitted to his brother one night, "I wasn't always on board with the strike . . . wasn't sure how I felt about the issues or how things were being handled in the early stages."

It was a bold admission. Risky, too. And one that Jack hadn't planned on divulging. Somehow, though, it all seemed safe now. There was no reason to shield Benny from his feelings. Not after all they'd been through. Not anymore.

"What're you tryin' to say, kid?" Benny asked.

"I'm saying that I wasn't totally committed to the strike at the start," Jack replied. "Frankly, I wasn't sure the reasons for striking were legitimate. Being new to the tugboat trade, I didn't understand the challenges the workers faced, and felt I was caught unfairly in the jaws of something I hadn't bargained for."

Benny grinned. "Think I didn't know that?"

"You did?"

"Hell, yeah. Felt bad about it, too. Felt all I did in helpin' you land your job was to plop you in the middle of a shitstorm that you never saw comin'."

"You didn't have to feel that way," Jack said. "Signing on as a tugboatman was my decision. I always knew there could be a price to pay."

"Ya mean like owin' me a favor that you feared you couldn't repay?"

"That's part of it."

"An' gettin' caught up in a labor war at home, months after fightin' a real war overseas?"

"That, too."

"I'm sorry 'bout all that, kid."

"Apologies aren't needed." Jack waved his brother off. "Truth is, tugboat work has suited me just fine."

"Even with all the shit that's hittin' the fan?"

"Uh-huh. Regardless of all that, tugboat work has been good for me in a lot of ways. And I don't see the strike as a 'shitstorm.' I'm involved it because I want to be . . . want to be for my crewmates, want to be for you."

Benny's stony features softened. "I'm grateful you see it that way, kid," he said. "Makes me feel a whole lot better."

"Why is that?"

"'Cause I know the kind of man you are—your principles, your integrity. I know that you wouldn't be on board with the strike unless you truly believed in it. I also know that, even if you had some misgivings, you'd be in the fight outta loyalty to me . . . an' the bond we share as brothers."

Benny grinned. "See, I knew all along that you took the tugboat job as much as a favor to me as one from me to you. I also knew you compromised your principles to help me feel good about it. But to tell you the truth, I'm happy you took the job, 'cause there's no one in the world other than you that I'd rather have in the trenches alongside me. An' that's the goddamned truth."

The two of them lapsed into a long, pensive silence.

"I've been doin' a lot of thinking lately," Benny confessed, "an' I've come to realize that this war we're wagin'—it ain't just between workers an' management. It's a class war: upper class versus workin' class, 'haves' versus 'have-nots' . . . both sides clawin' for a leg up."

"But more importantly," said Benny, "I've also come to realize that I'm in the war not just for myself, but for all the poor schnooks that no one gives a damn about, guys who are invisible when they wage their battles alone. I'm in the fight for guys like Pop."

Jack was stunned. He had never heard his brother voice that sentiment, never realized that Benny saw the battle through that lens. Like most men, the brothers rarely spoke about things that truly mattered: heartaches, aspirations, happiness, fear. And the subject that mattered as much as any—Benny's relationship with their father—was touchy enough to have been off-limits for years.

Except that suddenly it wasn't. Unexpectedly, unprompted, Benny had raised the subject as if he'd been mulling it over for a while, reassessing his longtime posture toward Gus. Perhaps, Jack thought, there remained hope for reconciliation, even after all this time. Perhaps when it came to their father, Benny could find room in his heart for something other than alienation and anger—perhaps even the forgiveness Jack had spent years lobbying for.

"For as long as I can remember," Benny said, "Pop pissed me off 'cause I thought he didn't have the guts to fight for what he deserved . . . 'cause he seemed to stand for everything I was fighting to change."

"And you've punished him for that, haven't you?"

"Maybe so," Benny admitted. "But maybe I should've seen things differently. Maybe this strike is changin' the way I see a lotta things."

"It's changing us all," Jack said. "In many ways."

And it struck Jack then that among the many personal changes wrought by the strike, he had begun to see his brother in an entirely new light. He'd always seen Benny as the quintessential fighter: tenacious, iron-willed, unyielding. But now he saw him on an even loftier plane. There was something noble in the way Benny fought for his beliefs, something commendable about his passion, his view of what his struggle was all about. Sure, he was hardheaded, stubborn, quick on the trigger. But beneath it all, his heart was in the right place. Jack couldn't help but admire his brother's commitment, his tenacity, his dedication to the cause he championed. Couldn't help but respect it, either.

The strike, for all its hardships and misgivings, had drawn the brothers closer, deepened their bond, reminded them of what they meant to one another—and more so, what they could mean going forward.

For most of their lives, Benny had endeavored to care for Jack, serving as benefactor, mentor, and guardian. But the tables had turned. Jack had become, in many ways, the mentor and guardian now. There was nothing he wouldn't do for his brother. He'd be there for Benny, whatever the situation, whatever the cost. Supporting him. Guiding him. Protecting him too, if necessary.

"Ya know," Benny said, "you havin' my back means the world to me."

"And it means the world to me," said Jack, "that you've always had mine."

"Thanks, kid." Benny grinned. "To tell ya the truth, without you I don't know how much longer I could carry the torch. But knowin' you're beside me, I can carry it as far as I have to."

Tentatively, awkwardly, the brothers embraced. It was one of the few times Jack could recall the two of them acting so spontaneously on that impulse. How difficult it was for most men, even brothers, to convey those kinds of emotions, Jack thought. He hoped there'd be other moments like that. Other reasons, too.

So many things in life, Jack thought, fell into place without rhyme or reason: Gabriel's death; finding Kate in the tumult of war; and now an unwonted tugboat strike leading Benny and him to a moment like this, drawing them closer—no longer as boys, but as men. Win or lose this battle, they had each other; win or lose, they'd always be brothers. Whatever the outcome of the strike, Jack thought, at least they'd have that. He couldn't think of many other things in life that could ever mean more.

CHAPTER 39

February 11, 1946

The strikebreakers arrived on the eleventh day—scores of them, many packing handguns, carbines, and other small arms. Bused to the city under the cover of darkness, they'd been quartered overnight aboard a specially equipped cargo ship anchored at the mouth of New York Harbor. By daybreak, they were gathering at Henry's North River docks, preparing to board a fleet of tugboats—and end the strike by force.

Henry was hardly surprised. Despite knowing that their presence would further stoke the labor tempest ravaging the city, Henry, behind the back of the owners' alliance ... etc. Knowing that their presence would further stoke the labor tempest ravaging New York, Henry, behind the back of the Alliance, had contracted with Otto Blackburn's Asset Protection Corp. to supply two hundred replacement tugboat workers, escorted by a protective team of ex-army mercenaries. Their objective, to Henry's way of thinking, was critical: they'd been summoned to fulfill his company's mandate to resume its trash-hauling duties, thus quashing the threat of a damaging lawsuit by the city.

There was more to Henry's latest anti-strike ploy, however, than merely a matter of expediency. He was going for the jugular now, aiming a symbolic rifle shot squarely at Local 88's heart, putting his tugboats back in service regardless of condemnation or consequence. He was beyond such considerations at this point, beyond the need for explanation or assent.

He had also ventured for the first time beyond the confines of New York to abet his union-busting crusade. Instead of relying solely on local business allies, or the operatives he'd procured through Paddy O'Boyle, the interlopers who had entered the fray now were out-of-town professionals: non-union tugboat workers jettisoned from their jobs by an oil-industry slowdown on America's Gulf Coast. Desperate for a paycheck, the idled tugboatmen had no qualms about accepting per-diem work in New York—even if it meant traveling hundreds of miles from homes in Mobile, Galveston, and Baton Rouge.

Even if it meant stabbing fellow tugboat workers in the back.

Nor did the invading workforce come cheap. Among the plethora of union-busting services that Otto Blackburn provided, strikebreakers of this caliber were top of the line. Henry would be charged eighteen thousand dollars a day, all of it bankrolled personally. Blackburn would garner a six-figure bonus if his replacement workers succeeded in breaking the strike.

But those costs didn't matter, either. Henry by now had lost all concept of money when it came to wreaking havoc on the tugboat workers' union. Driven by his thirst for capitulation and unremitting rage, he was utterly blind to the cost of his actions. His anti-labor vendetta was no longer defined by logic or reason, nor was it bound by dollars and cents. Henry was going to impose his will on the tugboat workers' union, come hell or high water. He was going to get his tugboats back in service, period! He didn't care who stood in his way. Not his fellow tugboat owners, or his business allies, or his protesting customers. Not the politicians or the newspapers, the public or the courts.

And certainly not the union.

Indeed, Henry was truly flying solo now, bound by nothing and no one. In the past twelve hours, he had formally cut ties with the Gotham Harbor Alliance, disavowing the syndicate in a rambling, bombastic diatribe to reporters. The tugboat owners' coalition, in turn, had also distanced itself from its founder and chairman, denouncing Henry for his unyielding stance in contract negotiations, while refuting his scurrilous charges that strike leaders were really Communists-in-disguise. Henry, the owners' coalition proclaimed, was no longer its figurehead, its spokesman, or its guiding force. He was on the outside looking in, an island to himself in every possible way.

But Henry couldn't care less about that, either. In many ways, he was forging his own destiny now, reverting to his longstanding persona as a gunslinging maverick who made his own decisions and dictated his own fate. In a perverse kind of way, he saw his latest action as honoring a corporate tradition. Both Liam and Aidan McFarland had taken extreme measures to quash work stoppages. They knew how to deal with uppity labor unions, Henry reasoned: forcefully and with no holds barred. Why couldn't he?

But opening New York Harbor in the face of the strike wasn't going to be so easy.

No sooner had Otto Blackburn's mercenaries begun massing at Henry docks than word spread like a firestorm across the waterfront. Reaction was equally swift. Telephones rang off the hook at City Hall, police headquarters, newspaper offices, and strikers' homes. Emissaries conveyed the news to union halls, job sites, and other blue-collar haunts. Picketing plans were instantly shelved, while carloads of striking tugboat workers—many toting lead pipes, ax handles, tire irons, and brass knuckles—began flocking to the McFarland docks, girding for a fight.

Union officials faced serious legal jeopardy now, aside from the specter of widespread injuries, even death. Property damage or bloodshed, the union had been explicitly warned, would instantly be labeled as criminal—the strike halted, protesters jailed, the union slapped with fines and other sanctions. Strike leaders could ill afford that. Within minutes, Benny and others were racing to short-circuit the budding confrontation.

But Henry was prepared for that, too. Having called in a favor from Police Commissioner William Dunne, a longtime ally, Henry had arranged for two hundred Tactical Patrol Officers—along with dozens of off-duty cops and hastily deputized security guards—to defend the entrance to his docks. He'd also padlocked the twelve-foot-high cyclone fence surrounding the complex, topping the chain-link barricade with reams of barbed wire.

When the mob of irate strikers descended on the fortress-like compound, they were met head-on by a rampart of helmeted, baton-wielding cops. NYPD paddy wagons lined nearby streets. German Shepherd police dogs tugged at their leashes. And all the while, strikebreakers on the opposite side of the fence went about their duties, ignoring an onslaught of epithets, taunts, and threats.

"Scabs! Lackies! Traitors!" the striking tugboat workers shouted.

"Drop dead . . . you strikebreaking bastards!"

"Rot in hell, you sons of bitches!"

The verbal onslaught, however, had little effect. Ignoring the venomous catcalls, the strikebreakers continued working under the watchful eye of their rifle-toting private army. Gear was loaded onto tugboats, equipment readied, assignments radioed to pilot houses.

Then, as if cued by a silent command, dozens of strikers began hurling rocks, bricks, and other debris at the strikebreakers. A rogue group of the tugboatmen then stormed the chain-link fence, attempting to scale the barricade, and whacking it with baseball bats and pipes. Police whistles shrieked. Guard dogs yelped. Bull-horned commands pierced the air.

Without warning, several dozen cops broke ranks and began pulling strikers off the fence, beating them with nightsticks, blackjacks, gunstocks, and fists. Strikers scrambled for cover. Others battled back. It was tugboat workers pitted against the police now, a wild and unruly brouhaha.

And Benny was trapped in the middle of it.

For the better part of two weeks, Benny had done an almost-heroic job of rallying strikers, preserving unanimity, lifting spirits, and leading the workers peacefully. But no longer. What for the most part had been a disciplined and organized work stoppage had spiraled out of control. Even some of Benny's most loyal acolytes were abandoning all restraint and joining what had become an irate, unruly mob. Benny could no longer suppress the strikers' anger and frustration. Nor could he control the rampaging police.

Desperately clawing his way through the frenzied crush of humanity, he shouted at the top of his lungs, imploring strikers to quell their billowing outrage. But his efforts had little effect. Inching forward, trying to contain the savage hubbub, Benny was sucked unwittingly into its vortex. Buffeted by the feverish horde, he was cursed at and goaded into shoving matches—his leadership challenged, his peacemaking efforts rebuffed. Insults were hurled, kicks and punches thrown. And within seconds, Benny was corralled by a cordon of rowdy cops, knocked to the ground, and whacked with nightsticks and billy clubs.

"Get off me, goddamn it!" he shouted, arms flailing, trying to fend off the blows. "All I'm doin' is tryin' to keep the peace!"

"Tell it to a fuckin' judge!" squawked a cop, pummeling Benny with a nightstick.

"Hey . . . cut that out!" shouted Jack, wading through the riotous throng.

Instantly, the cop spun about, nightstick at the ready.

"Want some of this, too?" He took a wild swing, barely missing Jack's head.

Then just as swiftly, Tommy Duggan angled in through the crush of humanity, wedging himself between Jack and the wayward cop. Big Mack

Nowak waded in too, wrapping Jack in a bear hug and carrying his crewmate through the angry mob to safety.

"You cops are supposed to be neutral in labor disputes!" Duggan bellowed. "You ain't supposed to take sides! 'Sides, some of you men are off duty . . . or ain't even real cops!"

"We've got a job to do!" a police sergeant barked. "Orders to follow!"

"An' what orders are those?"

"Maintain order . . . at all costs."

"Well, Hitler's army had its orders, too," Duggan shouted. "That don't make what you're doin' right! For Christ's sake, you cops are supposed to be public servants . . . not strikebreakin' goons! Who the hell are you men workin' for, anyway?"

The tightlipped sergeant looked away, and with good reason. Indeed, he was on more than just the NYPD's payroll—moonlighting as a security guard at Henry's docks. In truth, he had been following orders—Henry's.

Henry, in fact, had masterminded the entire confrontation, arranging for the presence of both strikebreakers and police, while baiting protesting tugboat workers into the confrontation—all while setting Benny up to be assaulted by his fellow union members, roughed up by cops, and arrested.

"You cops oughtta be ashamed of yourselves!" Benny excoriated the officers, as he was handcuffed and led to a paddy wagon. "You call yourselves public servants? Union men? New York's Finest? What a joke! You'd think, if anything, you'd be on our side in this labor war! Instead, you're nothin' but a bunch of sellouts . . . no better than them scabs!"

Benny's admonitions, however, had little effect. The strikers' protest had effectively been squelched. Dozens of tugboat workers were arrested. Others beat a hasty retreat. Still others, battered by the police, staggered around aimlessly or lay crumpled on the ground—all while the strikebreakers methodically went about their tasks. Equipment and gear were loaded onto tugboats. Engines were revved, mooring lines released. And one by one, Henry's tugboats, escorted by police-patrol vessels, left their docks and headed to trash-hauling assignments, all under Henry's watchful eye.

"Now that's how you handle a goddamned strike!" Henry exulted, as he monitored the incident through a pair of binoculars from the window of his office, several blocks away.

"That's how you deal with labor unions that can't be reasoned with . . . and with impudent, ungrateful workers who know no bounds!" he crowed, as his secretary Elena Karas stood dumbstruck, quaking at his side.

Henry lowered his binoculars, face flushed, voice nearly breaking. "You've got to be forceful with those union thugs!" he jabbered. "Decisive and strong!"

Miss Karas cringed as Henry rambled on.

"You've got to show your workers who's calling the shots—show them that labor insurrections won't be tolerated, and that businessmen like me will fight them tooth and nail . . . with every weapon at our disposal. Every weapon!"

But Henry's euphoria was short-lived. Within minutes, it became apparent that the tugboat czar had grossly misjudged the outcome of his anti-strike ploy. For even as Henry bore gleeful witness to the melee at his docks, dozens of police officers, including many on horseback, were cordoning off a nearby section of waterfront, while attempting to expedite a fuel delivery by government-owned tugboats. Union members had countered by marshaling several hundred strikers determined to prevent fuel trucks from leaving their waterfront depots.

Within minutes, the confrontation came to a head. Wading through a wall of protesting strikers, helmeted police set about clearing a path for the fuel trucks. Linking arms, the strikers resisted. Horses whinnied and reared. Police whistles shrieked. Then a rogue cop fired a shotgun blast to scatter the crowd, and a column of mounted police rushed the strikers. Rocks and bottles were tossed. Tear-gas canisters exploded. A second wave of cops surged forward, breaking through hordes of strikers, shoving them to the ground and stampeding them under horses' hooves. Patrol cars, paddy wagons, and ambulances rushed to the scene. Medics attended to victims lying on blood-spattered streets. Clouds of tear gas hovered overhead.

By the time the toxic fumes dissipated, two dozen strikers had been wounded—four of them struck by shotgun pellets, others kicked by horses, burned by tear gas, or pummeled by nightsticks. Sixteen cops had been injured, as well—several of them struck by tire irons and baseball bats, others felled by concussions, bruises, and broken bones.

And still, the violence persisted. Out in the harbor, a private speedboat pulled alongside a McFarland tugboat and four hooded men leapt aboard the vessel, pummeling replacement workers with axe handles before tossing them overboard and releasing the garbage scows in tow. Cinderblocks were hurled through the windows of several of Henry's tugboats. Zip guns were fired at others. A fully loaded coal barge, struck by a Molotov cocktail, burst into flames.

It was unbridled warfare now, lawless and bloody. Rampaging police and unruly union factions roamed the waterfront, skirmishes flaring and property under siege, while city officials struggled to quell the unrest. And Benny was on his way to a midtown jail, his peacemaking efforts thwarted, the union rudderless, its fate seemingly hanging by a thread.

By the time peace was restored to the waterfront, it was obvious that the tugboat strike had entered an ominous new realm. The crisis devouring the city had descended into a place darker and more menacing than anyone could have imagined, threatening to swallow everyone even remotely tied to the walkout.

Chapter 40

February 11, 1946

Dutifully requesting her leave, Elena Karas left Henry to his anti-union diatribe, retreating to the sanctuary of a lavatory adjacent to her work desk. Alone behind closed doors, she brushed her hair, powdered her face, applied lipstick and mascara—and then fell to her knees, her body racked by a torrent of sobs that had been pooling inside her for weeks.

Since long before the onset of the strike, Henry's longtime secretary had kept her billowing emotions firmly in check, tamping them down like the stalwart corporate soldier she was: diligent, unflappable, devoted to both her employer and its legion of striking workers. But the burden of the past few weeks was proving far too weighty. Her emotions laid bare, Elena was crumbling to pieces in the face of the labor war ravaging her city: pained by the struggle of her co-workers, appalled by the actions of her longtime boss, and deeply conflicted over the compliant, company-first role she'd been forced to play.

She hadn't always borne the weight of those emotions. Far from it. For more than twenty years, Elena had devoted her heart, her soul, and every ounce of her talent and energy to McFarland Marine Towing Inc., the only company for which she'd ever worked, at a job she'd loved as much as anything in her life.

Women weren't given much credence in the workplace when Elena came of age, the daughter of immigrant Greek parents who had eked out a living peddling currants and figs from a pushcart in the leafy working-class enclave of Astoria, Queens, heart of Hellenic life in Greater New York. But, heartened by a women's suffrage movement with her hometown as its epicenter, Elena, at eighteen, aspired to more than outworn archetypes and rigid glass ceilings. Women in America had finally earned the right to vote. A growing number, Elena included, were chafing at the gender-based roles they'd been forced to play for decades in the nation's corporate realm.

Founded seven years earlier in Rhode Island, the Katharine Gibbs School had opened a New York branch in 1918, and Elena was among the earliest enrollees in a pioneering program that combined a traditional liberal arts education with preparation for the modern business office. At Gibbs, Elena learned typing, stenography, letter-writing, telephone etiquette, and how to use Dictaphones, Comptometers, and other office equipment. She also learned the so-called "soft skills" of professional women then: punctuality, poise, and the p's and q's of secretarial grooming: white gloves, shirtwaist dress, matching necklace and earrings, and just enough perfume and makeup to walk the line between being stylish but never seductive, attractive but never over the top.

When Henry became the company's CEO upon the death of his father, he had specifically asked that a "Gibbs Girl" be hired as his executive secretary. Two years at the venerable secretarial school had armed Elena with the skills needed to land the job. Everything from that point on she'd mastered on her own.

Secretaries were known as "typewriters" then, but Elena quickly proved that she was capable of far more than fetching Henry's coffee and sharpening his pencils. Within months, she was juggling a plethora of key administrative functions: managing Henry's schedule, handling his correspondence, taking dictation, screening his phone calls, and handling the demands of McFarland's senior management. A year later, at age twenty-one, she was overseeing both the company's secretarial pool and its clerical staff, while serving as the primary conduit between Henry and others.

But there was more to Elena's position in the corporate hierarchy than that of an administrative figurehead. Despite its status as a blue-chip firm, McFarland Marine Towing was run in many ways like a mom-and-pop business. With Henry trusting only a tiny circle of associates, power at the company was tightly held, select employees often serving in roles that far transcended narrow job descriptions. As her tenure at the tugboat firm lengthened and her status heightened, Elena was granted nearly unfettered access to corporate confidentialities: sitting in on nearly all of Henry's meetings, preparing internal memos and reports, and interacting—often on a cordial, first-name basis— with city officials, key clients, and other high-level contacts. She also managed many of Henry's personal affairs, especially in the wake of Carolyn's death.

Through the years, Elena had also forged cordial, close-knit relationships with many of McFarland's tugboat workers, often assisting the men—at times off-the-record—with benefits claims and other personal matters. Trustworthy, ebullient, and eminently approachable, she was in many ways the glue that held the company together, an indispensable Big Sister and go-to person who fostered cohesion and trust. Most of her co-workers referred to her, with immense fondness, by the nickname "Lennie."

But Lennie Karas's work life, like so many others, had been turned topsy-turvy by the strike. For one thing, Henry had made it resoundingly clear that, even with McFarland Marine Towing in a state of partial closure, it would be business as usual to whatever extent possible for the duration of the work stoppage. Supervisory, administrative, and other non-union personnel were also required to sign loyalty oaths pledging unequivocal fealty to the company throughout the duration of the work stoppage. At-will employees who refused to adhere to those dictates or who failed to report to work were summarily dismissed—sacrificing salary, accrued benefits, and earned bonuses.

Reporting to work in the face of the strike, however, was hardly easy.

Within hours after the work stoppage had been ratified, picket lines were being manned at the entrances to both McFarland Marine Towing's tugboat docks and its corporate offices, with non-striking employees required to traverse those lines to access and depart their workplace, forcing them to symbolically stab striking co-workers in the back to protect their own jobs. Three of Henry's top lieutenants had resigned in protest of the mandatory attendance policy. Half the company's administrative employees had been fired for honoring the picket lines. And those who reported to work, their allegiances torn, were palpably disheartened, many of them sitting at their desks for much of their workday, glassy-eyed or crying. Worse yet, the mood of picketing strikers had grown uglier and more menacing by the day—as had their actions.

For nearly two weeks already, non-striking McFarland employees had been compelled, twice each day, to run a harrowing gauntlet of insults, epithets, and threats—in many cases emanating from longtime co-workers and friends. Company executives were cursed at and spat upon. Personal vehicles were struck by tomatoes, rocks, and assorted debris. Effigies of Henry and other corporate officials, hanging from lampposts and fences, were beaten with broomsticks and ceremoniously set ablaze.

Henry, as was his wont, fought back. Police were summoned to stand vigil over company property. Private security guards were hired to escort non-strikers across picket lines. Corporate attorneys were dispatched to court, obtaining restraining orders barring acts of harassment against non-striking employees.

Nothing Henry did, however, could halt the personal abuse. And nothing anyone did could assuage Miss Karas's anguish or heartbreak.

Each time she crossed picket lines—heart throbbing, body trembling, tears welling in her eyes—Lennie felt tortured and sullied, as if what had once been an act of dedication and loyalty had become little more than a gut-wrenching act of abandonment and betrayal. Strikers hurled expletives, shouted threats, spat in her direction. Cognizant of her sensibilities, they cruelly singled her out, begging her allegiance, swearing revenge.

"Of all people, Lennie . . . not you!" strikers shouted. "How can you stab us in the back like this, after all this time? How can you hurt co-workers who live and die for one another?"

"Rot in hell!" strikers chanted, singsong. "We'll never forgive you!"

"Lackey! Sellout! Scab!"

Elena was personally devastated by the insults, wounded by the loss of esteem. For twenty-plus years, she'd loved nearly every minute of her job; proud of how she had helped McFarland Marine Towing rise to the top of New York's corporate heap; proud of the role she had played as a pioneer and symbol of the 20th-century Liberated Woman; proud of the reputation she had forged, the relationships she had built, the salary she earned, the respect she engendered.

Now everything she had built across the breadth of her corporate life was falling apart. And all of it so quickly, too.

In the span of eleven heart-wrenching days, McFarland Marine Towing had been thrown into utter chaos: revenue evaporating, customers bolting, lawsuits pending, workers pitted not only against management, but against each other as well. It was impossible to assess the extent of the damage or to imagine how the company—so riddled by resentment, dissension, and mistrust—could ever again effectively function. It was equally impossible to imagine how its workforce could ever again co-exist.

Then there was Henry.

Elena's feelings in that regard had changed dramatically, too.

Henry—headstrong, autocratic, condescending—had always been a challenge to work for. Yet somehow Elena had managed for the most part to turn the other cheek, forgive her boss's delinquencies and indiscretions, put up with his idiosyncrasies, his moodiness, his boorish behavior. The work alone had energized her, its rewards far exceeding its downside.

But working for Henry had become all but impossible now. He'd become so jaundiced, so belligerent, vindictive and cruel and soiled beyond redemption. Elena was jarred by his malicious outbursts, offended by his actions, mortified by his values and beliefs. Most days, she couldn't stomach the sight of him.

But there was more to her growing dilemma than all of that. Through the years, Elena had made her share of personal decisions, sacrifices, compromises. In many ways, she had given herself over entirely to her work: putting in weekends and holidays; commuting three hours a day between Manhattan and Queens; often arriving home well past nightfall. Social connections had been stunted. Suitors had come and gone. Time, almost imperceptibly, had slipped away. Elena was forty-six now—single, childless, living alone in the modest English Tudor she had inherited from her parents, second-guessing her actions, lamenting her decisions—the entirety of her life crashing in on her.

Much to her consternation, she was facing a deepening emotional crisis, plunging headlong into an abyss of uncertainty and despair, awash in a tidal wave of regret. Suddenly, she felt as if all the years of devotion and diligence had amounted to little more than heartache and doubt, her entire future murky and somber now. She wondered how, after all this time, she could possibly continue at McFarland Marine Towing—dreading, even more so, the prospect of having to start from scratch at another company.

And so, behind closed doors in the powder room near her desk, quaking with the onslaught of her emotions, Elena stared at the sorrowful visage in the wall-length mirror, breathed a weary sigh, then fell to her knees and wept.

CHAPTER 41

February 11, 1946

Jack raced through the riotous, fractured city, fishtailing through runnels of slush as he drove Tommy Duggan's battered old Buick across the river to Williamsburg, where he could tap the remnants of his and Kate's bank account and post the hundred-dollar bail bond needed to free his brother from jail.

It was nearly noon already, and Benny had been languishing since 7 a.m. in a dreary police stationhouse, where he was being detained in the aftermath of the fracas at Henry's docks. Hundreds of police officers had since been dispatched to the scenes of the savage confrontations between cops and striking tugboat workers. U.S. Army troops and National Guard units were being mobilized. Roadblocks limited waterfront access solely to medical personnel, soldiers, city officials, and police. Picketing anywhere within a four-block radius of New York Harbor was prohibited.

But far more than simply those developments had transpired in the past five hours. Equally apparent by now was that crisis enveloping the city had reached its breaking point. Henry's most egregious anti-union ploy—the summoning of strikebreakers—had proven a weight too heavy to bear.

Screening for the strikebreakers' qualifications, as was now evident, had been grossly mishandled by Otto Blackburn's labor-relations consultancy. While the replacement workforce was comprised of experienced, non-union tugboatmen, as Henry had requested, most of the strikebreakers, accustomed to Gulf Coast assignments, were woefully unfit to handle the unique demands of New York Harbor, with its narrow channels, swirling currents, and jutting shorelines.

The results had proven nothing short of disastrous. No sooner had strikebreaking tugboat crews departed Henry's docks than a string of mishaps began to unfold. In one instance, a tugboat towing a garbage scow failed to ease up as it approached a drawbridge, crashing into a concrete abutment and spilling tons of trash into the harbor. Shortly afterward, another McFarland vessel, pummeled by an unexpected tidal surge, ran aground at the Statue of Liberty. A third maneuvered out of sync with the rail barge it was towing, allowing the car float to snap its towline and run amok.

But even those mishaps, egregious as they were, weren't what brought the strike to a sudden, unforeseen head. Instead, as news spread about the violent skirmishes that had erupted that morning between striking workers and police, radio bulletins clogged the airwaves, and again newspaper extras hit the streets.

BLOODSHED ON NYC WATERFRONT!

POLICE WAGE WAR ON STRIKING TUGBOATMEN!

PROTESTS OVER STRIKEBREAKERS TURN VIOLENT!

Reaction to the news was both powerful and swift. For years, New York City police, under the bailiwick of Commissioner William Dunne, had garnered a reputation for brutality, ineptitude, and graft. This time, however, the police had gone too far. The men who Dunne's officers had wantonly attacked weren't anarchists or revolutionaries. Nor were they criminals. Instead, they'd been fellow New Yorkers, law-abiding strikers who had been brutally assaulted by rogue, on-duty cops for exercising their constitutional right to protest.

Most New Yorkers were outraged that city police, in tandem with private security guards and untrained, hastily-sworn-in deputies, had been used in effect as a mercenary arm for strikebreakers. City Hall was bombarded by charges of collusion between police and corporate interests. Union leaders, politicians, and pro-labor newspapers screamed bloody murder. The Gotham Harbor Alliance was excoriated by labor watchdogs. Police headquarters was besieged by demands for a federal probe and Dunne's immediate dismissal.

Then the dam really burst. For eleven contentious days, the city's other labor unions had held off from staging job actions in support of striking tugboat workers—waiting, like most New Yorkers, for a negotiated settlement or a government-imposed end to the strike. But their patience had finally run out; so had their reticence about joining the fracas. Within hours of the violent waterfront clashes, the city's unions had barged full bore into the tugboat dispute, flexing their muscle in a show of unanimity that transcended anything America had witnessed since the mass strikes of the nineteenth century.

Longshoremen, defying Paddy O'Boyle, were first to walk off the job, their wildcat strike spreading swiftly from waterfront locals to fifteen hundred miles of Atlantic coastline. Other unions quickly fell in line. Within an hour, Western Union employees were disrupting telegraph communications to the city and teamsters were turning away trucks at bridges and tunnels. Textile workers quickly joined the protest, shutting down the city's twenty-four-block Garment District in Manhattan. Meatpackers, warehousemen, taxi drivers, and healthcare workers soon followed suit. Elevator operators struck office towers and high-rise apartment buildings. Work halted at shipyards, factories, and construction sites. The entire city—already impacted by an idled harbor, a crippled economy, political gridlock, and a snowbound landscape—was soon in a full-throated roar, brought to a standstill by an avalanche of workers' protests.

Sensing the dramatic shift in momentum, the weight of public opinion shifting toward their side, strike leaders summoned tugboat workers to an impromptu rally in Times Square. By late morning, legions of blue-collar New Yorkers were joining in—marching, chanting, unfurling banners, waving American flags, and flooding midtown in a tidal wave of dissent. By noon, America's preeminent city had ground to a virtual halt. Motorized police patrols roamed the streets. Hundreds of soldiers manned checkpoints. City officials on sound trucks moved through throngs of protestors, desperately pleading for calm.

Worker protests of this magnitude had been witnessed in the past, although tied to radical political currents that hadn't existed for decades in America. The nation, it was thought, was beyond mass protests like this. But New York was fully immobilized now, gripped by a general strike, the closest a twentieth-century American city could come to a bona fide worker revolution.

* * *

While the morning's drama was spilling onto city streets, Benny, detained at a midtown police precinct, was in the dark about what was taking place.

"Thanks for bein' there for me, kid," he said, emerging from the jailhouse after Jack had posted bail. "I'll make good on the money you laid out. You got my word."

"Don't sweat it," Jack said. "It's the least I can do."

For Jack, the cost of his brother's bail bond stung far less than the gross injustice tied to Benny's arrest. Clearly Benny had done nothing to warrant his jailing, having served strictly as a peacemaker during the free-for-all. His alleged infractions—conspiring to riot, disturbing the peace, and resisting arrest—were nothing more than trumped-up charges brought at Henry's behest, as had been the brutal reception afforded Benny when he had arrived for booking. A cadre of cops in Henry's pocket had seen to that.

"What happened to you?" asked Jack, aghast when he bore witness to Benny's blood-splotched, swollen face.

Benny shrugged. "Welcome wagon at the jailhouse, is all."

"The cops roughed you up?"

"Nothin' to it." Benny snickered. "Fuckin' cops hit like little girls."

"That's beside the point!" Jack protested. "What those cops did to you is bullshit!"

"I appreciate the thought, kid," said Benny. "But no harm done. Let's just get our asses outta here . . . now."

Grudgingly, Jack acquiesced. Under a freshly fallen layer of snow, the entire city looked whitewashed and pristine, idyllic as a Christmas greeting card. There wasn't a hint of how sullied and fractured it had become.

"Bastards!" muttered Jack, still angry at the cops. "New York's Finest? Like hell they are!"

"They were just followin' orders," Benny said.

"Whose?"

"Same guy who pulls all the strings in this city."

"Henry McFarland?"

"You got it, kid!"

Jack recoiled. "His tentacles reach inside the NYPD, too?"

"All the way to the very top."

"Jeez!" Jack said. "Is everyone in New York sucking McFarland's tit?"

"Seems like it," Benny replied. "Politicians, judges, reporters, gangsters, cops—most of 'em are crooked, bought an' paid for. Money greases the wheel in this city, kid. An' McFarland's got enough of it to keep the wheel spinnin' for a very long time."

"Even when it comes to using city cops as a private strikebreaking army?"

"If that's what's needed . . . then yes."

Jack shook his head, embarrassed that he'd been blindsided by everything that was unfolding. All of it seemed so hopelessly out of whack—the entire system rigged, everyone in bed with someone else. Nothing, he thought, would ever shock him again. Not after witnessing the machinations of a high-stakes labor war.

"McFarland's comeuppance will come soon enough, though," Benny predicted. "Double-dealin' scumbags like him eventually come crashin' to earth."

It was only then that Jack remembered what he'd been waiting all morning to convey. Excitedly, he recounted the past few hours: how working-class New York had risen in protest of the actions of police; how organized labor had finally lent its muscle to the tugboat workers' cause; how a tidal wave of union protests and sympathy strikes was rocking the city to its very core.

"Holy shit!" Benny exclaimed. "This could be the break we've been waitin' for . . . could end the whole damned strike in our favor!"

Then, roaring with laughter, he planted a lusty wet kiss on Jack's forehead, and the two of them made a beeline for strike headquarters, where exultant union leaders were breaking out bottles of champagne and toasting a breakthrough that now seemed both imminent and favorable. Tugboat owners, in the meantime, were gathering in an emergency session at Gotham Harbor Alliance headquarters, attempting to put the final touches on an amended contract offer, including a wage hike close to what striking workers had been seeking all along. And Henry McFarland, brooding and short of breath, sat staring at an idle, fog-shrouded harbor, the walls of his office closing like a vise grip around his neck.

CHAPTER 42

February 11, 1946

There was but a single scheme remaining now in Henry's bag of tricks—one last-ditch ploy that could potentially save his crumbling tugboat empire and strike a crushing blow against the union.

He had nothing else. He had exhausted every other tactic he could muster in his vengeful crusade against the union. And what had his efforts yielded?

Nothing but failure, frustration, and heartache.

Eleven days into the strike, the prospects for Henry could not have been more dismal. Not only had every decision blown up in his face, but between his company's revenue losses and the dirty money he'd doled out, the tugboat strike had cost him a fortune, far more than if he'd capitulated from the get-go to the union's demands. And that was the most maddening thing of all.

Indeed, for Henry, money had always been the lingua franca of business, an instrument of manipulation, persuasion, and power. Money bought favors, forged alliances, and induced people to do Henry's bidding or blind themselves to his actions. But like everything else, his money had proven fruitless in impacting the trajectory of the tugboat strike. Influence could no longer be leveraged, power no longer asserted. Longtime alliances were crumbling. Public and private attacks hadn't made a difference. Deception and duplicity had proven equally futile. And not only had every one of Henry's union-busting tactics sputtered, but his most audacious ploy of all—the summoning of strikebreakers—had yielded the worst possible outcome: galvanizing a tidal wave of support for the very union he'd been trying so desperately to quash.

The entire city was up in arms now, rocked by pro-labor rallies, crippled by sympathy strikes. Support for Henry's hardline position had completely evaporated. Newspaper and business apologists were ducking him. Tugboat customers were bolting. Politicians were crawling up his ass, the city's breach-of-contract lawsuit on its way to court. Federal officials were poised to act, as well. With New York teetering on the brink of anarchy, the White House had issued a directive for the Defense Department to seize control of the city's tugboat fleet, and order the strike ended by 9 a.m. the following day.

Henry's effort to poison Local 88 from within had also fallen woefully short. Despite the lure of easy money, not enough of Paddy O'Boyle's confederates had crossed picket lines or otherwise disrupted the strike to make a difference. Fissures within the union, while substantive, hadn't opened widely enough to swallow Benny and his fellow militants. To the contrary, the union's rank and file, thanks largely to Benny's leadership, was holding firm. Unable to assemble coordinated crews, Henry couldn't operate enough of his tugboats to make a dent in the walkout. Even O'Boyle was backpedaling now. His reputation squarely on the line, the union boss had no choice but to swim with the tide. Hours earlier, he'd formally endorsed the mushrooming wave of sympathy strikes, abandoned his covert efforts to sabotage the work stoppage, and turned his back on Henry. Their decades-long business relationship was kaput.

So, for all intents and purposes, was Henry's professional standing. Suddenly, it was no longer union militants but Henry who was being viewed as irresponsible and irrational, Henry whose actions and motives were being challenged, Henry who'd become marginalized.

In the span of eleven days, "Mr. Big," overlord of New York Harbor, had become a pariah, the very symbol of callousness, arrogance, and corporate greed, his once-thunderous voice reduced to an inconsequential whimper. Power, the precious commodity Henry fought all his life to preserve, was all but gone. No longer was the former Gotham Harbor Alliance chairman a saintly presence, a shining star around whom others willingly orbited. No longer did he rule by fiat. No longer were colleagues paying homage, or worshipping at his feet, or permitting him to use his bully pulpit. Shorn of obeisance, stripped of political capital, he'd been cast adrift. Even his most ardent loyalists were cutting ties, seeing him as a cranky, out-of-touch relic, a crackpot marching on a path toward self-destruction.

And there was seemingly nothing that Henry could do about it, however he tried. With replacement workers wreaking havoc on his tugboats, insurance deductibles soaring, and indemnity providers barking louder by the minute,

Henry abandoned his strikebreaking efforts as quickly as they'd been mobilized. By mid-afternoon, McFarland tugboats were ordered returned to their docks and Gulf Coast tugboatmen sent packing, escorted by police through mobs of cheering strikers and bused from the city.

Henry also pulled his most valuable tugboats—*Jupiter* included—from the water, citing fears that the vessels were potential targets for union-inspired sabotage. One by one, they were secured under round-the-clock protection at the Eagle Dry Dock & Repair Company, a McFarland-owned maintenance facility near the Brooklyn Navy Yard. But even that seemed too little, too late.

A settlement to the strike, squarely in sight now, was beyond Henry's control, in the hands of Desmond Quinn, who was finally making headway in resolving the issues that had spurred the walkout. Indeed, substantive progress had been made during nightlong negotiations at City Hall. Both sides, led by Benny for the union and George Steele for the tugboat owners, were fully engaged now. Animosities had faded, differences narrowed. With Henry's impact receding, Mike Sturgis had also assumed a more prominent role in collective bargaining, the young owner more sympathetic to workers' grievances, more progressive and amenable to compromise—and, to Benny, far less distasteful.

Adding fuel to the negotiations, Jack had been able to pinpoint a series of cost-containment strategies for the owners to consider, freeing up previously unforeseen money that could be applied to union wage demands. Jack's math prowess had similarly enabled him to discover untapped revenue that could be converted into a one-time, prorated bonus for striking workers, blunting their demand for a higher raise. Indeed, Jack's numbers, along with corresponding ideas provided by Mike Sturgis, had already been forwarded to Desmond Quinn, who was busy crafting contract proposals based on constructive input from both sides. Negotiations were moving in a positive direction now. A spirit of conciliation had taken hold. Hours earlier, the union had dropped its charge that the owners were engaged in unfair-labor practices and agreed to binding arbitration by a panel led by Quinn. The owners, in reciprocity, had withdrawn their request that Taft-Hartley be invoked, agreeing to raise their current wage offer by one percent. Union leaders had countered by softening their wage demand in exchange for the promise of a one-time bonus and retroactive pay from the outset of the strike.

A breakthrough seemed imminent. And while his hated rival Benny was at the center of the negotiations, gaining in power and prestige, Henry was miles away, ensconced in his Sands Point estate. Impotent. Floundering. Alone.

Doubtless, Henry would be forced to swallow a deal he'd resisted for months. Benny Logan and other union activists would be around to haunt him for as long as he remained in business. Local 88 would act with impunity, issuing whatever threats it deemed appropriate. The union would not just survive; it would also prevail. And Henry would be further isolated, discredited, disgraced. All the years he'd spent building his corporate empire, rising to the pinnacle of the business world—all that would be flushed away, his reputation ruined, his legacy tarnished, his image destroyed.

The goddamned, fucking union! he thought.

Imprisoned inside his mansion—exhausted, under siege, fearful of venturing anywhere near the harbor he'd ruled for decades—he fixed himself a Manhattan, lit a cigarette, and wandered the corridors of what had once been his pride and joy, its emptiness now a reflection of his very existence: a deep, dark cavern absent of reason, a lonely port of call bordering on madness. In losing control over the strike that he'd masterminded, he'd lost his grip on his sanity as well. He imagined people laughing at him, deriding him, disobeying his every command; imagined himself as a funhouse caricature, his nose pimpled, his chin drooping, his body crooked and bent. His breath came in shallow, labored gasps. His chest felt as if it was being stood on by an elephant. His mind bubbled and churned as he groped for some way, any possible way, to turn the tide.

That's when the idea struck him. Like a bolt from the blue.

No, he thought at first. *I can't do that!*

No rational person would conceive of resorting to a scheme like the one that had suddenly thrust itself upon him. Somewhere in the recesses of his mind, he knew the idea was misguided, deranged. And surely criminal.

And yet . . . he couldn't help himself.

Irrational or not, misguided or not, illegal or not, Henry was irresistibly drawn to the gambit. Reflexively, he picked up the phone to call the only source of support who might conceivably still be on his side, a trusted ally who spoke Henry's language, and whose loyalty could always be purchased.

"I need you to arrange something for me," Henry said.

And Otto Blackburn replied, half-jokingly: "I'm all out of labor spies. And God knows, out of strikebreakers, too."

"And I'm running out of tugboats, thanks to the bumbling imbeciles you charged me a goddamned fortune for!" Henry raged.

Blackburn's response—a long, uneasy silence—made it clear that he didn't find the retort funny. Henry didn't care. He hadn't meant it as a joke.

"I'm talking about something different this time," said Henry, calmer now. He couldn't afford to lose Blackburn, too. No one else was there to lean on.

"I'm not sure, at this point, what kind of services I can provide," Blackburn said.

"Just hear me out," Henry urged.

He then divulged the plot he had in mind.

Blackburn, once again, was rendered mute. Even after all his years in the union-busting business, all the nasty anti-labor gambits he'd employed, he seemed rattled by Henry's idea.

"That's, um . . . a special job," Blackburn stammered. "Beyond the scope of what my company usually provides."

"Understood," Henry said. "But can it be arranged?"

"I suppose so. But—"

"But what?"

"It'll require me to use people who aren't on my payroll. And it'll cost you through the nose."

"What kind of money am I looking at?" Henry inquired.

"Twenty grand . . . minimum."

Henry didn't consider the cost unreasonable. He was prepared to pay even more. And quickly enough, Blackburn requested the additional compensation, though in another form.

"The twenty grand," he said, "would simply be your cost in dollars and cents. The total price tag would be higher."

Even in his desperate state, Henry couldn't help but smile. He'd anticipated a response like that from a savvy operative like Blackburn—someone, like Henry, who knew how to employ leverage, angle for a better deal.

"What additional costs are you talking about?" Henry asked.

"What I'd like," Blackburn said, "is an ironclad pledge."

"Keep talking."

"My company," Blackburn said, "is primarily an insurance carrier—remember?"

"I'd almost forgotten," Henry said snidely. "But please proceed."

"And you own an entire fleet of tugboats, correct?"

"More than a hundred in all."

"And all those tugboats require insurance coverage, do they not?"

"They do." Henry chuckled, sensing where the conversation was headed.

"Okay," Blackburn said. "Then the pledge I'm seeking is that, should we be successful in what you've proposed, McFarland Marine Towing will transfer all of its insurance coverage to my firm . . . instead of spreading it around, like now, to different companies."

"The two of us exclusive partners, huh?" Henry said.

"Now and forever."

For the first time in days, Henry laughed.

"Sounds like a pretty lucrative deal you're angling for," he said.

And indeed, it was. The agreement Blackburn was proposing would potentially put millions of dollars in his pocket. But Henry didn't care. He'd be paying sky-high premiums to insurance providers for as long as his company remained in business. It might as well be Blackburn's firm who reaped the rewards. Especially since Henry, in exchange, would be receiving a service no other insurance carrier could provide. No legitimate one, anyway.

"Your terms are acceptable," Henry said. "We have a deal."

Henry could envision Blackburn struggling to contain his ebullience. Then, as if his curiosity was gnawing at him, the labor consultant asked: "Are you certain you want to go through with this?"

"I am."

"But that's a valuable asset that we're talking about . . . is it not?"

"Worth north of a million bucks."

"A lot to sacrifice in the interests of your 'crusade' . . . wouldn't you say?"

"It's my asset," Henry said. "And my money."

"Of course. But—"

"Don't worry," Henry said. "The insurance policy is handled by another carrier."

"Well, that's a relief." Blackburn exhaled. "I wouldn't like getting hammered for the payout on the loss."

"It won't impact your company in the least," Henry said.

"But still," said Blackburn, "doesn't the asset have, uh . . . sentimental value?"

"It certainly does."

"And you're willing to sacrifice that, as well?"

"I am."

Then, as if to justify his response, Henry said: "Those union fuckers drove me to do this. I've worked too hard to let them walk away from our battle without at least a black eye."

"Well, what we've agreed to," Blackburn said, "should certainly achieve that goal."

Henry felt reassured. "So, we can move ahead with the arrangements?"

"Absolutely. How soon do you want it done?"

"Is tonight possible?"

"I don't see why not. Is midnight a good time?"

"Perfect."

"Then I'll make the necessary arrangements," Blackburn pledged.

"And none of what we've discussed," Henry asked, "can be traced back to me?"

"Or to me," Blackburn said. "The people we'll be dealing with on this are willing to assume the risks. That's the way they stay in business."

"And the blame—?"

"Will be pinned squarely on the people you want to target. There'll be no logical conclusion other than that they were the culprits," Blackburn said. "Who else would have done such a thing? Certainly not you!"

Henry was more than pleased. "This will really hurt those bastards, won't it?" he asked.

"I can't see how it won't," Blackburn said.

"Good," Henry said. "Because if I'm going to lose this strike, and possibly everything else I value, you can be damn sure I'm going to take those bastards down with me . . . or drop dead trying."

Chapter 43

February 11, 1946

The report was discovered by chance. Enclosed in an envelope marked for union leaders' attention, its contents were presumably routine: the summary of strike-fund disbursements that Tommy Duggan prepared each day.

What Duggan had left atop his desk, however, was hardly routine. Local 88's recording secretary, as it instantly became clear, had made an egregious and damning blunder. Bleary-eyed from a succession of grueling, eighteen-hour workdays, Duggan had unwittingly left the wrong report atop his desk: one he'd prepared that day for the union—and one he'd clearly intended for another set of eyes.

Certainly not Benny's.

"What the fuck is this?" Benny recoiled as he leafed through Duggan's report. For several seconds, he stood silent, immobile. It was shortly after 11 p.m. Strike headquarters had been emptied for the night, except for Benny and Jack.

"I don't believe what I'm seein'!" Benny was glassy-eyed, drained of color. "Please tell me this ain't what I think it is!"

Benny handed the report to Jack, who eyeballed the document—and suddenly felt weak in the knees.

The report Duggan had left behind wasn't the anticipated strike-fund summary at all; it was instead a summary of the latest union leaders' strategy meeting, along with a detailed accounting of Local 88's strike-fund balance, and a commentary about the tug-of-war between Benny and Paddy O'Boyle for control of the union.

"For Chrissakes!" Benny exclaimed. "Not Tommy!"

Only once before, on the day that Gabriel drowned, had Jack seen his brother look the way he did then: his face so knotted in disbelief and pain.

Then his anger kicked in.

"That two-faced sonofabitch!" Benny fumed. "Tommy Duggan's a spy, a fuckin' stoolie who's been workin' for the other side . . . sellin' his union brothers out!"

New York's waterfront had forever been a hotbed of indigenous conflict, rife with rivalries, infighting, deception, and duplicity. Railroads, utilities, tugboat firms, shipping companies, labor unions—all were perpetually at odds with one another, adversaries in an endless struggle for money and power. Benny was keenly aware of that. The waterfront was a cesspool of shadow and deceit, a fetid swampland of schemers and scoundrels, weasels and turncoats. You never could be sure who you could rely on, or who would betray you— never knew when a trap might be sprung or what form it might take. All along, Benny knew he'd have to keep his eyes and ears open, his antenna tuned. All along, he'd believed he could smell a rat. Yet never would he have suspected Tommy Duggan of sticking a knife in his back. Never in a million years.

Not Tommy!

Tommy Duggan was nothing less than a pillar of strength in New York's tugboat workers' union, tried-and-true, a gung-ho, deeply committed lifer: eighteen years in the tugboat trade, half a dozen as a union official. In the trenches day in and day out. Standing shoulder to shoulder with Benny. Fighting the good fight.

Even more than that, Tommy was a friend, as much a brother to Benny as Jack. Tommy and Benny shared the same blue-collar pedigree: poor boys who'd come of age on the streets of New York, scrounged their entire lives for a buck, and found their purpose in a union they lived and died for. They'd been bound at the hip in other ways, too: played in the same poker game every Friday night; bowled in the same league; went to Dodgers' games at Ebbets Field and the Polo Grounds, the racetracks at Aqueduct and Belmont Park, the prizefights at Sunnyside and Madison Square Garden. Even their families were close, having vacationed together at Tommy's Pocono Mountains cottage, where Benny's wife and daughters were being billeted at this very moment.

But now, in the blink of an eye, that longtime bond had been obliterated. Benny's trusted wingman, his closest friend, was one of the two spies planted by Otto Blackburn inside Local 88. All along, he'd been leaking confidential union intelligence to Henry McFarland, betraying the brotherhood for a price.

"Wait till I get my hands on that no-good sonofabitch!" Benny paced union headquarters like a caged tiger. "I'm gonna tear his goddamned head off!"

But no sooner had Benny mouthed those words than a frantic, unsuspecting Duggan bolted through the front door.

"We gotta talk, Benny!" Duggan wheezed. "Now!"

"Goddamned right we do!"

Menacingly, Benny closed in. Duggan, befuddled, backpedaled.

"Something big is goin' down tonight!" Duggan sputtered. "Somethin' you gotta know about!"

Benny's response was both savage and swift. A guttural grunt rising from deep in his throat, he reared back and coldcocked Duggan flush on the jaw, sending Tommy reeling.

"You sonofabitch!" Benny raged. "I ought to wring your goddamned neck!"

"What are ya talkin' about?" replied Duggan, feigning innocence. "What did I do?"

But the pretense rang hollow. Duggan knew exactly what had sparked Benny's rage. Instantly, his body shriveled, his face going flaccid and flushed.

Benny hit him again, the savage blow landing on Duggan's temple. Staggering, Duggan tried to backpedal. But Benny was all over him, his fury fully unleashed as he pummeled Duggan with a volley of crisp, powerful punches, knocking him head over heels.

"I'll break your goddamned neck, Tommy!" Benny grunted. "I'll fuckin' kill ya!"

Then, like a torrential downpour running its course, the vicious assault subsided. Pulling back, Benny slunk away as Duggan lay writhing on the floor, his nose and lips oozing blood.

"Get this rat bastard on his feet," Benny told Jack. "Let's find out what he's been up to."

Jack helped Duggan steady himself, easing him into a chair and handing him a handkerchief.

"How long has this spyin' been goin' on?" asked Benny, waving the incriminating report in Duggan's face.

"A while," Duggan whimpered, handkerchief pressed to his nose.

"Don't fuck with me!" Benny warned. "How long is 'a while'?"

Duggan listed like a foundering ship. "Coupla years."

"Years?"

"Uh-huh."

Benny turned to Jack. "All of it makes sense now."

Jack shook his head, still in the dark.

"For the longest time," Benny said, "Henry McFarland seemed a step ahead of the union, like he was a fuckin' mind reader. Everyone knew he had Paddy O'Boyle in his pocket, feedin' him inside dope. But I always suspected there was more to it than that."

Benny glared at Duggan, Tommy's eyes glazed, his jaw swollen and misshapen.

"McFarland's a crafty sonofabitch, I'll give him that—but no one's that smart," Benny said. "For all the time we've been negotiatin' with him, it always seemed like he was aware of things that should've been confidential. I knew there had to be a canary inside our local, leakin' private dope. We even talked about it—wracked our brains tryin' to figure out who it might be. But I didn't have a clue . . . not till now anyway!"

Glaring at Duggan, Benny balled a fist, but quickly pulled back. Duggan had gotten his message, loud and clear. Besides, Benny was interested more in information than in retribution now.

"So, how did ya land your spyin' gig, Tommy?" he inquired.

"Through someone at the waterfront," Duggan mumbled.

"Who?"

"Some mob goon. I'd never seen him before that. Never seen him since."

"An' this goombah . . . he just approached you one day?"

"Uh-huh."

"Who does he work for?"

"Dunno."

"So whose payroll are you on?"

"Dunno that, either. That's the God's honest truth, Benny. I got paid . . . an' didn't ask questions."

"Course not," Benny growled. "Long as your pocket got lined."

Duggan looked away sheepishly.

"An' what did ya do for the money?" Benny probed.

"Wrote reports," Duggan said.

"What kind of reports?"

"Reports about what the union was up to—strike-fund balances, sign-in sheets, negotiating tactics . . . shit like that. Sometimes I just dropped a copy of our meeting minutes in an envelope an' mailed it."

"An' how often did you write these reports?" Benny asked.

"Once a week," Duggan replied. "More often once the strike got underway."

"An' you mailed 'em . . . where?"

"To a blind P.O. box."

"That was it?"

"No one ever asked for more."

Duggan, head bowed, seemed genuinely contrite.

"I swear on the lives of my kids." He raised a palm. "That's all I ever did."

"That's *all*?" Benny recoiled. "As if that ain't enough?"

"I mean, I could've done more," Duggan said, "but I didn't. I never disrupted a meeting or a picket line. Never spread discord in the ranks. Always worked my ass off for the rank an' file."

"You worked for us?" Benny slapped Duggan hard across his cheek. "Is that what you think you did, Tommy? All this time you were stabbin' your brother union members in the back . . . an' you call that workin' for us?"

Duggan, quivering, dabbed at a bloody lip with Jack's handkerchief.

"When it started," he said, "it didn't seem like such a big deal."

"Really?" Benny glowered at him.

"What I mean," said Duggan, "is that it seemed inconsequential in light of all that was goin' on. File a report every week? So what? There was nothing at stake. Our union already had a contract. Everyone was focused on the war. I thought what I was doin' was harmless . . . never thought it would reach a point where it might hurt our union. You've gotta believe me, Benny. Underminin' our men was never my intent!"

Benny shook his head, seeming dispirited, on the precipice of despair. Jack felt his brother's pain, the price he paid for his integrity, his commitment, his passion. More than ever, Jack wanted to see Benny vindicated—win not simply a favorable labor contract but a measure of satisfaction, absolution, and peace.

"I can't believe you did this, Tommy!" Benny trained his eyes on Duggan. "How could you throw your fellow union members under the bus like that? How could you do it to me?"

Duggan shrunk in his chair.

"Why do ya think I did it?" he said. "Same reason anyone would: family to support, sky-high debt, bills to pay."

"So you needed money?" Benny grimaced. "Well, how 'bout earnin' an honest buck, Tommy? Ever think of that? Hell, you could've swept sidewalks if you needed dough that bad!"

"What can I say?" Duggan sighed. "I got in over my head."

"How?"

"String of rotten luck with the ponies."

"So, you owed the turf accountants?" Benny asked. "Couldn't pay the bookies their goddamned vig?"

"Uh-huh."

"Then what?"

"They had me by the shorthairs."

"So they offered you the spyin' gig, as a way of gettin' out from under your debt?"

"That's about the size of it."

"But Tommy," Jack inquired, "why would the mob want to submarine our union?"

"Probably 'cause there's money in it," Duggan replied.

"Money? From what source?"

"My guess? The same guy who always greases the wheel at the waterfront."

Duggan was right. Mob-connected operatives, seduced by Henry's bribes, had helped Otto Blackburn recruit the two spies he'd planted in the union.

"How many snoops are involved in this?" Benny asked.

"Supposedly two," Duggan replied.

"Who's the other one?"

"Damned if I know. Neither one knows who the other guy is."

Duggan lowered his head contritely.

"You gotta believe me, Benny." He sniffled. "I was caught between a rock an' a hard place."

"An' the money?" Benny asked derisively. "How much were you pocketin'?"

"Fifty bucks a week," said Duggan. "Just enough to keep the wolves from the door."

Benny shook his head sadly. "Didn't what you were doin' eat at ya, Tommy?"

"Course it did!" Duggan's voice was quavering now. "You got any idea how many times I wanted to give the whole thing up?"

"Why didn't ya?"

"They squeezed my nuts, Benny . . . tol' me that if I stopped they'd rat me out to the rank an' file. Keepin' at it was the only way I could keep from gettin' whacked by our own men."

"I oughta whack you myself," Benny said. "But I'll spare you the wrath of our men, Tommy. We'll keep what happened 'tween the three of us."

Jack nodded in assent. Duggan exhaled in relief.

"But consider yourself finished in the tugboat trade, Tommy!" Benny said. "You're finished in the union! Finished on the waterfront! Finished as my friend!"

"An' all the work I put in?" Duggan stammered. "All the hours I spent bustin' my nuts for our union? All that means nothin'?"

"Not after this!"

"An' how about what I was rushin' in here to tell ya, Benny? Remember that? Remember how I was comin' here to see you . . . sayin' that we needed to talk, that there was somethin' big that I caught wind of, somethin' you needed to know about right away?"

"What about it?" Benny asked. "What's so 'big,' Tommy, that you were comin' to see me in such a rush?"

"It's somethin'," said Duggan, "that could sink our union."

"What are you tellin me?"

"First, I need a drink." Duggan reached inside a desk drawer and removed a silver flask. "What I'm about to tell you, Benny, could land me in a grave."

Duggan took a swig of whiskey. Then he divulged what he had learned was planned for that night. Benny nearly keeled over. Jack as well.

"I'm done lyin'," Duggan swore. "What I'm tellin' you now is the God's honest truth."

"When did you hear about this?" Benny asked.

"Coupla minutes before I ran here to tell ya."

"Who tol' you?"

"Buddy of mine."

"An' why would this so-called 'buddy' tell you?"

"Who knows?" Duggan shrugged. "Maybe he doesn't want to see people get hurt. Maybe he feels that the labor war we've been wagin' has spiraled outta control."

Duggan pulled on his flask. And both Benny and Jack stared at one another, trying to wrap their heads around the fiendish plot that Duggan had divulged—and devise a way to quash the plot before it accomplished what Duggan warned it could: bring the tugboat workers' union to its knees, if not destroy it entirely.

CHAPTER 44

February 12, 1946

Tommy Duggan sat slumped in the shadowy half-light of strike headquarters, draining his hip flask. The plot that he had divulged was fully in motion by now, the seconds to midnight ticking like a time bomb.

"Spill your guts!" Benny commanded. "Give it to us again! Every sordid detail!"

Duggan, wincing, dabbed at his brow with Jack's handkerchief, his face bloody and misshapen from the beating he'd endured at Benny's hand.

"It's about one of Henry McFarland's tugboats," Duggan said. "The one called 'Queen of the Harbor.'"

"*Jupiter*?" Jack recoiled.

"That's her."

"What about her?"

"They're gonna blow her up . . . sink her."

Benny's jaw went slack. Jack felt sick to his stomach. Duggan had conveyed his story twice already, but still the brothers had trouble believing it. The plot was that far-fetched, that devious.

"I'm tellin' ya how I heard it," Duggan said. "Bunch of saboteurs have been paid to board *Jupiter* at midnight, plant dynamite in her wheelhouse . . . an' blow her to Kingdom Come."

Benny stared out incredulously. Jack felt as if he had been kicked in the gut.

"These saboteurs?" Benny inquired. "Who are they?"

"Damned if know," Duggan said. "Mob goons, I'd guess."

"What about union members?"

"That, I don't know."

"Is it possible?"

"I suppose. Anything is possible when there's money involved."

Benny swallowed hard. "Who do you suspect is behind this?"

"Haven't a clue," Duggan replied. "Got my suspicions, though."

"Who?"

"You'd never be able to pin it on him, but it wouldn't surprise me if it was none other than 'Mr. Big."

"McFarland?" Jack blanched. "Doesn't make sense. Why would McFarland destroy a million-dollar asset . . . the most prestigious tugboat in the city's fleet?"

"Because the desperate bastard knows he's goin' down," Benny asserted. "He knows he's losin' the strike . . . an' a whole lot more."

"Bingo!" Duggan nodded. "McFarland realizes he's fucked. He'd sacrifice his most-valuable tugboat, though, to achieve his real end game."

"You think McFarland would destroy *Jupiter* in order to pin the blame on the union?" Jack asked, in shock.

"That's exactly the plan," Duggan said. "McFarland has become desperate, unhinged. He knows he's goin' down . . . an' he's hellbent on taking the union down with him."

"His insurance will cover *Jupiter*'s loss," Benny surmised. "Knowing that scheming prick, he'll probably even make money on the payout."

"You're right," Duggan agreed. "*Jupiter* means nothin' to McFarland in the larger scheme of things. He owns a hundred or more tugboats. He'll sacrifice his most-prized vessel, but his other tugboats will pick up the slack. His company won't skip a beat."

"In the meantime," Benny said, "he'll lay the act of sabotage at the union's feet . . . claim that we destroyed *Jupiter* in retaliation for him bringin' in scabs to quash our strike."

"An eye for an eye," Duggan said. "He'll charge that the destruction of his most-prized tugboat was an act of revenge by our union. The whole thing'll sound perfectly plausible."

"McFarland will turn public opinion against our union," Benny added. "He'll discredit us . . . say that we're common criminals who've gotta be quashed."

"But how could McFarland prove our union was responsible?" Jack asked.

"He won't have to," Duggan replied. "All he'll have to do is lodge the accusation. If the saboteurs succeed, no one will ever know who really did the deed. The union will have to prove it wasn't us. We'll never be able to do that, or prove it was McFarland. The truth won't seem plausible. Any way you slice it, we end up losers."

"It's McFarland's last chance to bust the union," Benny said. "That was always his goal, right from the start."

Jack shook his head, staggered by the scope of the plot. There really were no holds barred in labor wars like this, he thought. Not when desperate men were out for blood.

Benny turned to Duggan. "When did you say the sabotage is supposed to take place?"

"Midnight."

The men glanced at a wall clock. Already, it was 11:30 p.m.

"That's why I was haulin' ass to tell ya," Duggan said. "Ain't much time left."

Thirty minutes. That's all they had.

"I may've done things that I'll always regret," Duggan told Benny. "But I had to give you a heads-up about this . . . soon as I found out."

Benny nodded, seeming grateful that, even with Duggan's betrayal, at least one bridge between the two friends hadn't been burned.

"Where's *Jupiter* now?" Benny looked at Jack.

"Henry McFarland pulled her from the water as a supposed precaution against union sabotage," Jack said. "She's at the Eagle Dry Dock, in Red Hook."

"Now it all adds up," Benny said. "A McFarland-owned dock. Easy access to *Jupiter*. Hire a few goombahs to blow the tugboat up, while the sentries look the other way. Then point to our union members as the culprits."

The trio grew silent, pondering the implications of Henry's scheme.

"The destruction of *Jupiter* could blow our union to smithereens," Duggan said. "There's no doubt the public will buy McFarland's charge of sabotage. People will never believe that our men weren't involved. We'll be branded as a gang of lawless thugs."

"Unless," said Benny, "we stop it from happenin'!"

"But how?"

"Leave that to me," Benny said. "I gotta get to that dock."

"No way, Benny!" Jack protested. "It's far too dangerous!"

"I've dealt with dangerous shit all my life," Benny said. "This is nothin' new."

"Maybe not," said Jack. "But the people involved in this aren't in it for shits and giggles. They'll be desperate, armed, ready for anything."

"Jack's right," Duggan warned. "No way can you go anywhere near that dock, Benny."

"Yeah? Well, who else is gonna stop this thing?"

"How about the police?" Jack said.

"The police?" Benny scoffed. "You shittin' me? After the way they manhandled our men at Henry McFarland's docks? Threw me in the slammer? Roughed me up? Uh-uh. No way can we trust the cops. Half of 'em are on McFarland's payroll. Who knows what they'll do?"

Benny turned to Duggan. "Tommy, you said there might be union members in on this plot, didn't you?"

"I said it's possible," Duggan said.

"Well, even if there's a chance that union members are involved, the union's gotta be the one to stop it," Benny reasoned. "That's the only way we won't be held responsible."

"But if you go anywhere near that dock, Benny," Jack said, "you're either gonna get implicated in the scheme, get hurt, or maybe even get killed . . . along with other men, too."

"Then that's a risk I've got to take," Benny said. "'An' there's no time to fuck around. I gotta see if there's some men I can round up, to help me head this thing off!"

He moved toward a telephone, but Jack cut him off.

"If you go anywhere tonight, Benny," Jack said, "I'm going with you!"

"The hell you are, kid," Benny scoffed.

"Why not? Someone's got to have your back."

"Well, I don't want that to be you," Benny said. "There's no way I'm lettin' you near that dock. I already lost one brother on my watch. I'll be damned if I'm gonna lose another."

With that, Benny brushed past Jack, entered strike headquarters' private office, and slammed the door behind him. Within seconds he was on the telephone, calling in the cavalry, ready to go to war, while Jack stood in his wake, unsure what to do or how to do it.

CHAPTER 45

February 11, 1946

Jack pondered the dilemma from every conceivable angle, groping for a course of action he could piece together on the fly, anything he could think of to alter the current chain of events.

By now, Henry's last-ditch plot to cripple the tugboat workers' union was unfolding precisely as planned. Otto Blackburn's gang of saboteurs were en route to the Eagle Dry Dock Company, bent on destroying *Jupiter* and pinning the blame on organized labor. Benny was still on the phone, frantically attempting to rally a posse to thwart the sabotage. Men on both sides of the budding confrontation were likely to get injured, perhaps killed. *Jupiter*, a tugboat treasured by Jack, was earmarked for destruction, Local 88's rank and file similarly imperiled. And Jack, like so many times throughout his life, was being drawn unwillingly into the vortex, just as he'd been drawn into his family's dissolution, into World War II, and into the nation's most bitter labor conflict—all while wrestling with feelings of entrapment, helplessness, and a fate he couldn't possibly alter.

But maybe tonight could be different, Jack thought. Maybe, for once, it could be he—not destiny or the actions of others—who could shape the course of events. Maybe tonight he could be more than simply a hapless bystander, a victim of circumstances careening out of control. Maybe tonight he could determine his own fate.

He didn't have much time, however. Already, the clock read 11:40 p.m. In roughly twenty minutes, if Tommy Duggan had his story straight, *Jupiter* would be dynamited into oblivion, Benny and his partisans exposed to mortal peril, and the tugboat workers' union irreparably harmed.

Quickly, Jack pulled Duggan aside. Benny, still on the phone, was out of earshot.

"We can't allow a faceoff at that dock," Jack said. "It's way too dangerous."

"Benny knows only one way to handle things," Duggan demurred. "Fight fire with fire."

"Then the two of us will have to go around him."

"How will we manage that?"

By now, Jack had stitched together the semblance of a plan. Something at least worth trying.

"I've got some phone calls to make," he told Duggan. "I need you to make some calls, too. But not here. I don't want Benny catching wind of what we're up to."

"There's a phone booth right outside," said Duggan, desperate to make amends for his spying. "Who do you want me to call?"

Jack detailed the plan he'd cobbled together. Duggan nodded and made a beeline out the door. Jack then placed the first of two calls.

"What's cookin', matey?" Shorty Long chirped on the other end of the line.

"The union's facing a life-and-death crisis," Jack said. "I need your help!"

"Just say the word," Shorty said. "Whatever you need, you got!"

Jack explained the situation quickly and then asked, "Think you can handle what I'm asking?"

"Bank on it!" Shorty pledged.

Jack then placed the second of his calls.

Two rings later, a dispatcher at NYPD headquarters picked up the phone, identifying himself as a Sgt. Timothy Rattigan. Jack informed the sergeant that he needed immediate police assistance, and why.

"Uh-huh," Rattigan replied nonchalantly. "An' exactly who's callin'?"

Rattigan's voice dripped with cynicism, a burnt-out, callous disregard. Jack envisioned the sergeant at his switchboard at the butt-end of another tedious shift, bleary-eyed and anxious to hit the sack.

"Who I am doesn't matter," Jack said. "What does matter, though, is what's gonna happen in about twenty minutes."

"An' what did you say that was?"

Jack tried to remain measured in his tone. "As I've already informed you, a group of armed saboteurs will attempt to board a tugboat named *Jupiter*. They intend to plant dynamite on the tugboat and blow it up."

"An' why would they do that?" Rattigan asked, dubiously.

"So the blame can be pinned on the tugboat workers' union."

"And?"

"And the union's reputation and credibility would be destroyed."

"I see," said Rattigan, playing cat and mouse. "An' exactly who are these alleged saboteurs?"

"Men hired by people with anti-union interests in the tugboat strike."

"An' how do you know all this?"

"Trust me . . . I know."

"An' how do I know this ain't a prank call?" Rattigan sighed. "We get a lot of them these days, now that everyone in the city's got a phone."

"Then I'll put it another way," Jack said. "I'm a member of the tugboat workers' union that's been on strike for the past eleven days. My information comes from a reliable source. I assure you, sergeant . . . this is no prank! What I'm telling you is about to happen!"

Sgt. Rattigan began to reply.

"I can also assure you," Jack interrupted, "that if the tugboat I'm talking about is destroyed, the newspapers are going to want to know why a Sgt. Timothy Rattigan, half-asleep at the switchboard, disregarded a credible warning just so he wouldn't have to be troubled before clocking out for the night. And I'll be more than happy to tell them how you failed to do your job. Catch my drift?"

Rattigan went mute.

"Furthermore," Jack said, "I think the NYPD has gotten enough of a black eye from the way its officers have handled themselves with respect to the strike. Wouldn't you agree?"

Once again, silence.

"I'd say the public is pretty pissed-off over the way 'New York's Finest' roughed up tugboat workers while acting in cahoots with strikebreakers," Jack said. "The entire city is in an uproar . . . or haven't you noticed?

"It'll make a hell of a story when I inform the newspapers that the police knowingly allowed the destruction of the city's most prestigious tugboat—and a potentially deadly flareup between strikers and saboteurs. The press corps will have a field day with that! So will the politicians and the top brass! I see City Hall clamoring for an investigation, and just looking for some poor schnook to point to as a scapegoat. The NYPD will have another black eye . . . and you'll be the schnook they'll be looking to hang!"

"Okay," Rattigan finally relented. "When did you say all this is gonna happen?"

"Midnight."

"An' where?"

"The Eagle Dry Dock & Repair Company. In Red Hook."

"Okay," Rattigan yielded. "I'll have a squad car sent there."

"Better make it more than one! Half a dozen at least. And get 'em there fast, Sergeant." Jack said. "Your ass is on the line here!"

He hung up the phone and waited—though not for long. Within minutes, Shorty Long, Dutch Hendrik, Mack Nowak, and Luke Huggins barged through the front door to strike headquarters.

"Thanks for answering my call," Jack said.

"Thanks for callin' us," Shorty said. "I'd tear someone's head off before lettin' them do anything to destroy *Jupiter!*"

"No way we're gonna let that happen!" Dutch Hendrik chimed in.

"Well with any luck, it won't," Jack said. "If things play out like I've planned, *Jupiter*—and a lot of people—will survive the night. So will our union."

"You're callin' the shots, Professor," Shorty said. "Whatever you say goes."

Just then, Tommy Duggan rushed back in, flashing a thumbs-up, a sign that he'd made the phone calls Jack had requested. Seconds later, finished with his own calls, Benny emerged, Louisville Slugger in hand. Leaving strike headquarters wouldn't be so easy, however. Not with *Jupiter*'s crew blocking his path.

"Well, what've we got here?" Benny cocked his head defiantly.

"Men who've come to babysit you," Jack replied.

"An' who decided I needed that?"

"I did."

Benny, eyebrows raised, glared at the human wall before him.

"Is this some kinda fuckin' joke?"

"It's no joke, Benny," Dutch Hendrik replied.

"Well, that's a relief!" Benny's words were laced with sarcasm. "'Cause I ain't in the mood for laughs. Don't you guys know what's about to happen . . . what I'm tryin' to stop?"

"We're fully aware," said Jack. "We're here because we have a vested interest in *Jupiter*, as her crew. And I have a vested interest in you . . . as your brother."

Benny's face hardened like stone. "What does that mean?"

"What it means," said Dutch, "is that we're not gonna let anything happen to either you or to *Jupiter*. Like it or not, Benny, this is one fight you're gonna have to sit out."

"An' the shit that's goin' down at midnight?"

"That's being handled," Jack said.

"How?"

"Let's just say that when the saboteurs arrive at Henry McFarland's dry dock, they'll get a surprise greeting . . . from the cops."

"You brought the cops into this?" Benny recoiled. "After everything those scumbags have done to submarine our union?"

"My guess," Jack said, "is that they'll handle tonight differently."

"Like hell they will!" Benny snarled. "Fuck the cops! This is union business!"

"We see it differently," Shorty Long said.

Benny hesitated, as if trying to decide whether to back off or force his way through the wall of humanity blocking his path.

"Look, Benny," Dutch reasoned, "we're grateful as hell for how you've been busting your ass for the union. Win or lose this strike, we owe you for that. But you don't need to get yourself killed. There are saner ways to handle this situation."

"You fuckers don't have a clue how to handle this," Benny protested. "I've called in an army of guys ready to handle things our way. Fifty men are on their way to Red Hook while you clowns are standin' around jerkin' yourselves off."

"That's been handled, too." Jack nodded at Duggan. "Tommy has been placing phone calls of his own, spreading the word for union members to steer clear of Red Hook—regardless of what you might have said. The message has been passed through the ranks."

"This is bullshit!" Benny lurched forward. "I'm gettin' to that dry dock! It'll take more than you guys to stop me!"

That's when Big Mack Nowak—all six-foot-seven, two-hundred-and-sixty pounds of rock-hard muscle—stepped to the fore.

"I know you're a tough guy, Benny, a great fighter in your day." Nowak pointed to his jaw. "Go ahead . . . give it your best shot!"

Arms tensed, eyes bulging, Benny rose to his full height, the crown of his head level with Nowak's chest. Then just as abruptly, he backed away. Getting through Nowak, he knew, would be like moving a mountain. Even Benny, feisty as he was, saw the futility in that.

"You bastards!" he growled. "I'll have your fuckin' jobs for this!"

"We'll take our chances," Dutch Hendrik said.

It was a safe bet. No one was going to fire a skilled tugboat captain like Dutch—or any of *Jupiter*'s crew, for that matter. Benny knew his threat was empty. They all did. And now all five men inched forward, nudging Benny backward into the office, then closing the door behind them.

"This is where we're gonna pass the time," Jack said. "Anyone got a deck of cards?"

Benny didn't find the humor in that. "How long do you clowns plan on keepin' me on ice?" he snarled.

"For however long it takes," Jack replied.

"With me as a prisoner?"

"If that's the way you want to look at it."

"How else you want me to look at it?"

"As if we're trying to keep you from a world of hurt."

Benny cocked his head, eyeballing his brother. "Why're ya doin' this to me, kid?"

Jack smiled. "Let's just say I'm following the guidance you've always given me."

"An' what's that?"

"It's that brothers take care of one another . . . that they always have each other's back."

Jack saw an odd expression creep across Benny's craggy features: a mixture of surrender, acceptance, gratitude—perhaps even relief.

"You've always had my back, Benny," Jack said. "All I'm doing now is returning the favor . . . and showing you how much I care."

Chapter 46

February 11, 1946

Adrift in an ocean of solitude, Henry lounged on the drawing-room couch at his Sands Point mansion, steeling his nerves with a hefty pour of Pappy Van Winkle, the same bourbon he'd toasted tugboat owners with at his Waldorf-Astoria suite during the runup to the strike.

"So much for the triumph of good, old-fashioned capitalism!" he mumbled, his slurred words tinged in irony. He'd drained most of the bottle by now, minutes before midnight.

Henry raised his whiskey glass, mocking the sentiments he'd uttered a mere twelve days earlier, fully in control then, tugboat owners in lockstep, all of them giddy over the prospects for their carefully conceived, crushing blow against organized labor.

"And let's not forget free enterprise!" Henry murmured. "And the right for businessmen like me to control their companies' destinies and make a profit!"

Laughing derisively, he drained the bourbon in a single gulp.

"Hail to the entrepreneurial spirit!" He sniggered. "And to the values, institutions, and visionaries that make America the greatest nation on earth!"

He laughed so hard that he began to wheeze, phlegm clogging his airways and forcing him to hawk a gob of blood-tinged sputum into a pocket square.

Boozy, babbling, shrouded by a swirl of cigarette smoke, the tycoon who had accumulated wealth and power on a scale equaled by few men chuckled at the bitter irony of the past twelve days, the lofty perch from which he had tumbled so far so fast. His thoughts were addled, ricocheting off one another like pinballs. Sweat ran down his forehead and cheeks. His shoulders twitched uncontrollably. Alternately, he stared at the portrait of Carolyn over his fireplace, and then through patio doors to the rear of his estate, a string of lanterns illuminating a footpath to the water's edge where his canvas-covered sailboat *Sallie Ann,* christened in his daughter's name, lay moored to a floating dock.

Oh, how he longed to be out on his beloved sloop, under sail in the sun-spangled waters of Long Island Sound, hands on the tiller, balmy breeze raking a salty spray off the wave tips, the City of New York as distant as the sky. He'd give anything for that. Anything!

Instead, here he was, entombed inside his gloomy, lifeless manor. Captive to the beastly winter. Drowning in loneliness and grief. Foundering like a sinking ship. And losing!

Losing the toxic labor war he'd poured his heart and soul into, staked his reputation on, and plotted so diligently to win. Losing customers, business alliances, and boatloads of money. Losing face in the eyes of corporate allies, government officials, the public, and a press corps he had commanded for decades. Losing to the labor unions he abhorred—to hooligans, malingerers, and unkempt lowlifes like Benny Logan and his cohorts.

"Fuck those bastards!" Henry muttered, barely audible.

What an unmitigated disaster his anti-union crusade had become! So much energy, money, and passion squandered! So many plans gone awry! So much equity lost forever!

Emboldened at its outset, ascendant in its early days, Henry was utterly drained by the toxic and bitter strike, wounded by his own worst instincts and the arrogance of his power. Everything he'd spent decades building was crumbling beneath his feet. Allies, colleagues, and friends were abandoning him, newspapers vilifying him, politicians shunning him. Resentment ran rampant throughout his corporate ranks. Even the likes of crooked Paddy O'Boyle and devoted, reliable Elena Karas had cast him asunder.

The "captain of industry" was seen now as little more than a decrepit old fool, the butt of jokes, very symbol of callousness, overreach, and greed. Flummoxed by political headwinds, the gleam of his waterfront empire tarnished, unable to dodge a permanent stain, Henry felt humiliated, ruined, disgraced. It was more than he could bear. More than anyone could.

"Fucking labor unions!" he grumbled, the same vengeful sentiment that had governed his recent days and haunted his sleepless nights . . . and were defining his last few moments on earth.

Henry took his final swig of Pappy Van Winkle, inhaled his final Lucky

Strike, stared for the final time at Carolyn's portrait, and reflected for the final time on the twisted plot he'd contracted with Otto Blackburn to undertake, the details of which beclouded his final thought.

When the pain hit, it was sudden and jolting, like getting kicked in the shoulder by a mule. Instantly, it radiated to Henry's entire left side, and then to his jaw, before settling in the fleshy gut beneath his ribcage. The living room spun like a carousel, went blurry and then utterly black, as Henry lurched backward into the fold of his couch, engulfed by silence, a gaping chasm opening like a fissure in the earth before closing again and swallowing him whole. His body, splayed like a mannequin across the couch, would be found early the next day by Billy Murdock, arriving to pick the tugboat magnate up for their drive to New York.

CHAPTER 47

February 11, 1946

It unfolded precisely as Tommy Duggan said it would, down to the tiniest detail. Otto Blackburn's cadre of half a dozen saboteurs, toting gunny sacks packed with sticks of dynamite, arrived at the Eagle Dry Dock precisely at the stroke of midnight. The waterfront complex, per Henry's directive, was deserted, its team of security guards having been summoned to a hastily called meeting. *Jupiter*, along with several other McFarland tugboats, sat unguarded in their slips.

But Jack's phone call to Sgt. Timothy Rattigan had not gone unheeded. The NYPD dispatcher, spooked by the prospect of a public lynching, had acted on the anonymous tip. No sooner had the saboteurs boarded *Jupiter* than they were ambushed by a cadre of police officers lying in wait. Taken by surprise, they had but two options: surrender meekly or forcibly resist. Opting for the former, the men were promptly disarmed and placed under arrest. Dynamite and weapons were confiscated, the would-be saboteurs marched to jail, the entire incident over in minutes without a single shot fired or drop of blood spilled. More importantly, the potential clash between Benny's union partisans and the saboteurs never took place. Thanks to Jack.

Tommy Duggan, anxious to make amends for his union spying, had followed Jack's instructions to a tee, notifying Local 88's hierarchy to pass the word through the ranks that tugboat workers, contrary to Benny's entreaties, were to steer clear of Red Hook. All the while, Jack and his *Jupiter* crewmates had kept Benny safely under wraps. Not a single union member was anywhere in the vicinity of the Eagle Dry Dock when the sabotage plot was thwarted. Neither Local 88 nor any of its members could be fingered for what surely would have been a damning crime. Moreover, Benny was spared from harm— as were *Jupiter* and the tugboat workers' union itself.

Similarly spared from either injury or notoriety were the provocateurs of the foiled plot. Otto Blackburn, having skillfully covered his tracks, would never be implicated in the potential terrorist act. Henry remained similarly unblemished. No one in their right mind, after all, would ever suspect that *Jupiter*'s owner would willfully destroy his most valued asset; the idea was too preposterous to even consider. Indeed, no one outside a tiny circle of insiders was even remotely aware of what had transpired—and no one was spilling the beans. Sworn to secrecy, neither Benny, Jack, Tommy Duggan, nor *Jupiter*'s crewmates would ever leak a word about the incident. Union higher-ups remained clueless.

The saboteurs, a group of ex-cons oblivious to who'd hired them, accepted their punishment and, per the usual code of criminal conduct, stoically served their time. Similarly clueless, New York's press corps treated the incident as a minor blip on the city's police blotter: a group of small-time hoods arrested while attempting to pilfer tugboat supplies. The story either went unreported entirely or was buried in the midsection of the city's newspapers, overshadowed by coverage of the organized-labor protests rocking the city—and the news of Henry's untimely death.

The New York Times, in a front-page obituary akin to a hagiography, praised Henry as a once-in-a-generation corporate titan whose achievements were instrumental in propelling New York to its status as the world's preeminent port. *The Daily News*, referencing Henry's waterfront moniker "Mr. Big," cited the impact of McFarland Marine Towing and the Gotham Harbor Alliance on the city's wildly successful tugboat trade. Everyone quoted—public officials, fellow tugboat owners, even Paddy O'Boyle—expressed nothing but the utmost regard for Henry's business acumen, citing his brilliance, vision, and tenacity as among his most admirable traits. No one mentioned how those very attributes, coupled with vengeance and cunning, had driven him to engineer the tugboat strike crippling the city. Nor did anyone cite the most pertinent fact of Henry's existence: that he'd died as he had lived his final eighteen months—joyless and fuming, bitter and broken—and that his unrelenting animus and grief, more than principle, prudence or any other quality, had fueled his final days.

"It ain't like me to dance on a dead guy's grave," Benny said, when news of Henry's death became public.

"Then don't do it," Jack said. "It's over for McFarland, Benny. Just let it go."

"You're right, kid." Benny relented. "But even you gotta admit: McFarland was a ruthless scumbag who didn't give a shit about workin' folks, except to bleed 'em to death while rakin' in the dough. To McFarland and men like him, guys like us are field hands, an' organized labor is the enemy. McFarland used every trick imaginable to bury our union."

"And in the end, he failed," Jack said. "Bottom line, Benny, is that Henry McFarland is dead . . . and New York's tugboat workers' union still lives and breathes."

"Amen to that," Benny said. "I guess being a conniving prick doesn't mean you always win—no matter how wealthy an' powerful you are."

"And being like Henry McFarland, however successful you are, is certainly never right," Jack said. "Principles matter in the end, Benny. They matter as much as anything. Besides, find me a person who's entirely free of dirt. Anger, ego, jealousy, greed—pick your foible. Every one of us is corrupt, in one way or another."

Benny grinned. "'Cept maybe you, kid."

"Believe me," said Jack, "I've got my vices too."

"Maybe so. But you always manage to choose the high road, don't you?"

"I try."

Benny nodded. "Well, maybe that's somethin' I gotta learn, too."

"It's worth a try."

Benny grew quiet and thoughtful.

"Ya know," he said, "droppin' dead was probably the only way the strike could've ended for McFarland. I always had the gut feelin' that the schemin' bastard would rather croak than compromise. He just couldn't show weakness. Wasn't gonna cave in. Always had to do things his way."

"Sound familiar?" Jack smiled.

"Yeah." Benny chuckled. "Maybe that's another thing I've gotta learn."

Benny seemed deeply appreciative—not merely for Jack's support, but more so for his counsel, his loyalty, his love.

"I guess I owe ya one, kid," he said. "Ya know . . . for everything you've done for me."

"You've already done more than enough for me," Jack said. "You don't owe me a thing."

"That's where we disagree," Benny said. "In hindsight, you saved my ass by keepin' me away from that dry dock an' showin' me there was a better way of handlin' contract negotiations. You probably saved our union, too. Hell . . . the way I see it, I owe ya big-time."

Jack grinned. For an intriguing payback possibility had crossed his mind.

"Okay Benny," he relented. "Maybe there is a way you can repay me."

Patiently, as just as sincerely, he informed his brother of the quid pro quo he had in mind.

"Whoa!" Benny recoiled. "That's a helluva lot to ask!"

"Sure is. And it takes a special kind of person to do what I'm asking of you. Then again, Benny, I'd like to think that you're up to the task."

"How 'bout you lemme sleep on it?"

"Fair enough . . . but you better make your mind up soon."

"I know," Benny said. "Like you've been tellin' me for years: you never run out of time to do what you're askin' of me . . . not as long the people involved are still walkin' this earth."

CHAPTER 48

February 12, 1946

It ended with an Oval Office decree. Eight months of venomous contract negotiations had resulted in a divisive, historic strike that roiled the nation's preeminent city, sent ripples across the country, and sparked a nationwide debate about the balance of power between corporate interests and labor unions in postwar America. In contrast, a long-awaited White House edict put an emphatic halt to the work stoppage that had spurred the turmoil and torment.

Nearly two weeks of economic carnage, political paralysis, civic discord, and near-anarchy had finally proven enough. Early on day twelve, White House officials deemed New York's tugboat strike a grave threat to the public welfare, invoked the prohibitory provisions of Taft-Hartley, and mandated that the warring sides declare an immediate truce. Seized by the federal government was the city's entire tugboat fleet, along with related corporate assets. Defense Department officials, accompanied by U.S. Marines, marched into strike headquarters and ordered Local 88 members to return to work immediately or face arrest. Other labor unions were ordered to end their sympathy strikes. And within hours, tugboats manned by union crews were once again transporting fuel oil, food supplies, medicine, and other high-priority cargo through New York Harbor.

For union leaders, the presidential edict represented a mandate they had no problem accepting. For while it threatened punitive action against striking tugboatmen, and effectively ended their work stoppage, it was precisely the kind of governmental intervention that Benny and his supporters had hoped for all along. There were no more tactical maneuvers to consider, no need for further negotiations, no additional hardship for the city and its people to endure. Both Local 88 and the Gotham Harbor Alliance were legally bound to ratify contract-settlement terms crafted, in large measure, by Desmond Quinn.

After a last-ditch flurry of intense, round-the-clock negotiations, Quinn's diligence had indeed paid dividends in the form of a comprehensive labor pact that was groundbreaking, pragmatic—and eminently fair to both labor and management. Concluding that it was more constructive to grant union wage demands than risk another harbor-crippling strike, Quinn had convinced White House officials to award Local 88 a five-year contract containing an across-the-board, three-percent pay hike in year one, with substantive cost-of-living raises in years two though five—yielding significantly more money for New York's tugboatmen than the increase the union had been fighting for. Retroactive pay, a one-time bonus, and several worker-friendly protections—including incentives for greater productivity—were exchanged for a ten-year no-strike pledge by the union. Criminal charges against Local 88 for alleged acts of sabotage were dropped. Allegations against Benny and other strikers for their role in the clash between tugboat workers and police were similarly scrapped.

The Gotham Harbor Alliance made out equally well. Mediators sweetened the deal for the owners by granting tax breaks and other financial incentives, including a pledge of millions of dollars in government contracts and an end to wartime price controls, permitting the owners to raise their towing rates. The breach-of-contract lawsuit against McFarland Marine Towing was also shelved, along with the union's charges that the tugboat owners had engaged in bad-faith bargaining.

At long last, it was over.

The most schismatic and costly strike in the nation's history, a landmark case in U.S. labor relations, had finally run its course, accompanied by assurances that a similar set of circumstances would never reoccur. And in fact, the groundbreaking agreement established an entirely new set of rules for negotiating labor contracts in America, safeguarding the interests of both employers and workers. Wages, healthcare benefits, and working conditions were addressed. Staffing practices were redefined. Grievance procedures were established, along with protocols for disciplinary actions and other personnel issues. A labor-management council was formed to enforce procedures for contract administration. An independent fact-finding board was granted unfettered power to mediate future contract disputes.

At a City Hall ceremony marking the contract signing, Benny and other union leaders posed for photos alongside tugboat officials—including progressive young owner Mike Sturgis, newly elected as Gotham Harbor Coalition chairman, and Henry's sons Patrick and Paul, heirs to the McFarland Marine Towing corporate throne and symbols of a changing of the guard. Elena Karas, promoted to the newly created role of corporate administrator, was present as well. All of them, smiling and convivial, shook hands and offered lavish quotes to reporters, as Edmund Flannery formally revoked the mayoral edict that had shut down much of the city. Municipal offices, landmarks, and public schools were reopened. Businesses resumed operations. New York Harbor once again hummed with waterborne traffic, including a convoy of troopships from "Operation Magic Carpet," the return to America of servicemen who'd served in the war.

Consistent with most political theater, all sides emerged from the labor war bruised and chastened, yet triumphant and relieved. Union officials hailed the new contract as a victory for America's working class, a blueprint for future labor agreements. Corporate leaders applauded the pact as an innovative, enlightened agreement that protected the interests of American businessmen. Public officials lauded the face-saving compromise as an example of decisive government intervention in a public-health crisis. All sides pledged that they'd work more harmoniously in the future, ushering in an entire new era of labor peace.

Paddy O'Boyle laughably claimed much of the credit for the settlement. Similar assertions were made by politicians from the mayor's office and state capital to the White House and Halls of Congress. Insiders knew, however, that the true credit resided with others: Desmond Quinn for his perseverance and insight; Jack for his financial acumen, pivotal behind-the-scenes role, and quick-thinking actions. And, of course, Benny.

In the weeks that followed the settlement, Benny was afforded the widespread acclaim his efforts had warranted. Letters, phone calls, and telegrams expressing gratitude for his actions poured in from political allies and labor bigwigs across the country. New York's working-class newspapers hailed him for his foresight, toughness, and charisma. The *Daily News* said he was precisely the kind of passionate, street-smart, altruistic leader that union workers craved. *The Mirror* praised his loyalty to Local 88's rank and file, lauding him as a feisty, courageous

White Knight who'd shone a spotlight on the critical role tugboat workers played in the city's existence, and for inspiring them in the face of their challenges. The *Post* called him a bold, new breed of blue-collar champion, a likely successor to Paddy O'Boyle at the helm of the United Stevedores Association.

The latter claim proved nothing short of prescient. Within months of the strike, Local 88 was granted the right to become an independent union, winning its own charter from the American Federation of Labor, and emerging from under the thumb of its crime-riddled parent to become recognized as the exclusive bargaining agent for New York's tugboat workers. A series of anti-corruption measures were also implemented, assuring that the United Stevedores Association could no longer remain a magnet for racketeering, bribery, coercion, and other criminal activity. Old-guard union bosses, targeted by federal prosecutors, were stripped of their power, while a rank-and-file election toppled the union's longtime oligarchy. Paddy O'Boyle and his cronies, charged with embezzlement and fraud, were swept from office and soon jailed. Benny and a slate of fellow reformers were sworn in.

Basking in national celebrity and personal redemption, Benny also found time to attend to a long-delayed bit of personal business, repaying the favor Jack had requested of him, the gesture of forgiveness Jack had sought for years.

Two days after the contract signing, Benny—his wife and daughters at his side—made the hourlong subway trek from the Bronx to Williamsburg, to the hospital room where Gus Logan sat propped in bed. Gus's surgery, a lobectomy to remove a portion of his right lung, had proven lifesaving, albeit with lasting residual effects. Work at the Dixie Sugar refinery, with its respiratory hazards, was permanently ruled out. Social Security, augmented by a full-time sewing job for Agnes and financial support from his sons, would be Gus's source of income for the remainder of his life. But at least he was alive—and his family was once again intact.

Agnes, tears of happiness streaking her cheeks, abandoned her bedside vigil to greet Benny and his family the moment they entered the hospital room. Jack, too, rose from his chair to embrace his brother, sister-in-law, and nieces—his joy compounded by the fact that Kate, with Martin and Emily Sedgewick at her side, was resting comfortably in the hospital's maternity ward, having given birth to a healthy, six-pound, twelve-ounce boy, Gabriel Edward Logan.

Benny didn't say a whole lot when he approached Gus's bedside to embrace his father. He didn't have to. He'd come to mend fences. That was more than enough.

Jack, for his part, didn't linger at the hospital for very much longer. Within an hour he was seated in a classroom at Pace, snug inside a cocoon of linear algebra and differential equations, once again chasing his postwar dream. Morning would be just as sweet, reunited with his *Jupiter* crewmates, back on New York Harbor at the cusp of another bright new day.

Things might not stay that way forever. Jack fully grasped that reality now. Life, he understood, would not be forever ascending—never could be. There would be roadblocks and setbacks, challenges and battles he wouldn't see coming. But Jack could live with that too, and make it part of who he was—as long as there were sunlit mornings when the tide was slack and the harbor was tranquil and anything in life seemed possible: love, family, work, peace.

Anything at all.

ACKNOWLEDGEMENTS

Port City is a product in equal parts of history and fiction, memoir and research. Inspired by an actual occurrence—a 1946 tugboat strike that crippled America's most important city—*Port City* drew heavily upon personal remembrances of coming of age in post-World War II New York: attending its schools, riding its subways, reading its newspapers, and being shaped by the city's blue-collar neighborhoods, by working-class parents trying to reboot their lives after years of struggle, and by the bitter (and in many ways interminable) conflict between organized labor and corporate interests in the aftermath of the war.

Memories aside, I was aided in my storytelling by numerous books, newspaper archives, and other resources that served as the basis for research on a wide range of issues, including the Port of New York, the tugboat trade, and the role that organized labor played in shaping the city's economic, geographic, and political landscape.

Primary among those resources were the following books: *Tugboats of New York*, by George Matteson; *Working Class New York*, by Joshua B. Freeman; *New York Harbor*, by Andrew Britton; *At Sea in the City*, by William Kornblum; *The New York Harbor Book*, by Francis J. Duffy and William H. Miller; *The New York Waterfront*, edited by Kevin Bone; *The Tugman's Passage*, by Edward Hoagland; and *New York, An Illustrated History*, by Ric Burns and James Sanders.

Equally valuable were the insights, diligence, and unending patience of my editor and publisher A. D. Reed, as well as the resources of Pisgah Press and the North Carolina Writer's Network. A debt of gratitude is similarly owed to the Brunswick Forest Men's Book Club, whose members Tom Barbour, Fred Eckhauser, Dave McKee, Ray Murphy, Mike Nardella, Paul Ornstein, and Rob Robinson reviewed pre-press copies of the novel, providing both encouragement and valued insights.

Lastly, a heartfelt note of thanks goes to my wife Rosalyn for shouldering nearly the entire weight of our personal lives during the many months it took to write this novel. Sweetheart, you have both my heartfelt gratitude and my deepest love.

About the Author

Eliot Sefrin has been a journalist, writer and editor for more than 40 years. A native of Brooklyn, NY, and a graduate of The City College of New York, he began his career as a newspaper reporter, covering a wide range of topics, including politics, law, business, education, health, and the environment. He later served as a newspaper feature writer and columnist, prior to becoming an editor.

In 1983, he co-launched *Kitchen & Bath Design News*, a monthly trade magazine serving the residential design and construction trades, serving as its editorial director and, later, as its longtime publisher. He currently serves the magazine and several sister publications as Publisher Emeritus.

Sefrin has also written several award-winning novels, among them *Officers Down*, which last year won a Gold Medal for general fiction in an annual literary awards competition sponsored by Reader Views, a popular book-review website.

Eliot lives near Wilmington, NC, with his wife Rosalyn, a former NY City police officer.

About Pisgah Press

Pisgah Press was established in 2011 in Asheville, NC, to publish works of quality offering original ideas and insight into the human condition and the world around us. If you support the old-fashioned tradition of publishing for the pleasure of the reader and the benefit of the author, please encourage your friends and colleagues to visit www.PisgahPress.com. For more information about Pisgah Press books, contact us at pisgahpress@gmail.com.

Also available from Pisgah Press

Michael Amos Cody

Gabriel's Songbook	$17.95

FEATHERED QUILL BOOK AWARD, FICTION, 2021

A Twilight Reel	$17.95

GOLD MEDALIST, FEATHERED QUILL BOOK AWARD, SHORT STORIES, 2021

Reinhold C. Ferster & Jan Atchley Bevan

Letters of the Lost Children: Japan—WWII	$37.95

Robin Russell Gaiser

Musical Morphine: Transforming Pain One Note at a Time	$17.95

FINALIST, USA BOOK AWARDS, 201

Open for Lunch	$17.95

H.N. Hirsch

Fault Line THE BOB & MARCUS MYSTERY SERIES	$22.95
Shade	$22.95
Rain	$22.95
Winter (coming summer 2025)	$22.95
The Last of the Swindlers Peter Loewer	$17.95

Jeffrey Melvin Hutchins

Perpetuonics: A Novel	$19.95
Jerome v. God (coming summer 2025)	$19.95

A.D. Reed

Reed's Homophones: A Comprehensive Book of Sound-alike Words	$17.95

Dave Richards

Swords in their Hands: George Washington and the Newburgh Conspiracy	$24.95

FINALIST, USA BOOK AWARDS, HISTORY, 2014

Trang Sen: A Novel of Vietnam Sarah-Ann Smith	$19.50

RF Wilson

Deadly Dancing THE RICK RYDER MYSTERY SERIES	$15.95
Killer Weed	$14.95
The Pot Professor	$17.95
Murder on the Rocks	$19.95

To order:

Pisgah Press, LLC
PO Box 9663, Asheville, NC 28815
www.pisgahpress.com
pisgahpress@gmail.com